"I Knew Your Ship Was Coming," Matt Sikes Said,

the words sticking in his throat. He drove through the night, an alien beside him, thinking of the desert, the first time. The fear.

"But . . . that's impossible," Cathy said.

Sikes shook his head, eyes on the road, seeing the streets of the city as they had been six years ago. "I wish it had been impossible," he said, and he meant it. Maybe things would have been different right now if things had been different back then. Before the desert. Before Sam. The first Sam.

"How did you know?" Cathy asked quietly. Her hand sought him, touching his arm softly.

Sikes shifted in his seat. Even with the shortcuts, they were still a long way from the medical center where the ambulance had taken Susan and Emily, where George waited. There would be time.

"It was my first case," he began. "My first day as detective." And the years unrolled as quickly as the waiting city flew by, as Matt Sikes remembered the beginning . . .

#1 ALIEN NATION™

THE DAY OF DESCENT

JUDITH AND GARFIELD REEVES-STEVENS

POCKET **STAR** BOOKS

New York   London   Toronto   Sydney   Tokyo   Singapore

An *Original* Publication of POCKET BOOKS

A Pocket Star Book published by
POCKET BOOKS, a division of Simon & Schuster Inc.
1230 Avenue of the Americas, New York, NY 10020

ISBN: 0-671-73599-3

First Pocket Books printing March 1993

10 9 8 7 6 5 4 3 2 1

To those who welcomed us on our own
Day of Descent:

Lydia & Arthur, who invited us in,
Brynne & Michael, who fed us,
and Geri & K.W., who keep asking us to leave.

Aim see terrata yas rifym vacwa vots tla, dudes.

ACKNOWLEDGMENTS

Alien Nation first appeared as a 1988 movie written by Rockne S. O'Bannon. In that production, the roles of Matt Sikes and George Francisco were originated by James Caan and Mandy Patinkin.

On September 19, 1989, the Fox Television Network broadcast the two-hour pilot episode of the *Alien Nation* television series. This new incarnation of the Newcomer saga was developed by Kenneth Johnson and was brought to life through the talents of many fine writers—including Tom Chehak, Diane Frolov, Kenneth Johnson, Steve Mitchell, Andrew Schneider, and Craig Van Sickle—as well as a splendid new cast, including Gary Graham and Eric Pierpoint, who further developed the roles of Matt and George, along with Michele Scarabelli as Susan, Sean Six as Buck, Terri Treas as Kathy, Ron Fassler as Byron Grazer, and James Green as Uncle Moodri—all of whom appear in these pages.

For this book, we have referred to many of the contributions made by the writers for both the movie and television versions of *Alien Nation*. Where contradictions existed we chose to adhere to the more recent television continuity.

In particular, we have drawn upon the work of Steve Mitchell and Craig Van Sickle, writers of the episode titled

"The Game," in which many of the first tantalizing hints of the Day of Descent originally came to light. In this novel, the holding cell scenes involving George, his brother Ruhtra, the Overseer Coolock, and the Game are based on the script of that episode.

"Green Eyes," the final (so far) episode of *Alien Nation*, broadcast on May 7, 1990, was planned to be the first half of a two-part "cliffhanger," and the framing action of our novel takes place in the brief minutes occurring between the end of "Green Eyes" and the beginning of its direct sequel, "Dark Horizons," in which the fate of the Francisco family is resolved. Though "Dark Horizons" is yet to be filmed, both episodes will appear together as an upcoming novel, as will additional, as yet unproduced scripts. As Matt Sikes has come to realize, the story of the Tenctonese on Earth isn't over yet.

Our thanks to our editor, Kevin Ryan, for inviting us to take part in this third incarnation of the Newcomer saga. *Now* we know what all those phone calls just to "talk about" the show were all about. We also thank David Kurtz, composer of the series' main title theme, for kindly searching his files for the original lyrics to "Ee take naz nahj?" handwritten by Ken Johnson. And we are deeply indebted to the noble self-sacrifice of the members of the fabled Rubber Ears Society (even those who didn't know they were members) who toiled endlessly to provide us with insights into the obscure naming traditions of Tenctonese culture— another stunning proof of Hodgkins's Law.

J & G

EE TAKE NAZ NAHJ
            ee take naz

NAH SOOS GAH NIL PAH ET
nahj

EE TAKE NAZ NAHJ
            nah soos gah

NAH SOOS GAH NIL PAH
nil pah gah nil pah

EE TAKE NAZ NAHJ
            ee take naz

NAH SOOS GAH NIL PAH ET
nah soos gah nil pah et

EE TAKE NAZ NAHJ
ee   *ee take naz*

NAH SOOS GAH NIL PAH
nah soos gah nil pah

AH AHHH
ah ahhh

EE TAKE NAZ NAHJ
            ee take naz

NAH SOOS GAH NIL PAH AH
nah soos gah nil pah

ahhh ahhh ahhh
     AHHHHHHH

ahhh ahhh ahhh
AHHH AHHHHHH

NAH SOOS
nah soos

        GAH NIL PAH
        gah nil pah

nah soos
        NAH SOOS GAH NIL

gah nil pah
        GAH NIL PAH

gah nil pah
        GAH NIL PAH

AHHH AHHH AHHH AH
ahhh ahhh ahhh ah

AHHHHHHHYA
ahhh ahhhya

—KENNETH JOHNSON

PROLOGUE

It was the Ship.

It had no other name. It had thousands.

From Tencton legends, it was lesh, *the hell where the flesh of those who turned their eyes from the three moons was seared in waves of salt water, only to be restored with each rising of the sun.*

It was am dugas, *the pit that tempted Celine from Andarko, from which only their love had saved them.*

It was the wask'l reckwi, *the knowing death of ancient times for those who died yet remained forever awake to the darkness that trapped them in an eternity of remembrance of the evil they had done.*

And there were other names, their numbers legion, more ancient than any Tencton legend and not from any Tencton language. Words of hatred and fear and despair and helplessness that came from the languages of other races that had been cargo in its hull, now ghosts whose death cries still echoed from the bulkheads, whose terror still pulsed through the choking air like the fluttering heartsbeat of a hunted animal run to ground.

How many eons this abomination had plied the dark ranges was unknown. Some legends said the race that had built this ship and the uncounted others like it in its fleet were long extinct.

Whatever the truth was, the race that commanded them now was also unknown. In fact, in fearful, furtive conversations, sometimes it was whispered that the race that commanded had never existed, that the ships themselves were the sentient force behind the evil they propagated between the worlds—vast, formless things mindlessly cutting through space, decimating entire worlds and cultures, transplanting billions of beings for unknowable motives beyond commerce or greed or conquest.

In those whispers the ship's name was despair—despair that all that happened to those on board happened without reason.

It was abandonment. It was futility. It was the absence of all purpose—for good or for evil. It was the complete negation of all cause.

Pain.
Punishment.
Oblivion.
The ship.
And it was the sum of George Francisco's existence.

George Francisco pressed his hands against the smooth glass of the hospital observation window, six years free from the ship but never free from his memories of it. Yet now he looked into a vacuum even less forgiving than space, a void that was threatening to engulf him forever, yet end nothing.

Beyond the window, bathed in the soft purple glow of life-giving ultraviolet, misted in cool billows of soothing nitrogen, lay what remained of his new life and new destiny. On the charts clipped to their beds their human names were given: Emily Francisco. Susan Francisco. But to the watcher at the window they were his daughter and his wife and part of the reason for his life itself.

And this new world, this cruel planet and the aliens who called it home, even now were taking that reason from him.

George leaned his cheek against the window. Felt through the glass, the hum of the nitrogen misters reminded him of the subtle hull vibration of the ship's stardrive. Six years of freedom and nothing had changed—he and his people were still slaves to patterns unrecognized and forces unknown. The Day of Descent had not brought freedom after all. It had simply been the day that they had traded one ship for another. The only difference was that this new ship had a name.

The planet Earth.

"Has the doctor come out yet?"

George turned at the sound of his son's voice. Finiksa, whom the humans had named Buck for some unknown reason, cradled the soft and bundled form of his sleeping baby sister in his arms. The girl child, almost three months old, was named Vessna, in memory of her mother's mother. Alone among her family, she had no human name, as if her own heritage would be strong enough to serve her and her future born of Earth and Tencton. George bitterly recalled those so-recent days of optimism when the pod he had carried had finally hatched and Vessna had become the first of his children whom he had actually birthed himself. Then there had seemed to be a future for his people in this place. Now he saw those days for what they truly were—days of blindness, denial, degradation. George shook his head at his son—a human gesture they had all picked up almost subliminally, for there was so much that was negative here. "The doctor is still in with them," he said.

In the isolation room beyond the window a human doctor moved like a ghost through the purple mist, cloaked in a white lab coat, wearing protective UV goggles that made his alien expressions more difficult to interpret than usual.

"They should let us go in," Buck said. There was no disguising the anger in his voice, or the concern. He had still not realized how important it was to hide how he felt from humans. But George had learned that lesson a long time ago, the lessons of all slaves, no matter what their ship: The less one gave of himself, the less there was to have taken away.

George held his knuckles to his son's temple in shared grief. As father and son they shared almost the same pattern of red-brown cranial spots, but in Buck's dark eyes there was so much of his mother. "The doctor is afraid that they might still be contagious. It would be unsafe for us to go in."

Buck held Vessna to him tightly. His eyes burned into the isolation room with the fire of the stars seen in superluminal space. "Nothing on this *sl'mym* planet is safe," he said.

"Nothing anywhere is safe," George said. He touched a gentle finger to Vessna's tiny perfect fist, curled in fitful sleep. The scent of her, so fresh, so pure, drove away the awful stench of the so-called antiseptics and cleansers and heat-broken lipids that permeated this place. He wondered what he and Susan had been thinking of to bring a child into a world like this. How could he ever keep the promise of Vessna's birth for her? How could he give her life when there was nothing waiting for her here but—

In the isolation room Susan cried out.

The pigmented borders of George's spots constricted in sudden alarm, bringing a tingling tightness to the smooth and hairless expanse of his scalp. He pressed his hands against the glass, so close to his love, so powerless to save her. Stars passing by, detached, removed, beyond all hope.

Susan's voice was muffled, but some words were clear. *"Finiksa! Ee, nteega . . . nteega kat nos eeb!"* She sat up in her bed, her arms reaching out for a memory of her own, her eyes unseeing of the present, trapped only in the past.

And George knew what she saw, knew what she felt, because he had heard her cry those words before. *Don't take my baby!* In the ship. When they had come for Buck.

"She's calling for me," Buck said beside him. "I have to go to her."

From the room where the doctor was trying to ease Susan back against her pillows: *"Nteega kat nos eeb!"*

George took Buck into his arms, turning his son's eyes from the scene of his mother caught in the delirium of her fever. "No," George said. "She does not know you are here."

He felt Buck tremble in his embrace. "She's calling my name."

From the room: *"Finiiiksaaa!"*

"She cannot see us."

Buck tried to free himself, and in his struggle George felt a sudden wave of mortality as he sensed his son's muscles had become almost powerful enough to pull away from his grip. No longer a child. Almost an adult. Soon he would need a future of his own.

But not yet.

Susan called out again, plaintive, heartbreaking. George tightened his arms around his son and baby daughter, and for now the strength of his arms, and of his love, was invincible.

"Please, Buck, please," George said. "I do not want to lose you, too."

With those words George felt his son's body relax, and he did not know which emotion had more power over him—the relief he felt that his son would still obey him, or the sudden realization that the emptiness he had felt just moments earlier was not yet absolute.

George did not wish to lose his son and infant daughter.

He still had something left to lose. Something worth keeping. Somewhere within him there must still be hope.

"We should never have come here," Buck said angrily. "Back on the ship, when we still had a choice, we should never have come here."

Instantly George looked around to see if any human had been near enough to hear his son's intemperate words. The matter had been settled long ago in Quarantine by those Elders who knew everything that had transpired to bring the Tenctonese to this world. Their decision had been clear and absolute: There were some things humans were not meant to know.

But there were no humans present other than the doctor in the isolation room beyond the glass window, where Susan once again lay silent and unmoving on her bed. "Shhh," George whispered to his son. "You know that is not something we should discuss here."

Buck drew back from his father, and George, sensing that the moment of youthful rebellion had passed, released his hold.

"But you know it's true, don't you?" Buck said. "You know it was a mistake to come here. All we did was trade one ship for another."

George stiffened. It was one thing for him to think such thoughts. But to hear it come from his child . . . that was wrong. Buck was too young to feel that way. He *couldn't* feel that way. It wasn't fair, it wasn't right, it wasn't—

"No, Buck. Don't say that."

Buck's eyes bore into his father's. "It's what I feel, *Apod*. And it's what you feel, too, isn't it?"

George blinked. His son had called him *Apod,* not *Pod.* Father, not Dad. A sign of formality that hinted at the growing rift between them. George thought again of the slave's lesson— the less one has, the less there is to take away—and understood that Buck was attempting to distance himself from his father and his family. Cutting himself off now to prevent someone or something else from doing it for him later.

Did it have to come to this? George thought. Six years free from the ship, and we still act like slaves, not because of this alien world but because the fear the ship created still exists within us?

George looked back into the isolation room. The doctor was

palpating Emily's droonal flanges. It struck George that it was a miracle that a human knew enough to do that. It bespoke of hundreds of hours in classrooms, learning Tenctonese physiology and medicine. Why? he wondered. Humans still had so much to learn about their own medical needs. Why had this one, and hundreds of others, made the effort to learn about the Tenctonese?

"This world isn't like the ship," George said. Whether he was speaking for himself or his son, he wasn't sure.

"You know they're in there because of *terts!*" Buck said.

George could not argue with his son. He was certain that it was the human Purists who had sent the flowers to his home, doused with the airborne bacterium that had ravaged Susan and Emily when they had inhaled the flowers' scent.

"Because of *some* humans," George said, refusing to use the foul term for them his son did. "But because of other humans, like that doctor in there, your mother and sister are still alive."

Buck turned away from the window. "For how long?" he asked. "This is a nightmare."

Suddenly George saw it all clearly. With half his family on one side of the glass, half his family on the other, he realized that not everything rested entirely on him alone. There was death in this world. But there was life as well. Hope as well as despair.

Stars as well as the darkness they blazed against.

It was simply a question of where he chose to look.

"No," George said to his son, at last understanding. "This is not a nightmare. This is our dream a century in the making."

Buck's face screwed up in disgust. "What kind of dream puts us in a world where everyone wants us dead?"

"On the ship, Finiksa," George said, "it was our own people who became the *kleezantsun*. Why should we expect the humans to be any different?"

"You don't understand. It's not just *some* of the *terts,* it's *all* of them who are the new Overseers."

But George shook his head again. "Look at Dr. Quinn in there, treating Susan and Emily. On the ship the *kleezantsun* processed the sick through the recyclers."

Buck wouldn't look up to meet George's gaze.

"Finiksa," George said quietly, "we do have new enemies here. But we have new friends as well. And if we must die here, like this, then at least we will die free."

Buck shook his head as he stared down at the floor, Vessna still held close. "We should have gone on. We shouldn't have come here."

Again George touched Buck's temple. "You were so young then. You did so much for us. But there's still so much you don't know."

Buck looked up. "Moodri told me," he said, saying his great-uncle's name with a reverence George shared, despite the differences he had had with his uncle. "Moodri told me everything before he died. Everything he did. Everything *I* did and had . . . had forgotten."

George stared at Buck in silence, wondering if that could be true. Moodri had always been so full of mystery. George was not certain if he himself knew everything there was to know about *Crayg la Kenrudd*—the Day of Descent. The ancient system of *keer'chatlas,* so necessary on the ship, still held true to this day, providing safety and security by dividing knowledge so that no one person could reveal enough under torture to threaten the whole.

"Everything?" George finally asked.

Buck looked into his father's eyes then, and George could see that the teenager's anger had subsided. But was it being replaced by understanding? George paused for a moment, then spoke.

"Niss tel su bemry," George said, using the formal words of shared reflection. *"Niss tel su bemry otega . . ."* Then let us remember together . . .

"Kak bemry?" Buck asked.

George held out his hands to touch both of Buck's temples. "The Day of Descent," he whispered. *"Bemry,* Finiksa. Remember . . ."

And like the tears of Celine and Andarko, the years fell away, and father and son, together, remembered . . .

PART ONE

ACQUISITION

DESCENT MINUS 7 STANDARD DAYS AND COUNTING

CHAPTER 1

AT THIS TIME, IN THIS MEMORY, he was seven days and half a light-year from the world of the bored civil servants who would dub him Sam Francisco, and from the police officer who would change that name to George. For now, his only name was Stangya Soren'tzahh. Brother to Ruhtra, husband to Appy. A hull maintenance worker of no particular skill or importance. Son of slaves. Father of slaves. Another drone of the holy gas, bound for the recyclers at the end of his shifts. Or so he thought.

At this time, in this memory, less than an hour from the stardrive's final translation, George scanned the ship's hull. His tool was a narrow metal wand, no longer than his arm. The wand was connected by a triplet of slender wires to the heavy backpack of sealed equipment that he wore.

What he was doing, George wasn't precisely sure. The Overseers had instructed him in what circular sweeping movements he should make with the wand, how far from the beaded hull welds he should hold the wand's tip, and how long he must hold the wand tip to the weld when a green light glowed on the wand's handle. But typically they had not provided him with an explanation of what he was doing or why.

The Elders—an honorific for those among the Tenctonese who had been born on the home world more than a century earlier, before the coming of the ships—had told George that the wand was a molecular probe. Its purpose was to detect the beginning seeds of stress fractures in the hull-plate welds. When the green light glowed it meant a fracture seed had been found. By holding the tip at the fracture's location the mechanisms of the ship recorded the fracture's position and its size. The repair of the fracture—by molecular restacking, the Elders had told him, though the term had no meaning for George—was then undertaken by one of the machines that crawled along the outside surfaces of the ship, guided by the probe that George held in place until one had arrived.

George had often seen those machines through the portals. They were large oblong shapes, space black, broken up by inset panels, overlaid by wiring conduits, and gently curved like overturned plates. Each machine was as wide as four Tenctonese lying side by side, as thick as a single individual, and each skated across the outer hull on six metal legs, squatting here and there to press itself against the ridged and geometrically textured metal of the hull as orange-white light flared out from beneath its saucerlike body. The light had something to do with restacking molecules, George assumed. Whatever that meant.

George knew that some of the other slaves who had seen the machines on the hull believed that they were what commanded the ship. The Elders said that wasn't true, that the hull-crawling machines were as enslaved as the Tenctonese. But in some quarters of the ship the Elders' proclamations were beginning to carry less weight than before.

Also, from time to time, similar though smaller machines were sighted in the wide corridors leading to the restricted areas of the ship, resulting in intensified flurries of rumors that there were thousands of other machines hidden somewhere *inside* the ship. What more proof was needed that the machines were in command? But the rumors also said that there were alien races on board in sealed-off sections of the cargo disk, that Celine and Andarko's frozen bodies were on board, that the planet Tencton itself had been shrunk and that *it,* too, was on board. George had come to ignore all the stories. He only believed what he could see, and the only thing he could see was the ship.

For the moment, George stood by one of the portals that studded the ship's hull—a teardrop-shaped slab of transparent

material that the Elders were still unable to identify, twice as
tall as George and as wide as his outstretched arms. The Elders
often argued about the very presence of the portals on the ship.
They claimed it made no sense for so many windows to be
installed for the use of slaves. Some among them believed the
ship must have been built for purposes other than slave-
running. But whatever that original purpose had been, it had
been lost in centuries of time—the pitting and scarring on the
ship's outer hull spoke of thousands of years of travel, the
Elders said. And given the efficiency of the machines that
crawled across its surface conducting repairs, perhaps even *tens*
of thousands.

For his part, George sometimes had trouble envisioning how
something the size of the ship might have been *built* in the first
place. As he stared out through the portal at the leading part of
the craft its hulking outline seemed so tremendously large that
surely the ship had to be the size of one of the three moons of
Tencton.

In the terminology of the planet that was destined to be
George's new home, the ship was just over two miles long. The
disk-shaped cargo section in which the Tenctonese were kept
was approximately half a mile in diameter and, by volume, the
Elders estimated it to be little more than one tenth of the total
ship's size. In the more than a century they had spent on board
the Elders had mapped the cargo disk well, determining that
the Tenctonese inhabited only four of the five wedge-shaped
sections it contained. Some speculated that the other section of
the cargo disk might also contain living cargo—perhaps
Tenctonese, perhaps not. Though rumors of strange creatures
and devices ran rampant as always, no one had ever publicly
produced any reliable evidence that other cargo existed.

In any case, the Elders maintained that whatever else might
be living on the ship, if anything else *were* living on it, at least
part of the cargo disk had to hold maneuvering and landing
engines as well. When the ships had come to Tencton—by the
hundreds or the thousands, no one who had lived through that
time could be certain, so suddenly had they come—only the
disk sections of the ships had landed, leaving the bulk of each
vessel still in orbit around Tencton. So the larger portion of the
ship was most likely the stardrive engine, the Elders had
concluded, though by this point in the communal history
lessons George usually lost track of what the Elders went on to

speak about. Without the fabled calculating devices and thinking mechanisms that supposedly had existed on the home world George found it difficult to accept most of the arcane and unverifiable pronouncements that the old ones termed "science."

For some reason having to do with this ancient discipline, the Tenctonese who had lived at the time of the coming of the ships had believed that it was impossible to travel faster than the speed of light—though clearly that meant travel between most stars would take dozens if not hundreds of years, and George knew for a fact that it often took only a matter of months. But when, in his youth, he had had been brave enough to question the Elders on these matters, they had gone off into impenetrable discussions of faster-than-light dimensions, the impossibility of the artificial gravity fields that maintained up and down on the ship, vacuum energy extractors, and a dismayingly confusing assortment of other topics that had had no relevance whatsoever to the harsh realities of being a slave.

So George did now what he had done then, what all slaves did from time to time. He turned off his thoughts and simply stared at the passing stream of stars and the seemingly unmoving expanse of the ship and let time flow by him. Without conscious thought his fingers brushed the portal's smoothness, and, unknown to him, part of him wondered what it would be like to be free. Consciously he had given up that hope years ago.

"Step back from the portal."

The voice startled George from his reverie, and he jumped back on the metal grating that formed the ship's corridor floor in this part of the hull access zone. Reflexively his eyes closed, and he cringed, waiting for the burning sting of the Overseer's prod.

But nothing happened.

Fearfully he turned to face the person who had spoken to him.

It was Moodri.

Unlike George in his stiff and shapeless gray tunic and trousers, the frail Elder wore his prayer robes—immaculately white and trimmed with resplendent Tenctonese sine script worked in shimmering gold threads. They rustled softly in the constant wind that blew up through the open floors of the hull access zone, part of the ship's ceaseless circulation of its atmosphere.

The Overseers encouraged such shows of religion as Moodri's robes, believing that they kept the cargo controlled, mindlessly focused on a better day. Elders who were unable to take on heavy labor but who were otherwise healthy were permitted to carry out the services of their various traditions, provided the food stores were adequate. Nonworkers were usually the first to be recycled on the deep ranges, where port worlds could be years apart.

Normally George found some comfort in his worship with his wife and infant daughter, but he found nothing comforting in Moodri's robes. They were those of *Celenitipra,* a pre-Celinist religion dedicated to the goddess Ionia, for which George had no patience.

Moodri obviously saw the look of displeasure in George's eyes. "Do these robes offend you?" he asked. As always, he spoke with a smile hidden in his voice, another reason George disliked the old one, who always acted as if he knew more than he would say.

George glanced up and down the corridor, instinctively looking for Overseers, and was surprised that he saw none. Family contact was strongly discouraged on board the ship, except between mated *gannaum-ta* and *linnaum-ta* and any of their children younger than age ten. Overseers who happened along the corridor right now and saw the similarities between George's spots and Moodri's would know instantly that the two were related, and the punishment would be immediate.

"Your religion is one of acceptance," George said. He said the last word like a curse.

"What religion isn't?" Moodri asked, unperturbed. Even before the ships, Tenctonese culture had given birth to at least fifteen major religions and hundreds of smaller ones. Most lived in perfect harmony with one another. Indeed, many Elders had suggested that the Tenctonese traditions of peaceful coexistence were what had permitted the ships to so easily conquer their world.

"Andarko and Celine struggled against their adversity," George said, proud to be a Celinist. "They did not accept their fate."

"But is there not more to life than struggle? Once our people certainly thought so."

George felt all his frustration compress into a single burning point of anger focused on Moodri. "I am tired of your tales of the home world, Uncle. I don't care what life was like there or how many things you could choose to do in a single *crayg*. *Here* and *now* there is only struggle, and that's *all* that matters."

But the vehemence of George's words appeared to have no effect on the Elder. Instead Moodri gazed at George as if the younger Tenctonese had just proferred his eternal pledge of friendship. His smile was infuriating George.

"Here and now is but a single point in the vast continuum of existence," the Elder said serenely. "Time moves forward, Stangya. Space is mutable. Situations change. What is a struggle one day is meaningless the next."

George turned his back on Moodri, glaring out at the stars, unable to take the sight of the Elder's smile another instant. "If you came looking for me to tell me how meaningless my life is, I already know."

In the reflection in the portal George saw Moodri raise his hairless eyebrows. "Stangya, no life is meaningless."

But George recklessly pounded a fist against the portal. "You can look out at that infinity of stars and tell me that my life on this ship *isn't* meaningless?"

"You don't need me to tell you that," the Elder said. "You are your father's son. You already know the truth."

Now George wanted to pound his fist against the old one's spots. Always Moodri made mention of his brother—George's father—but he would never say anything more about him. Almost all George could remember of his father was the look of torment on his face as the Overseers took George away at age ten. Where his parents were now—another section of the ship, laboring deep in the caves of a port world mine, or recycled a thousand shifts ago—George did not know, and Moodri had never said.

"Why *are* you here?" George asked. He wanted Moodri to leave, to stop reminding him of what he had lost. Without memories there was nothing, and most times he preferred it that way.

"I have come to give you an important message."

George turned back to the old one. Coming from Moodri, a important message could be anything from an urgent plea from George's wife to return to their quarters to an admonition to refrain from eating meatgrowth for the duration of an obscure pre-Celinist festival honoring rocks and pebbles.

George narrowed his eyes suspiciously. "What message?"

"Turn off your probe and step back from the portal."

George checked to see if Moodri's spots were fading—a clear sign of the confusion brought by oversleeping, common among the old. "Why?" he asked, risking the convoluted answer he might get.

Moodri knew where George looked. "My spots are whole, Stangya." He glanced out at the stars. "Please do what I ask now."

George would be *karr-da* before he'd go along with any of Moodri's superstitions about the proper time for work. "Give me one good reason."

Moodri pursed his lips. "Stangya, the ship is about to translate back into normal space."

George leapt back from the portal and fumbled with the activator switch on his probe. No wonder there are no Overseers in the hull corridors, he thought frantically. And just as the ship shuddered around him he saw Moodri smile his inscrutable smile again.

What happened next was something George had experienced hundreds of times before and hated more with each occurrence. The sensation was similar to what he thought it must be like to be stretched into an endless flattened strand of vegrowth, as if being extruded by the rollers in a food dispenser. Deep within the ship, closer to the living quarters, the sensations accompanying translation were much milder. On the bridge the crew was somehow shielded entirely from their effects. But out by the hull they were agony.

Fortunately, Moodri had given him enough warning that he had been able to avoid a feedback shock from his probe. But from the sounds of electrical sparking and the cries of pain that echoed through the corridor, the other hull workers had not been so lucky.

Outside the portal the racing stars smeared into rainbow blurs of light, then coalesced into unmoving pinpoints of brilliance, so different from their appearance in what the Elders called the ship's superluminal mode. Slowly George felt his body return to its own shape again. He knew he had not actually changed configuration, but his muscles ached as if he had. His vision flickered with black sparks. He reached out a shaking hand to steady himself against the corridor's blank wall. He felt a thin trickle of blood escape from his nose.

Moodri, on the other hand, remained exactly where George

had last seen him, standing placidly with his hands neatly clasped at his waist, apparently unaffected by what they had both just experienced.

"We are now undergoing a course correction in normal space," Moodri announced.

George nodded, having no idea what Moodri meant by "normal" space. But a course correction meant the ship would not stop. No cargo would be offloaded.

"We will stay in this mode for approximately four *crayg-ta*. We will then be at our closest approach to the course correction star's gravity well and will translate back into the superluminal realm."

Superstitious nonsense, George thought. Long-dead Tenctonese magic. But still, the old one had known when the moment of translation would occur.

"How did you know?" he asked in spite of himself.

Moodri smiled enigmatically. George decided that his uncle would either say nothing or launch into a mystical explanation of some complex calculation derived from the phases of Tencton's moons. But the real answer was much simpler.

"The Overseers told me," Moodri said.

George stared at him blankly.

"We must always know our position in the heavens so the faithful can arrange their reclining platforms to face toward the galaxy of *Cen'tawrs,*" Moodri explained.

"The Overseers just *tell* you what our course is?" George had never heard of such a thing.

Moodri shrugged. "We have to ask, but yes, they will tell us what our heading is and when we will be changing course. It is but a small scrap of information that is of no importance to them, but quite important to us." He adjusted his robe, preparing to leave. "Are you all right, Stangya? I'm sorry I was not able to come to warn you earlier."

"I'm fine," George said. He stepped closer to his uncle, unsettled by what he had been told. Again he checked the corridor forward and backward for Overseers. Everyone knew how bad translation felt out by the hull. Naturally, the Overseers had not bothered to warn the hull workers what would be happening on this shift. But now that the moment of discomfort had passed, the Overseers would be returning to their duty positions. George knew he had to speak quickly.

He dropped his voice to an urgent whisper. "Moodri, tell me the truth. If the Elders have been told our course and all corrections since we left Tencton, is it possible that you know where Tencton is among the stars?"

Moodri showed no interest in understanding what George might be leading to. "Yes, the calculations are always kept current. We know precisely where Tencton is. Or was. With the movement of the stars—"

George had no time for the old one's meanderings and moved even closer, cutting him off. He could feel his hearts flutter with excitement. "And with such knowledge, would it not then be possible for . . . someone to pilot this ship home?"

Moodri drew back. "Don't speak such a thing. Don't even think it."

George leaned closer, speaking in agitated whispers. "Don't play games, Uncle. There is a rebellion on board. I know it. I hear the rumors as often as you do. You probably hear *more* than I do."

Moodri abruptly took George's hand in his and squeezed with more strength than George would have expected. "Trust me, Stangya. There *is* no rebellion. There is no *talk* of rebellion. There is no *chance* of rebellion."

George tore his hand away from the Elder's grip. "Then you're useless. Your spots are fading, and you're blinded by your spineless religion."

Moodri ignored the insults. "The goddess Ionia is not without her strengths, nephew. And if you persist in talking about such foolishness as a nonexistent rebellion, then you are bound for the recyclers and will leave your wife and children defenseless."

George opened his mouth to shout at the old one and then realized what Moodri had said. *Cate-al.* Children! Not *cate-un*—child.

Of the children George and his wife had been permitted to have *and* to raise, Finiksa had been taken by the Overseers a year ago, his fate as much a mystery as whatever had befallen George's mother and father. Little Devoosha—whom the humans would name Emily for reasons of their own—was now their only child. Yet Moodri had said "children." Was it possible?

"Do you *know* where my son is?" George asked. He could

not bring himself to ask about the other—the memories of what had happened were still too painful, even after all this time.

But Moodri dashed his sudden hope. "You know we aren't allowed to know the disposition of our families."

"But Uncle, you found me and Ruhtra years ago," George said. Even to his own ear valleys his voice had taken on the sound of desperate pleading.

"A fortuitous glimpse of your spots in a crowd," Moodri said, "nothing more." George had heard that tone of voice before. Moodri would not say anything more on the subject.

"I see," George said in a low voice. He hefted the wand of his molecular probe in his hand. The mindlessness of work was better than this agony of thought, this terrible cycle of hope and despair. He touched the activator switch on the wand and felt it come to life. "Thank you for your warning," he said flatly, without any inflection of gratitude.

Moodri bowed his head and turned to go. But then he hesitated, and without looking directly at George he said, "Stangya, remember what I've said. Your family needs you now. In the *crayg-ta* ahead that need will grow." And then, inexplicably, he met George's puzzled gaze, saying one thing with his words but another with his eyes. "Don't abandon them through foolishness. Don't speak of things that don't concern you."

Slowly, without quite knowing why, George raised his knuckles in a sign of farewell, and in the small smile that danced on Moodri's lips just as he turned away George suddenly grasped the real purpose of his uncle's visit.

George went back to his work barely able to contain his elation. Outside the portal the stars hung motionless. A sign that the ship had slowed, making an approach, to where or what George didn't know. The only thing of which he was certain was that the old one had been lying to him. About everything.

And that meant there *was* a rebellion.

And that Moodri was part of it.

And something would happen soon.

"In the days ahead," the old one had said. And for once George had no reason to doubt him.

CHAPTER 2

THE TENCTONESE YOUTH who would come to be known as Buck
Francisco ran along the catwalk with the other children, their
footsteps thundering through the dark and enormous food
reprocessing chamber. Two open-deck levels beneath them,
fifty huge, thick-walled, brown- and green-crusted vats of
meatgrowth and vegrowth steamed and bubbled, filling the
cavernous chamber with an almost choking overabundance of
the damp and pungent smells that usually wafted only from the
food dispensers.

The excited children were still in the aftermath of the
peculiar sensations of the ship's translation only minutes
earlier, which had not been painful this deep within the hulls.
Their exuberant voices echoed as their Watch Leader came to a
halt halfway along the catwalk and held her prod high, pressing
its alert signal. Down on the processing floor the vat workers
instantly ceased whatever they had been doing, looking nervously above, knowing that the high-pitched electronic whine
was inevitably a precursor to punishment.

Some of the younger children on the catwalk reacted as did
the workers and stopped talking and laughing, still remembering the painful lessons of the Overseers' prods. But Buck was
one of the older ones present—almost eleven Earth-years old

and a year gone from his parent's quarters—and he and his
crèche mate Vornho had come to understand that they had
little to fear from the Overseers.

As he watched the nervous vat workers Buck patted the
shoulder of the eight-year-old girl beside him. Her hands were
clenched tight around the catwalk's railing as she stared down
with large dark eyes at the motionless workers.

"Don't be afraid," Buck said with all the self-importance of
his years. "The alert is only for cargo."

The young girl glanced up at Buck. Her voice was small
in the presence of their Watch Leader. "But aren't *we* cargo?"

Buck smiled at her the way the Overseers smiled at him, as if
a blessing was about to be bestowed. "Cargo's down there.
You're up here," Buck told her. "Don't you get it? You've been
chosen."

The girl's face wrinkled in confusion. "Chosen?"

Buck tugged at the crisp black scarf he wore over his gray
tunic. It was the same space-black color as the Overseers'
uniforms. Even the silver clasp that held it in place was a
miniature reproduction of an Overseer's badge of rank.

"For the Watcher Youth Brigade," Buck said.

Vornho came over to Buck and the girl. He was Buck's age,
thinner, taller, with cranial spots that were smaller than Buck's
and distributed more like paint splatterings than Buck's distinctive strokes. But Vornho wore the same type of black scarf.
The girl looked from one youth to another, eyes fixed on their
silver clasps.

"I can . . . be a Watcher, too?" she asked tremulously.

"Well, not now," Vornho explained. "You're still too young,
and you can't be a member of the Brigade until you get away
from your parents."

"And you have to prove yourself worthy," Buck added. "And
the Chooser has to choose you."

"But then you can probably join, too," Vornho said.

The girl's mouth was open in wonder. "And the Overseers
won't . . . won't hurt me anymore?" she asked.

Buck and Vornho exchanged knowing looks. "You don't have
to worry about the Overseers," Vornho said. "They won't ever
do anything to *you*. Their job is to keep the cargo in line. I
mean, take a look down there at the vat workers. You can tell

they're lazy just by looking at their spots. They're only out to cheat everyone else out of their fair share." He dropped his voice to a whisper. "I mean, it's not like they're real Tenctonese or anything. Most of them have been . . . crossbred to *malsina* anyway."

The girl's eyes grew even larger.

Vornho nodded sagely, then went on. "But since you were taken out of the shift crèche for this outing, that means your bloodlines are pure. So you're okay."

"I am?" she asked breathlessly.

"Well, yeah," Vornho said. "The Overseers don't make mistakes about that kind of thing. They're really smart."

"Like the Elders?"

Vornho laughed and ran his hand over his skull as if wiping away his spots—a cruel gesture to indicate the absence of intelligence. "The Elders are a bunch of spotless wonders," he said. "Tell her, Finiksa." He and the girl looked expectantly at Buck.

Buck hesitated. His great-uncle Moodri wasn't a spotless wonder, though Buck knew he wasn't supposed to let on that Moodri *was* his great-uncle. All their talks and meetings must remain secret, Moodri had told him. But he felt Vornho's impatience, and he knew that hesitation was invariably a sign of weakness. Weakness was not tolerated in the Watcher Youth Brigade.

"Look," Buck said to the girl, "this is how it works. If your bloodlines are clean, then the Overseers keep a watch on you as you're growing up. If you turn out to be smarter and better than the other kids, then you get asked along on special shifts like today, so you can find out about the ship and how everything works and stuff like that. And if you learn fast and behave, then when you finally get free of your parents you can go to a special *luff* crèche and . . . you can wear one of these scarves, too."

There was a bit more to it than that, Buck knew. He had heard the stories other children whispered, of secret ceremonies with the Chooser *binn*self, strange metal bands that covered the temples, even hints of ritual sacrifice—though of what, Buck didn't know. But generally speaking, what Vornho was telling the girl was the truth. Just not the complete truth.

Vornho couldn't contain his pride. He continued the lesson. "And *then,* if you really do well in your studies and you show you know how to handle responsibility as a Watcher, *and* you show you know how to deal with cargo with a focused prod, *then* you can be an *Overseer.*"

The young girl let out a puff of amazement and wonder.

"Pretty neat, huh?" Vornho said.

The girl's face was transformed by the revelation Buck and Vornho had provided. "And then," she began to ask breathlessly, "when I'm an Overseer . . . I can . . . I can look after my mother and father so—"

Vornho pushed at the girl's shoulder. "Aw, forget about your parents. The Overseers are a better family."

The little girl clutched her hands to her chest, and her bottom lip trembled. "But . . . but I don't want to forget about my parents."

Vornho bent down to face her eye to eye. "Then you're just going to be cargo for the rest of your shifts, aren't you, you little *eeb?*"

Buck pulled his crèche mate away from the girl. "C'mon, Vornho, this is her first time out. She doesn't know anything yet."

Vornho leered at Buck. "What's the matter with you? Sticking up for cargo all of a sudden? She's a bit young for coupling, isn't she?"

"Eat salt," Buck said.

Vornho's grin didn't leave him. "You eat salt, mother hummer!"

The little girl gasped at the foul language. Buck jumped back as Vornho came at him with an extended finger, trying to jab it in under Buck's arm.

"Cut it out," Buck said, his anger turning to nervous laughter as Vornho was suddenly all over him, trying to get in at the sensitive nerve clusters under Buck's stiffly clenched arms.

Vornho started laughing, too, as the youths tussled against the railings. Vornho's finger hit home first, poking into Buck's armpit and causing the boy to double over with a gasp of shock and even more laughter. Then, just as Buck was rising to defend himself, a familiar deep voice said: "Boys! This is an educational tour, not a tournament."

Instantly Buck and Vornho stopped their fight and turned to face their Watch Leader. In less than two months an over-worked national guardsman in an overcrowded quarantine camp would call her Betsy Ross, and she would go on to become a formidable leader in the Los Angeles underworld, but for now her name was D'wayn, and she was an Overseer in charge of youth recruitment.

Her dark eyes twinkled almost merrily in her full and fleshy face as she gazed down, looking from Buck to Vornho. "Well, Watchers? What is your report?"

Vornho stammered something inaudible. Buck was the first to speak intelligibly. "Um, we . . . we were just explaining . . . how to . . . how we can . . . maybe . . . how we can get to be Overseers." Buck's feet began to throb with the pain of tension.

D'wayn lightly tapped her prod against the palm of her hand. She was a large female, and in her black uniform, studded with four heavy and gleaming silver rank badges on her left shoulder, she appeared to be as imposing as the hull crawler machines. She made a face of disappointment, and Buck was acutely aware of the staring faces of the other children who crowded behind her.

"And is becoming an Overseer something that is to be taken so lightly as to inspire you two to . . . playfight?" D'wayn asked.

Vornho and Buck bowed their heads as if they were wired together. "No, Watch Leader," they mumbled.

Vornho risked looking up. "The girl . . . she said she wanted to be an Overseer so she could . . . look after her *parents.*" He shot his head down again.

"I see," D'wayn said coldly.

Buck didn't like the thought of the young girl being punished for something so trivial. "Please, Watch Leader," he said, peering up without raising his head too far. "She's just a kid. She didn't know how any of this works."

D'wayn stepped in front of Buck and lightly tapped him on the shoulder with her prod. Buck twitched, though the metal tube wasn't even turned on to minimum charge.

"Are you trying to *explain* something to me, Watcher Finiksa?" she asked.

Buck dropped his head even lower. He could see no way out.

Overseers *never* explained anything. In their ranks it was the equivalent of mutiny. In the Watcher Youth Brigade it was cause for expulsion. And those who were expelled by the Watchers might just as well step into the recyclers, for they would never be accepted again by either the Overseers or the cargo.

"Were you?" D'wayn demanded.

Buck's voice was like a croak. "I was just trying to report all the details, Watch Leader."

After a long, long moment of anticipation Buck felt the prod lift off his shoulder.

"Very good, Watcher."

Buck was afraid to look up.

"I said very good, Watcher. Watcher Finiksa? Do you enjoy making me repeat myself?"

Buck brought his head up. Watch Leader D'wayn was smiling again. She winked at him, then turned to make sure all the others were paying attention.

"Now you all be sure to remember this, children," she said. "As Watchers your function is to be the eyes and ears of the Overseers. But . . . the best watching in the ship is useless if you do not combine it with full and detailed reports to your superiors. Do you understand?"

A mixed chorus of young voices saying "Yes, Watch Leader" came back, almost too faintly to be heard above the background hissing and gurgling of the immense vats.

D'wayn smiled broadly and nodded her head, creating fleshy rolls under her chin. She went over to the quaking child still standing by the railing.

"Now is this the little troublemaker responsible for all this commotion?" she asked. The words would be enough to purge the flanges of any child, but the Overseer spoke them in the same way a parent spoke nonsense to a baby.

Buck watched with horrified fascination as D'wayn lifted the girl in a careful embrace. He would not be surprised to see the Overseer toss the child into a meatgrowth vat below.

But D'wayn affectionately brushed her knuckles against the girl's temple. "What's your name, little spotty head?"

"Hambli," the child whispered.

"Well, Hambli, I understand that you want to help your parents. Is that true?"

By now Hambli had her hands pressed tight against her mouth and could only nod in the Overseer's embrace. That's it, Buck thought. She's used protein for sure.

"Well, that's an admirable thing to want to do," D'wayn said earnestly. "It's a good thing to care for your family." She glanced at the rest of her charges. "Isn't it, boys and girls and *binnaum-ta?*"

The children nodded, and Buck relaxed. Hambli wasn't going to end up in the vats after all. He could see the lesson that D'wayn was about to teach. It was taught to all in the Watcher Youth Brigade.

"But you know," the Overseer continued to the little girl lost in her arms, "I don't think you know just who your real family is. Take your parents, for example. They aren't your *real* parents."

Hambli's eyes looked as if they might explode.

"No, no, no," the Overseer said kindly. "We just found out about it a few shifts ago. Your real parents were brave Overseers who fought valiantly in the Tromus IV mine rebellion. The bad male and female who you *think* are your parents *killed* your real mother and father and then *stole* you when you were no more than a podling."

Buck could see drool running down Hambli's chin from her open mouth. She had stopped shaking, completely enraptured by the Overseer's melodious voice.

"And you know why that bad male and female did that, spotty head? Do you?"

Hambli bowed her head quickly.

"Because . . . they wanted to *trade your protein for extra food rations!*"

The younger children gasped. To encourage full reuse of all supplies, everyone on the ship was entitled to get as many extra ration credits as they could by bringing unclaimed waste to the recycling stations. For some reason Buck had yet to understand, that led many parents to make jokes about trading in misbehaving children at the stations the same way they might trade in uneaten meatgrowth for fresh slabs. And Buck had heard from many other kids who claimed that they knew someone who had a brother or a sister who had been recycled by desperate parents. He had never really believed those stories, but if an Overseer said it was true . . . who really knew?

"And that's why we asked you to come out on this tour," D'wayn said to the girl. "Because we know that you're much better than your pretend parents. And you deserve to know who your real family is." She let the child slide gently from her arms and deposited her safely on the catwalk. "So you're absolutely right to want to look after your family. That's a very good thing. But—you have to know who your *real* family is." D'wayn gazed down at the small child. "Do you know who your real family is now?" she asked.

Hambli nodded.

"Then tell me," D'wayn said.

"The Overseers," Hambli whispered, barely making the click at the end of the word.

D'wayn clapped her hands, and some of the children around her jumped up and down excitedly, making the catwalk rattle and tremble. Just as there were few things worse than an angry Overseer, there were few things better than a happy Watch Leader.

"Very good, little Hambli! Very, very good!" D'wayn slipped a hand into the opening of her tunic, looking for something. "I just knew you were so much smarter than those bad, bad people who stole you from your real parents. I just knew it." With a flourish she drew out a small green wriggling form that Buck recognized as a *tadlin.* He had loved those when he had been a child, and, like all real, unprocessed food on the ship, they were only available to the Overseers.

"Go ahead," D'wayn said to the child. "Take this treat for being such a good good girl, and we'll have a long talk about your parents later. Okay?"

Hambli tentatively brought the twitching creature to her lips. Buck saw her whisper a few quick words to thank Celine for this gift and bless the *tadlin,* and then she hungrily placed it in her mouth and sucked hard. Her delighted grin was contagious, and the other children began asking for treats as well.

As D'wayn doled them out Buck wondered how it could come to pass that people so evil as to steal a podling would then turn out to be the type of parents who would teach their child to say the blessings of Celine. It was a big ship, and there was still a great deal he didn't understand.

Vornho nudged Buck as the *tadlin-ta* were passed out. "I

thought she was going to be tomorrow's extrusion," Vornho said.

"Me, too," Buck agreed.

Vornho kept his eyes on the young girl. "I wonder if we're related."

"You and Hambli?" Buck asked.

"Yeah. My real parents were Overseers. They got killed on Tromus IV, too." Vornho nodded at the thought, even though Buck quickly realized that the math didn't work out. Hambli was eight. Vornho was eleven. Surely he'd remember if his parents had been killed when he was three. After all, if they had been Overseers, he would have been raised in better quarters, with better food and—

"So, have you two calmed down a bit?" D'wayn asked as she came over to them again. The rest of the children happily sucked and chewed their *tadlin-ta*. A few leaned over the railing and spit bones into the vats, laughing as the workers desperately tried to fish them out with stirring paddles. If the contamination levels were too high on any batch, the workers had to go without food rations until a replacement batch had been cultured—a process that could take up to twenty shifts.

Vornho squared his shoulders. "I apologize for disturbing the tour, Watch Leader."

Buck said the same.

But D'wayn waved her hand, dismissing their words. "There's nothing wrong with a little boisterousness from time to time. As long as it doesn't interfere with your duties, correct?"

Buck and Vornho nodded, two bodies with a single mind.

"And how are those duties progressing, boys?" Her smile left her. "Anything to report?"

Before Buck could speak, Vornho jumped in. "I overheard two water workers talking about diverting some flow to . . . uh, level fifty-seven," he said.

D'wayn looked thoughtful for a moment. "Fifty-seven? You're sure about that?" Vornho nodded. "Do you know their names?"

"No, but I'd recognize them again. Their quarters are near the *sawtel* hall by my crèche."

"You two like to play *sawtel*, do you?" the Overseer asked.

"A lot!" Vornho said.

"A little," Buck confessed. Using a stick to hit a ball through an overhead net struck him as a waste of time, but he didn't want to appear too different from the others. Moodri had told him that that was important, too—not standing out.

"Maybe this will help your games go a bit better, then," D'wayn said. She pulled two small packets from her tunic and handed one to each boy.

Vornho and Buck took the packets with trembling hands. Though they had never seen it before, from the distinctive iridescent purple luster of the small lozenges that lay within the crinkly transparent wrap they knew exactly what it was.

"What do you think?" D'wayn asked them. "Are you old enough?" Then she laughed as they earnestly nodded. "Well, don't take it here. You run off now. Give it a try, see what you think. Maybe find yourself a good game of *sawtel*. Or a girl who's . . . *sleema*. You understand *sleeeema*, don't you?"

Buck had never heard an adult use the word with that intonation before. He assumed it was play hall talk. Just for kids. But he knew what it meant—a girl who would couple for reasons other than those that had to do with bonding. It was hard to imagine that such females existed, but Vornho said he had a friend who knew someone who—

"So what are you waiting for?" D'wayn said, pointing back along the catwalk with her prod. "I can handle these podlings on my own. You two go enjoy yourselves, and I'll see you at the *luff* crèche in two shifts."

The boys turned to leave, both clutching their crackling packets in tight fists.

"Oh, and Vornho," D'wayn said abruptly. "Level fifty-seven? You're certain that's where the flow was to be diverted?"

"Yes, Watch Leader."

"Good work," D'wayn said. Then she looked directly at Buck. "We could use more of it."

The boys bowed, uncertain what other response might be expected. But apparently nothing else was required. D'wayn waved her prod again and then went back to her charges, who were busily tormenting the vat workers below.

As one, Buck and Vornho ran back along the catwalk. They didn't stop running till they came to a 'ponics hall and ducked into a passageway that ran between two towering walls of transparent crystal. Beyond the walls multicolored *sleefa* plants grew from an intricate network of crystal pipes that carried water and nutrients. The soft rush of the water and the transparent walls made this a good place to have private conversations—no one could get close enough to overhear a whispered exchange without being seen. Only here did Buck and Vornho dare unclench their fists and gaze at the prizes their Watch Leader had given them.

Vornho tightened his lips and gave off a short ultrasonic whistle. Buck tapped the packet in his palm, feeling the shape of the purple lozenge, wondering if he had the courage to unseal it.

But Vornho had no doubts. He split the packet and held the lozenge between two fingers. It glittered in the bright life-giving lights that flooded the 'ponics hall. The pure ultraviolet blended in with the other frequencies was beginning to make Buck feel light-headed.

"This is amazing, Finiksa. This is . . ." Vornho's teenage vocabulary apparently was exhausted as he contemplated the wonders that the lozenge could bring.

"Eemikken\," Buck said quietly.

The Overseers' drug. That which gave them their power. The antidote to the holy gas of obedience.

"Open yours," Vornho said. "Let's take it together."

Reluctantly Buck split the packet.

Vornho stared at his friend in amazement. "What's wrong with you, *siiks?* Don't you know what this means? It means the holy gas will have no effect on us. It means we can say no if we want to. It means we can do whatever we choose whenever we choose to do it. Andarko! We can even do what D'wayn said—find some *sleema* females and *couple, Finiksa."* He waited for some indication that Buck might share the excitement he felt, then frowned, stuffed the lozenge in his mouth, and swallowed.

Vornho took some deep breaths, looking around the 'ponics hall. His dry scalp almost glowed pink and brown under the intensity of the *sleefa* feeding lights. He gestured at the lozenge in Buck's hand. "If you don't take that, I will."

"It'll only last for half a shift or so," Buck said.

"We're only Watcher Youth," Vornho sighed greedily. "When we get to be Overseers, we can take it all the time. They all do."

"Not 'when,'" Buck said as he brought the lozenge to his lips. "By taking this, we *are* Overseers."

"Then act like one."

Buck placed the lozenge on his tongue. It had no taste.

"Tastes great, doesn't it?" Vornho asked.

Buck shrugged, then swallowed.

"Yeah, I can feel it working already." Vornho pounded on his chest. "Andarko! It makes the air smell different. I can't even smell the holy gas, not that it's been too strong this shift."

Buck inhaled deeply. The holy gas had never had much of a smell to him. He had never been able to tell when the concentration of it was being adjusted the way some of his friends could. And he noticed no difference now.

"I feel *great!*" Vornho exclaimed. He clapped Buck on his shoulder. "C'mon, let's get over to a *plaski* hall and find some girls. I heard that you can get a mat room all to yourself if you know whose spots to cross."

Vornho bounded forward without waiting for Buck's reply. Which was just as well, because Buck had no reply to give. He had no idea how coupling could take place without bonding. He didn't even know why anyone would want to. If you couldn't do it like Celine and Andarko, what was the point?

He decided Vornho's enthusiasm must have something to do with the *eemikken*. Maybe in addition to blocking the effects of the holy gas the drug made it possible to couple in a purely physical way, like *malsina* could. It was a big ship. Who knew? Perhaps the *eemikken* could even clear his mind enough so he would understand everything Moodri told him in their secret meetings. Buck decided he would like that and waited with more eagerness for the drug to take effect.

Twenty minutes later at a *plaski* hall, as Vornho engaged in heated negotiations with a maintenance worker for the private use of a mat room, Buck was very aware of the explosive change that had come over his friend. Vornho browbeat the old *binnaum* in charge of the hall forcefully, without patience or politeness. Buck decided he would not enjoy wrestling with his crèche mate when he acted in this manner. A single finger in the armpit was one thing in play, but Vornho looked as if he would no longer know when to stop.

Vornho got the mat room in exchange for the clear wrap the *eemikken* lozenges had come in—an exchange in which Buck saw no advantage, other than freeing the *binnaum* from having to continue talking with the obnoxious boy. Then Vornho came over to Buck, keeping his eyes on a group of young females about his own age who were cooperating in bouncing a set of *sawtel* balls off a wall in intricate patterns.

Now Vornho behaved as if he had been under the feeding lights for a hundred shifts, speaking expansively and bouncing from foot to foot as if ready to start a race. "This stuff is *great,* Finiksa. Do you feel it the way I do? I mean, it's almost as if the light is brighter in here, or as if I can see farther down the corridors, hear things more clearly. No wonder the Overseers know everything that's going on."

As far as Buck could tell, the dim lighting was no different now than it had been in the past eleven years. The cramped and narrow corridors still stretched out into mist-obscured points, and the background rush and rumble of fans and pumps and three hundred thousand Tenctonese going about their lives in a volume of the ship suitable for a third that number sounded just the same as it always had.

"Well?" Vornho asked.

"Actually," Buck said, deciding on his strategy, "I think it's upset my stomach. I'm feeling a little sick."

Vornho's mouth dropped open in disappointment. "Finiiiiksa. Look at the females over there. See the one with the ear valleys? The really curved pair?" Vornho crossed his hands over his chest and thumped his hearts in a crude rendition of a lover's greeting. "How *low* do you think her spots go?"

Buck knew he would have to leave. He wouldn't be able to talk Vornho out of what he wanted to do, and Buck wanted no part of it. "I'm going to have to go back to the crèche," Buck said, trying to sound ill.

"You're missing a real opportunity," his crèche mate said. "Who knows when D'wayn will give us another dose and we'll be able to feel this way again?"

Buck didn't know what his friend was speaking about. The *eemikken* had had no flavor and no effect. Either Vornho was imagining things, or D'wayn was trying out a trick on them and had only handed out one real dose of the drug. Whatever was going on, Buck didn't want to be involved.

"I really have to go," he said, and with that final protest he could see that Vornho was glad to be rid of him so he wouldn't be able to spoil the fun he had planned.

"I'll tell you *everything* that happens," Vornho said. "I'm not going to waste a chance to feel like an Overseer." Then he began to swagger over to the females without even raising a single knuckle in good-bye.

Buck turned away and headed through the corridors for his crèche. If this was what it felt like to be an Overseer, he thought, then what was the advantage? He felt no different now than he had on any other day of his life.

He'd have to ask Moodri what that meant.

Moodri knew everything.

INTERLUDE

SOMETIME IN THE LAST TWENTY MINUTES, Matthew Sikes realized, the rain had stopped, as if the whole world were holding its breath as it waited to find out what would happen next. It was the way he felt as well. And feeling that way, he could think of nothing else to do but keep driving. Through the city, through the night, toward the medical center where the ambulance had taken Susan and Emily, where George waited. No thinking. Just driving.

Driving with an alien beside him . . .

Sikes glanced to his right and saw Cathy Frankel fixed and rigid, staring straight ahead through the windshield. The passing headlights of cars and the dull orange flash of the streetlamps drew flickering arcs of light along the graceful sweep of her hairless, smooth, and spotted head.

Graceful? Sikes thought. He glanced again at his across-the-hall neighbor, the Tenctonese female who troubled his dreams and, more and more in recent days, his waking thoughts. The inhuman lines of her gently rounded skull *were* graceful. Odd how that had never struck him before, or that he had never admitted it to himself. And the sensuous curve of her ear valleys, almost trailing into a gentle S . . . George had once told Sikes how seductive that was to a Tenctonese male, and

Sikes could almost see why. The easy curve of it, the delicate fold, the shimmering sparkles of light caught along its soft ridges by a few shining beads of rain like dew on a flower. Dew on a flower? Sikes thought. Since when—

AARRROOOOOOOOGGGG!

A deafening airhorn blast captured Sikes's attention as if a thousand volts had shot through him, and he jerked the wheel of his sleek red Carralo to bring the car back across the double yellow lines and out of the path of an onrushing semi. The Carralo's alignment just hadn't been the same since his daughter's crazy boyfriend had driven it over the median on Sunset Plaza.

Yeah, that's what went wrong, Sikes told himself with a gulp. I wasn't distracted by Cathy. It was the damned car. He rubbed at his face, heart hammering, seeing Cathy stare at him from the corner of his eye.

"Are you all right?" she asked. Her sweet voice, usually both light and husky, was strained by tension.

"Yeah, sure, fine," Sikes mumbled. "The guy musta been falling asleep at the wheel."

"I can drive, if you'd like."

"I'm okay," Sikes said. His hands were tight on the wheel, his eyes fixed on the brake lights of the car a block ahead. Until now he and Cathy had said little to each other, ever since the odd radiance of the aurora borealis had flickered across the clearing night sky. An extremely rare event this far south.

As rare as an alien spacecraft crash-landing in the desert.

Every time Sikes looked up to the skies these days, everything up there seemed to have something to do with the Newcomers. Spacelab arcing by overhead, testing its communication laser; he had watched it from the roof of his building with Cathy. The night had been so cold, yet he had been gripped by a warmth he had been terrified to acknowledge. Spacelab was home to the first Tenctonese astronaut to return to space. Sikes had held Cathy close. The world had changed so much in six years. His hand had lightly glided over the perfect smoothness of her skin. Lasers flashing through the night. Brilliance against darkness. Their lips had met. The taste so different, the heat of her breath, the stars circling. Even the damn aurora tonight probably had something to do with the Newcomers. Everything in the world was caught up with the

Newcomers. Everything in Sikes's world was contained in Cathy's eyes, in Cathy's lips, in Cathy's arms.

Sikes wanted to pull the car over to the side of the road and kiss her again. To gather her tightly in his arms and mold himself to the secret ridges and curves hidden by her clothes and flesh. He wanted to tell her that no two people were *ever* alike. But that two lovers were always the same.

Two worlds, two lovers, two hearts—no, *three* hearts beating as one. He laughed at himself, breaking the tension that filled the car.

Sikes couldn't pull over. Sikes couldn't kiss Cathy. Because the truth was he was afraid of her, just as he had always been afraid of the Tenctonese, ever since he had met them, long before 'George, from that first time, in the desert. The desert . . .

"What is it?" Cathy asked. Her voice was brittle now. Tension surfacing. She didn't understand his laughter.

"Nothing," Sikes said. He looked at her. His heart ached for her. She frightened him.

Cathy looked into his eyes, and Sikes had no idea what she saw. But he could guess what she felt. The rain on her face made her look as if she were crying. Her expression said the same.

"They'll be okay," Sikes said, looking away, pretending that the tension between them was the result of their shared concern for Emily and Susan, victims of a Purist plot to kill prominent Newcomers.

"It's not them," Cathy said. Her hands picked at the shoulder strap of her seatbelt. She looked ahead. "It's everything . . . everything about this world."

Sikes couldn't stand to hear anyone, even Cathy, descend into self-pity. He had done it too often himself and knew now, from the clear and perfect vantage point of hindsight, that it had simply been a way to drive his wife and daughter away from him. Besides, Cathy wasn't the type to feel sorry for herself. She was building walls. Deliberately. Just like a human.

"Look, Cathy, things are bad. I'll give you that. But what happened to Susan and Emily, and Judge Kaiser and Dr. Bogg, for that matter, are just isolated incidents. Sooner or later the same thing happens to every minority, everywhere on Earth." He tried to smile but failed. "It goes with the territory."

Cathy watched the road. "Where we come from, we weren't the minority."

But you were slaves, Sikes wanted to say. But he didn't. He didn't want to hurt her.

Cathy sighed then. If she had been human, Sikes might have thought he had heard the prelude to tears needing to be released. But he couldn't be sure what that ragged, trembling sound might mean coming from a Tenctonese. Then, without knowing why, he wondered what Cathy's face looked like when she made love, how or even if her eyes closed, how he could possibly know what she might mean by any expressions she might make, how he could possibly know how to please her.

It's impossible, he told himself, shaking his head to drive the questions and the images from his mind, to think instead of all the traffic shortcuts that lay between home and the medical center. He had watched the "educational" tapes Cathy had lent him of Tenctonese lovemaking, videos made for her comparative sexuality courses at UCLA. Beyond the superficial sameness of gross body structure—what some experts thought might be the result of random though convergent evolution—Tenctonese did not look human, did not act human, were not human. And after watching the tapes forward and backward and in slow motion and freeze frame, Sikes couldn't see how a human male and Tenctonese female could ever even *attempt* to perform some hybrid blending of their species' respective acts of love without the human breaking his neck, besides other parts of his body.

Cathy sighed again.

He had to face facts. He actually feared involvement with Cathy. To make some form of love with her could be life-threatening. Yet her unhappiness was cutting through him, robbing him of his better sense. He reached out to hold her hand. "Are you going to be okay?" he asked, and he realized that he would do anything—*anything*—to make certain that she would be okay, for as long as he was able.

Cathy looked out the side window at the dark stream of locked and grilled storefronts they passed. "Oh, Matt. I don't know anymore. Nothing's right. Nothing makes sense. Nothing is how we hoped it would be." The sigh again. "Sometimes I . . . I don't think we made the right decision to come here."

Above all else—confusion, fear, and heartache—Sikes was a

cop, and he heard the one word in her statement that didn't belong.

"Decision?" he repeated. "I thought you guys crash-landed here when your ship went kablooie."

Sikes felt her hand tense beneath his.

"Cathy," he said, "your ship *did* crash-land, right?"

She squeezed his hand once, then slipped hers away. "Yes, Matt," she said. "The ship crash-landed here." She took a breath. If she had been human *and* a criminal, Sikes would have bet a week's worth of doughnuts that a confession was going to follow. "Because it was *made* to crash-land here." She looked at him, waiting for his reaction.

Sikes's only reaction was to wrinkle his brow in confusion as he expertly shifted gears to swing around a slow-moving van on the wet road before them. "What are you saying? That there was a mutiny or something on board?" The official reports were still no different from what had been on the news at the time. The Newcomers' slave ship had had trouble with its main engines as it was performing some sort of close approach to the sun to store up . . . whatever. Sikes couldn't remember. But the engine problem had led to the Newcomers' ship coming apart just past the moon, with the cargo-disk section being jettisoned and coming in to a rocky landing in the Mojave Desert. Yet Cathy had just implied that that story was wrong.

"No, not a mutiny," Cathy said evenly.

That's better, Sikes thought. He didn't need his fragile world rearranged again.

"We were slaves," Cathy continued, "not crew." She took another breath of confession. "It was a revolt."

The car slowed as Sikes turned his head sharply to stare at his passenger. "A revolt? No shit? I mean, I remember once you said something about some of you *trying* to organize a revolt . . . but with the holy gas and the Overseers and everything else, you guys actually managed it?"

"With the holy gas, the Overseers, and everything." Cathy kept staring out the window.

"How come nobody knows about it? Yow!" Sikes wrenched at the wheel as he narrowly missed another oncoming vehicle. George had told him more about Tenctonese history than he ever wanted to know, but his partner had never breathed a hint about there having been a revolt on the ship.

"There's so much we don't talk about. So much we don't . . ." Another soft sigh. "It's not something many of us even know about."

"But *you* know about it?"

"I know about it."

Sikes narrowed his eyes, almost as if he were trying to see a new image of Cathy. "Because you were part of it?"

Cathy nodded. "I almost wasn't." There was such sadness in her words. "But at the end, when they needed me—yes, I was."

"They? Who were *they?*"

Cathy shrugged. "We have a word. *Keer'chatlas.*"

Kirsch chitlins, Sikes heard. It sounded like something George would have for lunch.

"It's hard to describe," Cathy said. "Strength through weakness. Safety through division."

"Compartmentalization," Sikes said. He understood. "Like spies in a network of cells. If you don't know who you're reporting to, then you can't turn them in if you're captured and . . . well, questioned."

"Keer'chatlas," Cathy said softly. "No one knew who was in charge. No one knew if it all wasn't a plan by the *kleezantsun* just to lead us on, to keep us busy and confused, to find out who the troublemakers were and . . . deal with them."

"But it wasn't," Sikes said, trying to break the inexplicable spell of remorse Cathy was weaving around herself. "Hey, it worked. You brought the ship down."

"Down to Earth," she said bitterly. "In the end I had no choice. We had no choice. We were desperate. We were frightened. We knew exactly what we could expect if we stayed on board." She stared down at her hands, now folded motionlessly in her lap. All life seemed to have gone from her. "We just didn't know what to expect down here."

Sikes reached out for her again to break her mood. "Cathy, listen, I—"

She looked up suddenly and didn't let him finish. "It must have been just as big a shock and surprise for you humans, mustn't it? Waking up one day to find that a *starship* was landing, a whole ship filled with *aliens?*"

Sikes hated it when people changed the subject.

"Well," Cathy said, "am I right? How surprised were *you* when you heard what had happened?"

She looked over at him. He guessed she meant her expression

to be a mask over her true feelings, but there was something in her she couldn't hide. Not from him. And what was to be a mask became instead the fragile, hopeful, nervous smile she had given him that night on the roof. Brilliance against darkness. Their lips touching . . .

He could keep no secrets from her.

"Matt?" she asked hesitantly, as if sensing the turmoil within him, the decision he had reached. "How surprised *were* you?"

It's time, he told himself. If anything is ever going to come of this—of us—then it's surely time.

He took a breath then, and any other cop would know what was going to come right after it. *His* confession.

"I wasn't surprised," he said, the words sticking in his throat.

Cathy blinked as if he had spoken in a language she had never heard before. "I don't understand," she said.

"I knew the ship was coming." Sikes drove through the night, thinking of the desert, the first time. The fear.

"That . . . that's impossible," Cathy said.

Sikes shook his head, eyes on the road, seeing the streets of the city as they had been six years ago. November, he remembered. A week after Halloween? Maybe a bit later. "I wish it had been impossible," he said, and he meant it. Maybe things *would* have been different right now if things had been different back then. Before the desert. Before Sam. The first Sam.

Cathy was uncertain. This time her hand sought him, touching his arm as softly as sunlight. "How," she asked quietly, "how did you know?"

Sikes shifted in his seat. Even with the shortcuts he knew they were still a long way from the medical center. There would be time.

He took another breath of confession.

"It was my first case," he began. "My first day as detective."

And the years unrolled as quickly as the waiting city flew by.

CHAPTER 3

MATTHEW SIKES COULD SMELL the body already—sweet corruption and foul bodily wastes lightly blended and delicately mixed in the overheated confines of the gleaming white Continental parked too long in the morning sun. He felt what had passed for his breakfast begin to rebel within him, and he quickly turned away, bent over the fluttering yellow band that said POLICE LINE DO NOT CROSS, and splashily anointed the asphalt of the uppermost parking level with the fruits of last night's celebrations.

Sikes could hear the other cops at the scene snickering. He saw the bright flashes of the crime photographer's camera as she captured a few candid snaps of Sikes's first case, no doubt destined to find their way into the locked trophy case back at the station house. And Sikes knew that his pals, his friends, his oh-so-supportive coworkers, had done this to him on purpose.

It was his first day on the job as Detective Three, and it had begun with him barely able to wrench his eyes open and keep his thoughts in order. His radio alarm that morning had buzzed so long and loud that old man Booth had started pounding on the wall from next door. Gotta move out of here, Sikes had thought as he had slowly pushed himself out of his bed—a bed that had been giving him a good old-fashioned E-ticket ride four hours earlier when he had stumbled in from the party at Casey's to try to get some sleep for the big day.

In the shower he had alternately scalded and frozen himself under the weak spray of the water-miser shower head, trying to make his shaking hand find the magical temperature balance on the single faucet control. I really got to move outta here, he had thought then, a bit more coherently. And by the time he had managed to force down his breakfast—a partially defrosted bagel swallowed only with the help of incompletely mixed orange juice that left little frozen globs of concentrate at the bottom of the glass—he at least had been alert enough to remember to put on his civvies and not one of his uniforms. The uniforms were history, six years of it, and as far as he was concerned they could stay wadded in the tomb of their laundry bag for the next thousand years. Sikes had finally achieved his dream of being a detective, even though his friends had made certain he would not enjoy the day.

Then again, Sikes thought as he made his way to his car that morning, they made certain that I'll never be able to forget this day, either. His 1984 Mustang SVO hesitated slightly as he tried to start it, almost as if it, too, had spent six hours in Casey's the night before, drinking toast after toast to the next stage of his career.

Yet eventually the Mustang had started, just as Sikes had managed to do, even if the purring echo of the car's finely tuned five-liter engine had sounded much better than Sikes had felt. Though he had worked hard not to admit it to himself. The old-timers had solemnly told him that whatever went down on his first day as detective would set the tone for everything else that would happen to him in the years to come, and Sikes had been damned if he was going to start out by calling in sick.

At least I've only got a quiet day of paperwork ahead of me, he thought as he made his way out of the underground parking garage of his bland and characterless Studio City apartment building that morning after the Casey's blowout. I'll just sit at my desk, filling out all my first-day forms, drinking coffee till it's quitting time. Maybe even check the rental ads in the *Times* for a nice loft somewhere. And then I can go home and die in peace.

It had been a comforting plan for a hugely hung-over Detective Three to have for his first day on the job. Unfortunately, he had not thought to check that plan with Dispatch.

Sikes's first call for his first case on his first day had crackled over his car radio when he was all of ten minutes away from the station house. He had had the personal radio installed two days ago at the police garage, and he regretted that eager act of jumping the gun as soon as he heard the first electronic squawk warble out from the dash. But thirty minutes later he was standing on the top level of another parking garage, this one on La Cienega across from the Beverly Center where West Hollywood, Hollywood, and Beverly Hills pinched in to share their borders. And he was staring through his dinged-up Ray-Bans at his first body, wondering how uncool it would be to hold his nose. As things had turned out, his stomach had made sure that he kept his hands well away from his face until he was finished vomiting.

As Sikes stood up again, surprised by how much better he felt now that he had given in to what his body had been telling him to do since five o'clock that morning, his new partner came up to him. She punched him on his shoulder, handed him a thick wad of Dunkin Donuts napkins, and said "Welcome to Homicide, Sikes." Then Detective Two Angela Perez laughed, and her perfectly straight and even white teeth were almost as blinding as the mirrored aviator shades she wore. "Quite the party at Casey's, I understand."

Sikes took the napkins and wiped his mouth clean. "I was set up." He swiped at his tongue, too, trying to get rid of the sour orange juice taste he feared would be with him forever.

Angie pushed down her glasses and looked over the frames at Sikes. "You going to be okay?" Her large, dark eyes studied him. Their deceptive softness had led more than one cornered adversary to gamble that she would lack the guts to pull the trigger.

Sikes relayed the question to the rest of his body and waited for everything to report back. "It's just the . . . the smell . . . you know?"

Angie pushed her glasses back up with a single finger. "Oh, yeah, Sikes. I've been doing this gig for ten years. I know *all* about the smell." She took a clean napkin from him and wiped at a corner of his mouth. "Now you know why coroners smoke those big cigars." Then Angie nodded over at the Continental, parked all by itself, straddling three sets of lines that marked the asphalt into parking spaces labeled COMPACT ONLY. "Enough of the small talk," she said. "Time to work."

Sikes walked back to the victim's car with his new partner. He had met her six months ago when he had been the first officer on the scene for a robbery and shooting in a parking lot behind Mann's Chinese. She was quick, thorough, and—unlike a lot of the detectives he had worked with while in uniform—in her written reports she had given him full credit for the way he had secured the scene, found the shell casings, and canvassed the parking-lot attendants. That report had earned Sikes a commendation, and that commendation, in turn, had lifted his spirits enough that he had gone into his detective exams without his traditional feeling of examination panic. As far as he was concerned, that change in attitude had made all the difference, and he had aced both the written and the orals.

When his passing grades had been posted Sikes had called his mentor, Theo Miles—what other cops would call his rabbi on the force. Theo had taken Sikes off the streets at that mystical conjunction in Sikes's life where he still had the freedom to choose between hot-wiring muscle cars for the rest of his life—which undoubtedly would have been short and miserable—or finding a real direction to follow and a purpose to be guided by. With patience, trust, and—when all else had failed—a good left hook, Theo had pointed Sikes in that right direction and given him a purpose the young man could believe in—that he had it in his power to change not only his own life but the lives of others who were just as troubled as he had been.

After Sikes had screwed up college, Theo had even gotten Sikes into and through the academy. He had also become Sikes's first partner of sorts in a special drug detail that had lasted most of a year while Sikes was still in uniform but loaned out to Vice as a new face who wouldn't be recognized by the old-time dealers who seemed to know every undercover cop from Sacramento to San Diego.

But for now, Theo was still happily partnered in Vice, and he had told Sikes that a rookie detective's first partner should be someone who would be able to teach Sikes as much about the departmental bullshit of being a gold shield as Theo had been able to teach him about walking a beat.

After that conversation the first name that had come to mind for Sikes had been Detective Two Angela Perez, and though it was unusual for a rookie detective to be given the Homicide desk for his first posting, the recent commendation helped clinch his request at division headquarters. Sikes, however, suspected that the real clincher had been the photograph of Victoria he still had in his locker. Angie had wandered into the locker room one day at the end of shift to talk with Sikes about his request, which, he could tell, she was not inclined to support. While they had talked—Angie unperturbed by the cops who milled about nervously, wondering if they dared change in front of her—she had seen Victoria's photo and asked about it.

Sikes had told her flat out that being a successful detective was part of how he planned to get back together with Victoria and Kirby—his wife and daughter. At the time he had seen a look of cool calculation in Angie's eyes that said maybe she was willing to gamble that a guy hung up on getting back with his wife would be a guy who wouldn't hit on her each time they went out on stakeout. So she had agreed to his request to be her partner. Of course, one month after all the paperwork had been dealt with, Sikes was still trying to figure out how to tell Victoria that he had a female partner again. Especially such an attractive one, even if she was a few years older. The gender of his partner had been a sore point in the past and, Sikes knew, would be again.

"So what are we looking at?" Angie asked him as they stood looking at the victim's car, ten feet away.

Sikes was confused by the question. "I just got here. How should I know?"

Angie jammed her hands into her front pockets and frowned at him. She was shorter than Sikes, slender, and quite appealing in her jeans, white Reeboks, Gap shirt, and loose linen jacket. But her gold badge flashed from the folded-over case jammed in her jacket pocket, and her suddenly serious manner told Sikes that the lesson was about to begin. With any luck, it probably wouldn't last more than a year or two.

"You should know because you're a detective, detective." Angie nodded her head at the victim, slumped behind the wheel and just visible through the car's open driver's-side window. "Examine the scene and tell me what happened."

Sikes glanced at the others near the car, ignoring the parking garage attendants who stood fifty feet away, held back by another yellow tape strung across the ramp entrance to this level. Two S.I.D. technicians grinned back at him. Their standard-issue Scientific Investigation Division cases were open at their feet, so Sikes knew they had already examined the scene. The crime photographer was no longer taking her pictures, so her job was done as well. And Angie had been here at least a half hour before Sikes had arrived, so that meant that *all* the police work was finished, and it was up to Sikes now to duplicate that work and come to the same conclusion everyone else had come to before the M.E. and the meat wagon arrived to cart away the stiff.

Okay, Sikes told himself as he pocketed his sunglasses and squinted in the bright morning light. It's just like a test at the academy. He ran his hand over his bristled hair and had the pleasant thought that now that he was in plainclothes he could finally let it grow again. He walked over to the car and began to study the scene.

The white Continental was a model from the early seventies, back when they were the size of a small yacht and got about three miles to the gallon. It was in cherry condition, no sign of dust, maintained by someone who appreciated it. He stated his first conclusion. "I'd guess that this is the victim's car, not stolen."

"Why's that?" Angie asked.

"A car like this, wouldn't make any sense to steal it. Not enough demand for it. Miserable gas mileage. Obviously owned by someone who loved it and who'd report it gone in a flash. Plus it's too noticeable for someone to steal to use in a crime."

"Could it be the killer's car?"

Sikes studied the Continental. Whoever owned this car would be just as likely to kill someone in it as Sikes would be to kill someone in his limited-edition Mustang. Too messy. An act of disrespect for a superb piece of machinery. But just before he started to speak he realized that Angie had asked him a trick question.

He glanced back at her. "Do we *know* it's a murder?"

Angie licked her finger and marked off a point on an imaginary scoreboard. "That's one for the rook. Take a look inside and tell me what you think."

Sikes held his nostrils shut and leaned in through the window, being careful to keep his feet away from the chalk circles marked off underneath the car door. Blood spatters, he assumed.

After a few seconds he pulled his head out again and took a deep and cleansing breath. He was just about to put his hands on the car's window frame to steady himself when he saw the dull white powder from the technician's attempts to dust for prints in the same location. Of course, Sikes thought. If the killer steadied himself when he leaned in, that's where he would have put his hands, too. And he had seen enough to know what kind of crime had been committed here.

"It's a murder," Sikes said. "And going by the way the blood's coagulated, it happened at least eight hours ago."

"How do you *know* it's murder, Sherlock?"

Sikes glanced back at the victim. He still wore his seat belt. "Powder burns on the forehead," he said. If the victim had killed himself by holding a gun to his forehead—right between the eyes, Sikes noted—the small black spray pattern of burning gunpowder would be tightly grouped around the entrance wound made by the bullet, a .45, from the size of it. But the powder-burn pattern that did appear was sparse, almost nonexistent. Sikes guessed the killer had stood about five, maybe even six feet away. "Unless the stiff's got arms like an orangutan, someone else pulled the trigger."

"Two points," Angie said. "What else?"

Sikes bent down, held his nose again, and looked back inside the car. The driver's window was down, and the passenger-side window was open as well. But he could see the irregular fragments of segmented safety glass just where the window went inside the door. The other window had been shattered by the bullet after it had taken off the back of the victim's skull. "Okay. A murder. Gunshot wound to the head is the cause of dea—" He caught himself again. "Is the *probable* cause of death." Only the M.E. could rule on the cause of death. Detectives were only to state what they observed, not draw medical conclusions.

"Three points," Angie said.

Sikes began reciting from the procedural checklists he'd had to memorize. "I'd run the registration, check the roof and doorframe for the killer's prints in case he touched anything when he leaned inside, and check out the asphalt in that direction"—he waved to the other side of the car—"for bullet fragments."

Angie joined him beside the car. Sikes realized he almost

didn't notice the smell anymore. "We ran the registration. Car belongs to one Randolph Petty. Address in Westwood."

"Did you run the victim's license?" Sikes asked.

Angie looked over the top of her frames again. "Randolph Petty. Male, Cauc. White hair. Hundred forty pounds. Age seventy-two."

Sikes nodded. That fit the description of the body in the car.

Angie had another question for him. "What makes you think the killer might have leaned into the car?"

Sikes shrugged. "I'm guessing robbery, so . . . he reached in to take something. Right?"

Angie slapped a pair of surgical gloves into Sikes's hand, and when he realized what that meant he wished he had called in sick after all.

Within twenty minutes the late Randolph Petty was lying stiffly on a meat-wagon gurney, still more or less in a sitting position. His head was encased in a plastic bag, just in case any bullet fragments seeped out with what was left of his brains. His pants pockets had held a grand total of $1.27 in change and no wallet. There was nothing in the glove compartment, in the front-seat storage console, or on the floor, either.

"Four points for the rook," Angie said as she peeled off her gloves. Sikes didn't know why she had bothered putting them on, considering she had made him move the body and put it down. "No wallet equals robbery."

But Sikes was a dogged student. "Maybe he didn't need to carry his wallet."

"How was he going to pay for parking?" Angie asked.

"They validate here." Sikes nodded at Angie's skeptical frown. "I bought my daughter a Nintendo at the Good Guys. For her birthday, just a couple of weeks ago." The big electronics store was three levels down and connected to the parking garage. "First two hours are free, with or without purchase."

"Don't get carried away, rook. He'd still need to carry his license and insurance in something. And usually that means a wallet."

It was only his first day on the job, and he still had a headache that was ripping through his skull like the San Andreas Fault, but Sikes was no longer sure that theft of a wallet was enough to explain what had happened here.

"Look," he said testily, "if I wanted to rip off wallets, why would I do it up here? I mean, so I pull out my gun, get the guy to hand his wallet over, and then what? I'm on the fifth level of a parking garage. It's going to take a minute or two to get down to the exit, and then I've got a stop light and the traffic on La Cienega or Beverly or Third to worry about. If anyone sees anything, I'm nabbed within a block." Sikes shook his head emphatically. He had walked foot patrol around Sunset and Highland long enough to know how wallets and purses were best stolen—ground level, bad lighting, easy getaway.

Angie regarded him patiently. "So what does that wonderfully convoluted chain of reasoning suggest to you, Detective Sikes?"

"Uh, that something else was stolen," Sikes said.

Angie checked her watch, then glanced over at the S.I.D. techies who were shooting the bull with the meat-wagon drivers. "The rook hits pay dirt in twenty-seven minutes, boys. What do you think? Does he get another point?"

Sikes felt the tension in his shoulders ease. The techies gave him two thumbs down. The meat-wagon boys gave him one down and one up. He sighed and pulled his sunglasses back out of his pocket. The test was over.

Angie looked at Sikes as if to say, so what should I do?

"Good work," she told him. "Slow and plodding but good."

Sikes rubbed at his eyes and saw little fireworks go off. He put his sunglasses back on. "Can we save some time and you just tell me what else you've got?"

"Poor baby," Angie said pitilessly. And then the real lesson began. "Look, Sikes, thoroughness is good in its place, but in a murder case the trail starts going cold in thirty minutes. Now, I know you know that, because of the bang-up job you did back of Mann's six months ago. That was good police work because you acted fast, went on gut reaction. You stick at this and you're going to find out that sometimes it's better to just rush off and follow your instincts instead of sitting around deliberating and evaluating every possibility."

Sikes said nothing. It felt as if he should be taking notes, but he remembered he had left his notebook and pen back on his dresser in his bedroom. What a great way to start the first day of the rest of his life.

"So," Angie continued. *"I* come up here, *I* see the car and victim, and in *one minute* I know it's murder and that there's not going to be a wallet."

"A minute," Sikes said.

Angie smiled. "It's a gift. So anyway, you're right, this isn't the place for a perp to be ripping off citizen's wallets. So whatever the perp was after was something else. I knew that in a minute five. Now you tell me, what was the perp after?" She snapped her fingers at him. "C'mon, you've already almost said it."

Sikes nodded. "A Nintendo set."

Angie beamed. "Good boy."

"Or a stereo or a television . . ."

"Or any one of numerous fine consumer items on sale at the electronics emporium below," Angie agreed. "Me, I'm betting it was a portable stereo, maybe with a CD player."

Sikes waited for the explanation. He was certain she had one.

She did. "This is the fifth level, Sikes. With all those stairs, whatever happened up here was a young person's crime. Ergo, whatever was stolen was something that a young person might want to steal."

Sikes could feel sweat trickling down his neck. He decided he needed to get into the shade pronto. It was late October and unseasonably hot, even for L.A. "So what do I do now?" he asked.

"What do you think you should do?"

"I think you should *tell* me what to do."

Angie mercifully seemed to understand that she had prolonged the torture enough for one day. "Okay, Sikes, school is out for now. What we've got here is a random killing. That means we've got almost no chance of solving it, so that means it's not a high priority. You okay with that?"

Sikes nodded. Right now he was okay with anything that meant he could sit down soon.

"So the only thing we can do is to see if we can put ourselves into a position where we might get lucky. We've got three ways of getting lucky on this one." She held up a finger. "One, we find out that the late Mr. Petty was involved in a blood feud with some other old guy who threatened to kill him and who owns a .45. That's a long shot, but you never know." She held up another finger. "Two, there's a witness out there somewhere.

That's a real long shot." The third finger came up. "And three, we find out what was stolen, and by tracing it we find the perp. That's the longest shot of all."

Then Angie finally took pity on Sikes and led him over to the open door of the nondescript gray city hearse so he could rest on the back bumper in the vehicle's shade. The techies and the drivers were still waiting for the M.E. to show up so they could take the body away. Angie gave Sikes her notebook and pen so he could take notes on what he had to do next: mind-numbing, tedious legwork—the heart and soul of being a real homicide detective.

First Sikes was to go to Randolph Petty's home and find out if anyone in his life had a motive for killing him. Next Sikes would have to dig through Petty's personal effects to try and recreate what the man might have had in his wallet by way of credit cards, cash, and checks on the night he had died. Through court orders Sikes would then have to contact all the credit-card companies and banks to see what Petty might have purchased recently that might have made him a target for the killer. Maybe a credit-card slip or a chance remembrance by one of the sales staff in a nearby store would show he *had* purchased a portable stereo at the Good Guys or an equally enticing item somewhere else. Maybe a canceled check would show that his purchase had been traveler's checks from the American Express Travel office on the corner. Whatever, it was Sikes's job to track it down. And then, *if* Petty had purchased something that might have provided the motive for the crime, Sikes had to try to trace it.

Sikes dutifully wrote down everything Angie said, with visions of a blizzard of paperwork burying him in peaceful, cool whiteness.

"Think you can handle that?" Angie asked.

"Yep," Sikes said. Sitting down was good. The shade was good. The work she had just outlined for him was bad, but he'd worry about that later, maybe by the end of the week.

"Okay, then," Angie said. "I'm going to give you two days on it. If you don't turn up anything, then it goes to the bottom of the to-do list, all right?"

"Two days?" Sikes asked with real surprise.

"In the time we've been sitting here, rook, two other murders have been committed in our fair city. If we work hard, maybe we can solve one of them. See what I mean?" She punched him lightly on his shoulder. "I've got another call to roll on. You wait here for the M.E."

Sikes groaned. She had just given him two weeks' worth of digging to do in two days, and now she was making him sit out in the middle of a hot parking lot, unable to get started.

"You have a suggestion to make?" Angie asked.

A completely unexpected question leapt to Sikes's consciousness, proof that at some level his mind was set in a detective mode. It was the sort of detail that might make things a lot easier. "Did he have a watch?"

Sikes hoped Petty didn't. Sikes hoped Petty had a big red mark on his wrist where a heavy gold Rolex had sat on it. People were being held up for their Rolexes every day in L.A. being killed every week, it seemed. No need to check credit-card records then. One nice Rolex with a serial number and there was motive and an easy way to trace the stolen property, and it could all be taken care of in an hour, and then—

"Yeah, he's got a watch," one of the meat-wagon drivers said, leaning out of the window to look back at the two officers. "A funny-looking Japanese dooie."

Sikes did the right thing and jumped on the words "funny-looking" just as Angie did.

She went over to the body in its orange body bag on the gurney. "I looked at that watch," she said. "It was a cheap little digital with a black plastic strap." She unzipped the bag with a quick yank, then used the body bag plastic like a pot holder to pull out Petty's arm without touching it directly. "What's so funny-looking about that?" she asked when the watch was revealed.

Sikes saw it at once. "It's got two windows," he said.

Angie squinted down at it. "So? It shows two time zones. Lots of watches do that."

Sikes took off his Ray-Bans and was able to read the liquid crystal display at the bottom of the watch face. But the display at the top didn't show numbers. It was a picture—a series of nested ellipses with black dots. He laughed. He had an uncle who would like a watch like that. "That shows the position of the planets," he said. He bent down to look at the watch more closely. The ellipses were printed on the upper display, but the black dots were dark spots of liquid crystal.

"Does that make it something special?" Angie asked. "Expensive or anything?"

Sikes saw the printed ellipses also included one at a sharp angle overlapping the others. He knew what that was, too. The path of Comet Halley. He had gone out to the desert to see it five years earlier. Kirby had been with him, seven years old and bored with the whole thing. But Sikes had been fascinated. Uncle Jack had taught him all about the stars, back before—

"Sikes! Wake up!" Angie poked him in the ribs and brought him back to the here and now. "I said is that an expensive watch or anything?"

Sikes stood up and put his Ray-Bans back on. "It's a Casio, that's all. Interesting, but nothing fancy."

Angie dropped the arm. "Zip him up, boys." She was gone in under two minutes, having told Sikes she'd expect to see him back at the station house by five.

One of the techies looked at Sikes as Angie drove away. "Quite the party at Casey's, I understand," he said with a smirk.

Sikes grimaced and went back to take another look at the white Continental, mostly so he wouldn't have to make conversation. He stood in front of the car, staring through the windshield, imagining where Randolph Petty had been sitting, how he had turned, rolled down his window to speak to whoever . . . to whoever was five feet away? Five feet? Sikes could imagine rolling down the window if someone was standing right by the car. But five or six feet away, at night, on the roof of a parking garage? Must've been the gun, Sikes told himself. The killer waved the gun, and Petty rolled down the window.

Sikes rubbed at the back of his neck, still looking into the car. That didn't seem right. Robbers came up from behind, out of sight, so their victims didn't have time to pull their own guns from the glove compartment. Robbers want to take people by surprise.

He saw the bullet hole in Petty's forehead again. Dead center. The window down. The passenger window blown out by the bullet fragments. Petty had had his head turned ninety degrees. The killer had been coming at him straight from the side. *And Petty had rolled down his window.*

"Naah," Sikes said aloud. There were a dozen other explanations. The killer had sneaked up on Petty, made the old man hand over his wallet, then had started to walk away. Petty had yelled out something to him. The killer had turned, five or six feet away, and had fired. Yeah, that works, Sikes thought. But it was convoluted. And it wasn't what he had thought first. Wasn't what his instincts had told him.

He took off his sunglasses, looking for details. There was a thin line of orange just at the top of the windshield, barely detectable. Sikes went to the driver's side and leaned in. He used the pen Angie had given him to pull down the sun visor even though he knew the S.I.D. technicians would have done that as a matter of course when they searched the car. Nothing fell out. He pushed his head in closer, twisting his neck to peer up where the visor touched the roof, just where it met the windshield. There was an orange tag jammed in there, flush with the roof and not the visor. He wasn't surprised no one had found it.

Sikes poked it out with the pen and caught it in his palm. He held it gingerly by its edges and turned it over. It was Randolph Petty's parking tag from last night. He had entered the parking structure at 10:37 P.M. That would make sense to Angie, Sikes thought. The stores in the Beverly Center would all have been closed then, but the Good Guys ran twenty-four hours a day. Petty had bought something there, and it had been stolen by—

Sikes turned the tag over again. There was no validation stamp on it. Randolph Petty hadn't gone shopping anywhere. And since he had been wearing his seat belt, he probably hadn't even gotten out of his car before he was shot.

"Man, oh man," Sikes whispered. He remembered when he had bought Kirby the Nintendo. A Friday night. Almost midnight. The Good Guys and a few restaurants were the only action in the area, and the parking structure was almost completely empty. So why did Randolph Petty drive all the way up to the top level to park at 10:37 P.M.? Sikes asked himself. How many empty parking spaces did he pass to come all the way up here?

The old guy had been seventy-two. At the very least, he would have parked by the escalators or the elevators.

Unless, Sikes thought. He didn't want to think it. He knew all the extra paperwork he was going to make for himself if he continued thinking it. But headache or no headache, two-day limit or no two-day limit, Sikes was a detective now, and he had the gold shield to prove it.

And his fledgling detective's instincts, the ones Angie Perez had told him he had to learn to trust, said that Randolph Petty had not been killed in a random robbery.

Randolph Petty had driven up to the top level of the parking garage at 10:37 last night because he was planning to meet someone here. And that someone was someone he knew. Someone who could walk right up to him without bothering to stay hidden. Someone whom Petty would recognize and roll down his window for.

Randolph Petty was a white-haired, seventy-two-year-old guy who wore the planets on his wrist and who had been set up to be killed.

What a way to start, Sikes thought as his stomach rumbled uneasily. Here was a murder staring him straight in the face, and all he wanted to do was throw up again. If this truly was the way the rest of his career was going to go, then he suspected he was in deep trouble. But then, when wasn't he?

CHAPTER 4

To be a detective is to be bored. It took Matt Sikes most of his first day to learn that lesson, and he learned it well. He was in pain most of that day, too, though that had had nothing to do with his job. But it had also been a lesson, if not as rigorously learned.

He had sat on the roof of the parking garage a full half hour after Angie had left, before the medical examiner had arrived to pronounce Randolph Petty—stiff and ripe and missing the back half of his skull—dead. Then Sikes had climbed into his Mustang, cranked the air-conditioning up to high, and driven out to Westwood to Randolph Petty's house, stopping once for coffee and twice for a restroom.

Petty's house was not the kind of place Sikes had come to associate with a dead person. Most of the dead people Sikes had seen in his uniformed days had been young car-wreck statistics and teenagers caught up in petty theft, drugs, and gang warfare. If those victims had lived anywhere, they had lived in crowded tenements or small, dilapidated houses that were warped and flaking and peeling apart with brown scrub on their drought-corroded lawns.

But Petty's house was nice. Small, but nice. The neighborhood was nice, too. The flower-filled garden, the green lawns fed and watered by underground irrigation systems—it was all *nice.* People who live in this kind of house don't expect to get murdered, Sikes thought as he went up the walk, which was edged by tiny blossoms of white alyssum. But he had the unsettling feeling that he would see more of this in his days as a detective.

No one had been home at Petty's house, and Sikes hadn't been surprised. If the old man had lived with someone, no doubt he would have been reported missing last night. So once again it was time for Sikes to wait, this time for a black-and-white unit to arrive so two uniformed officers could provide continuity of evidence for when he used the keys on the chain from Petty's car to gain entry to the house.

In the meantime he called on the neighbors. The ones who were home were all nice, too. Shocked, upset, some moved to tears, but all pleasant and courteous and of an age with Randolph Petty, who, by all accounts, had also been nice. For the first time since he had become a cop Sikes had time to think about the consequences of violence, to think about how he as a detective could take the time to really investigate the causes of that violence. In fact, he was supposed to—that was his job now.

Without actually realizing it at the time, Sikes had felt the fire begin to burn more intensely inside him that day. Something every good cop felt eventually. And once that heat was experienced, it was never forgotten. Sikes *was* going to get the person who killed Randolph Petty. Not because it was his job. Not because the arrest would look good on his record. But because he had to. For the planets to remain in their orbits, for the sun to rise and the birds to sing, someone had to stop criminals. It was that simple, that elemental.

Without his actually realizing it, his feelings that day had proved that Sikes had what it took to be a cop. It would be years before he came to understand fully what had been unleashed in him. He still would have to struggle with his own prejudices, his own weaknesses and uncertainties in the years ahead, but the fire that had possessed Sikes's gut that day would not, could not be extinguished.

That baptism had happened in the few moments it had taken him to walk up the pathway to Randolph Petty's house for the second time that day, a dead man's keys in his hand, the two uniformed officers behind him, a small group of neighbors on a nearby lawn.

What had happened was wrong.
And he would make it right.
As simple as that.

An hour later the brighter flame inside him had been dangerously overfueled by the anguish of the silent house. It was as if Randolph Petty, just by turning the key in the lock as he had left his home, had triggered a freeze frame of his entire life. Everything in order, everything clean and undisturbed, everything ready for him to return. Yet he never would. And knowing that, Sikes found himself going through the record of Randolph Petty's life on earth with the reverence of an archaeologist in the tomb of an ancient king.

Petty had been a university professor, one of his neighbors had said. An astronomer, another had added. That explains the watch, Sikes thought. And the star field photographs framed and hung on the walls. The old amateur telescopes in the den. His photograph with Carl Sagan. The certificates on the wall.

Sikes had stood by one certificate for more than a minute, reading it over three times, staring at the small star field photo included in the frame—a scattering of white specks marred by one short streak, the time-smeared image of an object in motion against the stars.

"How about that," Sikes had said to the uniformed officer standing in the living room. "This guy had an asteroid named after him. Son of a gun, huh?"

The uniform had just shrugged, but Sikes had been awed.

There had also been other photos on the wall, and on the mantel, and in the bedroom. Photos of a younger Randolph Petty with a woman about his age. A wife, Sikes knew, and he judged from her absence in the more recent photographs that she had died about ten years ago. He never even thought that it might have been divorce. In the photographs of Randolph and his wife together Sikes could tell that nothing so final would have ever come between the two.

He had wondered then what conclusions others might draw from the photographs he still kept of himself and Victoria, taken while they were still together. Was their eventual fate as a couple so easy to see? Could a single image reveal the future?

At the end of two hours the small house had revealed much of Randolph Petty's life, but little that was of use to Sikes. He had a name and address and a whole set of what looked like telephone numbers for a daughter—Isabel—currently living in Australia. He had a name and number for a doctor, for a lawyer, for a bank manager. A bankbook and UCLA pension check stubs that showed Petty was comfortable, but not rich. He had the name of a neighbor to call in the event of an emergency, though that neighbor was out. He had neatly stacked and labeled boxes of old correspondence, a broken desktop computer on the desk in the den—which did nothing but bump and click when Sikes turned it on—and absolutely no indication that anything had been touched since Randolph Petty had set out for the parking garage on La Cienega last night.

At the end of those two hours the uniformed officers had made a point of looking at their watches. "Okay, okay," Sikes said. "That's it for now." He would have to come back to the house with a neighbor or a cleaner—someone who might know if there was anything he'd overlooked, anything disturbed or missing. But for now he had done all he could do. Which felt like nothing.

Disappointed, but not yet frustrated, Sikes stood out on the porch of Petty's house, watching as the uniformed officers sealed the door with their rolls of yellow tape. He had a wealth of leads, and he looked forward to having Angie Perez go over them with him, suggesting which ones might be the best to follow. He was going to get this guy. He knew it.

It was then that a second police car arrived, from Westwood Division.

Like wary dogs checking each others' tails, the five cops showed their badges and gave their precincts. Officer Rubia of Westwood Division was the officer in charge of this new call. She was a tough, no-nonsense Patrolman Two who seemed to be able to smell the fresh paint on Sikes's badge.

"What are you guys doing so far from home?" she asked suspiciously. She actually checked the ID photograph in Sikes's badge case.

"Randolph Petty was found murdered this morning in a parking garage by the Beverly Center," Sikes said.

Rubia pushed back her cap. "Well, that explains it." She glanced at her partner, a grim rookie who reminded Sikes of himself about five years ago. "Got a call from Dr. Petty's daughter asking us to look in on him."

Sikes's eyes narrowed. According to the letters and postcards he had found, the daughter was in Australia—some town called Woomera. How did she know her father was in trouble? Unless she had decided to speed up her inheritance.

"Did you talk to the daughter?" Sikes asked.

But Rubia hadn't. "The call came in to Dispatch about an hour ago. Seems the daughter's in Australia, talks with her father every day on some sort of computer network. Hadn't heard from him yesterday. He's seventy-two. She just wanted us to drive by and look in."

Sikes thought Angie was going to be proud of him. "The computer's broken," he said.

Rubia and her partner blinked without understanding what Sikes meant.

"If Petty talked with his daughter every day," Sikes explained, "doesn't it seem unusual that he gets killed *and* that his computer breaks at the same time?" Sikes felt a rush of adrenaline almost strong enough to wash away the dull throbbing pain of his slowly diminishing hangover. How many times had the lesson been pounded into him at the academy? In police work there are no coincidences.

Sykes told his uniforms to unseal the door. The broken computer in Randolph Petty's den had just become his first clue.

Angie Perez wrinkled up her face and frowned. "What the hell are you talking about, Sikes? *Everything* in police work is a coincidence."

That was the last thing Sikes wanted to hear. It was five-thirty. He had lugged Petty's computer, monitor, and keyboard back to the station house and set it up on what he had thought was his desk, just across from Angie's desk. That had been news to Sergeant Amrico, who had given Sikes one minute to find another desk, preferably in another precinct. And before Sikes had been able to straighten out his desk assignment—his was the beat-up one *beside* Angie's—Angie had come in with a fifteen-year-old boy in gang colors and booked him for murder. Not for Petty's murder, but for one she had been working on since last week. "I've been out earning my keep," she had said to Sikes as she walked by with her prisoner. "What the hell have you been up to all day?"

Now, half an hour later, she wasn't at all impressed by the broken computer.

"C'mon," Sikes said as he fiddled with an extension cord, making sure all the peripherals were plugged in. He knew the word "peripherals" because his daughter had taught it to him while he watched her set up her new Nintendo beside her Apple IIGS. "Don't you think that's just a little bit suspicious? Petty talks to his daughter every day on a computer network, and then the one day his computer breaks, he gets killed?"

Angie settled back in her chair and folded her arms. "Do they sell computers at the Good Guys, Sikes?"

Sikes hesitated. He thought back to the counter where he had bought Kirby's birthday present. What else had been there? He remembered. He frowned. "Yeah. They had a few."

Angie grinned. "Quite a coincidence that, hmm? Finding a guy murdered exactly where you bought something a few weeks ago." She rubbed her chin thoughtfully, exaggerating each motion. "Hmm. Hmm. Wonder what Lieutenant Columbo might make of that."

Sikes sat back in his chair, and it creaked ominously. "Okay, you made your point."

"And what point is that?" Angie asked like the teacher she was.

Sikes sighed. "That Petty's computer broke last night, and since he talked to his daughter every day, he went to the one store he knew would be open to buy a new one."

"Which makes his murder . . ."

"A coincidence," Sikes admitted.

Angie nodded, driving the point home. "He was just the wrong guy in the wrong place at the wrong time," she said. "If his computer had broken an hour earlier or a day later, none of this would have happened. How much more of a coincidence do you want?"

Sikes stared at the dark screen of the broken computer on his desk. It was the only thing on his desk. An ACROS 386 SX, according to the printing on it—a color monitor sitting on top of a dirty beige box with two disk drive slots, one large, one small, a mouse, and a grimy keyboard with more keys than Sikes could imagine needing on three keyboards.

"But what about where he parked?" Sikes asked, suddenly remembering his earlier suspicions. "Why did he go to the fifth level so late at night when there would be lots of other parking spaces down by the store's walkway?"

Angie leaned forward and leaned her arms on her knees. Her chair didn't squeak. "Sikes, you saw the car he was driving. If you had a boat like that, kept it in immaculate condition, where would *you* park it so it wouldn't get its doors dinged to ratshit?"

Glumly Sikes nodded.

"He was parked across *three* parking spaces, Sikes, just like people park their Rolls Royces and their Porsches, right?"

And their Mustang SVO's, Sikes thought. In public lots he always parked his pride and joy across two spaces, even if he had to pay double.

"So," Angie said. "Did you pull anything else out of a hat today?"

Sikes shook his head. He felt like he should go back to writing parking citations.

"Not as easy as it looks, is it?" Angie asked. But she said it kindly. She knew half the other officers in the busy room were listening in to what was going on here.

"I thought I was on to something," Sikes said. "That's all."

Angie unlocked a drawer on her desk and pulled out her purse. "That's the name of the game, Sikes: thinking we're on to something, then running smack dab down a blind alley. If you manage to get a lead to pay out one time out of twenty, you're par for the course." She stood; the shift was over. "You did good today, rook. You've got a good eye, an even better imagination, and your heart's in the right place." She waved her thumb over her shoulder, pointing toward the door. "Why don't you let me buy you a beer? I think they might remember you down at Casey's."

Sikes made a face. He wasn't ready to head back in there. Not for a couple of years at least. "Maybe tomorrow," he said, knowing he should have jumped at the chance to spend more time with his partner away from work. Theo Miles had taught him the importance of that. When split-second decisions were needed on the street, the odds were a lot better if your partner was someone you could count on to be able to read your mind. "I'm not feeling all that good."

Angie came over, leaned over, and put her hand on the arm of Sikes's chair. "To tell the truth, rook, after last night's winging the station house line was five-to-one you wouldn't make it through the whole shift without going on sick call. You just cost a bunch of your fellow civil servants a whole wad of money." She laughed. "Watch your back, Sherlock." And then she was gone.

Sikes sat at his desk. So much for following my instincts, he thought. He decided he wasn't up to facing the traffic in the canyons at rush hour. He turned on the computer, just as he had back in Petty's den.

And the same thing happened. Nothing.

The monitor screen came up blue. None of the keys registered on the screen. Something inside the box bumped and clicked for a minute or so, and that was all.

"Got a problem there, detective?"

Sikes looked up and saw an officious young man looking back. He had a white shirt, a painfully dull red-striped tie, and jet-black hair cut in an almost comically precise duplication of the official diagram in the LAPD Officer Appearance Manual. He also wore his badge and ID card around his neck, the way everyone was supposed to but few did. He thrust out his hand.

"I'm Detective Grazer," the young man said as they shook. "Bryon Grazer. And you are . . ." He made a show of trying to find the ID that Sikes was supposed to be wearing.

"Sikes," Sikes said. "Matt Sikes."

Grazer nodded gravely. "Ah, yes, the new man. Welcome aboard, detective."

"Uh, thank you . . ." Sikes had been about to add 'sir' to his thank you, but then he had noticed that according to his ID, Grazer's rank was also Detective Three, even though he was acting like a bloody chief.

"So," Grazer said imperiously as he came around to Sikes's side of the desk to peer at the monitor screen. "What have we got going here?"

"Not much," Sikes said. "It's broken."

Grazer pursed his lips. "May I?" he asked, and Sikes slid out of his way.

Grazer typed something on the keyboard. Nothing happened. "This yours?" he asked.

Sikes shook his head. "Evidence."

"I see," Grazer intoned. Sikes had no idea what there was to see, though. The unsmiling detective reached around to the back of the computer and turned it off. Then he made it apparent that he was counting down from ten by tapping the air with his finger with each number, silently warning Sikes not to talk so he wouldn't lose count. At zero he flicked the computer on again. "Don't want to cause a surge," he said, as if that would somehow be as bad as swallowing a mouthful of broken glass, and that everyone knew it.

Then Grazer listened to the bumping and clicking coming from inside and smiled knowingly. "There's your problem right there, detective. Your hard disk isn't mounted."

"Mounted?" Sikes asked.

But Grazer ignored him. "Be right back," he said, then shoved back his chair, got up, and marched off to one of the partitioned offices at the side of the common work area. Sikes looked at his own decrepit desk and wondered how much a Detective Three had to suck up to get his own office around here. From the looks of Grazer, though, he looked capable of sucking up big time.

Grazer came back almost instantly, carrying what Sikes recognized as another type of computer peripheral. "I'll just use my hard disk to give yours a jump start," he said as he switched off the computer again and attached his disk drive to the back of it. Then, as he burst into a flurry of activity that instantly produced type on the screen, Grazer also launched into a long and boring lecture on the future of the computer in law enforcement. Sikes had the impression he was listening to a well-worn speech. It certainly had no effect on how rapidly Grazer's hands flew over the keyboard.

"Yessir," Grazer said as he squinted at a complex patterns of ones and zeros that suddenly scrolled by on the screen. "You'd be wise to get computer literate as soon as possible, detective. It's the future, no doubt about it. And computer literacy will impact heavily on the career path of any officer who's on the fast track to command." He suddenly looked sideways at Sikes. "Do you have any ambitions for command?" he asked in an oddly flat tone.

Sikes shrugged. He hadn't bothered listening to half of whatever Grazer had been babbling about. "It's my first day," he said. Then he looked at the screen, where ones and zeros still rolled by. "What's all that?"

Grazer took on a professorial tone again. "Ah, well, that's your problem, isn't it?"

"My problem?"

"There's nothing on your disk, detective. Hadn't been mounted, just as I said."

"Nothing on it?" Sikes asked. "You mean it's been erased?" That might be something to look into.

But Grazer smiled smugly. "No, no, no, detective. Usually when a file is erased on a hard disk, the file isn't *really* erased."

"It isn't?"

"Just the index listing is deleted. The information itself remains on the disk until another file is recorded over it." Grazer tapped the screen knowingly. "Even if you had deleted the *entire* index, there would still be file fragments scattered over the disk, and with the program I'm using now we could read those files. But as you see, there's nothing here but random bits. *Nada.*"

Sikes thought he understood. "So you're saying that this disk has never been used." He tried to see how that would fit in. Petty's hard disk broke. He went out and bought a new one. Installed it. And that meant he would have had no reason for being in the parking garage *except* to have a meeting with someone!

But Grazer brought him down just as quickly as the idea had grown. "Oh, no. This disk has been used, all right. If it were new, let's say, all we'd be seeing now would be whole streams of zeros broken up by occasional regular patterns of ones."

Sikes was at a loss. "Well, if it's not new but it hasn't been erased, what else is there?"

Grazer leaned back and tapped his fingers on the edge of Sikes's desk. He made his pronouncement. "It's been overwritten."

How about overbearing? Sikes thought. "And what does that mean?"

"Every sector on this disk has been recorded over with a random assortment of zeroes and ones. Three times is the government encryption standard."

Sikes felt as if he were knocking down a house one brick at a time. "And why would someone want to do that?"

Grazer thrust out his bottom lip in thought. "To prevent anyone from recovering any of the information that might have been on the disk to begin with." He pressed a key, and the screen cleared. "That's it. There's nothing recoverable on the disk at all." He glanced at Sikes. "Any idea what might have been on it?"

Sikes shook his head. An old man's computer correspondence with his daughter? Tax records? How many different kinds of information could a computer hold? "Is it hard to do? Overwriting, I mean."

"Oh, no, not at all. There are lots of programs that do it. Utilities, they're called. Very simple to operate."

Sikes tried to go along with the idea to see where it might take him. "You just sort of tell the disk to erase itself, and that's that?"

Grazer looked at Sikes with a pitying expression. "You really should try to find out more about these machines, detective. If you asked the disk to erase itself, then in most cases you'd be erasing the program that told the machine how to run. No, you'd need a second disk to erase the first—something that would not be erased itself."

Sikes reached over to tap Grazer's hard disk drive. "So whoever overwrote the disk in the computer needed something like this to do it."

Grazer sighed. "It wouldn't have to be hard drive. It could just as easily be a floppy for in here." He pointed to the computer's floppy disk drive ports.

That's it! Sikes thought excitedly. He didn't have to go back through the house with a neighbor to find out if something was missing. Something *had* been missing right from the start. Not only had there been no other hard disk drive on Petty's desk, there had been no other floppy disks at all.

"You just think of something?" Grazer asked.

"Yeah," Sikes said. "My daughter's got a computer. An Apple—"

Grazer looked on Sikes with pity.

"—and she's got boxes of disks all around. Start-up disks. Game disks. CDs. Graphics. Programs. Hundreds of them. At least it seems like hundreds."

"So?" Grazer asked.

"So there were no other disks in this guy's den. Nothing on the desk with the computer. Nothing in the drawers. I know. I went through all of them." He looked questioningly at Grazer. "Does that sound unusual to you?"

"Oh, yes, very unusual. You almost always have at least one

set of disks nearby—emergency start-up, data storage, diagnostic programs. Just in case anything goes wrong."

"Goes wrong," Sikes repeated dreamily. Had something ever gone wrong.

Grazer raised one eyebrow. "What kind of case are you working on, anyway?"

"Murder," Sikes said.

Grazer's eyes widened enviously. "But . . . you're a Detective Three. You shouldn't be working Homicide."

Sikes grinned. Whatever had been stolen last night was something that could be stored on a computer. He was certain of it. Someone had set up Professor Randolph Petty in a late-night meeting, killed him, then gone back to his house to wipe out whatever was on his computer and stolen his loose disks at the same time.

"I said," Grazer repeated, "that as a Detective Three you shouldn't be working Homicide. Especially not on your first day."

Sikes shrugged. "I guess you just gotta know who to suck up to, Bryon."

Grazer leaned forward, eyes wide. "And who would that be?"

Sikes jumped to his feet, wondering if he could still catch Angie at Casey's. Or do I want to tell her so soon? he suddenly thought. Before I've had a chance to check it out so she won't shoot me down again? He still had one day left on the tight schedule she had given him.

"Sikes, c'mon. I helped you out here."

Sikes clapped Grazer on the shoulder. "Want to help me out again?"

Grazer looked at the hand that dared touch him. "Will you put me in your report?"

"Absolutely."

Grazer coughed. "But only . . . only if everything works out, that is."

"Only if everything works out," Sikes agreed. And he knew it would. It *had* to.

"So what do you need me to do first?" Grazer asked.

"First," Sikes said, "we need a computer like this one that works, and that will let us talk with the victim's daughter in Australia."

Grazer nodded. "I've got a modem. Paperwork to get

approvals for the long-distance charges should take more than a week to—"

"We've got twenty-four hours," Sikes said.

Grazer looked panicked. "But we have to follow procedures. I mean, it's bad enough that I'm taking time away from my assignments in forensic accounting to help you out on . . . on . . . what exactly am I helping you out on, anyway?"

Sikes patted the computer on his desk. "Twenty-four hours ago someone thought this computer held information that was worth killing a retired seventy-two-year-old astronomy professor for."

"Good Lord," Grazer said. "What kind of information?"

The answer to Grazer's question was just over three billion miles away, traveling at a speed beyond human science, and heading straight for the sun, the Mojave, and the rest of Matthew Sikes's life.

But seven days from descent and counting, Sikes still didn't know. In fact, the only being who *did* know was an ancient Tenctonese priest named Moodri.

Because the youth who would be known as Buck Francisco was right.

Moodri knew everything.

CHAPTER 5

FEW TENCTONESE HAD NEED for more than a single name. Each knew who he or she or *binn* was, and, to the trained eye at least, their spots told the story of their lineage, for the patterns formed by those patches of darker pigmentation were a blending of the patterns of their mother and father. In such a situation, how many names would any intelligent being need?

Thus there were hundreds of Moodris aboard the ship as it hurtled down toward its final gravity well where a single yellow star waited impassively at the center. But there was only one Moodri among them who carried the distinctive trident marking of the Family: Heroes of Soren'tzahh above his left temple counterbalanced by the graceful brushstroke of the Family: Third Star's Ocean, that adorned the crest of his skull.

That singular Moodri was an Elder, born on the home world before the coming of the ships. In the measurement of time on the planet that would be his final resting place he was almost one hundred and forty years old. Yet his spots remained dark, his eyes alert, and his mind far sharper than any exposed to the holy gas for so long had any right to expect—and far sharper than any Overseer would suspect.

As an Elder, Moodri worked his shifts in whatever crowded day crèche had need of an extra pair of hands, tending to the podlings and the toddlers of those parents who toiled elsewhere in the ship. When the Overseers came on their inspection tours he let his eyes go vacant and hummed old Tencton tunes softly to himself, changing diapers, cutting up vegrowth, playing simple games with two-year-olds who appeared to be smarter and more aware than he.

For twenty years he had played this role, until he had become nothing more than another gray wall support to the Overseers' eyes. A babbling old fool who sometimes donned priestly robes to calculate the position of the galaxy *Cen'tawrs,* and who other times recut his gray tunic and trousers into a skirt, just as he had worn a century before on Tencton. To the Overseers he was harmless, he kept the cargo blinded by the false hopes of a weak and passive religion; and as long as he could lift a child, he would not be recycled.

So the shifts passed, one after another, endlessly falling into the gray mist of the gas and lost memory.

At least, to the Overseers.

This shift, Moodri sat with five sick podlings in an isolation room off the level fifty-seven day-crèche infirmary. The podlings slept deeply, in no obvious distress, but across their tiny chests and thighs distinctive fan-shaped rashes of purple speckles grew—the first symptom of what might develop into an infection of the spartiary gland called *nensi* fever.

Nensi fever could be fatal but not often enough for the Overseers to automatically recycle anyone with symptoms, as they did those patients with other, more virulent diseases. More often than not, *nensi* patients recovered and were thereafter immune, just as Moodri was. Though because the lethargic symptoms of the disease could persist for several dozen shifts, seriously interfering with productivity, it was necessary to isolate the infected patients until the danger of contagion had passed.

From time to time an Overseer might peer through the small window on the door to the isolation room, but for the most part the sick podlings and the senile Elder dozing off in his chair among them were ignored. If the podlings lived, fine. If the podlings died, fine. The most important consideration for the Overseers was that the disease would not be permitted to spread, if in fact it was spartiary gland infection that had stricken the children. With the limited medical facilities on board the ship there was just no way to be certain.

But Moodri was certain. What had stricken the children was not *nensi* fever. They had simply been given a small dose of minced-up *ceel* root with their vegrowth. The *ceel* root made them sleepy and triggered a harmless rash that appeared to be the same as that caused by *nensi* fever, though any trained physician would see the difference at once. In a handful of shifts the podlings would reawaken, the rash would fade, and the isolation room would no longer be necessary. And no outbreak of spartiary gland infection would arise until the next time the Elders needed a secure and private place to meet and talk without fearing the approach of the Overseers. Thus, as the podlings slept in their swings and oscillators this shift, the Elders met in safety.

Vondmac was the eldest of the three who had assembled. Her spots were myriad—hundreds of tiny near-circles evenly spaced across her scalp. According to an old husbands' tale, children born with such a distribution were destined for the life of science, and though it annoyed her no end to give any sort of support to such superstitious nonsense, Vondmac was proof of the legend.

This shift, however, instead of wearing the narrow, shawllike tippet of a scientist, Vondmac wore her Ionian robes in honor of the goddess, as did Moodri and the youngest of the three, Melgil. Should any Overseer risk infection by intruding on this meeting, ancient star charts and ceremonial divining crystals were unrolled and scattered at the Elders' feet, giving weight to their well-practiced story that this was yet another of the endless rounds of religious debates that consumed most of the Elders' time and attention. Fortunately, none of the Overseers ever seemed to recall that on Tencton religious debates had been exceedingly rare, given the strong current of tolerance to which most Tenctonese faiths adhered.

But it was not religion being debated in the isolation room, it was the survival of the three hundred thousand Tenctonese aboard this ship. And Vondmac did not talk of the dual nature of the *serdos* or how the seasonal festivals of the goddess could be reconciled with the passage of relativistic time, but of planetary chemistry and distant atmospheric readings. On the home world she had been a biochemist and thus was the first to whom the stolen readings from the bridge were always given.

"In terms of distance to the primary, it is the second planet of this system that is better situated," Vondmac reported. "But initial scans show it to be completely cloud-covered and far too hot to support life as we know it. I suspect that it does not even support life as we don't know it."

Moodri and Melgil waited patiently, a trait honed by spending more than a century aboard the ship and in slave camps on distant worlds. Vondmac would say what she had to say and in as much detail as she felt necessary. It was the way of things, and they were content.

"But the *third* planet is possessed of minimal cloud cover. *And* an oxygen atmosphere," Vondmac said. She paused then, a subtle smile at play on her lips.

Melgil sat forward in his chair. His withered right arm was momentarily exposed by the wide sleeves of his robes. Melgil was a *binnaum,* and his spots were few but exceedingly large. "What is the planet's mass?" he asked.

"Point eight seven of one Tencton mass," Vondmac said.

Moodri asked the next question he was certain she was expecting. "And the percentage concentration of oxygen is . . ."

"At this distance and velocity, the spectrograph shows twenty percent," Vondmac said, "with a plus or minus error factor of two."

Moodri and Melgil exchanged a glance of hope, and of concern. With such a small mass the third planet could not be expected to maintain such a sizable portion of oxygen in its atmosphere as the result of purely mechanical and chemical means. The only explanation that would therefore account for that oxygen's presence was for the third planet to have an established biosphere of carbon-based life—a biosphere that might be capable of supporting Tenctonese life.

Their concern was for the hard decisions that would have to be made if, in fact, the third planet was the long-hoped-for refuge the Elders had suspected it might be.

For the moment, though, Melgil concentrated on the facts at hand. "Then the old charts *are* correct," he said. "This *is* a habitable system."

But Vondmac did not immediately confirm the old *binnaum's* conclusion. Moodri was afraid to guess why.

"The third planet is possessed of an organic biosphere," she said. "But that is not all."

Moodri was surprised by the force of the disappointment he felt. For almost fifteen years the Elders had had it in their power to disable the ship under certain conditions. Throughout that time, during each translation into normal space for a course-correction swing around a star, the Elders had searched for a world that could provide safe harbor for the wretched slaves on board.

So many stars they had swung about in that time, and fewer than one in three had met the combined conditions of emitting the proper range of light required for Tenctonese health *and* having planets the proper distance from their sun. Of those appropriate solar systems, almost nine in ten had supported some form of life on planets that were near the right size and temperature. But fewer than half of those had been planets on which the biosphere was organic—its life chemistry based on the carbon ring, as was the home world biosphere in which the Tenctonese had evolved.

Of the handful of planets that orbited a sun that produced the right light, were the right size, had the right temperature, and were home to carbon-based life, half again were already in the service of the ships—home to slave camps, mines, ocean farms, and energy converters constructed on a planetary scale, slowly transforming entire worlds into planetesimal debris.

Which left the Elders with fewer than six chances out of every hundred translations to find a world that might offer hope to their people. And of those six chances, how many had been lost to them because the atmosphere seethed with ancient radiation from a long-ago war? How many had been lost to biospheres corrupted by the sudden introduction of artificial life forms for which no ecological checks and balances had ever evolved? How many were cloaked by ice, devoid of free water, or poisoned by planetary oceans brimming with unimaginable concentrations of sodium chloride?

Too many, Moodri knew, for the dream of freedom to have remained alive in the younger among them—those who were the firstborn on the ship and thus the next to take over as Elders when the last generation of the home-born died.

And now it seemed that Vondmac was about to tell them that this world, too, was unsuitable for them.

"What else is this world possessed by?" Moodri asked.

"According to the spectrographic readings, fully two thirds of the surface is covered by oceans polluted by sodium chloride," Vondmac said.

Moodri sighed. They might just as well be oceans of sulfuric acid. But still, that meant that one third of the planet might be free of the poisonous liquid. And even at point eight seven the mass of Tencton, a planet was still a large place.

"Are the oceans alone enough reason for us to pass by this world?" Moodri asked.

"Alone?" Vondmac said. "No, not by themselves. They would add hazard and health problems to any resettlement, but I would assume there would be deserts enough to suit us."

"Then what else is there on this world?" Melgil asked. Moodri could hear in the *binnaum* the same sense of despair that he himself felt.

Vondmac stared at a podling in the gently rocking swing beside her. The small one made a fist and sleepily tried to shove it into his toothless and flangeless mouth. Vondmac smiled and brushed a gentle knuckle across the podling's spots. "At this distance, at this velocity," the scientist said, "the world is radiating strongly in the electromagnetic spectrum from three meters to three centimeters."

Moodri understood. "The world is home to a race of intelligent tool users," he said. Life was everywhere throughout the stars, but intelligent self-awareness was rarer than a three-fold lunar eclipse.

Melgil bowed his head. The Elders had discussed this possibility often. The only moral and ethical decision that could be made would be to pass the world by completely.

But Moodri was puzzled. The sun they were approaching was a regular course-correction star for the ships. It had been used dozens if not hundreds of times in the past. Moodri himself knew he had passed it before, almost a century earlier.

"Is this world not already in service to the ships?" Moodri asked.

Vondmac shook her head, acknowledging his quick appreciation of the conundrum they faced. "No, it is not," she said. She held up a slender hand. "And before you ask, this star *has* been on the ship's charts since we left Tencton, as has the third planet's orbit. In fact, were I to judge from the drift error between the star's projected position according to the charts and its actual position as established upon translation, I would estimate that the ship's builders originally charted this star more than ten thousand years ago."

"Ten thousand years," Moodri said softly. He wondered if in that time the message of the goddess might have reached this world, or even if Celine and Andarko might have left their touch upon it.

"I don't understand," Melgil suddenly said.

Moodri nodded. "How true. None of us understands the slightest iota of the universe around us."

But Melgil waved his sleeves at Moodri. "I am speaking literally, Moodri, not spiritually." To Vondmac he said, "If this world has been known to the ships so long, and if it does have intelligent tool users upon it, then why is it not in the service of the ships?"

Vondmac raised her empty hands to Ionia. "Why not, indeed? It is a very good question, and I have no answers for you."

Moodri didn't believe that for a second. "Come, come, scientist," he said. "We have a simple set of starting conditions here. A suitable theory to account for them should not be too difficult to formulate."

Vondmac gestured to Moodri. "I bow to your greater knowledge, scientist."

Moodri sighed again. More than a century in captivity, and Vondmac still knew how to play games. He decided he should admire her resilience and not be annoyed by her stubborness.

"Very well," Moodri began. "We set out the following conditions. So far, all other worlds that have an indigenous race of intelligent tool users are in service to the ships."

"All other worlds *of which we have knowledge,*" Vondmac qualified.

"Surely, that is a given," Moodri said. "If we know a world to have indigenous intelligent tool users, then it follows that we have knowledge of that world."

But Vondmac raised a finger. "Not if you—"

"Colleagues!" Melgil said loudly.

Moodri and Vondmac turned to look at him. The podlings stirred, disturbed by Melgil's sudden outburst.

"This is not a classroom, nor is it the hidden council," Melgil said testily. "Perhaps we should dispense with the debating tactics and get to the hearts of the matter."

Moodri and Vondmac regarded each other's eyes for long moments until both understood that a truce was in order.

"I shall begin again," Moodri said. "So far, of all the worlds *of which we have knowledge,* we have noted that each world with indigenous, intelligent tool users is in service to the ships.

The third planet of this world is home to such tool users, yet it is not in service. Therefore our pattern of knowledge has been broken, and we need to add new conditions to our initial statement."

There was a lengthy pause, finally broken by Melgil. "And what might those new conditions be, Moodri?"

Certain that Vondmac would not interrupt, Moodri continued.

"One, the electromagnetic emissions from the planet are the result of heretofore unknown natural phenomena, and the planet is not inhabited by intelligent creatures."

"Unlikely," Vondmac said.

"Conceded," Moodri agreed. "Two, the planet is like Korullus V."

Melgil nodded to indicate it was a reasonable assumption to him. Korullus V was a planet once inhabited by a species of intelligent tool users, and which was now inhabited only by the species' intelligent tools. The world had become little more than a landscape of mechanical contrivances similar to the ship's maintenance hull crawlers, moving from place to place, occasionally doing battle so that the loser's spare parts could be incorporated into the winner's configuration. The planet radiated powerful deep-space microwave beacons as if the mechanical thinking devices on the planet sought their creators and enticed them to return home, apparently with no knowledge that it was the thinking devices that had caused the creators to become extinct in the first place.

"Perhaps," Vondmac said thoughtfully. "But the devices of Korullus V are powered by fusion and conversion technologies. The atmospheric scans of the third planet indicate a great deal of biomass combustion is providing that world's energy needs. That type of energy production is not generally found to be concurrent with the advanced mechanical technologies that give rise to self-motivated machines capable of reproduction on a planetary scale."

Moodri accepted that. "Just a thought," he said.

"Have you no others?" Melgil asked.

"Two," Moodri said, though he did not wish to state either.

"Two should do it," Vondmac said, to let him know that she had already arrived at the conclusions he had.

"The third possible explanation for what we see is that the last time this ship—or any of its fleet—executed a course correction around this sun, the third planet was *not* radiating in the microwave frequencies."

Melgil's face wrinkled up in thought. "But did we ourselves not pass by this star just less than a century ago?"

"A great deal can happen in a century," Moodri said.

Melgil rocked back in his chair and waved his good hand, dismissing the theory. "If you're suggesting that the third planet's intelligent species developed radio technology in the precise span of time elapsed between our last passage of its star and this passage, you're ready for the vats, my friend."

Vondmac snickered. "The level of coincidence is extreme," she said.

"What level of coincidence?" Moodri asked. "The ship has known of this star for ten thousand years. If intelligence has grown on one of its planets, is it coincidence that it should do so in the ten thousand years of the ship's existence? Think of all the life we have seen and know of in this galaxy. Intelligence must have arisen millions of years ago in thousands of places. The goddess willing, it will arise again and again millions of years hence in thousands more. To ask why it is that in our passage in one ship of a fleet of perhaps thousands, over a span of years that might very well approach a million, one small planet should achieve a pinnacle of technological development *now,* is like asking how it came to be that any one of us was born where and when we were. Goddess! There are so many stars, so many planets, so much life"—Moodri dropped his voice to an angry whisper, so unlike him—"and so many ships that what we see is something that was inevitably to happen at some time. The only coincidence is that we are the individuals who are here to see it. And that is not coincidence, colleagues, that is fate."

One podling snuffled. Other than that, there was silence in the isolation room. Until Vondmac said, "Conceded."

Melgil cleared his throat. "And what of the fourth possibility?" he asked Moodri. "You said you had *two* more, did you not? So another possibility remains."

Moodri adjusted the prayer beads at his neck. "It is not a pleasant prospect, old friend."

Melgil's face clouded.

"If there is intelligence on this planet, intelligence that is not in service to the ships, then perhaps the reason is that . . . the ships are in service to this planet."

Moodri felt his spots pucker at their edges at even the thought of what he dared suggest.

Melgil reacted the same way and brought a hand to his scalp, rubbing his spots to relax them. He flexed his feet up and down as well, trying to relieve the pain of tension that must have cut through them.

"Are you *serious?*" the old *binnaum* whispered. "That this could be the world of Those Who Made the Ships?"

A podling who was too attuned to the emotional state of those around him began to cry at the sudden increase in anxiety that filled the room. Moodri got up and went to the child to comfort him. The hem of his robes brushed lightly against the textured metal of the floor. "A possibility only," he said as he lifted the babe. "A condition that might account for matters as we view them." He whispered to the podling, filling it with his love, for even here, even now, the goddess provided.

Melgil's eyes blazed with horror. "We must . . . we must tell the others," he said breathlessly.

But Vondmac raised a hand to calm him. "The power of science is such that those who have shared in the examination of the initial conditions will have arrived at the same range of possible conclusions," she said. "Most of the hidden council will know what we face by the end of shift."

"What we face?" Melgil said. "What we face? We face nothing! There can be no decision to be made this time." He stood up and hugged his withered arm tightly to his chest as he paced through the room. "We have already said that we will not inflict ourselves upon any world's indigenous culture, especially if our presence might then bring other ships to reclaim us and endanger the inhabitants of that new world." He stopped and wheeled to stare at Moodri, who softly cooed to the podling snuggled safely in his arms. "And to attempt to land on a world that is the home of Those Who Made the Ships . . . that's insane! Utter madness! Every last one of us will be recycled like . . . like that!" He made a frictive click with his tongue where a human would have snapped fingers.

Moodri said nothing, simply rubbed his knuckles against the tiny temples of the child. "We thank Ionia for this day," he whispered to the child, "and each day ever after."

"Have you nothing more to say?" Melgil asked.

"No," Moodri said simply.

"What more could he say?" Vondmac asked. She rose stiffly from her chair and walked uncertainly over to Melgil. At her age, the many sudden shifts from the artificial gravity field of the ship to the work camps of other worlds had caught up with her more quickly than it had the others. Quantum compression was what the Elders who once were physicists called it. "What Moodri has stated is supposition based on facts—possibilities to be examined until we can divine which is more likely or that all must be discarded for yet another, newer theory. His reasoning is solid, his explanations succinct. Until new data are available from the bridge, further pontificating is unproductive."

"But . . . but the decision we must make, the hidden council must vote and . . ." Melgil looked at Moodri. There was apprehension in his face. Everyone knew what the cost of that decision would be, especially for Moodri.

But Vondmac gently put her hand on Melgil's withered arm. "We don't know enough to vote yet. On the one side we have Moodri's four theories. On the other we have the certainty of Terminus. For now our course of action is clear and indisputable."

Terminus. Melgil trembled at the word as he had at the thought of meeting Those Who Made the Ships.

Terminus. A port at which this ship had never called, but a port each Tencton knew. The stories of its horror were as old as the alien names for this vessel, as dark as the hell of Tencton legend.

Terminus. A vast and artificial world system of linked and orbiting toroids larger than any planet. It was there that the ships were repaired and their machines exchanged. Where cargo was off-loaded, processed, and sent on its way to other sectors of the galaxy, to other worlds, perhaps even other dimensions and times. For the stories said that all manner of ships docked at Terminus eventually, including some that made what the Tenctonese rode now look like a pleasure cruiser.

And it was at Terminus that the cargo was culled.

Living beings from all different species and races and worlds were continually propelled down endless, gravity-free tunnels by technologies no sane mind could describe. The bleating and screaming and wailing of a thousand stolen cultures filled those lightless tunnels as individuals were plucked from the streaming, terrified mass of alien flesh to be surgically restructured, or medically blended, or even disassembled into a mist of conscious cells that would better be able to withstand a voyage that might take millennia through regions that were not part of space and time.

Some aboard this ship would survive this process, in body if not in mind, but once they had been off-loaded and selected and reprocessed, the stories made it clear that the survivors would never again return to their home sector of space. For how could a slave even think of home if home was so far away in space and time as to have no meaningful existence?

Terminus was the nightmare of the ships a thousand times over—the promise that they were not just an aberration of one small group of stars in one small galaxy at one short moment in time, but that their influence spanned the universe with mindless cruelty.

The stories made it abundantly clear. When this ship docked at Terminus what little culture the Tenctonese captives had maintained, what memories of their home and their history and their beginnings they had relayed from parent to child over two generations would be lost forever.

The Tenctonese would be no more.

There would only be soulless biological working machines. No past. No future. No present but pain and fear.

Up to now the Tenctonese had only been in transit, stopping off to take care of an odd job here and there.

But soon, only two course corrections away, the real horror would begin, the real nightmare.

What they had experienced, what they experienced now, was nothing compared to what awaited them.

All else was prologue.

"Terminus?" Melgil repeated in a whisper. "Are you certain?"

"I have seen the charts," Vondmac said. "We have been in transit long enough. This ship and its cargo are to be . . . processed."

Melgil staggered against the frame of a pod swing, seeking to hold on to it for balance. "What will we do?" he said plaintively. "What will we do?"

"For now," Vondmac said, "we will prepare as we have planned. We can always stop our preparations if need be, but we will not be able to stay on schedule if we do not begin now."

"But the hidden council . . ."

"The council will vote when we know more. It is too early to make any decisions now."

Melgil's spots had paled dramatically in the past few minutes, but as he took deep breaths they began to darken again. He looked to Moodri, still carrying the podling.

"You knew about Terminus?" Melgil asked.

Moodri nodded yes.

Melgil's breath caught in his throat. "And yet you appear so indifferent. Either way this goes we face doom, and yet you remain so unaffected."

Moodri smiled peacefully. "I have no burden because what happens next is not up to me," he said, blowing warmly against the podling's minute ear valleys, making it gurgle with delight.

Melgil calmed himself and adjusted his robes. "Yes, you are quite right," he said. "It is not up to us. It is up to the goddess, Ionia."

Moodri's easy smile never left him, but he knew his friend was wrong. In the final accounting, of course, what would happen would be up to the goddess, Ionia. But over the next few dozens of shifts what would happen was in a completely different set of hands.

Everything that would happen next was up to his grand-nephew, Buck. And it was time that Buck learned the truth.

CHAPTER 6

GEORGE CLOSED HIS EYES against the purplish glow of the ultraviolet light banks overhead, luxuriating in the soothing warmth they spread upon his scalp. He closed his ear valleys to the loud, low rumble from the furtive conversations of the hundreds of other off-shift workers packed into the metal-walled light bay. He concentrated only on the hand that was in his, squeezing it softly, feeling it squeeze back in turn.

Beside him on the hard metal floor, sitting so she was side to side against him, Appy made a subtle though surprisingly sexually explicit humming sound in her throat, so softly that only George could hear. The most sensitive spots in the small of his back immediately began to feel as if they fluttered against his skin, sending anticipatory thrills of pleasure radiating through his midsection. But he was acutely aware of those hundreds of other workers surrounding him, and so George did not do what he wanted to do, but only what he could do. He laughed, more from embarrassment than with amusement.

Appy's gentle laughter joined with his, and she leaned her head on his shoulder. George opened his eyes again and looked at her—his life partner, mother to his children, the hearts to which his own hearts answered, beat for beat. In the language of the world that waited for them, Appy would be named Susan

Francisco, and her relation to George would be categorized as wife. But it would not be the first time that a language of that strange planet did not do justice to the range of emotions it attempted to describe so simply. For now, George couldn't even find the words in his own, more complex language to describe all that he felt for Susan, other than that in the midst of this hell she remained the focus of everything. Sometimes, especially when they were in a privacy chamber and he heard that gentle hum building in her as she nuzzled his back, he could almost think that the two extremes of his life were in balance—that life on the ship was reasonable payment to be made to the universe in return for knowing Susan and sharing his life with her. In that, George knew that what they shared was exceedingly rare among the captive members of their race, and thus even more precious.

But for now George lightly tapped a knuckle against Susan's temple—a playful admonishment more appropriate to children than to two adults, unless the two adults were lovers. "Stop that," he whispered unconvincingly. "We are not alone."

Susan snuggled closer, fitting perfectly against him. "Mmm, I wish we were." She began to hum again, teasingly, and so much more loudly that George looked nervously around to see if any nearby could hear.

"Appy, shhh," George said, feeling his eyes begin to water in the Tenctonese equivalent of a human blush response. Another couple behind them in the crowded light bay were now grimly staring at George and Susan, and George was familiar with their expression because he had seen it often. Almost all the marriages on board the ship were arranged by the Overseers for reasons George had never been able to understand. Complete strangers were suddenly forced to spend their lives together, no matter how incompatible they might be, and such couples had little tolerance for that handful of true-mated Tenctonese who discovered that they would have chosen their assigned mates regardless of the Overseers' decision. As had Susan and George.

But, typically, Susan didn't care who was listening. "Shhh yourself," she said with a giggle. "I'm remembering the time we were in the privacy chamber with the *asha* lotions and you—"

In a panic George placed his hand over Susan's mouth. Tears rolled from his eyes. How could she even *think* of talking about the *asha* lotions with so many others so close? "People can hear," he pleaded.

Then Susan laughed again and took his hand from her mouth, giving his fingers a fleeting kiss. "Honestly, Neemu, sometimes I think you're turning into an old *binnaum* on me."

As she called him by her pet name for him George recognized the playful look in her dark eyes and understood that she was only teasing him once again. She had not planned to say anything more than what she had said, hoping only to get a reaction from him by pretending that she intended to say more. The *asha* lotions would remain their secret. They had to.

"But if you could see the way the others are looking at us," George said, struggling to maintain a semblance of dignity while registering his disapproval of her supposed joke.

"I don't care," Susan said.

"It is not safe to attract attention."

Susan narrowed her eyes. He recognized that look as well. "We're not doing anything wrong, Stangya." Her use of his real name indicated her abrupt change in mood.

"We must stop being—" George suddenly realized what he was going to say and stopped before he said it.

Happy. He was going to say happy. As if being happy were wrong. As if finding that some small part of his soul had real sunshine in it, not artificial wavelengths from naked overhead light banks, was somehow incompatible with how the universe was supposed to be.

Susan understood. She always did. It was her turn to whisper "shhh," and her face reflected the sudden onset of unhappiness that George felt. "Why don't we go back to the dorm?"

This time George didn't speak because he *didn't* know what to say. He and Susan still had a quarter shift of UV allotted to them. The Elders had explained that the lighting tubes in the bulk of the ship didn't provide the wavelengths necessary for Tenctonese health, so the Overseers had outfitted large chambers with UV lights like those in the 'ponics chambers in order that the Tenctonese could receive periodic megadoses to keep their spots dark and their faculties intact. George had never tried to understand how light could be nourishing. All he knew was that the periods spent sitting idly in the light bays were the closest thing to time off that any of the workers had, and that he and Susan were so seldom assigned the same UV schedule that this shift felt almost like what Moodri described as a holiday—entire remarkable days on Tencton during which whole tribes had not worked. George didn't want to lose a second of this time.

"Please, Neemu," Susan said. "Little Devoosha is with Peetmor and Laynzee." She tightened her grip on his hand. "Most of the others in the dorm are on shift. So perhaps"—she dropped her voice to the barest whisper—"there will be a privacy chamber free."

George looked deep into Susan's eyes and marveled at her. Like him, she had been born on the ship, lived all her life with its rules and its schedules, and yet she could circumvent them as easily as if she were an Elder. To suggest going into a privacy chamber during a shift break? It was so outrageous an idea that George was certain that there wasn't even a rule about it.

"Appy, the schedule says we're supposed to remain here until—"

Susan looked directly at him. *"Neck* the schedule."

George flinched at Susan's language. "You are talking like a vat worker."

"I want to be with my husband." She spoke in the tone that George knew meant there was nothing he could say to argue with her. Susan stood up without relinquishing her grip on his hand. "Come along, Stangya."

George felt the eyes of everyone else in the light bay turn to him. Susan was the only one in the crowded chamber who was standing. But an argument would only attract even more attention, so he reluctantly rose up beside her.

Susan began threading her way through the dense mass of bodies, heading for the short entrance tunnel that led to the corridor. George followed, feeling almost as if he were being dragged. As he carefully placed his feet between the scattered hands and stretched-out legs of the seated workers he mumbled over and over: "Early shift . . . I'm sorry, excuse us . . . early shift starting." He hated to stand out. It was only an invitation for trouble with the Overseers.

But when they reached the corridor George was almost sorry that there was no Overseer standing in their way to help convince Susan that it might be better, and less trouble, if they remained in the light bay. The corridor was deserted, filled only with a fresh, thick mist of low-lying holy gas. As he and Susan stopped outside the light bay tunnel it was still spewing forth from the overhead nozzles, dark purple in color and not yet oxidized to white, indicating that the gas had been released just in the last few minutes.

"That's odd," George said as Susan turned to the right to continue down the gray, pipe-lined corridor to a branching intersection. "The gas usually isn't this thick when we're in transit."

Susan's feet cut through the mist, making it roll away in slow waves of purple-white whorls. "At least it means there won't be any Overseers around," she said.

That was true, George knew. The holy gas of obedience was a double-edged sword. At high concentrations it made the Tenctonese passive and completely responsive to the Overseers' orders. However, it also reduced workers' stamina, strength, and reaction time and made them completely incapable of handling an unexpected situation. At low concentrations workers were almost unimpaired but were far more capable of resisting the Overseers' commands. The pattern that therefore had been established kept the gas at low levels throughout most of the ship most of the time, with greater numbers of Overseers on duty at the most critical work stations. During ship-to-ship rendezvous, or while orbiting planets, the gas concentration was increased in almost all areas of the ship except for the bridge and the power plant facilities in order to prevent any attempt at revolt. And during those times Overseers were seldom seen in the areas where the gas concentrations were highest.

Personally, George didn't understand the Overseers' reasoning. He had been off the ship often enough to know what it felt like to be gas-free. There was an unexpected, if mild, clarity of thought and feeling of increased energy that came upon him at such times—though that could just as easily be attributed to low-gravity fields and higher oxygen concentrations. But once back on the ship it really didn't seem to matter whether the concentration of the holy gas was high or low. He seldom felt any different. And certainly Susan didn't seem to be slowed down by the gas the way so many others were, except when she was freshly exposed after being off-ship for long periods of time. Under those circumstances she could succumb to the gas instantly. But after a long period of exposure she was almost as untroubled by it as was George.

George laughed out loud as a sudden thought came to him. Susan glanced at him suspiciously. "What?" she asked.

"I have just now realized the real reason why we are so much more content than other mated pairs," George said, squeezing Susan's hand. He gestured to the layer of mist that covered the floor of the corridor. "Here we are in the midst of full gas concentration, yet we are searching for a privacy chamber." That was the other common side effect of too much gas—most Tenctonese completely lost the desire to couple under its influence. But the more George thought about it, the more he realized that he and Susan had never felt so constrained. Certainly their intimate times together were infrequent prizes in the mind-numbing routine of the ship, but on those rare occasions when their schedules overlapped at the same time a privacy chamber was available, it had never really seemed to matter what the concentration of the gas was.

They reached the branching intersection, and Susan stopped in the middle of it with a thoughtful look on her face. In all eight directions the corridors were deserted, almost eerily. "You're right," she said. "I never really thought about it before." She gave a small cough—the first sign that the extremely high level of gas was finally beginning to have an effect on her.

George slipped his arms around Susan, knowing that within an hour at most the gas would take its toll on her. But an hour would be enough time for him to get her away from the highest concentrations.

He looked all around them, treasuring the feel of her within his arms. "It must be proof of our love," he said. That certainly made sense. To couple without love was almost unthinkable as far as George was concerned. And no doubt those who had been assigned to each other by the Overseers, without a chance for love to enter their unions, shared that feeling—which might explain the jealousy that George so often felt directed at him and Susan. It might also be the reason why the birth rate on board was so low. Dropping precipitously, the Elders said.

"Proof of our love," Susan repeated as she returned George's hug at the same time she gazed up and down the empty corridors. "Either that, or the *sardanac* I've been slipping into your meatgrowth is finally beginning to work."

George stepped back from Susan. She could joke about anything. But they had both long ago decided that *sardanac*—an artificial pheromone that could chemically bond any male and female—was not desirable or necessary for them. At least he hoped she was joking.

"Doesn't this strike you as strange?" Susan asked.

"Sardanac?" George replied, confused.

Susan shook her head with a sigh of exasperation. "No, Stangya. The corridors. The whole time we've been standing here there's been absolutely no one in them."

George shrugged. Now that they were beyond the watchful eyes of jealous others, the idea of finding a privacy chamber was seeming more and more like a good plan, particularly before the effect of the gas grew any stronger in Susan. "It's mid-shift," he said.

Susan frowned. "But still . . . there should be couriers, Elders, scavengers, off-shift workers . . . somebody. Even an Overseer."

George once again looked down each of the eight corridors. Susan was right, but he could come up with a partial explanation. "With the gas levels so high, the Overseers don't need to be in the corridors. The gas will make almost all the others stay where they are until they're given orders to move."

"All the others except for us," Susan said with a preoccupied tone. "I wonder if it's because we wanted to couple."

George reflexively looked around to see if anyone else had heard her blunt statement. "Appy . . ."

"Oh, relax, Stangya. There's no one here. But why? And if the Overseers don't need to be in this section, where *do* they need to be?"

She was right again. This wasn't normal. George tilted his head, straining to hear if there was anything wrong with the ship. Once, almost fifteen years ago on a deep range, a strange vibration had rumbled through the corridors, and the ship had violently translated into normal space hundreds of parsecs from any course-correction star. The lights and gravity had been out for almost an entire shift. During the nightmarish period of zero gravity all through the ship food-growth vats and sewage-processing units had emptied into the air-circulation system, which had taken more than a year to properly cleanse. The Overseers' response had been to withdraw to other parts of the ship and then to flood the corridors with copious amounts of holy gas to place most of the Tenctonese into a state of near catatonia. Thousands had died of starvation and dehydration during that time. George, with his brother Ruhtra, had been one of only a handful who were still able to move about, groggy, though not completely incapacitated by the gas. And he could remember that almost twenty shifts had passed before the ship translated back into its superluminal mode and the Overseers returned to the corridors. Near the end of those twenty shifts, as the effects of the overdose of gas began to wear off, many of the Tenctonese had come to believe they had been abandoned by the Overseers to die in space. Some had welcomed that fate. To this day, as far as George understood, no one knew what had happened to cause such a near disaster. He listened apprehensively now in case it was to happen again.

But in the empty corridors the constant background vibration of the ship's machinery was smooth and unchanged. There was, however, a noise of a different kind coming from one direction. George strained to hear it, to understand it.

Susan looked down the same corridor. She heard it, too. "Is it some kind of machine?" she asked.

The sound was regular enough to be mechanical in origin, but there was something more to it, something . . .

"It's marching!" George said. His spots puckered. It was the sound of Overseers' boots moving in perfect rhythm. Dozens of them. Perhaps a hundred.

He saw Susan rock gently from foot to foot, soothing the muscles of her feet. "Maybe we should go back to the light bay," she said nervously.

George kept his eyes fixed on the corridor from which the sounds of marching came. He sought out Susan's hand and held it tight. "Maybe we should," he said.

The marching grew louder, then began to lessen again. Whoever—whatever—was moving through the corridors still thick with holy gas had shifted directions.

Susan and George took a step forward at the same time, not even conscious of what they were doing until they turned to each other, first in surprise and then in immediate understanding.

There was something unusual occurring nearby. Something

that, judging by the gas concentration, the Overseers didn't want anyone else to see.

Given such a situation, George and Susan moved as one. They had to know what was happening. Hand in hand they cautiously edged down the corridor. It was the only act of rebellion of which they were capable.

For now.

CHAPTER 7

AFTER TWO HOURS IN Bryon Grazer's company Sikes was already beginning to regret ever talking to the detective. True, Grazer knew more than Sikes ever would about computers, but the only topic the forensic accounting detective wanted to talk about was how the political structure of the LAPD would be changing now that Chief Williams had replaced Daryl Gates. "The old boys' network of the past is on its way out, Sikes," was the way Grazer had begun his lecture on the drive back to Sikes's apartment. "The old loyalties are in disarray. Lines of communications are broken. In a way, the current conditions within the force resemble the start of the Wars of the Diodochi in 323 B.C." He had peered earnestly over at Sikes then. "You *are* familiar with the forty-two-year war of succession that followed the death of Alexander the Great, aren't you?"

Sikes's biggest mistake of the day was that he had confessed that he wasn't all that familiar with the War of the Dahoozits, and Grazer had immediately set out to correct that shortcoming, spending the next hour in a nonstop detailed discourse that appeared to touch on everything from Babylonian toilet habits to the contradictory reports concerning the performance of Patriot missiles during the Gulf War. In retrospect, Sikes was amazed that one person could talk so assuredly in such an incoherent manner for so long. But at the time he had only wanted to scream and hit the steering wheel, which was his traditional method of dealing with the frustrations of driving in L.A. traffic. About the time Grazer began describing the spread of animal-grease rumors during the Sepoy Mutiny of 1857 Sikes even considered for a few satisfying moments what might happen if he screamed and then hit Grazer.

Remarkably, as the two men rode up in the balky elevator in Sikes's Studio City apartment building, Grazer brought his entire surreal lecture full circle, comparing each of the LAPD's assistant chiefs to one of Alexander the Great's generals. "And, of course," Grazer grandly concluded, "I don't have to tell *you* who General Lysimachus compares to, because it is just *too* obvious." He chuckled knowingly, and Sikes, on the brink of mental suffocation, joined in weakly just as the elevator chimed and the doors opened on his floor.

Grazer hesitated outside the elevator, clutching the late Dr. Petty's computer to his chest, and sniffed the air. "What is that?" he asked. "Cabbage?"

Sikes had a sudden fear that he was about to be subjected to a seminar on Irish immigration and thus ignored the question, charging quickly down the L-hallway toward his apartment. The sooner he could get the computer set up and running, the sooner he could focus Grazer's rambling intellect on the Petty case.

But when he turned the corner he realized that the evening was not going to get any simpler or better.

"Where have you been?" Victoria Sikes, née Fletcher, said angrily. She was waiting by Sikes's apartment door, where it appeared she was in the process of writing a note on a piece of paper she had stuck over the security peephole.

Sikes froze at the corner and almost lost his grip on the cardboard box he carried, filled with stacks of Grazer's floppy disks and the monitor for Petty's computer. His eyes widened as he tried to remember what day it was. "Vic?"

His daughter, Kirby, stood behind his wife and waved at him, grinning. Except for her Guns 'N Roses T-shirt and three silver crosses dangling from her left ear, she looked to Sikes like the sweetest thirteen-year-old girl imaginable. Victoria, on the other hand, in her traditional severe business suit, looked as if she were ready to kill.

"Well?" Victoria said, placing her hands on her hips. "Do you know how long I've been waiting?"

"Twenty-two minutes," Kirby said. She grinned again at her father. "No big deal, Dad."

Sikes felt trapped. He was delighted to see his daughter but didn't know how he was going to handle working with Grazer if Kirby was supposed to spend the night. He was unnerved to see his wife, but as always Victoria's presence made his heart flutter, as if it hadn't been in communication with his brain since their honeymoon. "Um," he stammered, "this *is* Wednesday, isn't it?"

"Yeah, it's Wednesday," Grazer said as he came to a stop beside Sikes. "So, are you going to introduce me?"

"So what if it's Wednesday?" Victoria demanded.

Sikes nodded at his wife and daughter. "Detective Bryon Grazer, this is my daughter, Kirby, and, uh, my wife, Victoria."

"I didn't know you were married," Grazer said.

Of course not, Sikes thought, you've only known me two hours, and you haven't let me say more than a dozen words.

"We're separated," Victoria said sharply. "Well, Matt, I'm waiting for an answer."

Sikes thought feverishly. All his hopes for the future were riding on his determination never to screw up with Victoria and Kirby again. But from Victoria's mood, he obviously had, and he didn't know how.

"I thought," he began cautiously, "I thought Kirby was coming for the *weekend.*" Every other weekend during the school year. That was the arrangement. Sikes was certain of it.

Victoria crossed her arms and sighed dramatically. "Oh, Matt. I *told* you I had to go to Bern tonight." She looked at him accusingly. "The Oberth Pharmaceuticals account? Sound familiar?"

"That's the company with the new sugar substitute, isn't it?" Grazer asked. "An L-sucrose. Just as sweet as sugar. Can't be digested, so no calories. With aspartame's patent having run out they stand to break into a twenty-billion-dollar-a-year market with an initial eight percent penetration. Right now they're shopping for a California-based advertising agency that—"

Sikes stared at Grazer in bewilderment. "How the hell do you know that?"

Grazer blinked innocently at Sikes. "I take a money management course at UCLA so I can handle my investments more efficiently. I highly recommend the course, detective."

"You have *investments?*" Sikes asked incredulously. "On *our* salaries?"

"Don't you?" Grazer asked as if he were genuinely puzzled.

"No, he doesn't," Victoria said. "Now open the door, Matt. My flight leaves in two hours."

Sikes leaned down and placed the cardboard box on the worn floral print broadloom in front of his apartment door. As he straightened up to pull out his keys he could see that Victoria had been writing her message to him on a large yellow Post-it note. She always carried three different sizes of them in her purse. There had been times when he had thought she had intended to redecorate their apartment with them. The note began: *Matt, I'm not surprised that you have let me down again, but I can't understand how you can continue to disappoint Kirby in this callous manner.*

It was too much. Sikes's hand began to shake, and he couldn't get his key into the lock. He turned to Victoria. "Just *when* did you tell me that you were bringing Kirby over tonight?"

Victoria's lips pursed in restrained anger. She reached into the large shoulder bag she carried and pulled out a thick Filofax. She leafed through it quickly, then ran a long red fingernail—her own, not an extension—across a handwritten entry. "Last Tuesday. Our phone call about Kirby's summer school."

Sikes thought back to last Tuesday. He and Victoria *had* talked. She wanted him to contribute a thousand dollars to send Kirby to some sort of scuba-diving summer school in the Bahamas. Sikes had suggested that he could take Kirby to Sea World instead, and she could use the rest of the money for clothes and schoolbooks. Victoria hadn't been impressed. But had she mentioned anything about Kirby coming over on Wednesday?

Sikes finished replaying the conversation in his mind. "Vic, all you said was that you had to go out of town—to Switzerland—this week. That was it."

Victoria shoved her Filofax back into her shoulder bag without taking her eyes off Sikes. "Matthew," she said icily, "when I go out of town, who usually looks after Kirby for me?"

Sikes looked to the ceiling for guidance. "Nannies." He looked to Kirby for support. "Right?"

"Yeah, right," Kirby agreed. "I keep telling Mom I don't need them. I mean, I'm almost old enough to have sex, and—"

Sikes's breath exploded from him. *"Almost?"* he repeated. "Try eight years!"

"Oh, Daaad," Kirby groaned. "Everyone's doing—"

"Try *ten* years!"

Victoria placed her hand firmly on Kirby's shoulder. "That's enough, Kirby." She glared at Sikes. "And in the past, when I've hired nannies, have I not always informed you that I have arranged for Kirby's care? Well?"

"I guess," Sikes said, feeling himself on the edge of a long slippery slope.

"And did I tell you that I had hired a nanny this time?"

"But you *always* hire a nanny."

"*Did* I, Matthew?"

Sikes shook his head, turning the door keys over and over in his fingers. He didn't know how, but it was all his fault again.

"So you admit that you knew you were supposed to look after Kirby." It wasn't a question. Sometimes Sikes wondered how Victoria had decided on advertising and marketing and missed becoming a lawyer.

Grazer put the computer down on top of Sikes's box by the door. "I think she's got you there, Sikes."

Sikes jabbed a warning finger at Grazer. "Don't you start."

"It's all right, Dad." Kirby came up to Sikes and gave him a hug.

But Victoria wasn't about to let Sikes off that easily. "It's not all right, Kirby. And don't you dare think otherwise, Matt. If you're going to continue to behave in this irresponsible manner, I don't know—"

"Stop it!" Sikes exclaimed. He thrust his key chain into his daughter's hands. "Kirby, you open up and show this guy where he can set up the computer." He looked at Grazer. "Bryon, you go with Kirby." Then he turned to Victoria. "But you, you come with me."

"I said my flight leaves in two hours," Victoria protested.

"I'll walk you to the elevator."

At the elevator Sikes stood in front of the call button so that Victoria couldn't press it. "This will take less than five minutes," he said.

"I've already given you twenty-two today," Victoria said.

Sikes opened his mouth to respond but then realized that if he was to accomplish anything in the next few minutes, he couldn't waste time. He took a deep breath. "Vic, are you doing it to me on purpose, or do you really hate me this much?"

Victoria didn't have an immediate smart comeback, so Sikes knew he had broken the escalating progression of the argument. "I don't know what you mean," she said.

Sikes held up his hands to keep Victoria from interrupting. "I'll admit I screwed up on figuring out that Kirby was going to have to come here while you're in Switzerland. No, don't say anything. You're right, I'm wrong. But really, Victoria, even you have to admit that it was an understandable mistake. And now it's taken care of. I showed up—twenty-two minutes late, for which I apologize—but everything's okay. So why do you tear into me like that? Especially in front of Kirby."

He could see her jaw tighten, but her tightly drawn back blond hair remained immobile, as perfect as if it had been sculpted in place. Finally she spoke. "This isn't the first time you've screwed up, Matt."

"No. And it won't be the last. But I'm getting better, aren't I? I mean, it's not like when Kirby was born and I didn't know what the hell was going on or what I wanted or . . . or anything."

Victoria looked away for a moment, then grudgingly she said, "No, it's not like when Kirby was born."

He could sense she was calming down, becoming the Victoria who had forgiven him so often in the past. Until the day her patience finally ran out. He decided to take a gamble—a hard thing for him to do—and spoke the truth to her. "I *am* trying, Vic. And you know why, don't you?"

She stared searchingly into his eyes. She had looked at him that way the first time they had met, and he had lost his heart to her in less than a single beat. *"Do* you know what you want?"

"More than ever," Sikes said.

"Tell me."

It was all or nothing. Like drawing a gun in a dark alley, looking for shadows. "I want you. And Kirby. Back in my life."

"You had that once."

"But I didn't know it," Sikes said honestly. "Like the song says. It wasn't until you'd gone that I realized what I had."

For an instant it appeared as if Victoria's perfect composure might be cracking. Now it was her turn to have to look away. "We've had this conversation before, Matt. Why should I believe you this time?"

Sikes clenched his fists at his side. It would be so much simpler if she could just read his mind. He wasn't like Grazer. Words did not come easily to him. "Because I'm trying. I'm really trying to get my life in order. To make Kirby proud of me. To make *you* proud of me."

For a moment he saw a smile flicker on her lips. Then she looked away.

"What?" he asked.

She seemed embarrassed, but for the first time in this brief meeting he didn't feel her fighting him, denying him. "I was just remembering you in your uniform. The day you graduated." She looked at him, honesty in her eyes as well. "I was proud of you, Matt."

Sikes fumbled at his back pocket and pulled out his badge case. He flipped it open and held out the gold shield inside like a child offering a painting to be hung on the refrigerator.

"Detective," Victoria said, wonderingly.

"My first day," Sikes explained, trying to keep the excitement from his voice, not willing to risk anything interfering with the sudden connection he felt he had made with her. "That's what the computer's for. It's a lead in my first case. Me. A homicide detective."

This time, when the smile came to Victoria's lips, it wasn't fleeting. "Congratulations, Matt. Really. It seems it was a long time since you took those tests. I didn't actually realize that . . . well, that you'd finally made it."

There was no undercurrent of sarcasm in her tone, and Sikes didn't go looking for it. For him, making detective was the first step on a long road to personal rehabilitation—a road that ended with his family back together with him.

"That detective you were with," Victoria said, "is he your new partner?"

The lie was out of Sikes before he even had time to think about it. "Yes," he said. "Grazer's helping me out on this one. He knows a lot about computers. He, um . . ." He was faltering, and he knew it. The last thing he needed to do now was to tell Victoria that he had a female partner. An *attractive* female partner. That was another mistake in his past he was trying to recover from—one that was never too far from Victoria's thoughts, and for good reason. But Sikes knew he wasn't going to be able to get away with it this time. He could never lie to Victoria without stumbling and stammering and that was exactly what was happening now. She was looking right at him, and she would know what he was doing. There was only one conclusion she could reach.

But again Sikes was wrong. There were *two* possible conclusions. And Victoria preferred the second.

She put her hands around his hand that held the badge case. "Oh, Matt," she said, not a hint of reserve left anywhere in her. "I know what it means when you start sputtering like that."

Sikes felt his insides turn to ice. He had almost made contact, and then he had blown it again. "You . . . you do?" he said, dragging his defeat out as long as possible. Who knew? Maybe the Big One would finally hit, and the building would collapse, and that would be the end of his struggle.

"Uh-huh," Victoria said. Then, amazingly, she stepped closer to Sikes and gathered his hand to her chest and stared at him with her lips only inches from his. "I've always had that effect on you, haven't I?"

Sikes's throat was as dry as a Santa Ana wind. He tried to nod, but he seemed to have relinquished control of his body.

And then Victoria threw her arms around him, pressed her hands against the back of his head, and kissed him like their very first kiss, when the world had spun away from them, disappearing for hours.

Sikes felt his chest melt. His knees actually went wobbly. He kissed back, urgently, rapturously, matching her mood and her need moment by moment until he lost track of where he was and who he was, and even the smell of his apartment hallway vanished in the warm haze of Victoria's perfume and the taste of her.

When it at last seemed to Sikes that he would no longer be able to breathe Victoria pulled slowly away, still perfectly in tune with him. Sikes breathed through his mouth. Each beat of his heart echoed in his ears. Victoria's eyes were half closed. A small strand of hair had pulled away from her sleek chignon and danced softly against her forehead. Sikes reached out with an unsteady hand to brush the hair away. Victoria took his hand, kissed his fingers, and whispered throatily, "I'll see you when I get back."

She reached around him and pressed the elevator call button

behind his back. She stayed there, pressed tightly to him, hands running up and down his back until the elevator chimed. Then she left, blowing him a final kiss just as the doors slipped closed.

"Oh, man," Sikes said to the emptiness of the apartment hallway. "Oh, man, oh, man, oh, man . . ."

He rubbed at his face and could smell Victoria's scent still clinging to him. His entire body vibrated like the sweetest chord Springsteen had ever played. And all he could think was that he had done it. He had actually, finally, and incredibly won back Victoria.

He almost felt like dancing as he walked back to his apartment. He knew he still had extensive ground to cover with his wife. They had more to work out between them than anything a good dose of hormones could overcome—especially the matter about his *real* new partner, Angela Perez. But he knew he *would* be able to work everything out because Angie and his new position as detective and the Petty murder investigation—that whole jumble of potential barriers to his reconciliation with Victoria—were only minor, work-related details. Easily understood, easily dealt with.

After all, he told himself as he stepped into his apartment, it wasn't as if the world were coming to an end any time soon.

CHAPTER 8

"WE'RE HEADING TOWARD a water hub," Susan said as they crept along the mist-filled corridor. George had never seen the gas concentration so high. Great purple gouts of it sputtered thickly from the overhead nozzles, falling like slow water into a hazy, violet-streaked white river that was almost up to their knees.

"Which one?" George asked. He could actually taste the gas now. A strange sweet flavor that others seemed to sense all the time but that he only noticed when levels were extremely high or when he returned from an off-ship tour of work. The taste had an almost physical component to it as well, as if it were making his tongue and nostrils vibrate. If he paid too much attention to the sensation, he felt he might forget to keep moving forward.

"By the main 'ponics sector," Susan said. She coughed deeply, trying to mask the sound by holding both hands to her mouth. "I think."

George took her arm. "This much gas can't be good for us. We must go back."

From the end of the corridor, where it opened out into the water hub, the ominous sound of marching was breaking up into a mad pattern of running and irregular thuds and impacts. Susan and George heard screams. "Almost there," Susan said.

She touched George's hand, then moved on. He followed at her side.

Water hub was the name given to sixteen immense and puzzling cavities within the ship, each of which appeared to have been constructed to hold an enormous quantity of liquid. Baffle plates could be tightly sealed over each corridor entrance that opened into the hubs, and the bottom of each cavity formed a concave depression like an enormous bowl made from precisely curved segments of metal plating.

Overall, the hubs were circular, perhaps one hundred human yards across, and each extended vertically through at least ten levels of decks. At each level a wide metal-grille catwalk circled each hub's inner wall, connecting up to twenty-four corridors. At evenly spaced intervals steep stairways connected the catwalks so that the hubs became the most convenient way of moving between widely separated areas of the ship, enabling workers to change corridors and levels in one central location. As far as George knew, the Elders had thus far been unable to determine what the hubs were originally intended to be. Some form of liquid storage seemed most probable. However, since the hubs were not arranged in a regular pattern throughout the ship, if each had been entirely filled with water, it had been calculated that the resulting asymmetrical stresses would interfere with course changes and the structural integrity of the hull.

Whatever the hubs were, they were further evidence to support the theory that the ship had originally been intended for purposes other than the transfer of Tenctonese slaves. Though what those purposes might have been, none could guess.

As George and Susan approached the catwalk that ringed the water hub at their level a sign on the wall confirmed that they were in the main 'ponics sector on deck fifty-eight. From the sounds that echoed out from the water hub's center, it sounded as if whatever was going on was located two or three decks below. And whatever it was, it sounded bad. In addition to the clanging of Overseer boots on the catwalks George could hear the unmistakable sounds of fighting, of cries of pain, as if Tenctonese were being attacked with shock prods focused to their highest settings.

George turned to Susan. As yet they were not close enough to the end of the corridor to see what was going on below their deck, or to be seen themselves. There was still an opportunity to go back.

"We have to look," Susan said. Her voice was full of fear, but she would not shirk her duty to the others.

"I know," George said. Each Tenctonese was honor bound to report to the Elders about unusual activities they encountered on the ship. The Overseers would never provide such reports, and eyewitness accounts were the only weapon the Elders had against the terror of unchecked rumor.

"Let me go first," George said. They were ten feet from the corridor's end. Wafts of holy gas cascaded past the opening as if rushing down from the decks overhead.

But Susan would not let George face danger by himself. "You go to the right," she told him. "I'll take the left." That tone was there again. No argument.

When each was at one side of the corridor, a foot from the opening, they looked at each other once more, then carefully leaned forward to peer out to the catwalk. George instantly saw their chance. "Over there," he whispered, and he pointed far left to where a group of about twenty workers huddled at the catwalk railing, staring into the center of the water hub. Even twenty feet from them, George could tell from the workers' blank expressions that they were almost comatose from their exposure to the gas. If he and Susan could join their group, any Overseer that might happen to see them would think they were similarly affected. Susan nodded once, instantly understanding George's plan. Quickly they moved against the smooth curved wall of the hub to join the group of gassed workers.

From the carryall sacks the workers wore slung around their necks George knew that the work team was a scavenger group that patrolled corridors looking for abandoned material that could be recycled. George guessed they had been inadvertently exposed when the gas had begun pouring forth, and that no Overseer would question their docile presence. Susan must have reached the same conclusion, because she slipped off the sack of the worker closest to her and handed it to George. "Your disguise," she said, then she took another sack for herself. The two workers did not seem to notice Susan's actions.

Moving through the clump of workers was almost like stepping around the bodies in the light bay. George and Susan made their way easily through the unresponsive group until they both stood at the railing's edge.

"Act like the gas has gotten to you," George whispered as he let his face go slack and his shoulders droop.

"That won't be difficult," Susan said. George saw her slump as well, imitating the stance of the truly affected workers around them. "I've never seen anything like this."

Neither had George. The water hub was like a giant drain into which hundreds of streams of purple gas emptied. He could see the jets flowing through the open metal of the catwalks, pouring in from the entrance of each corridor that ran into the hub. Some of the jets appeared to glow, luminous with the corridor lights that shone behind them. A small pool of whitening gas was even beginning to form in the curved bottom of the hub eight decks below.

Past the falling ribbons of holy gas, on every catwalk level there were scattered knots of Tenctonese workers seemingly frozen in place, completely overwhelmed by the gas. Eight-person squads of Overseers marched around them on the lower levels, obviously preventing anyone from the lower decks from entering the hub itself. George guessed that the lower-level decks hadn't yet been gassed, or had not been gassed with the same high concentrations. The Elders had long known that since the holy gas was heavier than air, the Overseers typically released it in the uppermost decks first, letting it settle through the rest of the ship under the influence of whatever generated the artificial gravity field.

But George wasn't concerned with the Overseers' tactics. He was more interested in their intent and wondered why they had gone to such trouble to keep this particular hub clear. Especially since the only thing going on was the disturbance on the catwalk directly beneath George and Susan on level fifty-seven. That's where the disturbance was still in progress. George had never seen anything like that, either.

Off to the right on the catwalk below and across from them a squad of eight Overseers had formed a half circle around a huddled group of five workers who crouched with their backs to the hub wall. George was amazed that the captive workers seemed to be ready for a fight, shouting at the Overseers and making feints—as if they, too, were unaffected by the gas.

A few feet over from the Overseer squad an actual fight was still underway. Two Overseers were sprawled on the catwalk.

One had a shock prod shoved deeply in his mouth, and every few seconds the device discharged as if it had been focused on automatic. The body twitched each time the blue sparks arced out from the prod's handle, and pink blood frothed furiously from the body's mouth. In between discharges the body lay so completely still that George realized with a gasp that the Overseer was dead. The other fallen Overseer was still breathing, though there was a deformation in his skull that George could see even from his distant vantage point.

Near the bodies six other Overseers tried to subdue three struggling workers. Each of the workers wore shimmering gray membrane suits—one-piece skintight coveralls of synthetic iridescent material intended to insulate the skin of those who worked underwater in the sewage-purification chambers. Though why three water workers would come under Overseer attack on the fifty-seventh level was a question George couldn't answer.

Then George heard a sharp command ring out, strangely muffled by the cloaking presence of the mist, but quite clearly an Overseer code word. Instantly the six Overseers who fought with the water workers jumped back. The water workers hesitated, as if unsure whether they should take the opportunity to try to press the attack or to escape. But the choice was quickly taken from them as a startlingly thin blue beam of light sliced open the middle worker's chest with a hissing explosion of vapor. The middle worker collapsed without even having time to scream.

"Celine!" Susan gasped. "What *was* that?"

"I don't know," George whispered in reply without moving his lips or turning his head. Though the only weapons the Overseers were ever seen to carry were their prods, the ship was full of rumors of other, more frightening weapons the Overseers kept hidden so they wouldn't fall into the wrong hands. "It looked like a mining beam. But it was so small." George had seen crackling blue mining beams carve twenty-foot-wide tunnels from solid rock with huge explosions of dust and debris, but those beams were twenty feet wide as well, generated by machines that were even larger.

The two remaining water workers seemed as shocked as George and Susan were, and they slowly stepped back until they reached the hub wall and raised their hands over their heads. Then a new group of four Overseers came into view, approaching the workers. But as the new group stepped into a clear area between two falling streams of gas George saw that only two of the four were Overseers.

One was a tall male with a heavily lined face. He carried a metal rod connected by thick wires to a heavy backpack, reminding George of his own molecular probe. The second Overseer was a female, shorter than the first but, judging from her well-fed size, of equal mass. The other two figures with them were much smaller—only children, two males clad in gray tunics and trousers and not Overseer uniforms. But both wore the repellent black scarves of the Watcher Youth, which meant that someday they *would* be Overseers.

The tall Overseer with the metal rod appeared to be talking to one of the two boys as he gestured to the water workers. The boy nodded quickly, then the female Overseer pushed the children to the catwalk so they were well out of the way.

The male Overseer pointed his rod at the closer of the two water workers, and George realized that the small device was the beam weapon even as a second lance of light blasted the arm from the rebellious worker. Her instant shriek of agony echoed through the water hub as she crumpled to the catwalk deck, leaving a jagged spray of pink on the wall behind her. Before that first cry had faded her moans joined it.

Beside him George could hear Susan praying, her words stumbling over each other in her fervency. On the catwalk one of the two children turned away from the bloody scene and stared down into the gas-filled abyss of the hub as if looking for a way to escape. And on the child's head the distinctive brushstroke spot of the Family: Third Moon's Ocean was like a beacon. Susan stopped praying in the same instant that George recognized the child's complete cranial pattern and felt his hearts trade beats.

"No," Susan whispered.

The child in the traitorous scarf was their son. Buck.

CHAPTER 9

KIRBY WAS NEVER ONE to let a mouthful of Doritos get in the way of her passing on advice to her father. "Why doncha jus' call 'er?" she said, then went back to noisy crunching.

Sikes looked over at his daughter. She was sitting on one of the mismatched wooden chairs, hunched over his dining room table. The smoked glass panel on top of four fat black cylinders wasn't really a dining room table, but then his apartment didn't have a real dining room, so everything worked out. "Why don't you finish your homework?" he suggested. "And go easy on those things."

"Why?" Kirby asked, giving the word two syllables as if she had been brought up in a shopping mall.

"You'll spoil your dinner." Even as he said it Sikes couldn't believe he had actually stooped to something so lame.

"Yeah, right, Dad. Doritos are really going to kill my appetite for Domino's pizza. Gotta keep my food groups in balance, right?" She rolled her eyes and defiantly took another handful of the chips from the split-open bag in front of her.

Sikes sighed and looked back at Grazer. The earnest detective was sitting at the opposite end of the table, squinting at the hieroglyphics on Petty's computer screen, typing madly. Then Sikes heard an amplified rendition of phone tones, then ringing, then a bizarre electronic rushing sound. Grazer sat back. "Good," he said.

"That's good?" Sikes asked as the sound cut out. Grazer had been going at it for half an hour so far, connecting the computer to Sikes's phone line and then loading his own software onto the computer's blank hard disk.

"Of course it's good. That means we've connected with the service."

"Why don't you just phone her?" Kirby asked again.

"Because she's in Australia," Sikes explained for the fifth time.

"Big woo," Kirby said. "That's only three bucks a minute after six o'clock. Can't the department afford that?"

Sikes eyed her suspiciously. "How do you know how much it costs to phone Australia?"

"Dad-dee," Kirby groaned.

"Okay, here's the directory," Grazer announced. "What's his full name?"

Sikes looked down at one of the scraps of paper he had been forced to use instead of his notepad. "Petty. Randolph Ramey."

Grazer typed. "Petty, R.R., in Los Angeles," he said as the words on the screen changed. "Got it. Write this down: 712436,17."

Sikes wrote it down. "What is it?"

Grazer sighed this time. "It's his address, Sikes. For sending messages in the mail system."

Kirby stretched out over the table and slumped her head onto one hand. "Mail? This is the nineties, guys."

Sikes sighed. Somehow Kirby had been more fun when her questions had had more to do with how Santa managed to get into an apartment that didn't have a fireplace than with how police procedure operated. "Here's how it works," Sikes began. "The guy who used to own this computer was murdered last night."

"Gross," Kirby said.

"Now, it might be just a random robbery and shooting," Sikes continued, "but there's a chance that the guy's computer disks were stolen and someone erased his hard drive at the same time."

Kirby straightened up. "Hey, I know how to recover stuff from a hard drive. You see, it's not really erased until—"

"I *know*," Sikes said. But he wondered how Kirby did. She seemed to possess a great deal of information that was inappropriate for a thirteen-year-old. "But whoever blanked this guy's disk *did* erase everything by, uh . . ."

"Random overwrite. Three times," Grazer said without looking up from the keyboard.

Kirby nodded sagely. "That'll do it. But E-mail still seems like a slow way to get his daughter when you could call her on the phone."

"We don't want to get in contact with his daughter. At least not yet. What we're . . ." Sikes gave up and reached for the Doritos bag. "Bryon, explain it to her."

"The daughter called the police and asked them to look in on her father when he didn't send her an electronic letter at the regular time," Grazer said. He typed something more on the keyboard, and then the screen blanked. "So, according to department procedure, we have to automatically consider anyone who reports a crime to be a suspect. Until we can specifically rule her out."

"But how could she murder him? You said she's in Australia," Kirby reminded him.

Grazer shook his head. "Listen carefully. *She* said she was in Australia when she called. She may live in Australia, but she could have made that call from anywhere."

Sikes added, "We've already asked Immigration to look for her passport number on recent admissions to the country. Can't take anything for granted."

Kirby sat up and moved her chair closer to Grazer's end of the table, her interest increasing. "Cool. So you think the daughter really could have killed her own father?" She smiled winningly at Sikes.

"Don't get any ideas," Sikes said. "We just can't rule out anything at this time."

"So the computer mail . . ." Kirby prompted.

"Before we talk to the daughter," Grazer said, "I thought it would be a good idea to see if we can find out what she and her father exchanged letters about every day. Maybe they were arguing about his estate or something else that might give her a motive."

Kirby rested her head on her hand again, interest flagging. "How do you do that?"

"A lot of people who use computer-mail services will send

copies of electronic mail to themselves or store copies of their own or others' letters in the system's memory. I'm going to take a look for any copies."

"Don't you need a search warrant or something?" Kirby pulled the remnants of the Doritos bag away from her father. Orange crumbs sprayed out across the smudged surface of the table's glass top.

"That's a gray area," Grazer said, looking up from the keyboard. "Your father has a search warrant for Dr. Petty's house—that's automatic in a murder investigation. It covers correspondence, even from third parties. But there's never been a case to establish if such a warrant applies only to correspondence that *exists* in the searched premises as opposed to correspondence that can be *read* in the searched premises." Sikes recognized the familiar glassy look that came into Grazer's eyes. "You see, under current precedent, if correspondence can be read in the searched premises, then the court presumes that the correspondence *exists* within said premises. Technically, however, electronic correspondence *doesn't* exist in the premises—"

"Uh, Bryon," Sikes said, trying to break the detective's rhythm while there was still a chance.

"—even though it *can* be read there. It's actually quite a fascinating legal conundrum. One that I've devoted considerable study to because of the way it will impact on future cases. Interestingly enough, it goes back to a case in Boston in 1892 when a Civil War veteran—"

"Uh, Bryon, I think the computer wants you to do something." Sikes waved his hand back and forth at Grazer to bring him back to the here and now. Something was making that strange electronic rushing sound again, and it wasn't stopping.

"Oh, yes, of course," Grazer said. He turned over the keyboard, looked at something on its bottom, then flipped it right side up again and typed. The rushing sound ended. "That should do it."

"Do what?" Kirby asked.

Sikes glared at his daughter. "I don't think you should ask Detective Grazer any more questions," he warned. "You're distracting him."

But Grazer had no compunctions about undermining parental authority. "Not a problem, Sikes. How's she expected to learn if she doesn't ask questions?" Kirby smiled smugly at

Sikes. "The first time I logged onto the service I did it under my own account so I could get Dr. Petty's user number from the public membership index. What I've just done now," Grazer continued, obviously pleased with himself, "is to sign on to the service under Dr. Petty's account so that the service will think I'm Dr. Petty and give me full access to his mail."

Kirby lifted her head from her hand. "Don't you need a password or something to do that?" she asked in a strangely formal way.

"Of course," Grazer answered. "User number and password."

Kirby's eyes were wide. "And . . . you know how to figure out people's passwords?"

"There are certain psychological techniques that can be applied to recreate likely choices," Grazer said pompously as he stared at the screen.

"What are they?" Kirby asked with admiration in her voice.

"Didn't I ask you about your homework?" Sikes said. The last thing he needed was a hour's lecture on psychological techniques.

"Daddy, this is important. I take computer science in school. This counts as homework."

Sikes narrowed his eyes. "Nice try, but I don't think so."

"I'll tell you one technique," Grazer said, as if Sikes didn't exist. "A lot of people are afraid of forgetting their passwords, so they write them down. All you have to do is go looking for them someplace near the computer." He flipped over the keyboard again and showed it to Kirby. Sikes saw there was a piece of beige masking tape stuck to the bottom with handwriting on it. "Red motor. As easy as that."

"Under the keyboard," Kirby repeated. "All right."

"Other good places to look are on disk labels, inside a drawer, bottom of the monitor or a desk lamp."

"How's it going, Bryon?" Sikes felt that Kirby had had enough of an education for one night. He tried to put together her interest in overcoming computer password protection, her knowledge of erasing hard disk drives, and her familiarity with making international phone calls. He wasn't able to decide what she was doing with all that information, but whatever it was, he was certain he wouldn't like it.

"Disk labels," repeated Kirby. "Great idea. People would think it was just a file name or something."

Grazer tapped at the keyboard again. "It's going fine, Sikes. You might want to make a note of this." He read from the screen. "The last time Dr. Petty logged on was at two-thirty-seven yesterday afternoon. The way his account is set up, that would have been during the peak rates, so unless the guy was rolling in money you could probably conclude that he was logging on for an important reason. Something that wouldn't wait for six o'clock."

Sikes wrote that down. For all of Grazer's overbearing self-importance, Sikes grudgingly had to admit that the forensic accounting detective had a fine eye for detail.

"Okay," Grazer said, "now I'm going into the mail, and . . . there we go." He tapped at a few more keys. "He's got two unread letters waiting for him and . . . five older letters stored." Grazer slipped a floppy disk into one of the computer's drives. Sikes didn't know why they called it a floppy because it was in a hard plastic case. But he knew that if he asked Grazer how the name came about, Grazer would probably start his answer with the social implications of the invention of electricity and move on from there.

"I'll save the letters on this disk, and then I can print them out for you back at the station tomorrow," Grazer said.

Kirby was running a moistened finger through the few remaining Doritos crumbs in the bag. "Hey, if this is an official investigation, how come you're doing this here and not at the station?"

Sikes looked at his daughter. If only she would pay attention like that in school. "Like the man said," Sikes told her, "it's a gray area."

"By accessing the mail from here," Grazer added, "your father can make the case that he was following his own interpretation of his search warrant. If we had logged on under Dr. Petty's account at the station and a higher-ranking officer had looked over our shoulders, we might have had to desist until we got a definitive ruling from a judge that the search warrant applied to the computer system. Since the system might only store letters for a few days after they've been read, we might have lost important information."

Kirby stared at her father knowingly. "In other words, you didn't want to get caught. I can understand that."

"What's that supposed to mean?" Sikes asked.

"Nothing," Kirby said innocently. "So what do the letters say?"

"We'll read them off-line," Grazer said. "No sense adding a lot of time charges to the poor guy's last computer bill."

Two minutes later Grazer had logged off, and Sikes sat beside him so they could read the letters together. Kirby politely asked if everyone would like a beer from the kitchen, and after a moment's hesitation both men said yes. The regular work day was long over, and Sikes thought a beer might be just the thing to take the edge off the remaining roughness from last night's celebration. Come to think of it, he hadn't noticed any remaining ill effects from the party at Casey's since Victoria's passionate farewell at the elevators. Could be proof of our love, Sikes thought dreamily. Either that or my hormones have overwritten my brain three times at random.

The first unread letter was from Petty's daughter a short note asking her father to at least send back a "hello" even if he didn't have time for a full note. She was worried about him, she said. The time code on the message showed it had been sent about five hours after Petty had been killed and about twelve hours before she had called the Westwood police station. There was nothing unusual or suspicious about its contents.

"Did she have to be in Australia to send this from her computer?" Sikes asked. Grazer said that the daughter could have sent it from anywhere. All she needed was a portable computer. Then he scratched at his chin and said that the computer system could probably run a trace to see which communications port had accepted the message and began to explain how that might lead to them identifying in which area code the message had originated, but before he could launch into all the stupefying technical details Kirby returned with the beers. Sikes took a grateful swig from his. Grazer stared at the second bottle Kirby held, then asked her if she could bring him a glass as well.

Kirby looked at Sikes. "Daddy, do you *have* any glasses?"

"Kids," Sikes muttered after he had told her where to find them and she returned to the kitchen. "How about the second letter?"

Grazer brought it to the screen. It was a sales message from the computer service itself informing "R.R. Petty" that he could qualify for a trip to Hawaii by logging on to another part of the service each day during the coming month. A new prizewinner would be randomly chosen daily from all participants.

"Electronic junk mail," Sikes said, grateful that there appeared to be at least one benefit of not being computer literate.

"Maybe," Grazer said. "Could be a coded message, too. Tomorrow we'll have to check to see if everyone else on the service got the same message."

Sikes looked at Grazer and took another sip from his beer. He would never have thought of that on his own. Grazer was good.

Kirby returned with a glass for Grazer. Grazer glanced at it, frowned, carefully put the glass down beside the computer, then drank from the bottle after all. "Now I'll call up the stored letters."

A list of five messages appeared on the screen, none older than five days. One was from Petty's daughter. Two were from Petty to his daughter—copies, Grazer said, to confirm delivery of the originals. The fourth letter was from Petty to someone called Amy. And the last was from Amy to Petty. That final message was the most recent of the five, having been sent about two o'clock yesterday afternoon. Grazer said that it was probably the last letter Petty read when he had logged on thirty-seven minutes later. Apparently Petty had never had the chance to send a reply.

"Which one first?" Grazer asked, holding his fingers poised above the keyboard like a concert pianist about to explode into a scherzo by Liszt.

Sikes shrugged. "Start with number one, I guess."

As Sikes had feared, the boredom of being a detective set in early, as the first three letters between father and daughter contained only inconsequential trivialities. Isabel Petty, apparently an astronomer herself, recounted her days at Woomera, where the most exciting event seemed to be going to the pub where astronomers went early each morning after long nights of observation. Randolph Petty wrote in return about the trouble he was having getting his doctor to do anything about his arthritic knee, and—

"Hold it!" Sikes said excitedly. He began to scrawl a note to himself as he explained his excitement to Grazer. "If Petty had a bum knee, then there's no way he would have parked at the top level of the garage." Let's see Angie talk her way out of that one, he thought happily. "Okay, keep going."

But there were no other important details in any of the first three letters. Petty talked about food shopping, a restaurant he had been to recently, working with a group of graduate students, and his beloved car. That was all. There was no sign of any conflict between father and daughter.

"Next letter," Sikes said. His beer bottle had only one more swallow in it, and he told himself to slow down.

But Grazer hesitated. "Didn't you say Dr. Petty was retired?"

"Yeah, so?"

"So how come he's working with students?"

Sikes nodded and made another note to himself. "Good point. Maybe he was advising them or something. I'll check it out."

"Do that," Grazer said. "Students coming over to his house. Maybe they see something they want. Cash. Coin collection. You never know."

Sikes half expected Kirby to chime in with some observation about students killing an old man and was surprised when he didn't hear anything. He shifted around in his seat as Grazer called up the next letter in the list.

"Hey, Sikes, this might be something," Grazer said.

Then Sikes saw what his daughter was doing. "Kirby Sikes! Put that down!"

Kirby instantly slammed a beer bottle down on a small table beside the living room chair she sat in, looking up guiltily from a copy of *Penthouse* magazine. Sikes was instantly out of his chair and in front of his daughter. "And put that down, too!"

Kirby slapped the magazine shut. Sikes grabbed it from her. "You don't need to be reading that."

"I think I really got something here, Sikes," Grazer said, apparently oblivious to the scene taking place five feet away in the living room half of the tiny apartment.

"Well, you read it," Kirby said. "It's not like I don't know what the letters are about or—"

"And who told you you could have a beer?" Sikes rolled the magazine into a tube. All he could think of was that somehow Victoria's flight had been canceled and that any second she would walk through the front door and see her daughter in her father's capable care—swilling beer and reading a skin magazine.

"You said it was okay," Kirby said.

"When did *I* say it was okay?"

"I asked if everyone could have a beer, and you said yes, so—"

Sikes put a hand over his eyes and groaned. "You and your mother. I can't stand it."

"Definitely we got a possible motive here, Sikes," Grazer called out.

"What's wrong with drinking a beer?" Kirby asked.

"You're not twenty-one."

"That's just in bars and restaurants, Dad. At home, with my parents' permission, I—"

"You don't *have* your parents' permission. You will *never* have your parents' permission."

Kirby folded her arms obstinately. "Fine. You want me to drink beer at raves, then that's what I'll do."

Sikes stumbled in his outrage. "What the hell is a rave?"

Taking him by surprise, Grazer was beside him. "That's an underground party, Sikes. You know, organizers rent a warehouse, pass out secret instructions. All the kids go to them." He looked meaningfully at Kirby. "But as much fun as they seem to be, they can be extremely dangerous, young lady. Usually the buildings they're held in don't conform to fire safety codes, and there is a great deal of illegal drug activity. You could get into a lot of trouble just by being on the site if there's police action. And according to the memos I've seen, the department is making a major push to step up its efforts to stop raves."

All the defiance was gone from Kirby's face. She had that look of intense interest again. "Yeah?" she asked. "I could get into trouble just by being there? Even if I wasn't doing anything illegal myself?"

"I'm afraid so," Grazer said.

"That's good to know," Kirby said thoughtfully.

Sikes witnessed the exchange in amazement. Kirby never listened to anything he said, yet here she was, buying the whole law-and-order deal from someone she had never met. What was it about Grazer? What was it about Kirby, for that matter?

Grazer put his hand on Sikes's shoulder. "Anyway, Sikes, I really think you should take a look at these next two letters. They could mean something."

"Yeah, okay," Sikes said. He began to turn away from Kirby

to go back to the computer, then spun around and grabbed Kirby's beer bottle from the side table. "Read your schoolbooks or something, would you?"

Kirby sighed with forbearance.

Sikes went back to the computer and put the beer bottle and the *Penthouse* beside it. Grazer sat down, moved his chair forward, glanced at the unrolling magazine, then exclaimed, "Hey, it's Kiki!"

"Kiki?" Sikes asked in bewilderment.

Grazer tapped the forehead of the woman on the cover of the magazine—an impossibly proportioned woman in an impossibly small macramé bathing suit that looked more like a Boy Scout assignment in knot tying than anything intended to be worn. "Yeah, good old Kiki," Grazer said. "We used to go out a year or so ago. Calls me up every time she comes to town." He picked up the magazine and flipped through it until he came to a series of photographs of good old Kiki with not a bathing suit to be seen. "She's been trying to get a cover from Bob for a long time."

"Bob?"

"Guccione," Grazer said. "I kept telling him, Bob, a woman as lovely as Kiki *deserves* a cover, and he'd keep saying, Bry, if you knew the pressure—"

"Let me get this straight," Sikes said. "You *know* Bob Guccione?"

"Sure," Grazer said.

"And you used to date a . . . a Pet?"

"That's right," Grazer said again. He looked puzzled. "Why do you ask?"

Sikes shook his head. "No . . . no reason." He sighed as he stared at the computer screen. Why is it, he asked himself, that everyone in the world seems to have an exciting life but me? Petty gets an asteroid named after him. Victoria flies halfway around the world for free on business. Grazer hangs out with Bob Guccione. And I live in a hovel and look forward to watching Rolling Stone videos on VH-1.

"You okay, Sikes?" Grazer asked.

Sikes sighed again. "Oh, yeah, just fine. Now what was this about a motive or something?"

Grazer turned back to the computer and danced his fingers across its keyboard. "Two letters. One *to* Amy Stewart. One *from* her. Read them from the top."

Putting aside his own glum musing about his life, Sikes

began to read, and his uncle had managed to instill in him enough lay knowledge of astronomy that he was intrigued from the opening paragraph. And when he had finished reading the second letter—Amy Stewart's troubled, urgent reply to Dr. Petty—Sikes was forced to admit to himself that the multi-talented Bryon Grazer might have done it again.

The electronic letters could very well establish the motive for Dr. Randolph Petty's murder. A motive that had nothing at all to do with cash or coin collections. A motive that would undoubtedly come to play a part in more and more murders in the future as computers became more commonplace.

If the letters pointed in the right direction, then it appeared that Petty had been killed for information. What that information was, exactly, the letters didn't state. But whatever it was, Sikes knew it had to be important. Deadly important.

The questions remaining were: To whom was the information important, and why? Fortunately, the letters told Sikes where he could begin his search just as, more than two billion miles away, Buck Francisco's search was about to end.

CHAPTER 10

AS THE OVERSEER'S WEAPON cut the female's arm from her body in a crackle of blue energy, Buck had to turn away. The worker's shriek filled Buck's ear valleys as the sound echoed through the water hub, making him shudder. He fought back tears of shame, trying to tell himself that this was Vornho's fault, not his. But it was a lie, and he knew it.

"Well?" Coolock said to the last of the three water workers to remain standing. "Are you convinced now?"

Buck could imagine how the Overseer's ravaged face looked as he brandished his cutter wand, hissing out his threatening words with a cruel leer. Coolock wasn't what D'wayn said an Overseer was supposed to be—a peacekeeper among combative, less-developed and less-intelligent sub–Tentonese. Buck had come to understand that Coolock was someone who enjoyed causing pain whether he had a reason to do so or not.

But the last water worker didn't say a word.

"Finiksa," Vornho whispered to Buck, "you're missing it. Coolock's gonna slice another one."

Vornho grabbed Buck's arm and spun him around to make him watch. Buck felt his stomach churn as he gazed through threads of falling holy gas at the scene before him.

The first water worker appeared to have exploded from

within—his chest was a mound of gelatinous blue and green organs, streaked and glistening pinkly with blood. Beside him the female was sprawled on the metal catwalk, one hand limply grasping the stump of her arm as slow dribbles of blood weakly pulsed down through the open deck. It was a nightmare, as if Tagdot Cur Hiya himself had walked among them.

But in the midst of the carnage the third water worker was defiant. He was backed hard against the curved metal wall, holding his hands high, and Buck could see his chest wall heave in the changing shimmers of the gray membrane suit he wore. Yet his eyes blazed with hatred for Coolock and D'wayn, and his spots remained dark.

"This is your final chance," Coolock threatened. "Tell me: Who ordered you to divert the water flow? Who is the leader of your revolt?"

"You want to know my leader?" the water worker asked. He smiled grimly. "We thank Celine for this day. We thank Andarko for—"

Buck jumped as blue energy exploded against the wall beside the water worker. The worker jerked sideways, smoke rising from his membrane suit in a dozen places where molten droplets of metal had sprayed him. But his defiance never wavered.

Why? Buck wondered. It would be so easy to tell Coolock what he wants to know. What does it matter? How can anything matter? No one can defeat the Overseers.

"Are you in that much of a hurry to join your goddess?" Coolock sneered.

"Celine is not a goddess," the worker answered. "She is but a Tenctonese like you or I, who with Andarko showed us—"

Another beam blasted a glowing pit in the wall on the other side of the worker. Buck was astounded. This time the worker hadn't even flinched. Coolock raised the cutter wand so he could sight along its length, indicating that he wanted his next blast to hit precisely on target.

"Yeah," Vornho breathed excitedly. "Cut the mother hummer."

D'wayn tapped her shock prod on the railing beside Vornho and Buck. "Settle down, Watchers."

Coolock looked over his shoulder at the two boys in their Watcher scarves. He flashed his acid grin, keeping his cutter aimed at the third worker. "Eager for the kill, are we?"

Buck knew better than to look away—that would be an unforgivable sign of weakness. But he didn't know how to answer the Overseer's question. Fortunately or unfortunately, Vornho did.

"I want to see him get what he deserves," Vornho said.

Coolock's smile never left him. "You're the one who reported the plot to divert the water flow?"

Vornho stood tall and straightened his shoulders. "I am, Overseer."

Coolock stared at Buck. "And what about you?"

Buck copied Vornho's pose. "I did not hear the conversation, Overseer."

With those words it was as if Buck had made himself invisible. Coolock turned his attention back to Vornho. "Are you prepared to finish what you have begun?"

It took Vornho a moment to understand the question. D'wayn tapped his shoulder with her prod. "Answer the commander."

Vornho swallowed loudly. "Yes, sir."

Coolock held out his hand. The black sleeve of his uniform fell back to reveal the angular, jagged strokes of his Overseer's tattoo of authority. "Then come here, boy. Show me how you'll deal with cargo when you become an Overseer."

D'wayn tapped Vornho's shoulder again. Vornho stepped forward. Coolock handed him the cutter wand, still connected by wires to his backpack, then crouched down beside Vornho to help the boy aim.

"It's important that you only take him off at the legs so we can still interrogate him in the med lab," Coolock explained matter of factly. "But no matter what you do, you want to be certain you don't let the beam contact the head. We need to keep the brain lobes intact so we can measure how much *eemikken* the beast has ingested to enable him to withstand the holy gas." Then Coolock began to point out the firing studs and discharge levers on the wand.

"Tell me, Finiksa," D'wayn asked, surprisingly conversationally. "Did you enjoy your first taste of *eemikken\?*"

Buck stared in sick fascination at the water worker, who in turn watched as a child was instructed in using the weapon that could cause his death.

"Finiksa?" D'wayn repeated.

Buck nervously looked up at the corpulent Watch Leader.

"I . . . uh, it made my stomach sick," he said. Was Coolock really going to make Vornho cut off the worker's legs?

"It will do that," D'wayn said. "But you're feeling better now?"

"Yes, Watch Leader." Buck glanced back to Coolock and Vornho. They were laughing about something to do with the shape of the cutter wand. Buck had missed the joke.

"You *did* take the drug I gave you, didn't you?" D'wayn persisted.

Buck felt her powerful hand grasp his chin and turn his head back toward her.

"Y-yes," he stammered as he was forced to look up at her. "Vornho and I took it together."

"Good," D'wayn said, though she didn't release her grip on him. "You see, for the cargo to be able to withstand this amount of gas in the air, as you and Vornho are able to resist it for now, we know that they must be taking the *eemikken*, too. But we don't know where they're getting it. Someone suggested that some Watcher Youth might be passing it along to them." She squeezed Buck's jaw enough to cause pain. "You wouldn't do anything like that, though, would you, Watcher Finiksa?"

"No," Buck said. Why would anyone do anything against the Overseers? Nothing good could ever come of it.

D'wayn nodded over at Vornho, who was drawing a bead on the already maimed body of the female water worker. "How about Vornho? Are you sure you saw him take his dose?"

Buck suddenly understood that the Overseer was asking him to report on his crèche mate, as if there were no difference between that and reporting on the cargo. Is this what it means to be an Overseer? he thought.

"Yes," Buck said. "I saw him." And he was frightened to realize that he knew he would have answered the same way even if he hadn't seen Vornho take it. Just as he couldn't mention that he had seen Vornho trade the drug's crinkly wrapping to a maintenance worker in exchange for use of a *plaski* hall's mat room.

"Very good," D'wayn said. She turned back to Coolock and Vornho just as Vornho fired the cutter.

A lance of blue fire tore into the body of the female water worker, carving open her rib cage with a hiss of superheated vapor. Buck felt dizzy as he saw what could only be the twin fists of her hearts exposed, and he was grateful he did not see her body give any sign that it had still been alive when the beam cut into her. The blood loss from her severed arm must have already done the job.

Coolock tapped his knuckles against Vornho's temple in recognition of a task well done, then had him aim at the third water worker, who held his body proudly erect as if unafraid of death.

"What is your decision?" Coolock asked the worker. "Do you embrace the reality of the ship and tell me what I need to know to maintain its safety? Or do you embrace your Celine at the hands of this child?"

The water worker looked into Vornho's eyes. "Put down the the weapon, child. You know it is not right to act in this way."

"Aim right above the knees," Coolock said calmly. "The vapor explosion will cauterize the major arteries."

"Open your hearts, child. Ask Celine and Andarko if what you do is their will."

Without immediately knowing why Buck found himself silently repeating the prayer of guidance the worker referred to. It had so long been a part of Buck's life that he couldn't remember when he had first learned it.

"Fire the weapon," Coolock commanded.

"That is not what Andarko will tell you if you ask," the worker said.

Guide me in that which I do not understand, Buck thought. Give me strength to find answers that are just.

"Above the knees," Coolock said.

"Join me, child. Repeat these words: We thank Celine for this day. We thank Andarko for the future."

Buck gasped as his thoughts were answered. *No, Finiksa, this is not the path to be followed.* Buck felt his spots pucker. But the words had not been said in anything like what he imagined the voice of Andarko might be. The words had sounded more as if they had been spoken by Moodri. Yet wherever those words had come from, he knew he could not refuse their wisdom. With that, everything happened all at once.

"Vornho!" Buck cried. "Don't! He's—"

"Silence!" Coolock's rage was as sudden as the cutting beam Vornho fired.

"Little fool!" D'wayn shouted as Buck heard her prod click into focus and begin to hum.

Vornho's cutting beam aimed wild, crackling uselessly against metal, not flesh.

D'wayn's prod slammed into Buck's shoulder, sending him against the railing with a gasp of pain. He looked up to see the prod beginning to descend on him again, this time going for his forehead.

"FIIINIIIKSSAAA!"

The prod stopped in its descent as the deafening cry filled the water hub. Buck, D'wayn, Coolock, and even Vornho whirled to see from where the cry had come.

Buck slumped against the railing and looked out across the water hub's void. There! On the next level of catwalk above them among a group of gas-stunned scavengers, Buck saw two figures leaning over the railing. One waved frantically down at him. Through the violet mist of the gas they were hard to make out. A male and female he saw. Like paintings of Celine and Andarko ascending from the pit of *am dugas*. But who were they really? And why had—

A blue beam sliced through the air above Buck's head, angling up to explode in gouts of sparks against the next level's railing. Buck saw the two figures above jump back, the male pulling on the female's tunic as if to stop her from attempting to leap through space for Buck.

Behind him Buck could hear Coolock shouting orders to the other Overseer squads that were in the hub, telling them to seize the two slaves on level fifty-eight. The beam kept slicing back and forth. Buck saw a half dozen inert scavengers collapse in sprays of vaporized blood as the beam ripped through them.

Then Buck felt himself lifted painfully by one arm. D'wayn held him so his feet scraped against the catwalk. She held the sparking tip of her prod inches from his face. "Who were they?" she hissed. "How did they know you?"

Buck couldn't talk. He didn't know. The prod tip came closer.

Then there was another scream, the pounding of metal, Coolock shouting in anger. Buck twisted his head in time to see the third water worker burst across the width of the catwalk and flip over the railing and plunge down through the layers of holy gas and—

—Coolock's beam caught the worker in his back—

—the worker vanished in an enormous eruption of flame unlike any other effect of the weapon Buck had seen.

Then Buck felt the explosion's shock wave rip him from D'wayn's one-handed grip. His ear valleys rang with the metallic reverberations of the blast. He had no idea what had happened. No clue to whom the male and female had been. Nor why a worker would choose to defy the Overseers by suicide.

All he knew was that D'wayn now towered over him, slowly lowering her prod to his head with a ferocious expression of rage distorting her quivering round face.

Then the prod made contact, but instead of the crackle of pain Buck's last sensation was of his great-uncle's voice telling him to be at peace because there was nothing left to fear.

CHAPTER 11

GEORGE DRAGGED SUSAN back through the gas-filled corridor, away from the catwalk, the scavengers, and their son.

"They're going to kill him," Susan wailed as they ran. "We have to go back."

"They won't kill him!" George said, clamping his fingers around Susan's arm with the solidity of hull metal. "Didn't you see what he was wearing?" In the distance he could hear the clang of booted feet on the water hub's catwalks. He had heard the tall Overseer give the orders. A squad was coming for them.

"Not our son," Susan sobbed, each word resonating with the rhythm of her running feet. "Not Finiksa."

"He wears the black scarf of the Watcher Youth Brigade," George said bitterly. "Our own son is as good as being an Overseer himself."

"No," Susan said. "They must have *forced* him to wear it. They—"

"He was present for an execution," George said, his words coming between gasps for breath. He knew he was being cruel, but he had no choice. Susan *had* to accept the truth, no matter how painful it might be. Once again they had lost a child to a horrible fate.

"But the female Overseer, she was going to use her prod on Finiksa. He *couldn't* be one of them."

George skidded to a stop in the corridor, sending billows of white gas roiling ahead of him. He grabbed both of Susan's arms and pulled her close.

"It's their *way!*" he snapped at her. "They take our own children from us. They turn them against us. Just as they turn the stories of our own past against us. Whatever we have that's good they take from us and pervert."

Susan's face was streaked with tears. "Then what can we do?"

The word tore at George's hearts even as he spoke it. *"Nothing!"*

He felt Susan sag against his grip. "Stangya, no . . ." She began to cough again. The gas was strong within her.

"He's gone, Appy. We have to let him go or else they will kill us, too!"

"Then let them kill me. Let them—"

"Shhh!" George pleaded. He pulled Susan to him and held her tight. He listened carefully. There was running in the corridor, coming up on them quickly. George made his decision. He hugged Susan a final time, then pushed her away from him. "You go on. I'll hold them off here. Try to get back to the light bay and—"

"I'm not leaving you," Susan said. Her eyes were unsteady, unfocused. Another few minutes of exposure to the holy gas and she would be powerless to reject any suggestion George could give her. But for now she was still fighting, still refusing to give up control of her life.

"Appy, you must. Otherwise . . . they'll have won everything."

"They already have."

The running grew louder. Any moment the Overseers would be close enough to see their quarry through the mist. Then it wouldn't matter how fast George and Susan could run. The ship was a closed space, and their capture would be inevitable. There was only one thing George could say.

"Appy, listen to me: They haven't won. They're nowhere close. There's a rebellion on board. Do you understand? Some of us are fighting back!"

Susan reacted as if she'd been slapped. "No. That's impossible."

"Go now! Get to safety. Then contact Moodri. He's involved somehow. Or at least he knows about it."

George could hear shouts among the running.

"Moodri?" Susan's eyes were wide. "Moodri's talking of rebellion?"

"Appy, please go! I don't want you to die."

Susan tried to take a step away but faltered. "I can't. I can't leave you."

A new sound filled the corridor. Another pair of running feet. This time coming from the opposite direction. They were surrounded. There was no escape.

"Andarko," George cried. He had no other words. He pulled Susan close to him, wrapping her in his arms as if to protect her from everything. "I'm sorry," he whispered to her. "So sorry."

A powerful hand fell on his shoulder. It was over. George turned to face his captors, determined to take as many of them with him as he could.

"Stangya! Appy! This way!"

George's mouth fell open. "Ruhtra?"

George's brother aimed a small black device down the corridor toward the sound of the approaching Overseers. A red light glowed on the object. "Eight of them. Fifty meters and closing."

"What is that? Where did you come from?" George hadn't seen his younger brother for years. He hadn't even been sure that Ruhtra was still on the ship. Yet here he was now, dressed in slave's tunic and trousers but with an odd belt from which mysterious objects dangled, and wearing a intership communications headband and microphone. George was too shocked to do anything more than stare.

But Ruhtra understood the situation even if George didn't. "Come with me or be recycled!" Then he turned and ran back into the mist.

George didn't hesitate. He took Susan's hand just as she took his, and they both ran after Ruhtra.

They only had to go ten feet. George stared up in amazement. A ceiling plate was open, hanging down like a hatchway. Ruhtra was already up inside the opening it led to. He held out his hand. "Appy first."

Susan leapt for the opening eight feet overhead, hooked her hands inside, then disappeared inside as Ruhtra lifted her. "Now you!" Ruhtra called out.

George jumped. The edge of the opening was rough under his

hands, as if it had been imperfectly cut. He pulled himself up partway, then felt Ruhtra and Susan latch onto the waistband of his trousers and haul him up the rest of the way.

They were crowded into a small access tunnel, four feet by four feet. Ruhtra pushed by George, reached through the ceiling opening again, then pulled up the hanging ceiling plate. He locked it shut with a latch, bringing total darkness just as George heard the thundering feet of the Overseers pass by below.

For long moments George sat in the tunnel gasping for breath, hearing Appy catch hers. Then he heard a small click, and Ruhtra whispered, "Protein retrieved."

George stared into the darkness in the direction from which his brother's voice had come. *Protein retrieved.* Even George knew it was a code, like the indecipherable commands the Overseers shouted to one another. He felt a sudden chill of anticipation as he realized that he might at last have come into contact with a group organized like the Overseers, but working *against* them.

"I have a thousand questions for you, Ruhtra," George whispered into the darkness.

A small red light appeared in the darkness. Ruhtra's face was dimly lit beneath it. "Then move quietly and follow me," Ruhtra commanded, "and I shall try to answer them."

Ten minutes later they came to an intersection node in the access tunnels that was large enough for them to stand in. Seven other tunnels led out of the node at different angles, and beside each opening a single yellow light glowed. Something was written beside each light, but George couldn't see clearly enough to read any of the markings.

"We'll be safe here for a few minutes at least," Ruhtra said. He moved carefully over to George—the floor of the intersection node was covered with thick bundles of cables and pipes—and embraced his brother tightly. "I thought you had been off-loaded on Antagonus. I thought I would never see you again."

"Nor I you," George said. The emotions of the day were threatening to overwhelm him. To find his son and realize he was lost all in the same instant. To face certain death at the Overseers' hands and then to be saved by a brother he had thought was gone forever. George felt a sob rising within him. It had been so long since he had allowed himself to feel sorrow or sadness, because he knew that would proclaim the ship the final victor. But now, with Ruhtra's presence, with Moodri's hints, with the discovery of a network of tunnels in the ship of which it appeared the Overseers had no knowledge, sorrow and sadness seemed finally permissible because each feeling held the promise of hope.

George held his brother at arm's length, drinking in the sight of him. Ruhtra's face had aged dramatically in the time since they had last seen each other, yet his still-familiar features brought back strong memories of their days with their parents in the dormitory, before the Overseers had come for George.

But that was the past. It was the present that was important now. And the future.

"Is there a revolt?" George asked.

Ruhtra looked pained. "Please, Stangya. I can't answer that. Even if I knew what the answer was."

George was momentarily confused. Ruhtra slipped from his grasp and went to Susan. She was sitting on a thick bundle of pipes that snaked from one tunnel into another. She had wrapped her arms around her legs and was rocking slowly back and forth, staring blankly ahead of her.

"The gas has taken her," Ruhtra said as he crouched to look into Susan's expressionless eyes. "Has she no more *eemikken* she can take?"

"Eemikken\?" George said. "Only the Overseers take that."

Ruhtra stood up and stretched. His various implements clinked against one another on his laden belt. "No," he said. "The Overseers dispense *eemikken* lozenges to those whom they wish to reward or to coerce, but their own ability to resist the gas is linked to their tattoos." Ruhtra idly traced a finger around his own bare wrist. "Some sort of dermal transference, the Elders say. High dosage of the antidote to the holy gas released through the skin at a constant rate."

"I did not know that," George said. "But what of me? I have taken nothing, but the gas has yet to affect me."

Ruhtra smiled—an expression seldom seen upon the ship. He pointed a finger at the trident-shaped spot above his temple. "That's because you're like me," he said. "Family: Third Star's Ocean. Most of us are resistant to the gas, except to very high doses, of course. There are other families as well. I've heard an entire tribe was resistant, and they were among the first to be off-loaded."

George traced his own trident-shaped spot, just like Ruhtra's, almost identical to their father's. And to Moodri's. "Resistant?" he repeated. That would explain so much.

"But trust me, Stangya, if ever there are Overseers around, act as if you have accepted the release of the gas." Ruhtra read the question in George's eyes. "For a long time, the Elders say, the Overseers have refused to believe that any of us could be resistant. But as the generations have passed, and the Overseers have been mating the best workers with the best workers, they have strengthened this capability within certain families."

"Appy was right," George said. It made perfect sense. In a gas-dulled work force the best workers would naturally be those who were most able to withstand the effects of the gas. And like George and Susan, those who were most resistant were more able to couple and more likely to bring forth podlings who in turn would share both their parents' resistance. George wanted to laugh. It was such perfect justice. "The Overseers have been breeding the very workers who will rise up against them!"

Ruhtra smiled but held two fingers to his lips to signal for silence. "It is not quite as simple as that. They're beginning to suspect what is happening. They are trying to reformulate the gas. Break apart breeding couples who show resistance."

George looked at Susan. He knew why she would not abandon him in the corridor as the Overseers neared. He would never abandon her, either. "Let them try," he said fiercely.

Ruhtra put his hands on George's shoulders. "This is not your fight, Stangya."

George felt the sting of quick anger. "This is every Tencton's fight."

Ruhtra's gaze bored into George with the power of the Overseers' cutting beam. "Listen carefully, Stangya. You don't even know if there is a fight."

"Ruhtra, how can you say that? How can—"

"Keer'chatlas," Ruhtra said. And that one word explained everything. Strength through weakness. Victory through division. A network of spies and cells impervious to betrayal. A network of hope.

George paused. "Then there *is* a revolt."

Ruhtra dropped his eyes. "If there is, I do not know it." He drew his hands back. "I receive my orders. I do what I am told. Why I do it, for whom I do it, I don't know. And because I don't know, I cannot betray anyone when I am caught."

"No one will catch you," George said vehemently, with his newborn hope.

But Ruhtra did not respond to George's conviction. "I am frightened, Stangya. I started out reporting on the Overseers' movements. Like you, I could move through heavy concentrations of gas. Then an Elder instructed me in how to defeat the locks on certain equipment bins." He looked down at his belt and ran his hands over the devices that hung from it. "Now look at me. Possession of any one of these is grounds for instant death." He looked back at George, and the fear he felt was clearly evident in his haunted eyes. "There's no going back for me, Stangya. It's like sliding down the recycler chute or facing the sixth nozzle in the Game. My capture is inevitable."

"But why?" George protested. "With *keer'chatlas* you are protected. Someone must be planning everything, organizing everything. You can't *expect* defeat, or that is what you will earn."

Ruhtra shook his head at George's naïveté. *"Keer'chatlas* is breaking down. There are too many activities going on at once. Too many raids. Too many killings. The pace has increased ever since the last translation."

George's mind reeled. Raids? Killings? What was going on in the ship? Why did no one know? "The last translation? That was when Moodri came and—"

Ruhtra pressed his hand against George's mouth. "Please!" he said. "Tell me nothing." His hand trembled against George's lips. "I did not choose this. I am not some *chekkah* born and bred for battle. I dream of Tencton's purple fields of grass, of farming beneath three moons, of feeling my podlings kick within me, full of life." Tears fell from Ruhtra's eyes as he bared the secrets of his *serdos* to his brother. "And I shall have none of that, Stangya. None of that."

George took his brother's hand in his. "None of us will ever have the dreams we cherish unless some of us fight for them."

"Don't you think I know that?" Ruhtra pulled his hand from George's grip. "You will have to take Appy and leave," he said. "The Overseers know that the incident at the water hub has been witnessed. They will be searching for likely suspects."

"What was the incident at the water hub?" George asked. "And why was my son there?"

Ruhtra blinked in surprise. "Finiksa? You saw Finiksa in the hub?"

"In a Watcher scarf."

A bleak look came into Ruhtra's eyes. "They take everything from us, don't they?"

"Only if we don't fight them," George said. "Do you know why there were Watchers present? Do you know what the Overseers wanted?"

"No, Stangya. And you don't want to know either. My assignment was only to ensure the safety of workers from another cell. By the time you and Appy made yourselves known those workers had completed their assignment, and I was told to help you escape."

"By whom?"

Ruhtra tapped the small device that extended down from his communications headband to cover an ear valley. "By whoever talks to me through this. I don't know. I can't know. And I don't want to know." He turned away from George and went to Susan, gently compelling her to stand up. She was completely under the spell of the gas and complied at once.

Ruhtra pointed to a dark tunnel crowded with pipes. "Take this tunnel straight through past three intersections. You'll find a wall hatch that opens into a garbage sorting chamber. You'll only be a few sectors from your dormitory. Go there immediately before the search reaches it."

"How do you know where our dormitory is?" George asked as he guided Susan to the tunnel entrance. There were so many other questions he longed to ask his brother, but Ruhtra was signaling them to hurry to obey him.

"I don't know," Ruhtra said. He tapped his earpiece again. *"He* knows."

George crouched by the tunnel. "I want to help, Ruhtra. Tell *him* I want to join the revolt."

Ruhtra tried pushing George on his way. "They don't want you, Stangya."

George felt the acid wash of long-suppressed frustration and resentment move through him. "Why?"

The answer strained at Ruhtra's lips.

"I know you know," George said. "Tell me!"

Ruhtra shoved George into the tunnel. "In case of defeat, the Elders will not risk losing entire families," he said quickly, regretfully. "One from each line must be spared."

George stared at his brother. If what Ruhtra said was true, then everyone else from the union of Family: Heroes of Soren'tzahh and Family: Third Moon's Ocean was involved in the revolt—except for George.

He looked at the wall, trying to find a place to rest his hand for balance. He saw one of the signs that was mounted beside a tunnel entrance light. It was faded and smudged and not written in the sine script of Tencton's major language groups. It was alien.

"Everyone else in our line is involved?" George asked. Fighting their own kind in an alien construct, he thought. Was this what tens of thousands of years of Tenctonese history had come to?

"Go now," Ruhtra said. He stepped back from the tunnel entrance, away from the light. "Dream of Tencton for me."

George heard Ruhtra's soft footsteps rush away.

Everyone else in my line, he thought with a sudden chill. Ruhtra, and Moodri, and—he gasped in horror as he realized the full meaning of what his brother had said—Finiksa.

The very revolt he dreamed about seethed around George, and he knew now that he had been deliberately kept from learning anything about it.

But now that he did know, nothing could stop him from joining. No matter what Moodri said, no matter what Ruhtra said, George made up his mind that nothing could keep him from fighting for his people, his family, and his son.

He ran through the tunnel with Susan, and his hearts hammered with new purpose.

For George Francisco, the revolt had finally begun.

CHAPTER 12

SIKES ALWAYS FELT NERVOUS when he was on academic grounds. From his long stretches of permanent detention back at Belmont High to his abortive semesters at college when he was struggling with a new marriage, a new baby, and trying to find some direction in his life, school had never been a pleasant experience for him. And even now, driving slowly along the winding roads of UCLA on official police business, he felt his stomach tightening up just as if he had been called to the principal's office for smoking in the bathroom, or to the dean's office to explain his grades.

"Get a grip," Sikes muttered to himself as he slowed by a sign with a list of buildings and a confusing collection of arrows. He squinted through his sunglasses, trying to find Royce Physics Hall on the sign. Then he jerked upright as someone blasted a horn behind him.

Sikes looked over his shoulder at two tanned weight lifters in a red Miata waving at him to get off the road. Sikes muttered some more and pulled over to the curb to let the little sports car pass. His own school experience still led him to strongly dislike anyone who could afford college *and* a sports car at the same time.

The Miata squealed past him. The weight lifters laughed. Sikes gritted his teeth and memorized the car's license plate.

Maybe he'd run it through the computer later to see if there was a citation or two outstanding.

Twenty more minutes of searching brought Sikes, now on foot, to the entrance of a pleasantly designed building constructed of deep red stone. Unusual for southern California, it wasn't built in a Spanish design, but Sikes had no idea what other style it might be. Victoria would probably know, he thought. Or Grazer.

Sikes shuddered as he thought of his fellow Detective Three. How could anyone know so much without also knowing the definition of an insufferable bore? After they had read Randolph Petty's electronic mail on the computer last night Grazer had actually explained the development of the computer chip to both Kirby and Sikes for almost two hours. Kirby had taken the easy way out and fallen asleep, but Sikes, as the only adult in the room, had felt obliged to keep his eyes open.

After the first hour of polite "uh-huhs" and "reallys" Sikes had perversely decided to not say anything more that would encourage Grazer. Incredibly, the man had continued talking without any feedback from Sikes for almost another whole hour. In desperation Sikes had called up humorous mental visions of Grazer at home, practice-lecturing his goldfish or even a sofa. Then he had begun creating even more diverting visions of what it would be like when Victoria came back from Switzerland.

Whether Grazer had finally gotten the hint or his voice had given out, Sikes didn't know. But when the detective had finally left, it seemed to Sikes as if his own dismal, cramped apartment was suddenly twice as large and soundproofed. Maybe I don't have to move after all, Sikes had thought as he had gently wakened Kirby so he could make up the sofa bed for her. Maybe I just have to have Grazer over more often so I can appreciate what I've got when he's gone. That final thought— appreciating what he had only when he no longer had it—had made him think of Victoria again, and he had spent another restless night searching for her imprint beside him in his bed.

But this morning was far better than the previous morning had been. Sikes's head felt its normal size. The sun was warm and not a glaring interrogation spotlight. He had his official notebook with its numbered pages in the inner pocket of his sports jacket. He had driven through the canyons with the

Mustang's top down. *And* he was about to interview his first potential witness to his first murder case, all on his own.

Angic Perez hadn't even asked for details when Sikes had spoken with her at the station house this morning. "If you think you're on to something," she had said, "go get 'em, Sherlock." Then she had added, "Just remember that you only have until quitting time today before you start taking on other cases."

Sikes had groaned at the healthy dose of reality his new partner had inflicted upon him, but if the lead he had come up with last night did end up being worth something, he was certain he could talk Angie into giving him some more time. After all, the name of the game was solving crimes, and Sikes was determined to solve this one.

As pleasant as Royce Hall had looked on the outside, inside it was falling into disrepair, the fate of all schools in a system that worried more about the next quarter than the next generation. But the signs on the walls made more sense than the signs on the road had made, and Sikes quickly found the minuscule office of the woman with whom Professor Randolph Petty had exchanged his final electronic letters—Amy Stewart.

The door was open when Sikes arrived. Stewart's name was handwritten on a piece of cardboard held in a metal frame above the door number. She was identified as a Tutorial Leader. At first it looked as if the room beyond the door was a locker of some kind and not an office. It was that small. But there was a narrow desk crammed into a corner, wedged between floor-to-ceiling bookshelves that sagged under piles of magazines and papers. There were a number of certificates and framed color photographs of people on the walls' few unobstructed areas. And there was someone working at the desk, peering into an inordinately large computer screen on which a complex colored graph was displayed. Sikes had to knock twice on the door frame before that person realized she had company and turned around.

"Amy Stewart?" he asked.

The woman at the computer looked up at Sikes over the thin red frames of her large round glasses. Sikes stared back, at a loss for words. He realized then that he had had no expectations as to what kind of a person Amy Stewart might be. Perhaps, because Petty had been seventy-two years old, Sikes had expected Stewart to be of similar vintage. And perhaps, because the letters had indicated that she was an academic, he had expected her to be someone indistinguishable from the dusty piles of books that she worked with. But he hadn't expected the striking young woman who looked at him now.

Dimly he knew that she was waiting for him to say something more, but Sikes was at a loss. If he had had to put out an APB on her, he would have failed. She was female, most assuredly, but . . . Caucasian? Hispanic? Native American? He couldn't be sure, there were elements of so many different origins in her golden complexion, intense dark eyes, and jet-black hair feathered close to her skull. Her eyebrows were almost nonexistent, adding a look of permanent and childlike anticipation to a face graced with lips that made Sikes think only of adult pursuits.

"Yes?" the woman said.

"Umm," Sikes replied, two years worth of interrogation classes suddenly flushed from his mind.

Surprisingly, instead of turning back to her computer in impatience, the woman flashed Sikes a sly smile. "I'm Amy Stewart. That *is* who you're looking for, isn't it?" Her subtle accent was as unidentifiable as her heritage, and that smile further delayed the return of Sikes's verbal abilities. He fished around in the back pocket of his jeans and pulled out the leather folder he found there. Then he held it out to her.

"I'm, ah, Detective Sikes, LAPD?"

She looked at what Sikes held in his hand. After a moment all his credit cards fell from it and clattered on the floor.

"Uh, wrong pocket," Sikes said. He found his badge folder and brought that out, then squatted down to gather up everything that had fallen from his wallet.

Amy Stewart leaned back in her chair. Her smile grew broader. Two credit cards fell out of Sikes's hand.

"First day?" she asked.

Sikes decided her low, husky voice was as striking as her appearance. "Almost," he mumbled.

"Well, I don't drive. I have a green card. And I'm sure the statute of limitations has run out on any major felonies I've committed, so what can I do for you?"

Sikes got to his feet and jammed his wallet and its debris into an outside pocket on his sports jacket. He'd worry about sorting it out later. "I'm, uh, I'd like to ask you a few questions. If that's all right?"

Without consciously looking for it, Sikes noticed a small

flicker in her eye. Maybe it was a tic. Maybe it was a hidden reaction to the idea of answering questions for the police. He tried to discount it. But it *was* exactly what the textbook said he was supposed to be looking for.

"About what?" she asked. Her voice was as easy as before. No sign of tension.

"About who," Sikes said. He pulled out his notebook and pen to give his hands something to do. "Randolph Petty. You exchanged some—"

Amy Stewart pushed her chair back with noisy force and got to her feet. "Who are you really?" she demanded.

Sikes stepped back from her. The astronomy student was surprisingly tall, almost his height. "I told you. Matt Sikes. I'm a detective." Hold on, he thought. This isn't supposed to be happening. I'm supposed to put *her* on the defensive.

Amy Stewart held out her hand. "Give me that badge again."

Sikes was over the impact of her appearance. Warily he opened his badge case and gave it to her. She studied it intently, looking from the ID photo to Sikes and back again. She handed the case back to him.

"Where's Dr. Petty?" she asked.

Sikes took the case and returned it to a pocket. "That's what I want to talk with you about. I've got some bad news."

She swayed slightly.

"Dr. Petty was killed two nights ago," Sikes said, as gently as he could. There was never an easy way to say such a thing.

She stumbled forward.

Sikes grabbed her. He felt her tremble along the length of him, and the shock of her was as if he had been tasered. Their faces were inches apart. He could smell a scent rich and herbal coming from her hair. He guided her back to her chair, bending over her as he carefully lowered her to it. She gripped the arms of her chair, and Sikes felt her strength return. Regretfully he let go of her and stood back. He could still feel her against him. Sweat formed on his brow.

"Are you . . . are you okay?" Sikes asked. His voice was unexpectedly dry, as if he and not Grazer had done all the talking last night.

Amy Stewart gazed around the small room as if she had been sucker punched. "How?" she finally asked.

Sikes found a second chair, moved a stack of books from it, sat down, and told her.

When he was finished she tensed as if she were fighting back tears. Sikes told himself that he must remain emotionally detached from her—she could be a source of a motive in a murder case. But her obvious distress was getting to him. Unless she's faking it, Sikes cautioned himself. That possibility was enough to shock him back into being a detective. He began to watch her more closely.

"So why did you come to me?" she asked. Her taut fingers were like claws on the arms of her chair. She didn't look at Sikes.

Sikes reached into his jacket and brought out five folded pieces of letter-sized paper—the printouts he had made at the station house of the letters Grazer had saved to floppy disk. "These," Sikes said. "Your last computer letter to Dr. Petty and his reply to you." He offered the pages to her.

But the astronomy student had no interest in looking at them. "So you've come to me because I might have been . . . one of the last people to talk with Dr. Petty?" Her voice ended on a rise, as if that's what she *hoped* had brought Sikes to her.

"No," he said, studying her. "It's because I think that the material you and Dr. Petty mention in these letters might have been the motive for his murder."

Amy Stewart's face fell forward into her hands. "That's impossible," she said in a muffled voice. "How could . . . how could *anyone* do that? For *what?*"

Sikes forced himself to remain sitting. She might be a suspect, he kept telling himself. This might be an act. But he wanted reach out to comfort her.

"I was hoping that's what you could tell me," he said, allowing her time to regain her composure. He glanced through the printouts, reading the phrases he had underlined. "Your letters say something about 'the material.' How critical it is. How important it is that the original computer records be protected so others can verify them. How cautiously you will have to proceed to publish this information." He flipped a page. "You seem quite upset that Dr. Petty hasn't responded to you as quickly as he said he would. You keep stressing how significant 'the material' is." He flipped over two more pages. "And then Dr. Petty sends you back a quick note saying he has passed along 'the material' as he said he would and has arranged a meeting to discuss it"—Sikes looked up from the printouts and found Amy staring intently at him—"on the night he was murdered."

Amy said nothing.

Sikes asked her the question. "Ms. Stewart. What is 'the material'?"

Amy looked up at him and bit her lower lip. Her cheeks seemed flushed.

Sikes tried again. "Is it something valuable enough that Dr. Petty might have been killed for it?"

A breath escaped her.

"Ms. Stewart, please. If Dr. Petty *was* killed for something he got from you, you might be in danger, too. You have to tell me what it is."

Amy Stewart stared at Sikes in apparent indecision. He was caught by the intensity of her gaze. He had no explanation for the way she was making him feel. He had no desire for it. But he also couldn't stop it.

"Can you tell me?" Sikes asked, not certain if he knew to what the question referred.

"Better than that," Stewart said finally. "I can show you."

Thanks to his Uncle Jack, Sikes could recognize all of the constellations and knew the names of hundreds of stars, but the dense star field on the computer screen was a mystery to him. He couldn't find a single familiar pattern.

"I don't recognize anything," he said.

Amy turned to him with a look of surprise. She had left her office for a few minutes—leaving Sikes nervously wondering what kind of idiot he would look like if she didn't return—to wash her face, she said. But Sikes could still see the turmoil in her face. The old guy had definitely meant something to her.

"Why would you expect to?" she asked.

Sikes felt foolish. The words had slipped out of him. He'd forgotten he was just an amateur who only looked at the stars through a pair of binoculars these days, and lately only when he could persuade Kirby that there was something worth seeing. Amy Stewart was halfway through her Ph.D. in astronomy and physics. Who was he trying to kid?

"Well," he said in a voice that was awkward and stumbling once again, "I know a bit about . . . where things are and that."

Amy studied him for a few moments, then looked at her

computer monitor. The image was high resolution, almost as clear as a large film transparency. No wonder the screen is so big, Sikes had thought when the first star field had come up and he realized the detailed work it was used for.

Amy pointed to a large glob of white, bristling with spikes of light and ringed by a halo, that Sikes recognized as a low-magnitude star that had been too bright for a long exposure. "This is Bellatrix. Is that any help?"

Sikes stared at the screen, trying to figure out if the orientation of the field was standard. He pointed to a second overexposed star on the opposite side of the screen. "Betelgeuse?" he asked.

"Very good," Amy said, clearly surprised.

Sikes traced his finger across the screen, drawing the constellation's imaginary link lines. "So this is the top half of Orion." He pointed below the screen. "Alnilam and Rigel are way down here, and right about where this keyboard is, that's where the nebula is." He now knew why such a familiar constellation had looked so odd—there were too many stars. "So all the other stars in there, they're magnitude six or dimmer. Stars not visible to the naked eye."

Amy stared at Sikes again and tapped her finger against the side of her keyboard.

"Is something wrong?" Sikes asked.

"How did you get assigned to investigate Dr. Petty's death?" There was a definite edge of suspicion in her voice.

"My partner's name was next on the rotation," Sikes said, trying to understand her sudden change in mood. Sitting so close to her, two chairs pulled up to her narrow desk, it was easy to pick up on her feelings. And her perfume. And the heat of her body so near his. "Why?" he said, making a heroic effort to sound unaffected.

Amy hesitated. "I don't know. An astronomer dies. The officer assigned to investigate knows astronomy. Seems like an odd coincidence to me."

Sikes realized that now *she* was watching *him* for a reaction. He tried to think of a question that Angie might ask. "Do you have some reason for thinking that it's not a coincidence?"

Amy thought that over. "I'll show you what I've got here. Then you can tell me." She turned to the screen. "This is a plate taken six days ago as part of an asteroid mapping project."

"Dr. Petty had an asteroid named after him," Sikes said. "I saw the certificate in his house."

Amy flinched, and Sikes decided not to interrupt her again.

"It was his specialty," she said after a moment. "Deep-space tracking. He developed most of the search algorithms and observation techniques used in the field today." She typed something on her keyboard, and the star field shrank to about a quarter its original size and slid up to the left-hand corner of the screen. "Since he retired, Dr. Petty was part of an unofficial group of astronomers and space researchers who lobbied for the creation of Spacewatch—an automated asteroid tracking network to identify Earth-crossers." She glanced at Sikes. "You understand 'Earth-crossers'?"

"Asteroids that, um, cross the Earth's orbit?" Sikes guessed.

Amy nodded. "Back in eighty-nine one missed us by about a hundred million kilometers." She eyed Sikes. "At the speed it was traveling, that meant it missed us by about a day. *One* day. It was somewhere between one hundred to four hundred meters across, but if it had hit, it would have been like a thousand-megaton bomb. Flatten everything for a hundred and fifty miles. Could have taken out any city on the planet. Tens of thousands dead, if not millions."

Sikes whistled silently.

"So far we've got good data on about a hundred of them. But the best guess is that there could be at least a thousand. And for all that, there's only one observatory doing any crucial work in the field. Kitt Peak's got a thirty-six-inch Newtonian and a CCD camera. If we had three more telescopes around the world, we could probably track ninety percent of the Earth-crossers in a decade. And it would only cost about two million a year. Less than the cost of a science fiction movie for the whole ten-year effort." She typed again, anger evident in each keystroke. A second small star field appeared on the screen, opposite the first.

And then Sikes's stomach tightened. He realized that Amy was going to put two almost-identical star fields on the screen. He knew enough to understand that by flipping rapidly from one star field to another and back again, the parts of the fields that were different would appear to move back and forth like the cartoons in the small flip books Kirby used to play with. Sikes's mind raced. An astronomical discovery? Earth-crossers? Important information worth someone's death?

"You've found something, haven't you?" Sikes asked, leaning forward.

"That's the understatement of the century."

On the screen, in response to Amy's commands, the two star fields reversed to make each point of light a black dot against a white background. Then both fields expanded again to overlap and fill the screen until it appeared there was only one field on display.

Sikes put his hands on the edge of the desk. He had just gotten used to the idea that the United States and the late Soviet Union weren't going to nuke all life off the planet. But what if something else was about to?

The computer screen began to flicker. Sikes watched it intently. And after a few moments he found it—a small black dot that jumped back and forth, back and forth, like the tolling of a bell.

Sikes touched the image on the screen. "Is that it?" he asked.

Amy nodded. "Speckle data tells us it's about five kilometers across."

Sikes swallowed. If four hundred meters could equal one thousand megatons, then what would *five kilometers* do to the world? "And . . . and it's coming for us?" All he could think about was Kirby. She was only thirteen. How could he have brought a child into a world about to be—

Amy shook her head.

Sikes blinked. "I beg your pardon?"

Amy leaned back in her chair. "On its present trajectory it will just graze the sun, but it'll miss us. Comfortably. Won't come anywhere near the Earth."

Sikes sagged in his own chair. "Then what's the big deal? I mean, the way you were talking, I thought I was looking at doomsday coming for us or something. What's so important about one more asteroid?"

Amy took Sikes by surprise and put her hand on his arm, as if to anchor him in place.

"I mentioned the Spacewatch program only to let you know how I happened to come upon the data. But this isn't an asteroid."

Sikes stared at her blankly.

"From its size and shape, the spectrum it's emitting, and its speed," Amy said, "this object is inescapably artificial."

"Artificial?" Sikes said. "You mean like manmade?"

"Oh, God, no." There was some odd combination of regret and determination on Amy's tense face that Sikes felt he was finally on the brink of understanding. "Whoever built this thing," she said, "I guarantee you they're not human at all."

PART TWO

CORRECTION

DESCENT MINUS 4 STANDARD DAYS AND COUNTING

CHAPTER 1

BUCK FELL. FIELDS OF BLUE lay beneath him. He didn't know what part of the ship he saw. There were stars in the field. Thousands of them. Calling to him.

Finiksa.

He fell to the blue fields. To the stars scattered through them. Somewhere deep within him he knew he fell to Tencton, the home he had never seen. He didn't want to stop. But the voice was insistent.

Finiksa. It is not your time.

The stars drifted through the fields, caught in the same effortless current that drew Buck down. They called to him just as the voice did.

All things come from the Mother. All things return to the Mother. Your time will come, Finiksa. But your work is not done.

Buck opened his eyes, and the stars vanished from his knowing.

"I have no work," he said, surprised by how his throat hurt and his lungs ached. "I'm just a boy."

"We are all children." The voice spoke to him in words this time, not as feelings in his mind. He recognized the voice.

"Uncle Moodri," Buck said.

The Elder's slight though comforting hand gripped Buck's firmly. "You are not alone," Moodri said in soothing tones.

Buck's voice was a weak sigh. "It was . . . so beautiful."

"And it will always be there for you. No need to rush."

Buck realized the sleeping platform he lay upon was wider than the one in his crèche. He knew that Moodri would never risk visiting him in the crèche, either. So he must be somewhere else. He tried to lift his head to see where he was, and stars of a different kind burst before him as his neck cramped in pain.

Buck moaned, and both of Moodri's hands pressed gently on his shoulders. "Do you remember what happened?" his great-uncle asked.

Buck closed his eyes. He remembered the water hub. The billows of holy gas, more than he had ever seen. Watch Leader D'wayn had found him and Vornho. Another Overseer—Coolock—had been with her. They'd been on level fifty-seven. Something about water workers. Something Vornho had said about the flow being diverted and—

"Vornho was going to kill someone!"

As Moodri's hands pressed harder it seemed the strong fingers found places to push that eased the sudden panic that welled up in the boy.

"But he did not," Moodri said. "Do you remember why?"

Buck opened his eyes again. The lights above him were brighter than usual. The bed was softer. He tried moving just an inch to find Moodri. "I tried to stop him." And with those words Buck knew he was marked for recycling. He had dared defy the Overseers. Only one punishment was possible.

"What happened then?" Moodri asked.

Buck struggled to remember. The realization that Vornho was going to kill without justice. Coolock's rage. D'wayn raising him high . . . and then what? Dimly he recalled seeing . . . seeing . . . "Celine and Andarko came from the mist and saved me," Buck said. His voice filled with awe as he grappled with the implications of his vision. "Celine and Andarko." Against the pain he rolled his head to Moodri and with a shaking hand reached out to grip his great-uncle's white robe. "Uncle Moodri! I saw them! I saw Celine and Andarko, and they . . . they saved me from the Overseers!"

Through the black explosions that obscured his sight Buck could see Moodri's loving smile like a blessing.

"I . . . I know you don't believe in them," Buck added as he remembered the Ionian robes his great-uncle wore, "but I *did* see them."

Moodri's finger lightly pressed against a point between Buck's eyes, and the boy's sight cleared of black stars and pinwheels. "All things come from the Mother," Moodri said, "even Celine and Andarko."

"Then you believe me?" Buck asked.

"Never look to others for what you know is true within your own two hearts." Moodri touched his knuckles to Buck's temple. "I know what you saw, and what you saw is true. For you."

Buck looked past his great-uncle at the bright ceiling lights, thinking about those words. "So . . . what I saw might not be what I *think* I saw?"

Moodri laughed. "You are your father's son, Finiksa."

"My father?" Buck asked. "Andarko!" He tried to sit up. Waves of pain shot out from his forehead down his arms and his back. "And Celine! Celine was my mother! They were there, Moodri! My parents were on the level above me! And they *saved* me!"

Gently Moodri eased Buck back against the unusual bed he lay on. "For now you mustn't think of them. But soon, Finiksa, I promise that you may."

"Why?" Buck asked. His body thrummed the way it had when his Watcher Brigade had toured the power plants. But it was not a physical vibration this time. It was the afterimage of pain. "I was shocked by an Overseer's prod, wasn't I?"

"Focused very high," Moodri confirmed. He leaned forward so that Buck could see him without having to move again. "You understand the danger you are in?"

"I acted against the Overseers."

"Exactly," Moodri said. "And just as Celine and Andarko saved you in the water hub, soon you must save yourself."

Buck was confused. "But you said it *wasn't* Celine and Andarko. You said—"

"I said nothing, Finiksa."

Buck sighed. He was used to this. Everything Moodri said, everything he did was a lesson to be studied. "How do I save myself, Uncle?"

Moodri smiled again. "Listen carefully. The Overseers will come for you soon. They will question you. They will demand to know why you tried to stop your crèche mate from cutting the worker. They will demand to know who called to you from the catwalk. And you will have to answer them."

Buck closed his eyes in despair. He had tried to stop Vornho because he had said the prayer for guidance and knew that what Vornho wanted to do was wrong. He knew he had seen his parents on the catwalk, though as a Watcher he was to have no family but the Overseers. "They will recycle me."

"Not if you give them the right answers," Moodri said.

"What answers?" Buck asked. He opened his eyes again, but Moodri and the bright lights were nowhere to be seen. Instead Buck saw a gleaming crystal, no larger than a child's fingertip, spinning above his head as if dangling from a cord held by an impossibly distant hand. The crystal sent out brilliant streamers of light into space. He couldn't stop looking at it.

"Listen well, Finiksa. Remember what you *truly* saw."

The streamers of light swallowed Buck whole, and he fell again.

CHAPTER 2

IN THE END, AFTER HE had listened to all the evidence and carefully weighed the pros and cons, Matt Sikes had no choice when it came to making his decision: Amy Stewart was as crazy as she was gorgeous.

"You're looking at me as if you don't believe me," Amy said. She sat in her chair by her computer, loosely dangling her large red-framed glasses from one hand as she leaned back against her desktop looking exhausted. There had been a spark of something vibrant in her when Sikes had first seen her that had not returned once he had told her about Petty's death. He regretted its passing.

Sikes had pushed his chair back to the other side of the tiny office after he had looked at all twenty-four astronomical plates Amy had displayed on her computer. Then he had listened for more than thirty minutes as the astronomy student had painstakingly laid out all the technical observations and logical conclusions that had led her to believe that the rapidly moving point of light she had photographed with her own experimental asteroid tracking system was some sort of UFO made by second cousins to Mr. Spock. Sikes had stopped making notes after the first ten minutes. He could see no point in following this line of inquiry.

"You're right," he said, though he didn't like the frown that creased her face. "I can't believe you."

"Did you hear anything I said?"

"Every word."

"Do you think I'm making it up?"

Sikes had already asked himself the same question. "No," he said. "At least not the photographs."

Amy straightened up in her chair and crossed her arms. "So my *analysis* is wrong?"

"You'd make a good cop," Sikes said, admiring the way she was directing their conversation.

"Don't change the subject. If you accept the plates as real, then your argument is with my interpretation of them. Correct or incorrect?"

"Correct, I guess," he admitted, though he couldn't think how she was going to make him accept what couldn't possibly be true.

Amy looked up at the ceiling. The old acoustical tiles there were dingy gray and marked by orange-rimmed water spots, in discordant counterpoint to the thousands of dollars' worth of state-of-the-art machinery on her desk. "Look, I have an object approximately five kilometers across with a mass of approximately nine-times-ten-to-the-sixth tonnes. That indicates it's either made of something with the overall density of balsa wood or that it's mostly hollow." She lowered her gaze and stared at Sikes as if daring him to disagree with her.

Sikes took the dare. "So maybe it's a comet nucleus," he said. He had read all about them before he had taken Kirby out to the desert to look at Comet Halley. Most comet nuclei were thought to be masses of ice and dust, he remembered. Nowhere near the density of an iron-nickel asteroid.

Amy jammed her glasses back on. "Pardon me. I forgot. You're the detective who thinks he's an astronomer."

"Well, *could* it be a comet?" Sikes asked.

Amy lifted an invisible eyebrow. "All right, Galileo, let's use the scientific method, then." She held up three fingers, just as his partner, Angie, always did. "First, is its mass over volume consistent with known cometary nuclei? No. Still not dense enough." She folded down one finger. "Second, could it be a looser collection of dust and ice than we have seen before? Sort of like an interplanetary whirlwind? Again, no." She folded down a second finger. "It's cleanly occulted three stars so far, and in each case the spectrum drop-off has been laser sharp. Whatever's passing in front of those stars has a *solid* edge." As she folded down the last finger Amy leaned back with a sigh and stated her conclusion. "It's got a solid shell. It's got a hollow interior. It's *not* a comet."

Sikes decided he might as well get into this. "Okay, if it's solid, then maybe it's one of those, uh, other kind of asteroids."

Amy frowned. "Other kind?"

"You know," Sikes said. "The ones that aren't made of metal."

"Ah," Amy said. "You mean carbonaceous chondritic asteroids."

Sikes grimaced at all the syllables. "Do I? Are they the ones that aren't iron?"

"That's right, but wrong again," Amy said. "The object has too little mass to be one of those, either." Amy shifted in her chair and made it creak alarmingly. Except for the computer, Sikes realized that everything else in the office was on the brink of falling apart. "Look, it's not just this thing's mass or size that makes it wrong. There's its albedo." She paused and looked at him questioningly.

"Ah, its brightness, right?" Sikes said.

"Close enough. The fact is, I'm not just basing everything on the plates I showed you. I've run polarimetric analyses on it, comparing its albedo with known polarized samples. I've done a radiometric observation to look at it in infrared. I've cross-correlated everything, and *it's all wrong.* Its reflectance is wrong. Mass. Size. It's covered with infrared hot spots, radiating *unevenly.*" She rolled her shoulders dejectedly as if there were nothing more that could possibly be said. "It is not a natural object. It's as simple as that."

Sikes thought back to the arguments he had had with his Uncle Jack, long before Jack had shipped out that last time without telling his nephew, shattering forever a young boy's faith in all adults. During his last summer with Uncle Jack, when Sikes had been almost thirteen years old, they had had long discussions about the possibility of extraterrestrial life. Jack, Sikes remembered, didn't doubt that life existed elsewhere in the universe. But he wasn't convinced that any of the stories of UFO sightings or crashes were true. Sikes, on the other hand, full of the enthusiasm of a child eager to know more than an adult, fervently wanted to believe in such things. So over that summer Jack had led him through a long and logical examination of the study of UFOs. They had read all the books together. Discussed them endlessly. Years later Sikes had used his uncle's rigorous outlook on the nature of scientific investigation to survive his academy classes on evidence and deduction.

But most of all from that last magical summer Sikes remembered Uncle Jack's favorite argument-ending statement. It worked just as well now as it had then, too.

"Just because *I* can't say what it is," Sikes said to Amy, "doesn't mean that *your* conclusion is automatically right." As he waited for Stewart's reply he wondered when he had lost his boyhood desire for UFOs and aliens to be real. About the time *I went back home to my father for the last time,* he thought. UFOs were just another dream of childhood that had been beaten out of him by his father's drunken rage. Sikes cleared his throat. He decided he had remembered enough about the past for the moment. Despite the occasional letters his uncle still sent, Jack was out of his life forever.

"I think you understand what I've got here," Amy said urgently, as if it mattered to her that he did. Sikes felt pleased that she still wanted to prolong their discussion, even if he was no longer sure that it was giving him anything useful for his case. "Science can never say what something *is,* it can only say what something *isn't.* We look at a phenomenon. We describe a hypothetical set of circumstances that might allow for that phenomenon to exist. And then we try everything we can to chip away at those circumstances. If they can't stand up to our scrutiny and they fall, good. That's how science gets better, more detailed, and more insightful. But if the set of circumstances withstands our scrutiny, then we have a powerful piece of information we can use to create new hypothetical sets of circumstances to explain other phenomena." She looked behind her and tapped the screen where the final plate was still displayed. "Every question you're asking me I've already asked myself. And I've ruled out *everything* natural."

"It's a big universe," Sikes said, feeling foolish for refusing to accept her word. Though not as foolish as he would feel if he did believe in spaceships. "There're bound to be millions of things out there that we don't know anything about."

Stewart nodded. "I agree with you one hundred percent. But this object *isn't* one of them. Because just as it does not exhibit any of the characteristics of an asteroid or a comet, it *does* exhibit many of the characteristics of a self-propelled space vehicle."

Sikes shook his head. He *couldn't* accept her reasoning. It was impossible. It *had* to be.

Amy wasn't finished with him. "Detective, this thing has performed *three* course corrections during the time I've tracked it. Asteroids don't correct their courses. I plotted its general trajectory and checked back for other exposures that might have caught it in the past few weeks, and it *wasn't* there, indicating that it's undergone even more extensive course corrections in the past. This thing just *appeared* sometime in the past ten days, and it's got somewhere specific to go."

Sikes countered with the most important question he could think of—the one that made him want to discount what Amy claimed. "So how come you're the only one who knows about it? I mean, *if* that is some sort of bizarre spaceship heading for us, why haven't the big observatories called press conferences? Why is it just you and no one else?"

Amy met his gaze directly, thrillingly. "You said it yourself. It's a big universe. Telescopes can only watch so much of it at any given time. And as I told you, other than a couple of experimental rigs like the one I've put together, there's only *one* thirty-six-inch telescope actively involved in the full-time search for objects like this." Amy stood up and rubbed at the back of her neck. "Back in January, 1991, an asteroid passed within 170,000 kilometers of the earth. That's closer to us than the moon, for God's sake. And you know when we found out about it?" She didn't wait for Sikes to answer. "Three days *after* its closest approach, when someone finally got around to developing the plates. We don't see a tenth of one percent of what's out there."

Sikes stood up as well. He wasn't sure what to do next, but he knew it was important that he take the lead. Time was running out for his investigation. "Do you think anyone else *is* going to be able to see this thing?"

Amy hit a key that made her screen slowly dim until it was blank, except for a moving watch face. "It's big enough that it's bound to screw up a lot of time exposures eventually. But it's going to pass through Earth's orbit so far away that I doubt anyone will realize what they've seen until it's on its way out of the system again."

For the first time Sikes thought about what was going to happen to this object. He found it somehow terrible that if it were a spacecraft of some kind, it would just pass by, as if it were ignoring Earth.

He saw that Amy was watching him again with that same peculiar intensity and urgency. "Now you understand, don't you?"

But Sikes wasn't sure what she meant. He looked at his watch in frustration. Angie's deadline was approaching rapidly, and his most promising lead had just gone down the proverbial rabbit hole.

"Give me the benefit of the doubt for a minute," Amy said quickly. "Let me construct a hypothesis. What if the object *is* a spaceship? Since it didn't originate in this system, then it was built by creatures who have solved engineering problems that are hundreds if not thousands of years in advance of our science. Think of just the energy source it must have to let it cross between the stars. Think of . . ." She sighed. "I'm sorry. I'm getting carried away, and you obviously think I'm nuts. The point is, even if there's only a one percent chance that my analysis is correct, would you be willing to gamble away a chance to discover the secrets of that kind of technology?"

Put that way, without requiring him to accept that the thing definitely *was* a spaceship, but only to consider the *possibility* that it might be, Sikes found Amy's scenario easier to deal with. It still wasn't convincing enough. But it was easier.

Amy pounced as if she had spotted a weak point in his armor. "Here's your bottom line, detective. It doesn't matter what you think about what I'm telling you. What matters is that I told Dr. Petty exactly what I've told you. He believed. And someone else must have believed it, too."

"Who else?" Sikes asked.

Amy paused as if she didn't want to answer. "Whoever killed him, of course," she said at last. Then she pulled a short red jacket from a pile of books on the floor and lifted the purse that was hidden under it. "I've got to get out of here," she said. "You coming?"

Then she walked out of her office, and Sikes followed. He

wasn't willing to let Amy Stewart go yet. Professionally or personally.

Sikes felt ancient as he walked among the students on the UCLA campus. They all looked to be fifteen years old, full of superhuman energy. He felt out of place, as if he didn't belong there, even with the authority his badge gave him.

Amy seemed to know where she was going, so he walked beside her in silence. Her airless office *had* become oppressive. The bright October sunshine and lush green leaves of the trees that lined the concrete pathway they walked were a welcome break.

"How long have you been enrolled here?" Sikes asked, to hear her voice again.

"That doesn't sound like an official question."

"It isn't," Sikes admitted.

Amy slowed and looked at him. "Anyone ever tell you you look like Mick Jagger with short hair?" she asked unexpectedly.

Sikes made a face. He got that all the time. "That doesn't sound like a scientific observation."

"It isn't," she said, then she picked up her pace again.

Sikes wanted to ask Amy if she liked Mick Jagger but decided she had been making a point about the boundaries his questions must fall within. He wondered if she had felt the same rush of instant attraction he had felt when they had seen each other for the first time. Probably better not to know the answer to that one, he thought. But there were many other questions for which he *did* need to know the answers. He glanced at his watch again. It was becoming a nervous habit. But there were only a few hours before he had to report back, with or without making progress. He touched the sleeve of Amy's jacket to slow her stride.

"Leaving the spaceship stuff aside, what makes you think there's a connection between what you've observed and Dr. Petty's death?"

This time Amy stopped on the path. "I thought *you* were the one who said there was a connection. That's why you're here, isn't it?"

"Well, yeah," Sikes said, momentarily thrown off balance. This was the second time he had begun to suspect that she was hiding something. "My connection was that he had important 'material' and that he was killed the night he was going to meet with someone about it. So what I really wanted to know was, what was the content of the 'material,' which you've told me, and who did he meet with?"

"No idea," Amy said, jamming her hands into her pockets. She started walking again, and they passed a large bronze bear in a courtyard. Then they climbed a few steps and were on a broad walkway that ended at a large stone-sided building.

But Sikes didn't want to continue his interrogation indoors. He asked her if they could sit for a moment, outside, where they wouldn't have to worry about anyone overhearing them. Amy didn't seem to care one way or another. She just wanted fresh air. They sat on a concrete bench off the path, ignored by the nonstop parade of students.

"Why did you give the material to Dr. Petty in the first place?" Sikes asked.

"I didn't know what else to do with it."

"Why not call a press conference? Phone up "Sixty Minutes" or something?"

"I'm just a graduate student, detective. Who's going to listen to me? Dr. Petty's reputation was strong enough that he could have called the media and gotten away with it. But I couldn't."

Sikes realized there was something more hidden between the lines in that answer. "What do you mean by 'gotten away with it'? Get away with what?"

Amy hooked one arm over the back of the bench and half turned so she could face Sikes. She held a hand at her forehead to shade her eyes from the sun. "Ever hear of the SETI Protocol?" she asked.

Sikes shook his head.

"It's like a contingency plan," Stewart explained. "An informal international agreement that was originally drafted by the State Department of Advanced Technology and amended by astronomers around the world. Basically, it sets out the procedures to be followed if and when signals are ever detected that might indicate the existence of an extraterrestrial civilization."

"SETI," Sikes said. "The Search for Extraterrestrial Intelligence?"

"That's it," Amy agreed. "The Protocol's been ratified by almost every country capable of supporting a national astronomy program, except this one. And the steps it lays out are pretty straightforward. Essentially, the Protocol calls for immediate public disclosure and the creation of a civilian group of scientists who would then control all attempts to communicate with the signal source."

Sikes screwed up his face. "Scientists spend their time thinking about stuff like that?"

Amy moved again to angle her eyes out of the sun. "You'd be amazed what scientists think of in their spare time."

"So does your object qualify as a signal source?" Sikes asked, enjoying the warm sunshine and finding himself more and more drawn into this strange conversation with this very appealing woman and thinking less and less of his impending failure to crack his first murder case.

"It's as good as any."

"Then why the need for secrecy? Why not do what the Protocol says—contact lots of astronomers or the State Department or something?"

Amy made a sound that was almost like a snort. "Did you believe me when I told you what I had found? No, of course you didn't. So what makes you think the State Department's going to believe me? Half the astronomers in the world aren't going to believe me."

"I don't get it," Sikes said. "If you show the experts your plates and your polarized radio . . . stuff, they'll look at it, and it'll convince them. Right?"

"That would take weeks, detective. The object will be long gone by then."

"So?"

Amy shook her head. "Look, if I had detected intelligent signals coming from near another star, no problem. I'd post a couple of notes on Internet telling other astronomers where to look, and in a couple of weeks or months everything'd be fine. Or maybe if I'd found a crashed spaceship, I could just start taking people to it and let them look at it. In both cases my conclusions would be based on reproducible evidence. It wouldn't be going anywhere. People might scoff at me at first, but all they'd have to do is examine the evidence themselves."

Sikes saw what she was getting at. "But in this case the evidence is going to disappear."

"And forever after I'd be the wacko student who saw a UFO and wrecked her career. Dr. Petty would have kept that from happening."

Sikes knew what it was to face ridicule, and he could sympathize with her, yet there still seemed to be something she wasn't telling him.

"But that's not the whole thing, is it?" he said. "I mean, if you've been able to figure out so much about this thing in only a few days, somebody else must be able to do it, too. If it were me, I'd be jumping up and down and screaming and raising such a big stink that *somebody* would have to take a look in the same direction."

Amy looked at him, and this time it was with sadness. "You still don't get it, do you? That's what Dr. Petty was going to do. And look what happened to him."

Sikes lost it. She had been dragging him around the same bush for the past hour. "So what *did* happen to Petty?" he said in frustration. "*I* don't know. That's why I'm here listening to this crazy story you're dishing out. On the one hand you're acting like it's the biggest discovery in all history, and on the other you're telling me you can't breathe a word of it to anyone else."

"Because I *don't* want what happened to Dr. Petty to happen to me!" she retorted. "Didn't you hear what I said about the Protocol? It's been ratified by every country in the world *except* for the United States. The U.S. government has refused to let an international group of civilians take responsibility for communicating with other civilizations. The government wants the military to do it. *Our* military. Do you realize the implications of that? Just try." Amy's face flushed as if she were about to cry. "I went to Dr. Petty because I thought that *he* could stand up to them. He could get the word out, and more people would listen to him than me, and others would take plates, and . . . and who knows? Maybe even beam some lasers or some radio bursts at it and try to get it to change course. And if it *did* keep going, and it left the system, and there wasn't definitive proof of what it was, and the military wanted to come after someone for breaking the regulations that say we're only supposed to report these things to the government, *they wouldn't be able to do a thing to Dr. Petty.* Christ, detective, it would be like locking up Carl Sagan or Stephen Hawking." Amy took off her glasses and rubbed at her eyes. "Don't you see? Dr. Petty was supposed to be *untouchable,* and they *killed* him." She covered her eyes with one hand. "Because of what I found . . . because of what I found by *accident,* they killed him."

Sikes forgot all about professional detachment. He slid across to her and placed his arm around her shoulders. There was only one question left to ask. The only question that was important.

"Who killed him?" he said. "Who killed Petty?"

Amy drew back from him. "Who do you think?" she said bitterly. "It was the government. Our own goddamned government."

For Matt Sikes, everything he had been struggling to comprehend fell into place with the brutal force of a hurtling asteroid plunging from the sky with the power of a thousand-megaton bomb.

It was his first murder case, and he was suddenly afraid that it would also be his last.

CHAPTER 3

GEORGE FRANCISCO AWOKE to the cold pressure of a shock prod against his ribs, just at the edge of the sensitive nexus of nerves in his underarm. Instinctively he froze.

But the prod pressed deeper. "Up, cargo!" The rough voice could only be that of an Overseer. George instantly sat up. "On your feet!"

George coughed as he swung his legs over the side of his sleeping deck. The deck was nothing more than a narrow ledge in a stack of three, without privacy or comfort—one of hundreds of inset platforms that lined the dormitory's dimly lit, narrow, and claustrophobic corridors.

The Overseer cracked his prod across George's knees, but George barely noticed the pain of the sharp blow. The holy gas of obedience had been kept at its exceptionally high levels all through the sleep shift. Resistant or not, the buildup of waste products from having breathed so much of it was making George's head feel as if someone were gouging his spots out one by one and filling the holes with sodium chloride.

With great effort George managed to stand unsteadily, stealing a quick glance at the tormentor before him.

His hearts sank. The Overseer was T'ksam. Though scarcely out of his twenties and with but a single silver badge of rank on his black uniform, T'ksam was rapidly developing a reputation for mercilessness even amongst the older, more brutal Overseers. George kept his head down and prayed he would survive this encounter.

As George waited for whatever demand might follow, he dared a fast look down the dark and silent dormitory corridor. It was oddly empty of other Tenctonese. Generally there was a constant ebb and flow of workers on sleep shift, forlornly trying to engage in some form of social interaction during the few hours free from labor. But the low-lying mist was still unusually heavy—though the gas had oxidized enough to turn completely white—and from the sounds of retching that echoed from the long line of sleeping platforms George knew that others were having as much difficulty as he was in dealing with the effects of the gas.

"Is this your husband?" T'ksam's harsh voice said.

George couldn't help himself. He had to risk raising his eyes to the Overseer, fearing what he might see. And he saw T'ksam's hand gripping Susan's neck as he shoved her forward.

"Is this your husband?" the Overseer said again, giving Susan's head a violent shake.

George's hands trembled at his sides, but he forced himself not to react. He knew there was no action he could take that would not result in an instant sentence of death. Susan was obviously even more affected by the shift-long exposure to gas than he was, her eyes half closed, a thin line of drool sliding from her open lips. A female Overseer stood behind her, holding Susan up by her arms. The second Overseer was also a child to George's eyes, and she smirked at him as she saw him struggle to subdue his helpless fury.

T'ksam yanked Susan back against him and used his powerful fingers to roughly open her eyelids, not caring that the handle of his prod scraped at the fragile skin on her forehead. The profane words of the sine-script tattoo that darkened his wrist were all the more obscene so close to Susan's beauty.

Susan cried out in pain, and her hands jerked up to try and push the Overseer's hand from her face.

"Don't," George said. One minute word of protest escaped from the immeasurable sea of rage that churned within him.

The Overseer smiled like a podling with a pouch of *tadlin-ta*. "What did you say, cargo?"

He knew what he risked, but George could not remain silent. "Look at her. She is barely conscious."

"And what concern of yours is that?" T'ksam said.

George did not back down. "She is my mate."

"Good," the Overseer said. "Then perhaps this will make her wake up."

Even as the prod's dreaded tip descended for him George heard it clicking into focus. The shock made him grunt in pain and threw him back violently against his sleeping platform, smashing his head against the sharp edge of the platform directly above his own.

George's entire body shook with the aftereffects of the prod. His vision blurred. Both Overseers pushed Susan's limp body closer to him again. "Who is he?" T'ksam demanded of Susan.

Susan blinked rapidly. The Overseer's hand was tight against her throat. She looked at George, and he could see in her tear-filled eyes that she did not know if the answer T'ksam demanded would lead to George's betrayal.

"It's all right, Appy," George said softly. They had already discussed what they would do if the Overseers came for them. They had made each other promise to feel no shame in giving in to whatever cruel demand was made, provided that at least one of them could survive to protect little Devoosha, safe for now in the care of her day crèche.

"Who?" T'ksam said, shaking Susan like a *coska* trapped in the jaws of a predator.

"Stangya," Susan whispered. "He's my mate, Stangya."

The Overseer threw Susan forward so she fell over George, and her face slammed into the metal wall behind him. George swept his arms around her and swore to her that nothing would make him release her again.

"Staaangyaaa," T'ksam said, insultingly drawing out each syllable. "Family: Cowards of Soren'tzahh. Family: Third Moon's Cesspool." He twisted the focus knob on his prod to click it to a dangerously higher setting. Behind him the female Overseer drew her own prod from her tunic. "You didn't spend a full shift in the light bay last cycle, Stangya," the Overseer said. "Where did you go?"

George prayed to Andarko that his anger would mask the sudden fear in his hearts. Somehow the Overseers must have already guessed that it had been he and Susan who were in the water hub calling out for Buck. But how? Could it have been Buck who betrayed them? The young Watcher turning in his own parents? Andarko knew that had happened before on the ship. The Overseers stole children as easily as they stole lives and hope.

"What is your problem, cargo?"

"The gas," George blurted out desperately. "The holy gas of obedience," he said. "It was so strong. I can't . . . I can't remember."

T'ksam's reaction was instant. In a vile act of sexual aggression the Overseer jammed his prod against the small of Susan's back and fired it. Susan screamed and twisted in pain, and George swung out vainly to grab the prod. But T'ksam avoided him easily.

"Try again," the Overseer said menacingly. "The blessing of the holy gas took a long time to filter into the light bay, and we have a hundred eager witnesses who saw the two of you leave before the shift was over."

"We came here," George said plaintively. "At least, we wanted to come here. To look . . . to look for a privacy chamber."

T'ksam's eyes took on a fixed and icy stare. "Wanted to do a little spot licking, did you?" He used the tip of his prod to force up the back of Susan's tunic to expose her smallest and most delicate spots.

Tears fell from George's eyes. "Please, don't . . ."

"Just who do you think you are, cargo? Please this. Don't that. I see no tattoo on your wrist."

George tried to pull down Susan's tunic, but T'ksam knocked his hand away with the prod, then reached out with his hand and wrenched at the tunic's cloth so that it ripped apart and exposed the length of Susan's back. He held his prod tip inches from Susan's spine, just above the waistband of her trousers.

"Not so fast, Stangyaaa. Maybe I want to do a little spot licking of my own." He pushed Susan's body closer to George.

"I answered your questions!" George pleaded.

T'ksam turned to his female partner. "I don't think this cargo's been breathing his holy gas," he said. The female glanced at George, then slowly drew another object from her tunic. It was a short metal cylinder that ended in three long needles. George had seen devices like it in the infirmaries.

"Stand up," T'ksam commanded George.

Carefully George began to slip out from behind Susan. With his movement Susan winced in pain, her body still convulsing from the shock to her back.

"I said *stand stand stand!*" The Overseer grabbed at George's arm and pulled him forcefully from the sleeping platform, throwing Susan to the deck, where she curled into a defensive position, weakly holding the ruins of her tunic to her chest.

"Why do you do this?" George asked. "We've done nothing."

T'ksam twisted George's arm to push back his gray tunic sleeve. Then, before George could know what was to happen, the female stabbed his forearm with the cylinder's three needles.

"Andarko!" George gasped as he tried to pull back. But the Overseer held him firmly as the needles drove home.

Then, just as savagely, the female ripped the needles out from George's flesh, leaving three bloody gashes. She began to adjust the control dials on the cylinder's side. T'ksam released George's arm and reached for his prod.

George clutched his forearm to his chest, gasping for breath with each throb of fiery pain.

T'ksam waved his prod back and forth in front of George's eyes, slowly. "So, Stangya, how much *eemikken* did you take last cycle?" he asked.

"I've never had *eemikken\,*" George said through clenched teeth. "It is forbidden to cargo."

"Yet in this past cycle, when the blessing of the holy gas was at its peak, you were seen in the water hub in the 'ponics section." The Overseer held the prod directly over George's forehead. "Explain that, cargo!"

"We were not in a water hub last cycle," George said jerkily. "I told you: We came here looking for a privacy chamber. But by the time we got here, all we could do was sleep." George knew that all he could do now was to rely on the portion of his story that was true to convey his conviction to the Overseer. Susan and he *had* left the light bay in search of a privacy chamber. By the time they had reached the dormitory the gas had robbed them of all ability to do anything other than sleep. The fact that they had been in the water hub earlier, pursued by Overseers, then rescued by Ruhtra, was not something that George dared think about right now. And because these two were still interrogating them, George knew that the other

Overseers were not yet certain who had been in the water hub after all. Perhaps there was still a chance for survival.

The needle device made a musical tone. The female Overseer stared down at it, frowning. "Nothing," she said. "Not a trace of *eemikken*. Only normal gas by-products."

T'ksam took the device from her hand and used his thumb to readjust its controls. Again the musical tone came forth. He looked coldly at George, then handed the device back to the female. "Do his mate," he said.

George began to turn toward Susan in an instinctive attempt to protect her. But T'ksam brutally rammed his prod into George's gut and fired, sending him moaning to the deck. He lay there within the thick mist, shaking with futile rage as he heard Susan scream when the needles gouged her flesh.

With a curse George drew his arms beneath his chest, and he tried to push himself up, to rise again in Susan's defense. But the boot of the Overseer crashed down on his neck, pinning him helplessly on the cold metal floor. The cold, rough-ribbed texture of the deck plates dug into his face.

Trapped, George tried to pray, but all he could think of, all he could imagine were the names his people had given the ship—that which had no name, that which had thousands.

Susan shrieked as the needles were ripped from her skin and George was bound in *lesh,* feeling his flesh bubble in waves of salt water.

Susan sobbed as T'ksam adjusted the device's controls, and George tried to move one final time, beyond conscious thought in his rage and his grief. But T'ksam's heel bit deeper into his neck, grinding bones and stretching ligaments beyond their imagined limits. George's hands splayed out against the unyielding metal deck. He began the long fall into the endless black pit of *am dugas,* swept away by the curse of the *wask'l reckwi*—to be dead yet forever conscious of his fate, beyond even the rescue of Celine and Andarko.

Then, in the far distance, from without his inner darkness, George heard a musical chime, the same as before, and after a moment the pressure of T'ksam's boot was miraculously gone. Next George heard the Overseers footsteps clank away.

His tear-filled eyes opened slowly. Recklessly he lifted his head, half expecting to feel the prod hit him again for having fallen for the trick. But there was nothing—no final punish-

ment, no Overseers, no sound other than the faint crying of his
mate and the constant far-off thrumming of the ship's power
plants.

George sat up. The back of his head was sticky with blood.
His forearm pulsated with angry pain. His stomach cramped
with the aftershocks of the prod's assault, making it difficult to
draw a full breath. But nothing stopped him from dragging
himself across the corridor floor to be beside his wife.

Susan's arm was awash in blood. Her head slumped onto her
chest. She could no longer even hold the shreds of her tunic to
her, and her pale flesh was exposed.

It was all George could do to place his hand over Susan's.
Beyond that he could only sit beside her. Hearing her breathe.
Hearing his own ragged breaths.

The soft white river of gas eddied around them.

Neither moved.

And after a few minutes, when the Overseers did not return,
other Tenctonese finally dropped to the floor from their
sleeping platforms and began to shuffle along the dormitory
corridor.

They were *sonah*, without sense of self or direction, and none
stopped for George and Susan. The bloodied, semiconscious
couple leaning half against each other, half against the wall,
quaking with fear and pain and exhaustion, were nothing new
to the dormitory or the ship.

The Overseers had come. The Overseers had left. If there was
a purpose to the Overseers' actions, no one knew or wanted to
know. For to look too deeply into the meaning of anything that
happened on board the ship was to risk discovering that there
was no reason for any of it.

In a daze George watched the legs and feet of the others from
his dormitory as they flowed past him and Susan in both
directions. He was barely conscious of the others' presence and
never once thought that any one of them should stop and offer
help.

He was alive. Susan was alive. The ship moved on. What
more was there? What more could he expect?

But a new realization was also entering George's mind, the
idea that somehow a final step had been taken, a final barrier
had been breached.

This will end, George thought suddenly, startled by the new

lucidity of his mind. One way or another, through revolt or oblivion, this will end.

For the first time in thousands of cycles George felt the sweet touch of peace as he realized that his future was no longer uncertain.

He had lived with fear too long. He had seen his mate brutalized too often. He had lost at least one child to evil and would not risk having the same fate snare a second.

His breath caught in his throat. In an organized revolt if he could, on his own if he must, George realized that he would no longer submit to the Overseers.

He was going to fight back, and he knew he could win because he had nothing left to lose.

One way or another, the end of this life was near.

It was an overwhelming thought, and despite his pain George lifted his head and laughed tremulously.

After more than sixty years on board the ship, he finally had something to look forward to.

CHAPTER 4

THIS TIME BUCK AWOKE suddenly, with no dreamlike transition. He was immediately aware of a gentle hand on his shoulder.

"Moodri?" he asked, his voice still thick with sleep.

Urgently a female's voice whispered, "There is no Moodri here. Don't speak of him again." The gentle hand squeezed his shoulder sharply for added emphasis.

Buck tried lifting his head to see to whom he spoke. There was little pain left in him. Vaguely he remembered Moodri pushing at odd areas along his neck and across his shoulders. The residual pain from the Overseer's shock prod had vanished with that touch, back when . . . when . . . Buck couldn't remember when Moodri had come to him. Nor did he know where he was or what had happened after D'wayn had shocked him.

"Who are you?" he asked of the tall female who leaned over him. Her spots were small and myriad, an elegant pattern considered by some to be a sign of great beauty. For a moment Buck forgot that he had even spoken and simply stared dumbly up at her.

The female, plainly garbed in the ship's standard gray uniform, didn't appear to notice her effect on Buck. Her manner was abrupt, businesslike, unsmiling. In less than a month she would be given a new name to go with her new home, but for now Cathy Frankel gave Buck the name she had been born with. "I am Gelana. A cargo specialist."

That explained it. Cargo specialists were charged with maintaining the proper functioning of the cargo. Buck realized he must be in one of the ship's infirmaries.

"Where's Moodri? When—"

Instantly Cathy placed her hand over Buck's mouth and glared at him. She turned to speak to someone out of Buck's line of sight. "He's still confused," she said. "Still incoherent."

The black form of an Overseer pushed her aside. It was Coolock.

"He looks fine to me," Coolock said. He peered intently at Buck, his small eyes dark and unreadable in the shadows from the bright overhead lights. *"Are* you fine, Watcher Finiksa?"

Buck had been trained well in the Watcher Youth Brigade. At once he moved to jump off the infirmary sleeping platform and stand in readiness. But as he struggled to sit up, he felt the infirmary wheel around him, and he began to fall forward off the platform.

Cathy caught him. She held him steady on the platform. "What setting did you use?" she asked. Her voice sounded angry.

"The appropriate setting," Coolock said. "We always use the appropriate setting. Now let go of him."

Cathy released her grip on Buck. Confused, Buck saw another message in her eyes but didn't know what it meant.

"You may remain sitting for now, Watcher."

Buck swallowed to relieve the dryness of his throat. "Thank you, Overseer."

"Though when I am finished my questions I might require you to walk over there." He pointed with his prod to the other side of the cluttered, blindingly lit infirmary.

Buck looked in the direction the Overseer indicated, past a central work area filled with physical treatment harnesses and haphazardly stacked healing devices. His body stiffened in fright. Coolock was pointing to a medical recycler—a large, transparent tub of bubbling salt water in which medical waste and corpses were disposed. He turned back to the Overseer in horror.

"Who called to you in the water hub?" The corner of Coolock's mouth twitched as he waited for an answer.

Buck turned to Cathy, but the cargo specialist looked away.

"You have been asked a question, Watcher. Report."

"I . . . I don't know who it was," Buck stammered.

"They called you by *name!*"

Buck fought his fear to keep his head up. "I don't know."

"He's just a child," Cathy said. "The prods disrupt memories. There's a chance he'll never remember what happened just prior to the shock."

Coolock turned his head sideways, not enough to see Cathy, just enough to indicate that he barely recognized her presence. He closed his eyes. "Have I asked for your opinion?"

"No," Cathy said.

Coolock looked at Buck again. "Let's try an earlier memory. Why did you try to stop Vornho from cutting the water worker?"

"D-did I?" Buck asked. He tried to remember but could draw on nothing.

Coolock stepped forward until he loomed over the boy. His voice was as icy as a portal exposed to space. "You know there is no room for defective cargo on this ship, don't you? Are *you* defective, Watcher?"

Buck's neck ached as he looked straight up at his tormentor. He almost seemed to see a flash of light from somewhere, like a reflection thrown from a spinning crystal. There was something familiar about it. Something that tugged at his memory. "The water worker," he began uncertainly.

"This shift is almost over," Coolock said. "Neither of us has much time."

Buck tried to make sense of the sudden visual images that came to him. Something about—"The membrane suit!" he said excitedly.

"What about it?"

"It was tight," Buck said.

"They are designed that way."

"But on his side, about here"—Buck reached around and grabbed his own back just under his ribs—"there was something under the suit."

For an instant Coolock's cruel gaze lessened. "What was under his suit?"

Buck closed his eyes and saw everything with perfect clarity, almost as if a picture had been drawn on his mind. "I wasn't sure, Overseer. But it was long and blocky, as if three cylinders had been melted together." Then it all came back to him. His words fell over one another in his eagerness. "And I couldn't be sure exactly what it was, but the others didn't have it, and I didn't think Vornho could see it, and then I remembered the clearing charges that we saw in the power plant stations, the ones they use to clean the concentrates out of the fuel-cell pipes."

Coolock studied Buck. "You *saw* the clearing charges strapped to his back under his suit?"

"I wasn't certain, Overseer. But I was worried that if they *were* clearing charges and if the cutting beam hit them, then they might explode, and . . . so I tried to stop Vornho so the worker could be searched first."

Coolock stared at Buck without blinking. He slowly ran his tongue over his teeth. "Did you see the worker explode when the beam hit him?"

Buck's eyes fluttered as he sought another image from the past but found nothing. "I'm sorry, Overseer. I . . . I don't remember an explosion. I remember Watch Leader D'wayn calling my name—no! That was one of the scavengers on the next level! It was one of the scavengers who called me. And then . . . then . . ." He remembered the final detail. "The water worker ran past me and jumped over the railing, and . . ." He faltered. His words slowed. "And Watch Leader D'wayn shocked me before I had a chance to explain what I had seen."

Coolock rubbed at the bridge of his nose. "One of the scavengers called you? You're certain of that?"

Buck cleared his throat. "Whoever called me was standing where I had seen scavengers stand before."

Coolock nodded. He clapped his powerful hand on Buck's shoulder, making the boy wince. "A careful report! Facts only. No false conclusions. Well done, Watcher!" Then he moved his hand to Buck's chest, crushed a handful of Buck's tunic in his grip, and lifted Buck from the sleeping platform until the boy's feet dangled off the infirmary deck and Buck's ashen face was only inches from Coolock's.

"But how did the scavengers know your name? Report!" he said. Buck could smell fresh blood on Coolock's breath. The Overseers ate real food, not meatgrowth.

Buck's voice was only a terrified whisper. "I don't know. I don't."

Coolock's face was transformed by a huge grin, revealing

large teeth stained pink by blood. "Of course you don't, Watcher. Of course you don't." With surprising gentleness he lowered Buck back to the sleeping platform. Then he gave Buck the highest praise any Watcher could receive. "Good work, Watcher."

Buck tensed, waiting for another reversal in the Overseer's mood. But this time it didn't come.

"D'wayn acted too hastily in shocking you. I shall see that she is disciplined and—"

"Please, no," Buck said even before he knew he was going to speak.

Coolock remained amused. "You'd rather she was fed into that?" He nodded over at the frothing bubbles of the medical recycler.

"No," Buck said, shocked by the idea. "She . . . Watch Leader D'wayn I mean—she acted for the good of the ship." Buck could hide his shame no longer. He hung his head. "I did not give her a full report about my observations. Her actions were my fault."

Coolock laughed again. Buck saw him turn to speak to Cathy. "You see why we will *always* prevail?" He reached out to brush his knuckles against Buck's temple. "Relax, boy. You are at one with your true family."

Buck almost sobbed with relief as he realized that Coolock had accepted his answers. He would live.

"What additional care does he need?" the Overseer asked.

"Three shifts of rest," Cathy answered, making no attempt to hide the hostility she obviously felt. "Real food would help as well to make up for the disruption in his electrolyte balance, and—"

She stopped as Coolock raised his hand. "Requisition what you need on my authority." He smiled down at Buck. "The future of our race is here on this platform. Be sure you take good care of him."

Cathy remained silent, which seemed to amuse Coolock even more.

"Enjoy your rest, Watcher," the Overseer said in parting. "When you return to your crèche, you will find a new badge for your scarf."

Buck looked at him incredulously.

"You are moving up the ranks," Coolock said. "Such quick

thinking deserves recognition and reward. Though next time, *do* make your report more quickly."

"Thank you, Overseer," Buck said, and he meant it. He was moving up hundreds of shifts ahead of schedule—an unheard-of accomplishment for one so young.

Coolock moved closer to Cathy. "What joy it brings to my hearts to bring such delight to the face of a child. See? What have I told you about us? We can bring pleasure as well as discipline. To those who work for us."

Buck was puzzled as he saw Coolock's hand disappear behind Cathy, as if he meant to caress her as his mate. But whatever Coolock's intent, it was not, Buck saw, to give a caress of love on the part of a female's back that males were not supposed to touch in play. Instead of giggling or sighing, the way Buck remembered his mother reacting when he had sometimes seen his father caress her when they thought Buck wasn't watching, Cathy jerked as if she had been shocked herself. Then she turned her head away from Coolock with an undisguised look of hatred. Buck didn't understand how an Overseer could tolerate such an expression without exacting punishment, but Coolock only laughed—a different laugh this time. Harsh, as if he didn't mean it. Yet his hand remained behind Cathy, and she didn't move away. Or couldn't.

Coolock pulled Cathy close to him and brought his lips to her ear valleys. "Think of what you need for your infirmary," he hissed, loudly enough for Buck to hear. "And then think of the pleasure I can give you."

Buck was confused. Cathy responded to Coolock's offer by turning away and continuing to refuse to look at him.

"Keep playing your game," Coolock finally said. "But I know what your answer must be eventually." He laughed again, then saw Buck staring. "You don't understand what we're talking about, do you, young Watcher?"

"No," Buck answered truthfully.

"Don't worry," Coolock said. "You will soon enough." He fingered the silver badges of rank he wore. "You see, these have a special power that you've never imagined. And someday you might have one for your own." He leered at Cathy. "And then he'll have *many*, won't he?" The Overseer laughed uproariously. "Better not let this one get too close to your *lingpod* flap, boy. She's got a hungry look to her!"

Then Coolock strode to the infirmary's pneumatic door, which flew aside with a puff of air. And the moment the door had closed behind him, Cathy rushed over to a work station where there was a chamber of water and began to wash her face and, Buck was fascinated to see, her back beneath her tunic.

Buck sensed it was impolite to watch a female wash herself in such a way but found it difficult to look elsewhere. She was very attractive, and he felt a vague stirring desire to see exactly what the pattern of her spots was at the lowest point of her back. Though why Coolock had warned him about letting Cathy get close to his *lingpod* flap—the pouchlike opening into his midsection beneath which he might someday bring a pod to term—Buck didn't understand. He was just a child. His flap hadn't even opened for the first time. Though thinking about what Coolock had said, and seeing Cathy's hand move over her back, and remembering Vornho's determination to find a *sleema* girl with which to couple, Buck felt a small shiver rush deep behind his flap, something he had never felt before.

Dreamily he ran a finger across the almost invisible *lingpod* ridge beneath the skin of his upper abdomen. Cathy was so engrossed in washing that she acted as if Buck weren't present, and Buck forgot any pretense of polite behavior. He just kept watching, catching a brief glance of Cathy's spine where her spots were so small that—

"Where are your manners?"

Buck was so startled that he lurched from the sleeping platform and almost fell to the floor as he turned to see who had surprised him.

It was an Elder, dressed in the flowing white robes of the goddess Ionia, just as Moodri wore. But this Elder was a *binnaum,* heavy of spots, who limped as he walked, cradling a withered right arm to his body.

Buck stared. He had never seen anyone with a disability before. The Overseers would not permit such to live.

"I understood you were raised within the teachings of Andarko and Celine," the old *binnaum* said gruffly.

"Yes, I was," Buck said guiltily. Then he looked over at the infirmary door. He hadn't heard it puff open, yet when Coolock had been present Buck was certain that no one else had been in the large room. Where had he come from?

"Don't worry where I have come from, young one," the

Elder said. "Worry about where you are going. Do not Andarko and Celine teach you to have respect for all living things?"

"Yes," Buck said in a low voice, wondering how the Elder had been able to know what he was thinking.

"And don't worry how I am able to know what you are thinking," the Elder said. "Instead, worry how you will be able to show respect to *all* living things if you are unable to show respect to another person."

"Yes," Buck said again, and he bent his head. It was somehow easier to display his feelings of shame to an Elder because the Elders had never punished him for admitting a wrongdoing.

The *binnaum* shuffled closer to Buck. "And if you're going to start fingering your flap like a *soshal* in heat, then do it in private." He made a dismissive harumphing sound in his throat, and Buck felt his eyes sting with tears of embarrassment.

"What are you two going on about?" Cathy walked quickly over from the work station to join them. Her face was flushed with the results of her rough scrubbing.

Buck held his breath as he waited for the Elder to reveal what he had been doing behind the cargo specialist's back. But the old *binnaum* simply said "We were discussing the goddess" and left it at that. "I'm Melgil, by the way, a friend of your great-uncle's." Buck leaned back against the edge of the sleeping platform in relief.

"I told you not to come here until it was time," Cathy said to Melgil. "Coolock was just here."

"Coolock has just left," the Elder said. "He will not be returning."

"But others might. After the gas levels we had last cycle, the accident rate is going to be triple what it normally is. By the time this shift is over all the infirmaries will be overflowing with the injured and their guards."

"Then a lone Elder giving the blessings of Ionia will hardly be noticed," Melgil said.

Cathy folded her arms across her chest, and Buck couldn't think why she would be so agitated. "Until the time comes for me to operate on you! Then what happens? One shift the Overseers see you wandering around my treatment hall. The next shift you're in a healing harness. Don't you think they might get suspicious?"

The Elder eased himself down to sit on the sleeping platform beside Buck. "Suspicious of what?" he asked.

"That I've been treating you!" Cathy kept glancing over at the closed pneumatic door as if she expected it to open at any moment. "You know they're letting you live on borrowed time as it is. As long as you give your peaceful sermons and don't consume too much foodgrowth, they'll let you alone. But if they suspect that you're taking up *any* of my treatment resources . . ." She didn't finish. She didn't have to. Even Buck knew what she meant.

"But I am not taking up any of your resources," Melgil said. "And after the operation, what happens to me won't be of concern."

Buck looked from one adult to the other, trying to fill in between the lines. He knew that operations were medical procedures performed on workers to repair them and enable them to continue working. But he didn't know why any Overseer would permit an operation to be performed on an Elder. It would be a clear waste of medical resources.

"What happens to this *infirmary* after the operation is *my* concern," Cathy said. There was anger hidden beneath all her words, Buck realized. He decided that was why Coolock had let her act that way toward him. She must act that way toward everyone.

"You know they're not allowing us to train any more cargo specialists," Cathy went on. "Another ten years and there'll be fewer than one hundred of us left to maintain the health of everyone else."

But Melgil waved his one good hand dismissively. "This voyage will not last ten more years," he said.

Buck was stunned by Melgil's words, at the thought that the voyage of the ship could ever have an end. But he saw that Cathy wasn't. Instead she glared at the Elder.

"What's that supposed to mean? Has someone *else* had a vision?"

Melgil did not react to the derision in her voice. "Gelana, you have a kinder *serdos* than you know, and thus your anger and your contempt have no strength against me."

"I don't know what you're talking about," Cathy said.

"Of course you do," Melgil said. "Against the Overseers you have erected formidable inner walls. As strong as hull metal they are. But in your desire to save the children and the sick and the injured you have come to forget who is your enemy and who is your friend, and so you exclude *everyone* from your life."

"I have my work, and I do it," Cathy said stonily.

"There is more to life than work."

"Not on the ship there isn't."

Melgil reached out and placed his good hand on Buck's arm. His hand felt cool. "Neither of you will be on the ship forever," he said. "And when you are free, you must be able to open your hearts to a new way of life." He stared intently at Cathy. "A new way of feeling."

Cathy took a half step away. "It is cruel to talk of freedom in front of a child," she said.

Melgil gazed up at her questioningly. "Is it cruel to give children hope? To give children dreams? Do you believe you have denied them to yourself for so long that you have lost the capacity to feel their power? That is not true, Gelana. You must look more deeply within yourself."

"I have no time for this, old one. Leave now, while you're still able."

Melgil patted Buck's arm. "I must talk with Finiksa first."

"And if the Overseers come?"

"I will leave long before they return."

Cathy shook her head. "You honestly think there's going to be a revolt, don't you?"

Buck's ear valleys almost twitched at the word "revolt." Was *that* what all this tension was about?

"Do you have faith in the goddess?" Melgil asked.

"No," Cathy said.

"Do you have faith in Andarko and Celine?"

"No."

"Do you have faith in your people?"

Cathy faltered.

"Do you have faith in the children of your people?"

Cathy looked sharply at Buck. "I have faith in nothing, old one. I do my work."

Melgil nodded his head. "The words you speak are not the words you feel. Someday you will admit that to yourself as easily as you admit it to me now."

"If you don't leave me now, I will refuse to perform the operation!" None of Cathy's anger was hidden now. It was all out in the open.

"You would let the Overseers win?" Melgil asked. "After all that they have done to you? All that they have taken from you?"

Cathy put her hands to her face. "Stop it!"

Melgil stood and went to her. "That is exactly what I intend to do," he said, touching his knuckles to her temple and not reacting as she jerked her head away. "But I cannot do it alone." He looked back at Buck. "We must all work together. And then it *will* stop, Gelana. I promise."

Fascinated by the interaction, Buck watched as Cathy choked back tears behind her covering hands. He wondered what it was the Overseers might have done to her. No one on board the ship had anything, so what was there to take?

"Just leave," Cathy finally said. "As soon as you are able, leave." She went over to a work station and began to arrange bundles of rolled-up bandages that sparkled with antiseptic crystals. The stacks she made looked no different from the stacks she disassembled.

For a few moments Melgil watched her, then he sat back beside Buck on the platform. Buck wanted to ask him about Cathy and why she was crying. But Melgil held up his hand before Buck could speak.

"Later you will understand," the Elder said. "For now you must respect her privacy." Then Melgil placed his hand across Buck's chest. "Moodri tells me you are brave, that the hearts of the Heroes of Soren'tzahh beat strongly within you."

Buck felt embarrassed. The Elder's hand now felt unusually hot through his tunic. "Sometimes Moodri says things I don't understand," he said.

"Perhaps you just don't listen closely enough." Though Buck might have thought Melgil's words were a criticism, the Elder spoke in such a friendly fashion that it almost seemed as if he were telling a joke.

"I try," Buck said.

"We know," Melgil answered. He moved his hand a few inches higher as if searching for Buck's pulses. "Moodri also says that you have never betrayed the secret of his visits."

"Never," Buck said emphatically. He knew the Overseers had proclaimed that family members must not keep in contact with one another once the children were old enough to be raised independently. It had been explained to Buck in such a way that it made perfect sense. Everything must be done for the good of the ship. If the traditional tribal family structure of

Tencton was allowed to exist on board, unproductive strife might arise, wasting resources and endangering everyone. To be fair, Moodri had said that the tribes of Tencton had not experienced significant strife for thousands of generations—an interesting idea if it was true, Buck thought—but since his relationship with his great-uncle didn't make him any less willing to do things for the good of the ship, Buck felt the visits did no harm. Buck was certain that if he had an opportunity to explain his situation in detail to the Overseers, then they would understand and allow him to continue to meet with Moodri. But since Moodri was so concerned that Buck not do anything to endanger his status in the Watcher Youth, Buck had done as he was told and had so far kept their meetings secret.

"Good," Melgil said. "Because now I am going to ask you to keep another secret." He pressed his hand more tightly against Buck's chest so that Buck had to brace himself to keep from being pushed away.

"What kind of secret?" Buck asked warily.

"An important one," Melgil said, staring so deeply into Buck's eyes that Buck couldn't look away. "We will ask you to perform a task for us."

"You mean work?" Buck understood work. Everyone must work when they were old enough.

"In a sense," Melgil said. "Though it will be a simple task. Something you will have to do but once."

Melgil's breathing matched Buck's. Buck felt an odd connection with the Elder.

"What do you want me to do?" the boy asked.

"You must want to do it, too," Melgil said, "so we can be sure you will not hesitate."

Buck said nothing. He kept breathing, becoming more and more aware of each breath and each alternating beat of his hearts.

"In eight cycles the ship will prepare for translation."

"Translation," Buck repeated.

"You will be on the bridge—"

"No," Buck said, momentarily breaking the rhythm Melgil had been building.

"—as part of your Watcher Youth Brigade," Melgil continued. "Just a tour, Finiksa, like your visits to the power plants and the food-processing chamber. Watcher Brigades are always invited to the bridge for translations. It is nothing out of the ordinary. Nothing unusual. And now it will be your turn to go, and you will act as you always act and obey the Watch Leader and do all that you are told." Melgil paused, his eyes unblinking. "And then you will perform a task for us. For Great-uncle Moodri. For the goddess and for all your people."

"For Andarko and Celine?" Buck asked. His voice seemed to come from far away.

"For your father and mother as well," Melgil said.

Buck felt a wave of comfort settle over him. The warmth of the Elder's hand on his hearts. The dimly remembered infant security of sensing shared breathing. The knowledge that he would do work for the good of all his people because he knew that anything that benefited his people would be good for the ship.

"What shall I do?" Buck asked.

Melgil told him about the key.

And Buck was shocked back into separate awareness. For what the Elder asked him to do was definitely *not* for the good of the ship, and by the time Melgil had finished Buck knew he had no choice but to go to the Overseers and tell them about Moodri. The revolt. And everything.

CHAPTER 5

SIKES DIDN'T KNOW where to look. Beside him Theo Miles was tricked up like a Las Vegas pimp—gold chains, purple shirt opened three buttons too far, and black leather pants four sizes too small. To the other side a half-crazed audience lathered into a frenzy by equal parts alcohol and lust hooted in unison for the performers on the strip club's stage. The stage with its gleaming chrome poles was right in front of Sikes, but there was no way in hell he was going to look up there either.

Instead he stared at the beer in his glass, watching the concentric circles of the ripples made by the rhythmic pounding of the audience's feet. A shout suddenly went up from a hundred throats. Even Theo yelled. Sikes glanced up in time to see a pair of skimpy red underpants fly through the air toward a forest of waving arms and straining hands and immediately wished he hadn't when he saw what their absence had uncovered.

Theo pounded him on the shoulder and shouted over the blaring, thumping music. "Loosen up, Matt! It's a stakeout! Have some fun with it!"

Sikes shook his head and kept his eyes on his beer, praying for the music to stop so that he could have a chance to talk with Theo. Then something black and covered with sequins hit the table, and Sikes cringed, hoping that it wasn't what he thought it was.

But it was.

Theo, however, was definitely living the role his undercover persona demanded of him. He picked up the G-string, twirled it over his head, yelled, "Hey, ladies!" and tossed it into the middle of the audience.

The women in the audience almost started a fistfight over the apparel, but on the stage the men kept dancing. The fellow who had tossed his G-string at Theo and Sikes was now wearing only a hard hat and a carpenter's belt. Sikes cringed as he thought about where that hammer was bouncing.

Then the music finally faded, and the dancers scooped up their piles of clothes and props and ran offstage as the audience members whistled and thumped their tables. The lights came up on a sea of women's faces punctuated here and there by a few male companions, all of whom looked to be thinking the same troubled thoughts Sikes was thinking.

"It's safe to look now, Matt."

Sikes took a deep breath. "How in hell did *you* get this assignment anyway?"

"Because," Theo said gravely as he placed his hand on Sikes's, "I asked for it." He laughed, deep and booming, as Sikes yanked his hand away.

Theo finished off a shot of whiskey, then leaned close to Sikes. "Seriously, though, pal, we got reason to believe this place's got a coke ring workin' out of it. I'm doin' the preliminary scopin', and next week two female cops'll take over for the buy." He moved his eyebrows up and down. "It's called spreadin' out the resources. Who's gonna pay attention to a dumpy fifty-year-old guy in a place like this?"

"Fifty?" Sikes said. "Since when did you lose ten years?"

"Don't get smart, kid." Theo made a show of adjusting the chains around his neck. "I still got what it takes."

Sikes didn't get it. "They think you're here to pick up the dancers?"

"Hell, no," Theo said. "The women in the audience. After a couple of shows and a few gallons of beer you'd be surprised how many of them think I'm just what they need. But until closing nobody gives me a second look."

Sikes stared down at his beer again. "Sheesh," he muttered.

"Oh, right," Theo said, "as if it never goes on in any of the clubs where the women are on stage and the men are in the audience."

"That's different," Sikes said, though he doubted he could defend his position on anything other than an emotional point of view. Raising Kirby was having a much more profound effect on his life than he would ever have thought possible.

Theo called over a server—a bodybuilder in black tights and formal collar and bow tie. "Get with the program, Matt. It's the nineties. Equal opportunity for everyone. Black folks. White folks. Male and female. Even dumb micks like you. It's like I keep tellin' you, kid: You gotta keep an open mind."

Theo ordered another round and watched as the server walked away, squeezing his way through the closely packed tables and the reaching hands of his excited clientele.

"I'm starting to think you're getting into this," Sikes said.

Theo frowned at him. "And what the hell would it matter if I was? But just 'cause you're so worried, keep a close watch on the redhead in the leather jacket—fourth table over from the bar. See her?"

Sikes scanned the crowd. Theo elbowed him under the table. "It's a stakeout, fool. Don't be so obvious about it."

"Yeah, I see her," Sikes said as he found her, then glanced away.

"Then watch what happens when the server goes past her."

Sikes watched from the corner of his eye. The server stopped by the redhead. Put a drink on her table. She put what looked to be too much money on his tray, and then he fished something small and silvery out of his tights and dropped it beside her drink.

"That's enough," Theo said. "Look at the stage now."

Sikes did what he was told.

"I've made three of the servers already," Theo explained. "No regular customers so far, so it should be easy for my compatriots to arrange a good buy and a solid case." He leaned back in his chair and rested his head against the wall and his hands across his stomach. "So what's up, kid? Tired of Homicide already? Want to get into the real action in Vice?"

Sikes hadn't rehearsed anything. He just said the first thing that came into his mind. "I'm scared, Theo."

Theo nodded sagely. "I figured it was somethin' like that for you to track me down here. How bad is it?"

Sikes shrugged. "I don't know. It might even be nothing."

"It's not your partner, is it? Angie's not up to anything IAD should know about?"

Sikes shook his head.

"But it's not anything you can go to her about?"

"What worries me is where *she'd* have to go with it."

Theo sighed. "Better give it to me from the beginning, kid. You got ten minutes before the next set starts."

Sikes left out the technical details, so it only took him five minutes to explain the dilemma he faced. And Theo Miles, Sikes's mentor and first partner, didn't make a single crack about how ludicrous the premise was.

By the time Sikes had finished, the second round of drinks had arrived. Theo waited for the server to leave before he asked his first question. "So what I gotta know is, do you believe her? About the spaceship?"

"No," Sikes said. He had thought over what Amy Stewart had told him, long and hard. He *couldn't* believe her. "But *she's* convinced. And that makes me think that maybe other people could be convinced, too."

"Like government people?"

Sikes nodded.

Theo rubbed the side of his face, a gesture Sikes had come to associate with intense concentration.

"So the problem you're looking at is: What if this Petty guy *was* whacked by government agents because . . . well, not because of no spaceship, that's for sure. But who knows, maybe the junior astronomer got some photos of some top-secret aircraft or something, like that Aurora whatsit making the oddball sonic booms out in the desert every other Thursday. The astronomer doesn't know what she photographed, but the feds aren't willing to take any chances, so they . . ." Theo put his hands flat on the table. "Naah, it just don't make any sense. I mean, I've been on the force long enough to have had my own run-ins with the feds. FBI, CIA, DIA, you name it. And no one's gonna argue with the idea that the government *has* taken out people in the past and then forced the department to close its investigation. But those were always left-handed cases, Matt. Some Soviet trade attaché falls off a balcony in his hotel. A businessman with CIA connections gets found with a half kilo of dope shoved up his nose. They were housecleaning hits, you know? Strictly in the family. Spy versus spy crap. Never any civilians involved unless they were bystanders or something."

"So what are you saying?"

"If Petty got whacked on purpose, it wasn't a government hit."

"Even with that stuff about the Protocol and the government saying that the military is supposed to be in charge of all"— Sikes felt embarrassed discussing this part of it in public— "outside communications?"

"C'mon, Matt. Takin' a picture of a spaceship isn't the same as communicatin' with it. If this thing's only supposed to be around for a few weeks, why kill anybody? Just nab 'em and lock 'em up. No need to kill anyone. Naah, whatever this astronomer's got going, it's not what she thinks it is. I'd look into the possibility of it being a secret aircraft or spacecraft or something. Maybe it was industrial espionage. Lot of ex-KGB types working for Japanese corporations these days. Raising the stakes on industrial espionage something awful."

"Are you trying to cheer me up?" The prospect of going up against ruthless ex-KGB agents or industrial spies who were willing to kill was as disturbing to Sikes as facing a murderous government agency.

"As a matter of fact, I am," Theo said. "If whoever killed Petty isn't government, then they can't put any pressure on the force. You get public affairs to call a press conference about the case, spread the investigation around, and you're in the clear." He punched Sikes on the shoulder. "I mean, I'm not saying you don't have a problem. If the killer was a pro, I don't think you'd have a pig's chance in a Jimmy Dean factory. But who says this has to stay your problem?"

Sikes felt so relieved by that pronouncement that he even forgot his embarrassment at being in a male strip club. Good old Theo had come through for him again. Now he could go to Angie with what he had put together so far, and his investigation would go forward like any other case. He took a celebratory sip of his beer.

"I take that back," Theo suddenly said.

Sikes nearly choked.

"You do have something to worry about."

Sikes put his glass back on the table and waited for the bad news.

"The way you were talking about that astronomer. Amy, was it?"

"Yeah," Sikes said warily.

"Sounds to me that you're going to fall off the wagon, kid. Head over heels hot for her bones."

Sikes opened his mouth to deny Theo's charges, but the look Theo gave him told him he shouldn't waste his breath. Theo Miles could read his thoughts at twenty paces.

"That obvious?" Sikes asked grumpily.

"Might as well have her name tattooed on your forehead, kid." He finished his second shot of whiskey. "Things not working out between you and Vickie? Thought you were gonna try getting back together."

So did I, Sikes thought. "Jury's still out," he said.

"Well, listen to your rabbi, kid. If you think there's the slightest chance the astronomer's stringing you along about this spaceship government agent crap, you got to ask yourself why. And the first obvious answer to that question is that she had something to do with the hit and she's trying to muddy the trail."

Sikes gave a quick nod. He had thought of that possibility but hadn't found it necessary to pursue it. Amy wasn't a murderer any more than she had taken photographs of a spaceship.

"So," Theo concluded, "if she's a suspect, you got to stay away from her. Hand her off to Angie or something. But whatever you do, don't get involved."

The lights began to dim, and the background din of the audience's conversations suddenly stopped, replaced by scattered cheers and whistles.

"Thanks, man," Sikes said. He grabbed Theo's hand for a farewell shake and squeezed. "You always manage to set me in the right direction."

"I got no choice," Theo said. "After Angie's got you housebroken, you 'n' me are going to be partners again."

Sikes liked the sound of that and said so.

"Just don't get personally involved," Theo added, raising his voice against the sudden volume of a loud rap number. "At some point you got to remind yourself that it's just a job, and then you gotta draw the line, Matt. Remember that. You always got to know when to draw the line. Otherwise . . ." An unexpected sadness came to Theo's eyes then. Sikes didn't know what to make of it. Something to do with the changing lighting in the club, he told himself. "Otherwise you got nothing holding you together."

The audience screamed as the first dancer burst out on the stage in a red spotlight and not much else. Sikes didn't look. Theo did. But Sikes saw that the undercover vice detective was constantly moving his eyes from the dancer to the audience and back again, working all the time.

"Go get 'em, kid," Theo said out of the corner of his mouth.

Sikes moved through the tables, completely unnoticed by the women who stared raptly at the stage. He paused at the entrance and looked back toward Theo at his small, secluded table by the far wall. The server was back, dropping off another shot of whiskey. Theo appeared to be putting too much money on the server's tray. Sikes looked away before he could see if the server pulled anything small and silvery from his tights. The female cops would be making the buy next week, he told himself, so there was no reason Theo would be making a buy now. It was something he didn't need to think about, so Sikes didn't. Wouldn't.

Sikes walked out to the fresh night air of the parking lot, thinking about knowing when to draw the line. Theo had told him that before. Know your limits, he had said. Just don't accept anyone else laying them on you.

Sikes looked up into the night sky. A paltry handful of stars shone weakly through the soft glow of Los Angeles's thick haze. With Theo's help he now knew how to pursue the investigation. The only question remaining was how to pursue his own life. How *could* he want to get back together with Victoria yet experience such sudden and overpowering attraction to another woman? What did that say about his readiness to face the future? About his desire to be a family again for Kirby's sake?

Sikes walked out of the strip club's parking lot and along Sunset Boulevard to where he had parked his Mustang away from the rough treatment of the lot attendants. He was out of answers for tonight. Kirby was waiting for him back at his apartment, and pizza and a video sounded like a good way to close the day. Just like Theo said, he thought, treat it like a job. But he realized that he didn't know how to do that yet. He wondered how his ex-partner managed it. Too many thoughts for too late at night, Sikes told himself as he reached his car, and the first thing he did when he got in was to crank up the stereo—some classic Motown to purge his brain cells.

Sikes drove through Laurel Canyon with the top down, mindlessly drumming his hands against the steering wheel. When he crossed over Mulholland and headed down to the Valley he stole a glance at the sky to see if any more stars might be visible from higher up in the hills. And as he scanned the haze he found himself almost wishing that Amy Stewart *had* found something up there.

But that was just a dream, and he had never had much room in his life for those. He kept his eyes on the road all the rest of the way home and didn't look up once.

CHAPTER 6

TWELVE HOURS AFTER his meeting with Theo Miles, Sikes was ten minutes from UCLA, already feeling as if he was in the principal's office and that Angela Perez was the principal.

She sat beside him in his Mustang, held tilted back to the late morning sun, sunglasses glinting painfully bright, a smile on her lips as the wind blew through her fluttering short hair. She looked like someone on vacation, but she was interrogating her new partner like the ten-year veteran detective she was.

"How many computer disks did Stewart pass over to Petty?" she asked. The questions had been nonstop for the entire drive.

"I don't know," Sikes said. That had been his typical answer for the entire drive.

"Where did she pass the disks over?"

"I think at the university. Petty shared an office there with—"

"No one's interested in what a detective *thinks*, Sikes. What do you *know?*"

"I didn't ask her." From the corner of his eye he saw Angie staring at him.

"What's the matter with you? You miss writing parking citations so badly you want to start wearing a uniform again?"

Sikes kept his hands firmly on the steering wheel, telling

himself he would not punch any part of his car while Angie was in it.

Then Angie asked her first question that didn't specifically pertain to police procedure. "You fall for this Stewart or what?"

Sikes winced. First Miles, now Angie. *Did* he have Amy Stewart's name tattooed on his forehead?

Sikes's lack of a response was answer enough for Angie. "Jesus, Sikes. You do anything about it?"

"No!" Sikes said, far too emphatically, he realized.

"But you want to, don't you?" Angie shifted in her seat as if she were suddenly uncomfortable. "What got into you, Sherlock? I thought you were a straight shooter. Got that photo of your wife in your locker. A kid, even."

That was too much. Sikes swerved the car into the right lane and took the first turn off Sunset, ignoring the blaring horns behind him. The Mustang squealed to a stop on a residential street in Bel-Air. He yanked on the emergency brake, switched off the ignition, then twisted in his seat to face his partner. Only then did he realize that he had nothing to say.

"Yesss?" Angie asked. "You think I'm digging around too much in your personal life?"

"Yeah," Sikes said as he realized she was right. "That's it."

"You think what goes on between you and your wife is off-limits? You think I have no right to concern myself with your romantic and/or hormonal interests? That I should just mind my own you-know-what business?"

Sikes felt some of the indignation ease out of him like a slow leak in a tire. Angie was as good as Theo. She knew what he was going to say even before he knew it himself. Was he really that transparent?

"You got anything to add, or you want me to keep this going for the both of us?" Angie asked.

Sikes summed it up. "What goes on in my personal life has nothing at all to do with how I do my job."

Angie took off her sunglasses and stared at Sikes as if she were about to book him for murder one. "You get this straight, rook. You're not a shoe salesman. You're not a car mechanic. You're a *cop.* And *everything* you do in your personal life has to do with how you do your job. You get too happy, too depressed, too horny even, and you start getting distracted—and that makes you ripe for making a mistake. Shoe salesmen can make mistakes. They just go back and get the right size and color. But when a *cop* makes a mistake, somebody can get hurt or killed. And that could be a citizen on the street. Or that could be your partner. Am I making myself clear?"

Sikes looked up at the thick mass of leaves rustling in the tree he had parked beneath. "I've got my life," he said, "and I've got my job. And—"

"And if you try to tell me that they're two different things, you'll be working forensic accounting with that sphincter Grazer so fast you'll think it's yesterday."

Sikes knew if he tried to say anything more he'd be yelling. So he kept his mouth closed. He didn't have to take this crap. He could always ask for a transfer.

"C'mon, Sikes. Don't be looking at me like you're already writing up your transfer request."

Sikes gave up. He punched the steering wheel. Was *every* detective on the force some kind of mutant mind reader?

"Think of old man Petty," Angie said unexpectedly. "He was *murdered*, Sikes, and we still don't know who did it. How do you feel about that?"

Sikes scowled. "It sucks."

"Damn right it sucks. But this is your baby. You're doing the digging. You still want to make the case, don't you?"

"Damn right."

"You try to stop thinking about it, but you can't, can you? You drive home, and you see Petty in his car. You try to sleep at night, you see Petty's house, you go over those letters you got from the computer. That's not a *job*, Sikes. That's a calling. That's your goddamned *life*. And if you're trying to tell me you think it's anything else, you're not being honest with me, or yourself, or anyone else in your sorry little circle of friends."

The only sound on the street was the distant rush of traffic behind them on Sunset and the wind through the leaves overhead. Sikes kept his hands on the steering wheel, squeezing and relaxing his grip, squeezing and relaxing.

"You know I'm right, don't you?"

Sikes had had enough. He shook his head and slumped in his seat. "How do you *know?*" he asked. "It's like everyone else but me can read my mind or something."

"Look at me, Sikes."

Reluctantly Sikes turned to his partner.

"It's called being a detective. You understand that? It's called being honest with yourself, being in touch with yourself"—she touched her fist to her chest—"listening to what your gut tells you as much as what your eyes see and your ears hear. Because when you do that, when you listen to what's inside, you're going to find out that *everyone's the same*. Everyone. We all have the same needs and the exact same motives. The only thing that makes us different is what triggers us to act on those needs.

"Trust me, Sikes. If we find the guy who nailed Petty, when you talk to him and get him to tell you why he did it, you're going to *understand* it. You're going to listen to him, and you're going to look inside yourself, and you're going to know why it is we humans do the god-awful things we do. And if you really understand it, the only thing you can do is try to stop it.

"That's in you, Sikes. I saw it in the parking lot behind Mann's the first time I met you. Something in your past—whatever that was, whenever it happened—it made you a cop. You can't be anything else but a cop. So the only choice you have is to walk away from what you're supposed to be and live your life like you're half asleep and never going to wake up, like most of the other people who stumble through life, or to accept the inevitable and bear down and become the best cop you can be."

Angie held her sunglasses in one hand and wiped at the bridge of her nose with the other. "Christ, I should be able to give out course credits for a speech like that."

They sat in silence.

"So we going to be okay, Sikes?"

Sikes glanced at her, studied her eyes. He asked himself what *he* would be thinking now. He surprised himself by knowing the answer. "You wouldn't be wasting all this effort on me if you didn't think I was worth it, would you?"

Angie smiled beatifically. "You read my mind, Sikes." She put her sunglasses back on and leaned her head back against the headrest.

Sikes restarted the engine.

"Of course, you still screwed up the Stewart interrogation," Angie added.

"Thanks. I already figured that one out for myself," Sikes said as he made a U-turn and headed back onto Sunset.

"But not to worry," Angie said. "We'll take it from the top, and this time you let me do all the talking. Maybe I'll even give you an extension on your deadline."

"Whatever you say, Professor."

But when they arrived at the Royce Physics Building Angie didn't have much talking to do. Amy Stewart was gone.

The Astronomy Department had one overworked office assistant on the third floor who was attempting to keep up with the normal flow of work as he answered Detective Perez's questions while also trying to entice a shorthaired kitten with tightly curled orange and cream fur back into the cardboard box that sat open on the floor beside the counter. The label on the box announced: I'M GOING HOME. Beneath it, the name SAMP-SON had been handwritten.

The nameplate on the assistant's desk read: JOHN K. OHLIN. He looked young enough to be a student, though the cut of his dark blond hair and fashionably draped jeans seemed well beyond the student budgets that Sikes remembered. He also was acting as if he would rather be anywhere else than behind the desk in Royce Hall.

From behind the mounds of files on his desk, John put another phone call on hold and hung up the handset. "I can't give out her home address. The university has a strict policy about that." John bent down to push Sampson away from his leg and toward the box. The kitten's response was to purr madly and leap up the assistant's leg. He made it all the way up to John's shoulder. John sighed in defeat and turned back to Angie.

"You just told me that Amy Stewart missed two tutorials this morning," Angie said patiently. "You told me that she's never missed a tutorial before." Sikes stayed in the background to let her work. Besides, he was more of a dog man himself.

"Not without phoning in to cancel them," John said, checking the record book.

"Doesn't that worry you?" Angie asked.

John shrugged. Sampson swayed but held on. "Yeah, but she's an astronomer. They all keep these weird hours. Up all night and that sort of thing." The phone rang and he answered, taking a message for an absent professor.

"Did Randolph Petty have an office here?" Angie asked when John had hung up again.

"Yeah, he shared it with three other part-timers."

"You know Dr. Petty was murdered, don't you?"

"Yeah, that was terrible. Never know, do you?" John looked at the flashing lights on his multiline phone. He lifted the receiver and went to press down a button.

But Angie leaned forward and rested her knuckles on the only two clear spots on the desk. Sampson regarded her with interest, as if measuring the distance to another empty back. "So where were you on the night Dr. Petty was killed?"

John screwed up his face at Angie's persistence, but Sikes could see that Angie had finally gotten John's attention. "Why would you want to know?" the assistant asked. He placed a restraining hand on the kitten.

Angie looked over her shoulder at Sikes. "What about you? You thinking what I'm thinking?"

Sikes had no idea what Angie was thinking, but he wasn't about to interfere in whatever it was that she had planned. "Absolutely," he said.

Angie stood away from the desk. "Okay, John, I'm afraid you're going to have to come with us."

"What?"

"You figure it out. Dr. Petty gets killed, and you won't tell us if you have an alibi. Now Amy Stewart's missing, and you're not helping us track her down. It looks awfully suspicious to me." She held her hand out like a surgeon waiting for a scalpel. "Sikes? Cuffs, please."

Sikes automatically fumbled under his sports jacket for the cuffs on his belt. He couldn't be certain, but it looked as if Angie were risking a harassment charge. There was no way that the assistant could be considered a suspect just for following university policy. Besides, any judge would issue a warrant over the phone to obtain Stewart's address from university records. Then Sikes saw the look in Angie's eyes as he slapped the cuffs into her waiting hand. *He* knew what procedure was, and *Angie* knew, but the important point was that *John* didn't.

Angie rattled the cuffs. "You carrying anything besides the cat I should know about before I search you?"

"Are you *serious?*" John still held onto Sampson and the phone receiver as he stared at the two detectives.

Angie began walking around John's desk. "There's a murderer loose. It doesn't get much more serious than that."

John looked at the dangling cuffs as if he were about to be

hypnotized by them. He hung up the receiver swiftly, swung a protesting Sampson down into the cardboard box, and latched the lid shut. He straightened up. "Uh, what if I give you her address? Confidentially." A warning yowl rose out of the box.

"I'd consider that a sign of cooperation."

"I'm only subbing this week for a friend," John said as he flipped hastily through his Rolodex. He pulled Amy Stewart's card off the metal rings and handed it to Angie. The cardboard box at his feet began rocking back and forth.

Angie read it. "Did you try calling her at this number?"

John nodded, putting out his foot to keep the cardboard box from tipping over. "I just got her machine." A small orange-and-cream-striped paw punched a hole in the side of the box.

Angie copied the information from the card into her notebook. She handed it back to John. "Looks like you could use a set of cuffs yourself," she said with a nod at the box. "Stewart lives out in Santa Monica," Angie said to Sikes. "You ready to roll?"

"Let's check out her office first."

Angie frowned. "For anything in particular?"

Sikes shrugged. "First time I was in it I don't think I was looking at it the way I should have been."

"Fair enough," Angie said. She thanked the assistant for his help, then let Sikes lead the way down the hall to Amy Stewart's office. Behind them the assistant sighed with audible relief to no longer be the focus of Angie's attention. Sikes knew how he felt.

Amy Stewart's office appeared to be unchanged from Sikes's first visit. The clutter was about the same. All the pictures were still on the wall. And the computer was still on the tiny desk, though its screen was completely blank, without even the image of a watch face slowly moving across it.

"Anything missing?" Angie asked as she stood in the doorway and looked around. Sikes could tell she was already seeing the small room in more detail than he had the first time he had looked. "As if anyone could tell in this mess."

"Nothing obvious is gone. But then that's what I thought at Petty's house until I tried to look at the computer."

Angie walked over to the desk, studied the computer's keyboard, then pressed a single key on it. The computer chimed, and in a few moments the screen began to glow.

"You know about computers?" Sikes asked as he joined her at the computer screen.

"They're the future, rook. But don't tell that nut Grazer that I said so."

They watched the screen. Nothing came up on it. "This is just what happened at Petty's," Sikes said. "It wouldn't do anything because the hard disk had been erased." He began to search the desk's single row of drawers.

Angie knew what he was looking for. "Any disks?"

Sikes rummaged through the bottom drawer. "Nothing. Let's check the shelves."

Their search wasn't helped by the chaos in the crammed bookcases, but eventually the two detectives satisfied themselves that there were no computer disks hidden among the jumbled stacks of journals and papers and books.

Sikes began to feel a sense of frustrated panic grow in him. "Whoever killed Petty must have traced the material back to Amy," he told Angie. "We should get a black and white over to her place right now."

Angie handed him her notebook. Two wide elastic bands made it open to the latest page. "You're still jumping to a couple of sweeping conclusions, but I agree, let's play it safe. Call it in." Sikes pulled the desk phone out from behind two mounds of file folders and called Dispatch. When he hung up he was ready to head back to his car. Quickly. He kept picturing Amy dead in a parking lot, just like Dr. Petty. But Angie wasn't ready to go. She stared at the framed photographs on the wall between two bookcases, just above the chair Sikes had sat in the day before.

"This her?" she asked, pointing to a photograph of Amy standing in a group of four other people. The picture had apparently been taken on a mountaintop somewhere. Behind the group was only clear blue sky, and all four were dressed in sweaters and heavy jackets.

Sikes took a quick look at the photograph—an 8 x 10 color print. It was the same one he had seen yesterday. They all were. "Yeah, that's her. We should get moving."

"Slow it down, rook. The uniforms will get there way before we will. Have you ever seen this guy before?" She pointed to one of the figures beside Amy in the photograph.

Sikes was almost bouncing he was in such a hurry to leave, but he took a look at the person Angie indicated. "I, uh, I don't know," he said. Then he looked more closely. "But . . . he does sort of look familiar."

"Yeah, that's what I thought," Angie said. She lifted the photo from the wall, turned it over to see if anything had been written on the back, then looked at the picture again. "I know I've seen him before. What do you think? An actor or something?"

"Yeah, sure, maybe," Sikes said. That was one of the odd things about living in L.A.—the place was crawling with not-so-famous actors whose faces were vaguely familiar, though their names were not. Walking into a supermarket could be like walking into a high school reunion. A familiar face would suddenly jump out of the crowd, though it was impossible to say where or when it had been seen before.

In this case the person in question was a Caucasian male, about fifty, Sikes guessed. Dark hair, dark eyebrows, clean features that even he recognized as handsome. And there was a pleasant sense of quiet and calm to him, too. Everyone else in the photo, even Amy, was smiling broadly. In contrast, the mystery man had only a slight smile but appeared to be having just a good as time as the others. Whoever they were. "So she knows a movie star," Sikes said impatiently. "Is it important?"

"That's the fun about being a detective, Sikes. You never know what's important till the fat lady's locked up." She put the photograph under her arm and started for the door. "We'll stick it up at the station, maybe run it by someone at the *Times.*"

"You can just take it like that?" Sikes asked.

Angie frowned. "It's not *evidence,* Sikes. It's the picture we'll need if we have to put out an APB. Maybe we'll get a better one at her place, but why waste time?"

"Right," Sikes said. But he felt that was just what they had been doing.

Amy Stewart didn't have a *place* in Santa Monica. She had a house. Correct that, Sikes thought as he walked through the gate in the high, nondescript fence that edged the property, it's a mansion.

"Not bad for a student," Angie said as she walked up the path at Sikes's side. The house was an ultramodern assemblage of three large cubes joined in an apparently haphazard but curiously balanced pattern. The cubes were faced with strips of dark-stained wood—some sides striped diagonally, others checkerboarded. Elaborate plantings of dwarf and standard palms and monstrous bird of paradise plants erupted from the corner of each cube, as if the house were a gift freshly burst free of its multicolored wrapping.

Sikes stared at the spiky plants enviously. He had once been part of a task force that had broken up a stolen plant ring. Ten-foot-tall plants could cost more than he made in six months. He started up the wide wooden steps that led to an inset porch where two uniformed officers waited. There was an elaborate wall sculpture to one side of the porch—various angled pieces of heat-stained metal down which several trickles of water ran, creating an almost musical rush of splashing in a tiny rectangular pool.

"It's got to be her parents' house," Sikes said.

"Or her boyfriend's," Angie suggested. Before Sikes could respond to her barb she addressed the officers. "You check all the windows?"

"No sign of life," the younger of the two said. He had a fresh, eager look to him, and Sikes vaguely remembered he had had that look once himself, back in his first year with the department. "We can see in through about half the ground-floor windows. No indication that anything's amiss. But there is a large dog run out back, and no dogs."

Angie studied the front door. She and Sikes had known that no one was home here as soon as they had radioed in for a report from the officers sent to check the house. She looked at the two officers again, then held out the photograph she had taken from the office wall. "Either of you two recognize this guy?"

The officers peered at the photograph. The older of the two pushed back his hat to reveal a few silver tufts of hair against a freckled brown scalp. Sikes recognized the pattern—young cop with old, passing on the tradition.

"He's someone from television, isn't he?" the rookie asked. "Wasn't he on a sitcom or something?"

"Naah," the old hand said. "He's from the movies. Been in war pictures, back in the old days when they still made 'em."

"But you've seen him before?" Angie asked.

Both officers decided that they had, though neither knew where.

Angie put the photograph under her arm again and turned to

Sikes. "Okay, Sherlock. I've heard that you had an interesting childhood. Can you get us in here without causing too much damage?"

"Without a warrant?" Sikes asked.

"I don't know about you, but given what we found in her office, I'd say there's a chance that Stewart might be facing the same kind of trouble that Petty faced. That's clear and probable grounds provided we go in looking only for signs of foul play."

"Uh," the rookie uniform said, "there's a Westec sign out front on the wall."

"Then one of you go out front to meet them when they get here," Angie said. "And find out if whoever lives here said anything about going on vacation." She nodded at Sikes. "Let's go."

Sikes and Angie walked around the odd-shaped house to check all the possible entrances, and Sikes settled on a back patio where he would only have to break one small pane of glass in a pair of French doors. A shrill siren sounded as soon as they stepped inside, but both ignored it as they did a quick room-by-room search. There was nothing out of place, no signs of struggle. It was just a house where, judging from the closets and the enormous sacks of Dog Chow in the kitchen, one woman and two very large dogs lived. And none of them was home at present.

By the time Sikes and Angie left the house to check out the attached garage, a Westec Security car had arrived with a private guard. The guard, helpfully accompanied by the two police officers, went into the house to shut off the siren, then started taking down badge numbers for his report.

There was a convertible BMW in the garage, stone cold. Angie considered the car for a moment, then told Sikes to use one of the gardening shovels on the wall to smash the lock on the car's trunk. It took five swings. The trunk was empty.

Sikes had no idea what to do next other than to issue a missing person report. But Angie patted his shoulder and had him follow her out to the Westec guard to ask who was on file with the company as the person to be notified in case of an emergency at this address. The guard went to his car radio, and the answer came back from his head office in seconds. Sikes recognized the phone number that went with the name. It was the Astronomy Department at UCLA. The contact was the professor for whom Amy worked as a student assistant and tutorial leader.

"Shit," Angie said. "Full circle."

"What's that mean?" Sikes asked.

"What do you think it means? It means our leads have run out."

"So what do we do now?"

Angie chewed on one arm of her sunglasses as she watched the uniformed officers stretching yellow police crime-scene tape over the empty pane in the French doors as a temporary repair. "That depends. We have to ask ourselves what we're facing here."

Sikes didn't understand her uncertainty. "It's obvious, isn't it? Amy's missing because she's either already been murdered or because she's running for her life."

A look of pity came to Angie's face. "You're thinking with your pants again, rook. That's only *one* possibility. The other is that we're dealing with someone who's covering her tracks."

Sikes snorted in disbelief. "Amy? That's crazy, Angie."

"She pulled a pretty good vanishing act."

"She's afraid she'll be next!"

"Why didn't she come to the police?"

Sikes waved his arms as if he were trying for lift off. "What good can the police do if the poor kid's being hunted by her own government?"

"Sikes, do you honestly believe the government had anything to do with Dr. Petty's death? Over some UFO a billion miles out in space that's supposedly going to disappear in another week? Let's get real here. Either Stewart is genuinely certifiable or she's made up the whole story to disguise the real motive for Petty getting hit."

"Or," Sikes said angrily, "she really *did* photograph something out there, and someone else really wants to kill her for it!" Sikes was still finding it difficult to consider Amy Stewart a likely suspect in Randolph Petty's murder.

But the more worked up Sikes became, the more composed Angie appeared to be. "Uh-uh, Sikes, this isn't the fifties. Remember E.T. phone home? To boldly go? May the force be with you, and all that junk? People *want* there to be real flying saucers and real little green men. Hell, if Stewart actually took photos of a real UFO, she'd be able to sell them for a fortune, and the government would probably be giving her a medal, not trying to silence her."

Sikes looked at the expensive house Amy lived in on her own. "Well, maybe she doesn't need a fortune."

"Now you're thinking like a detective!" Angie said approvingly. "You met her. You talked with her. What *does* this woman need? What drives her? Why would she lie about any of this? Why would she think she was telling the truth? If she's a victim, why would anyone be after her? What could she have that's important or dangerous? And *if* she's the murderer, then why would she kill Dr. Petty? Quick, Sikes, before you can think about it—go with your first reaction. Why would Amy Stewart kill Randolph Petty? A man and a woman. A young astronomer and an old astronomer. Why, Sikes?"

Young and old, Sikes thought. Like himself and Theo Miles. Two uniformed cops. Like himself and Angie Perez. A teacher and a student. He stared at Angie. She was right. He'd been influenced by personal reactions again. Amy Stewart might be Petty's killer. He did what she told him a cop had to do—make the connection. So he made it personal. Why would I kill my teacher? he asked himself. He thought of how angry Angie made him. The way she pestered him with questions. But that's part of the learning process, Sikes thought. I expect that. And any student would expect that, especially one who works in a university.

"C'mon, Sikes, let's have it," Angie prodded. "Tell me what you're thinking."

Sikes shook his head, everything a jumble, worse than Stewart's office. It's not her questions, Sikes thought. It's not the fact that she can see through me, knows more than I know.

Angie was at his elbow, urging him on. "If you're stuck, Sikes, then whatever you're thinking about, turn it around. Come at it from the other side."

Okay, Sikes thought, I *wouldn't* kill Angie because I respect her. But what if I *didn't* respect her? Why wouldn't I respect her?

"Turn it around, Sikes."

I respect her because she gave me a break, Sikes thought, and he suddenly felt as if he had hit upon the core of the problem Angie had set for him. He understood what was inside him that made him *like* Angie so much—the shooting back of Mann's

Chinese. He had done good work for her that night, followed procedure straight from the book and contributed to the perp's arrest and conviction. And Angie had given him the credit he deserved. He had gotten his commendation. She had included him in her report. She hadn't taken anything away from him. She hadn't—

"One of them stole something from the other," Sikes said.

Angie encouraged him to continue. "Go with it."

"If Amy did it," Sikes said slowly, "then it was because either Dr. Petty stole something from her or she stole something from him."

Angie waved an arm at Amy Stewart's house. "Look at the size of this place, Sikes. What would she need to steal? What would be important to her? Think, man, think."

Sikes screwed his face up as he recalled his talk with Amy Stewart. She had definitely been edgy. Was that because she had been trying to hide how she felt about Petty, or because she had been truly upset and frightened?

"Her career," Sikes said suddenly.

"Astronomy?"

"Whatever was stolen had to do with—" Sikes turned away and dragged his hand through his short, spiky hair. "This is no good, Angie. It just brings us back to the photographs."

"But take it from the other side," Angie urged. When Sikes turned back to face her his partner was waiting for him. "What if Petty was the one who came up with the photographs—or whatever the *real* material is—and *he* passed them to *her?*"

"So every word she said to me was a lie?" Sikes asked.

"Maybe some of it was true, maybe none of it was, but at least we can see a way through it."

Sikes frowned. "You can see a way through all this?"

"Wouldn't be the first time an academic type bumped off a coworker over research, rook. It's the stuff careers are made of. An important career move might trigger some people into wanting to kill, wouldn't you say?"

"Yeah," Sikes said. He guessed he could understand the urge to kill—if not the action—when it came to preserving one's job. And he could certainly understand the need to make up wild stories for self-protection.

"So what do we do now?" Angie asked.

Sikes grinned despite himself. She had done it to him again.

"I go back to the university and find out what the old man was working on and what Amy was working on and interview other faculty to see where their interests might have overlapped." He sighed.

"Pretty boring stuff, hmm?"

"I hated college," Sikes said.

The uniformed officers had finished with their serviceable but makeshift repair of the broken pane in the French doors, so Angie threw an arm around Sikes's shoulders and steered him across the perfectly manicured lawn toward the front gate. "If you think interviewing faculty is dull, rook, wait till you start doing the paperwork that will let you track Stewart by monitoring her credit-card use and bank transactions." She shook her head in condolence. "You know you have to file more than thirty different forms for that? Looks like I'm going to have to give you an extension after all. Maybe even a whole week just to do the typing."

Sikes was aware that he felt much lighter leaving than when he had arrived. Everything had been a jumble—alien spaceships, government agents, losing his detachment, Amy Stewart missing. But Angie had managed to sort through the garbage and lies and cut the whole situation down to size. The most likely explanation was that this was simply a personal incident between two professionals—one old and at the end of his career, one young and on her way up. For whatever reason, bad blood had arisen between them, and one had attempted to kill the other. Whether Petty had set out to kill his student and had died in the attempt or whether the student had gone after her professor remained to be seen. He sighed again as he thought of Amy and the instant effect she had had on him. But still, on the face of it, the scenario worked. Randolph Petty's death might just be what Sikes had first thought it to be—a deliberate killing, not a random one. Now all that remained to be done was to put in the necessary hours of plodding, detailed investigation that would bring the last few pieces together. He shifted restlessly from foot to foot, eager now to get the tedious follow-up out of the way and get back to his own life.

"Jesus, Sikes," Angie said as they reached the Mustang, "the way you're hopping around, you look like you're ready to fly or something."

"I don't like mysteries," Sikes said. "And thanks to you, this one looks like it's on its way to being solved. That's making me feel good. Like at least something in my life's under control . . . or something.''

Angie glanced at the photograph she was still carrying— Amy Stewart, the mystery man, and two others. "Let's hope so. Got time for a beer at Casey's before you get started?"

Sikes checked his watch. He still had two hours before Kirby would be home from school. "Why not?" he said. "We can celebrate this case finally getting back to earth."

Angie tossed the photograph into the Mustang's backseat. "Let's hope so," she said.

CHAPTER 7

IT HAD BEEN YEARS since Moodri had been forced to use the complex network of half-size service tunnels to move undetected through the ship, and his ancient joints creaked with the strain of his doubled-over gait. But he had no choice. In time, as it was measured on the planet the ship was approaching, fewer than four days remained until the moment the Elders' plan must be set in motion, and without even knowing it, the Overseers were successfully counteracting that plan by searching for all who bore the markings of Moodri's lineage in their spots. Moodri was certain the goddess would share his appreciation of the irony of his predicament.

At last he saw a dim glow up ahead and knew that he was near the eight-way intersection where the meeting had been set. Melgil and Vondmac—the other two members of his cell of conspirators—were already there waiting for him. He had moved more slowly than he had estimated.

Vondmac smiled wistfully as Moodri gathered his simple skirt around him and settled on a wide pipe. Moodri's customary robes had proved too cumbersome for easy movement in these confines. He had abandoned them near the hidden entrance hatch he had used to escape the pair of Overseers who had appeared at his dormitory to question him.

"Doesn't this remind you of our youth?" Vondmac asked.

She gazed around at the spherical intersection, which was lit only by the eight dull lamps that glowed by each tunnel entrance, over the timeworn signs written in alien script. "The whispered secret meetings? The fervent plans for an armed revolt?"

"The ease with which we were infiltrated," Moodri added. "The quickness with which the Overseers identified and executed the conspirators."

Vondmac nodded in sad remembrance. "But in the end, the Overseers didn't succeed. They simply accelerated the evolutionary pressure that would inevitably force the birth of a conspiracy that could overthrow them, just as their breeding program has created family lines of workers that are naturally resistant to the gas."

"Exactly," Moodri said. "And while an armed revolt by the masses is not practical in these circumstances, a single act by a lone individual—"

"Will not happen," Melgil stated flatly.

Moodri turned to Melgil. As soon as he had entered the intersection Moodri had seen that the old *binnaum*'s mood was foul, but he had assumed it was the pressure of the decision they would soon have to make that had affected his colleague and friend. It was often difficult for Moodri to judge the moods and thoughts of those of his own generation who had achieved the same oneness with Ionia that he had, and apparently he had misread Melgil badly.

"What do you know?" Moodri asked calmly. At his age, after all this time in these circumstances, there was little that could disturb that calm.

"I have talked with your great-nephew."

"His interrogation by the Overseers went as we had hoped?" Moodri asked, though he had few doubts that it had.

"Yes, yes, fine," Melgil said, as if anxious to get this part of his report out of the way. "Finiksa told Coolock the story you imprinted in his mind—seeing the clearing charges beneath the water worker's membrane suit, hearing the scavengers call his name. Coolock accepted the story just as you said he would."

Moodri was pleased. "Then the operation at the water hub was successful."

"Seven of our best people were killed," Melgil said.

Moodri closed his eyes. "They returned to the mother so

their people could have a chance at freedom. Even now they move within the currents of stars in the fields of home."

Reflexively the three Elders touched their fingers to their hearts in a sign of blessing.

"Rest easy, Melgil," Moodri said reassuringly. "We knew the Overseers could not help but discover that we were planning diversions in the water hubs all through the ship. All of our workers who volunteered to be the visible part of the operation and be caught knew what risks they faced—death in the hub or in the Game. But because of their heroism our other diversions went as we planned, and the Overseers obviously feel no need to search further. We are in control of the ship's water system, Melgil. Our plan will succeed."

But Melgil looked more despondent than Moodri had ever seen him look before. "Not if we are to depend on Finiksa."

For a moment Moodri sought the peace of the goddess. Then he asked his old friend to explain himself.

"I told him about the key," Melgil recounted. "I told him when it would be given to him and how he was to use it when he was on the bridge."

"And you told him those were my wishes?" Moodri asked. With the Overseers patrolling for him he had not been able to risk moving through the open corridors into the service tunnel system that linked the infirmaries to reach his great-nephew himself.

"Of course," Melgil said. "He has great love and respect for you. But he also respects the Overseers. He is third generation, and the flames of hate do not burn in him as they did in us at his age." Melgil reached out his one good hand imploringly. "I told you, Moodri, this has been the flaw in the plan from the beginning. Only *we* lived on Tencton. We *know* what was taken from us, and so we alone are willing to risk everything to win it back. But our children's children know only this ship." His voice echoed against the pipes and cables of the intersection. "And to those who are in the Watcher Youth, the Overseers are a source of rewards, not punishment." Melgil shook his head. "Moodri, when I told Finiksa about the plan he said it was not for the good of the ship. He intends to report us all to his Watch Leader."

Vondmac, who had been listening quietly, started in alarm at Melgil's words. Her watchful gaze fell on Moodri.

Moodri closed his eyes in silent prayer. He had seen that

possibility in Buck's nature. The ship was his world. The Overseers brought order to it. Not knowing what had been stolen from him, he could not regret its absence. But still Moodri had seen the spark of the goddess in the boy. He had not been wrong about that. Buck was the key to the plan's success and had been ever since Moodri had gently guided him to say and do the things that would bring him to the Overseers' attention as a possible recruit for the Watcher Youth.

For the plan to succeed, the rebels needed access to one of the most highly secured areas of the ship. Overseers alone performed bridge functions. The maintenance workers who were allowed past the security precautions were either lobotomized or drugged. Only the children in a Watcher Youth Brigade could get through without difficulty. So the oldest among the captive Tenctonese had created a plan that relied on the youngest.

"What have you done with him?" Moodri asked, knowing full well that Melgil could not have left Buck without ensuring that the child would not make his report to the Overseers.

"He sleeps," Melgil said. "In order to be rid of me, Gelana, the cargo specialist, gave him drugs as I requested. Coolock had already agreed to have Finiksa excused for three shifts. He will not be missed for another cycle."

"I will go to him before that," Moodri said. He knew that if he had a chance to talk with Buck, the boy would understand why the Overseers could not be informed. Why the plan was necessary.

"Too dangerous," Melgil protested. Vondmac nodded agreement. "The Overseers are looking for anyone with spots remotely resembling Family: Heroes of Soren'tzahh and Family: Third Moon's Ocean. Your nephew, Stangya, has already been interrogated."

Moodri was surprised that Melgil had not added *and executed*. "He survived the interrogation?"

"They checked his blood for traces of *eemikken*\. They found none."

Moodri took a moment to smile wryly at the predictably lockstep blindness of the Overseers. The tattoo around their wrists had long been suspected of cutting the flow of blood to their brains.

"What about Ruhtra?" Moodri asked.

Melgil looked at Vondmac for the answer to that question. "No word," she said tensely. "The Overseers have been to his dormitory, but he was not present. You realize what that means, don't you?"

Moodri did. "Two workers were seen calling to Finiksa in the water hub. That means they recognized him, implying that they knew the pattern of his spots, suggesting that they were of the same family. And now two of that same family are missing from their dormitories." Moodri sighed because the situation, no matter how personally dangerous, could be of no importance so close to the culmination of their plan. "The Overseers have therefore concluded that Ruhtra and I were the observers in the water hub."

"If we had allowed Stangya to operate within a cell as I urged, he would have known about the importance of staying away from the water hubs," Melgil said.

"And if the revolt had been compromised, then an entire family line would have been eliminated," Moodri said. "You know the rules we set for ourselves. At least one from every family involved must remain untainted."

Vondmac cleared her throat and adjusted her position on the pipes she sat upon. Moodri knew her well enough to simply wait for her to say what she felt she had to.

"Moodri, it distresses me to have to relay this," she began.

"As I can see," Moodri said kindly.

"But there are those on the council who suggest that it is no accident that Finiksa does not appear capable of using the key. Especially in light of the Overseers' sudden interest in those who share your spots."

Moodri felt a sudden flare of temper rise up in him, and he quickly squelched it. "Does the council accuse me of cowardice?" he asked blandly, though he could feel his spots darken at the implied insult.

"Can you find fault with them if they do?" Vondmac asked in return. "We all know what the plan's success will mean to you."

"Freedom for our people," Moodri said, no longer bothering to maintain the essence of the goddess in his words.

"And certain death for you."

Moodri gazed at the curved and mechanistic walls of the intersection. They did remind him of his youth, in the first years of his people's captivity, when the fires of Tencton's clearly remembered sun had burned within all of them and they had sworn to give their lives for the defeat of their enemies.

"Have you forgotten the vows of our youth?" Moodri asked. "Made here, in these same tunnels?"

"Our people's hearts were full of passion then," Vondmac said sadly. "But as our wisdom has grown that passion has faded. I feel it. I know you feel it, too."

"Perhaps that is the nature of things," Melgil added. "Thus the old pass on their wisdom to help those generations who follow, those in whom the passion has not yet been extinguished."

Moodri studied his two friends closely. "Is this what the peace of Ionia has brought to you? Acceptance of one's own fate may well be the key to inner peace, but how can you accept the fate of all our people?" He stood unsteadily on the bundled wires and cables beneath his feet. "If we do not act now, there will be no children to follow us. I *can* accept my own death—at my age it is just a matter of time. But I cannot accept that my race will die. And shame on those who think that I do."

Melgil looked embarrassed. "It is not so much your death as it is the *nature* of your death." He turned away so he would not meet Moodri's gaze. "We do not even know if you *will* die. Ever."

"So it has come to this," Moodri said, letting them hear the anger and the disappointment that he felt. "The spots of the council have grown so pale that they cannot believe that any of us still believes in the ideals of our youth. Well, you tell them this: I will not consign my race to the extinction of Terminus. Finiksa *will* be on the bridge at the appointed time. He *will* insert the circuitry override key at the proper moment." Moodri's eyes seemed to blaze in the dim light of the intersection. "The superluminal drive *will* activate improperly. The cargo disk *will* be jettisoned. And when the drive translates into superluminal space in an uncontrolled trajectory, I *will* be on board to transmit the messages the rest of the cursed fleet will need to hear to know that this ship has apparently been lost in an unforeseen accident, never to be found again." Moodri sat down again, voice trembling. "And if it is my fate to be drawn into a never-ending spiral deep into the gravity well of the star we approach, then so be it. Eternity will be but a single, relativistic instant to me, and eventually even the stars will fade and the universe will collapse, and when time ends I shall return to the Mother knowing I have done what I must do."

Melgil and Vondmac looked at each other as if each wanted the other to speak. Vondmac was first. *"We* do not doubt you, old friend," she said. "We only relate the concerns that were raised in the council."

There was something more to what she had said, but Moodri knew it would come out in time, when she was ready. He looked at her sharply. "I trust you will relate back to them that their concerns are unfounded."

"For you, yes," Melgil said with difficulty. "But for Finiksa . . ."

"I will talk with him," Moodri said through clenched teeth. "He will know his duty as clearly as I know mine. What other choice do we have?"

Unexpectedly Vondmac spoke. "There is another plan."

Moodri felt his hearts trade beats. "And I have not been told?"

"Keer'chatlas," Melgil whispered.

"A plan kept from *me?"* Moodri asked in amazement.

"A precaution," Vondmac said. "There are those who have never trusted the involvement of a child. It was a backup plan. Merely a contingency."

Moodri twisted the hem of his skirt in his fists. "How does this new plan get the circuitry key to the bridge?"

"Among the stores of *eemikken* we have accumulated over the years," Vondmac said, "we have also . . . another drug."

Instantly Moodri understood. Instantly he was appalled. Vondmac could only mean *jabroka*—the miner's drug. A narcotic that affected the mind as well as the body's genetic structure. "You would turn our people into monsters," he said in horror.

"An assault squad of twenty only," Melgil said. "Enough to storm the bridge by force."

Moodri shook his head. "There are five pressure doors between the cargo section and the bridge."

"The miner's drug unlocks the unexpressed genes that make our species so adaptable," Vondmac said. "Under its influence the assault squad will draw on the hidden strength. They will be able to move fast enough."

"But not fast enough to prevent the Overseers from sending a distress signal indicating a revolt," Moodri snapped. "What good will it do to find freedom on a new world if we know that in less than a Tencton year a new ship will arrive to reclaim us?"

"It is a technologically developed world," Melgil said. "We will teach them, help them create defenses."

"Defenses? Against ships? From a world that has only developed *radio* in the past hundred years?" If it was not so pathetic and desperate an idea, Moodri would have laughed.

"We have no other choice," Melgil said.

"We have Finiksa!"

Melgil and Vondmac both bowed their heads. "The council has already decided. We cannot trust the fate of our people to a child in the sway of the Overseers."

Moodri lifted his head defiantly. "I refuse to accept the council's decision."

"As you wish," Melgil said. Then he stroked his withered arm with his good hand. "But you forget that I control the key. And I shall give it to the assault squad, not to your great-nephew."

"Then you will doom us all," Moodri said. "Even if the assault squad reaches the bridge, even if the key survives the battle and is used on time, more ships will come for us."

"I am sorry, Moodri," Vondmac said. "But it is our last opportunity. We must choose to pursue the plan that will give us the best chance for success. And we have chosen."

Moodri now understood the betrayal that Vondmac had concealed in her words. "You voted against me, didn't you?"

Both Melgil and Vondmac nodded. "I am sorry, too, Moodri," Melgil said.

The female and the *binnaum* stood. "We have arranged for a supply of vegrowth and water to be hidden in the third intersection by the inner food chambers," Vondmac said. "You will be safe there until we begin our descent. After that, we doubt if the Overseers will have much interest in trying to find you." She smiled briefly. "All other aspects of the plan will proceed as before—the search for the beacons, the capture of the Overseers."

"If a distress call goes out," Moodri said, "the beacons will not be necessary."

"We will still need your help then," Vondmac said. "We hope you will give it."

"Then," Moodri repeated grimly. "But not now."

"You are no longer needed by the council," Melgil said. "Rest for the next four days. You deserve it."

They left Moodri then, alone in the intersection and the tunnels he had not traversed in years. Had he not had the goddess within him, he would have begun ranting in the empty intersection, listening to his words resound down darkened tunnels built by unknown intelligences unknown ages ago. But that was not his way. Despite what the council had voted, despite the well-intentioned betrayal by his friends, Moodri knew his options were not at an end.

"An assault squad," he whispered, and he knew it was two generations of brutality that had led the council to adopt the very same measures that the Overseers would.

But force was not the answer here. It could not be. Whoever, whatever had built the ship had known more about force than the peaceful Tenctonese ever would, and safeguards against its use were built in at every key point.

Moodri straightened his skirt and hobbled off down the corridor, scanning each set of alien signs beneath each light, searching for the tunnel that would lead him toward the hull. If the council had abandoned him, then he would have no chance to tell them how important it was that they place their trust in the original plan and Finiksa. His only choice was to *show* them.

And he set out to do exactly that.

CHAPTER 8

ON THE FOURTH DAY of his first homicide investigation, Sikes arrived at the station house to find a stuffed E.T. the Extraterrestrial doll handcuffed to his chair. There was a handwritten confession stapled to the doll's chest, asking for a four-billion-dollar phone chit so he could call his lawyer back home. It was signed Commander BozoNuts of the Fourth Galaxy, but Sikes recognized the handwriting. He was impressed. He had never known Theo Miles to get up this early before.

Angie Perez came in a minute after Sikes, carrying a takeout coffee cup from which a tea bag tag fluttered. She looked over her sunglasses to squint at the doll as Sikes unthreaded its arm from one half of the cuffs.

"Since Grazer has the sense of humor God gave a dead frog," Angie said, "I'd have to say, as a detective, that you've been talking to someone else about your case." Then she waited for Sikes to come clean.

Sikes knew he had broken protocol by going to Theo about his concerns before he went to Angie, but now that the Petty case seemed to be under some kind of control he didn't see what harm could come of it. "Well, yeah," he admitted as he held the doll in his hands, wondering if it was too babyish for Kirby, "I sort of ran into my old partner and told him about it."

"Theo Miles?" Angie asked. Sikes nodded. "He's undercover Vice now, isn't he?" Sikes nodded again. "So you were hanging out someplace real nice where you just *happened* to run into an undercover vice cop? Sikes, what would your daughter think?"

"Okay, okay," Sikes confessed. "I went looking for him. I got spooked when Amy Stewart mentioned the possibility that the government might be involved. Theo's dealt with a couple of cases like that."

Angie shook her head and dropped her silver-lensed sunglasses into place again. "And what did good old Theo tell you?"

Sikes dangled E.T. by his upward-pointing finger. "That the government has better things to do these days than whack civilians. And that there ain't no such thing as little green men."

"Ah, not even in Vice?" Angie asked sarcastically.

Sikes ignored her. "And that Amy probably had taken a photograph of a secret airplane or something. Maybe got caught up in industrial espionage. Something like that."

Angie cocked her head to one side. "That's an interesting take on it. Industrial espionage. I hadn't thought of that."

"But it fits in with what you did think of," Sikes pointed out. "One of them stole something from the other. I suppose it doesn't matter if it's astronomical or industrial research. The motive's still the same."

Angie nodded. "Have you found out what Petty and Stewart were actually working on at the university?"

"Hey, I just got in. Gimme a chance."

"I'll give you one more day," Angie said. "But then you really do have to help me out on a couple of shootings on Robertson. Back of a restaurant stuff. Looks like two partners went for each other's throats, but it could have been a third-party setup."

"Yeah, okay," Sikes said noncommittally as he plunked E.T. on the corner of his desk.

Before Angie could get settled at her own desk next to Sikes's, a young khaki officer came into the ready room and handed her an interdepartmental document envelope. Inside was the photograph she had taken from Amy Stewart's office and copies of the APB flyer that the Documents Division had made from it. The khaki told her that Public Affairs would have the photograph to the television stations in time for the noon news and the newspapers in time for the afternoon editions.

Angie tossed the flyers onto Sikes's desk. "Note that I put *your* phone number on the bottom of it," she said with a cruel grin. "As soon as it shows up on the TV screen you're going to be hearing from every wacko in the city. You'll probably even get a couple of Black Dahlia confessions. I always do."

Sikes thanked her profusely and began to write out a list of the phone calls he had to make before that happened. Grazer walked in a few moments later carrying a briefcase and two newspapers and dressed in a three-piece pinstripe suit as if he were a bank manager on his way to a board meeting. He stopped to take a puzzled look at the E.T. doll, then saw the APB fliers and the framed color photograph.

"So that's Amy Stewart," he said grandly.

Sikes and Angie exchanged a glance of mutual forbearance. "That's what it says in the fine print," Angie agreed.

Sikes had an idea. "Hey, Bryon, you know everything. Come on over here."

Grazer straightened his collar in an attempt to act embarrassed and didn't fool anyone.

"Take a look at this guy beside her." Sikes pointed to the mystery man in the framed photograph. "He look familiar to you or what?"

Grazer gave the photograph careful scrutiny. "Well, yes. He does look like someone I've seen before."

"Good," Sikes said. "Who?"

Grazer frowned. "How should I know? He's familiar, that's all."

Angie got up and walked around to stand beside Grazer, looking at the photograph over his shoulder. "That's what we're all saying. But the question is, *why* is he so familiar? Do you recognize him from television, or—"

"Hardly," Grazer said imperiously. "I never watch it."

"Never?" Sikes asked suspiciously.

Grazer coughed. "Well, the news of course. CNN. PBS. Worthwhile programs."

Sikes and Angie raised their eyebrows together. "Okay," Angie said, "so it's someone either from the movies or from 'worthwhile' television."

Grazer laughed knowingly. "I pride myself on not having seen a movie made since nineteen sixty," he announced. "They really knew how to make them back then." He peered again at the E.T. doll. "What the heck is that thing supposed to be, anyway?"

Angie sighed. "Well, at least this is narrowing down the possibilities. If Grazer thinks he's familiar, the mystery man has got to be somebody from 'worthwhile' television."

"Impossible," Sikes said. "I never watch anything worthwhile, and I recognize him, too."

Angie shrugged. "Grazer, how about sticking the picture up on the bulletin board by the can with a sign asking if anyone can identify this guy?"

Surprisingly, Grazer shook his head. "That won't be necessary. I have an excellent memory. I took the Ryan Memory Control Course three times."

Angie made a face. "If you have such a good memory, why did you have to take it more than once?"

Grazer looked wounded. "Practice," he said in a hurt tone. "Practice." Then he took the photograph into his office.

"How *did* he manage to get his own office so fast?" Sikes asked as he watched Grazer leave.

Angie sat back at her desk. "What can I tell you? The guy knows how to fill out a requisition form just the way the Resource Allocation Office likes to read them." She made a rude kissing noise. Grazer spun around in his doorway. But he was too late. Both Sikes and Angie had their heads down and appeared to be working furiously at their desks, successfully hiding the snickers that threatened to escape them.

Sikes whistled as he made his first phone call to the Astronomy Department at UCLA. It was a good start to a good day.

But by the time he had finished that first call, he had no desire to whistle at all.

"Nothing makes sense," he reported to Angie as they stood by the ready room's decrepit Mr. Coffee. "The university says that Amy's specialty was"—he glanced at his notebook—"planetary nebulae."

"So?" Angie said. She stared intently at the spout of the electric kettle beside the stained coffee maker, watching for the first appearance of vapor.

"So she didn't use optical telescopes to study them. She used radio telescopes. In fact, she didn't even use them herself. She used computer tapes of what other astronomers observed."

The kettle began to make a sighing noise. Angie didn't look up. "I'm not getting it, Sikes."

"She couldn't have taken those photographs she showed me. They were optical plates."

"Then you were right. Petty took the photographs, and she stole them from him." She glanced at Sikes. "If she wasn't a suspect before, she sure is now."

"But Petty didn't take the photographs either," Sikes said. "He gave lectures in the history of astronomy for first-year students. The university says he didn't have any viewing time on any of their telescopes. Spent all his extra time helping people lobby the government for research funds."

Angie gave up on waiting for the kettle to boil. "Then where did the photographs come from, Sikes?"

"I don't know."

"In other words, a third party."

"With a humongous optical telescope," Sikes said. "I saw the plates. They were crisp, detailed. Whoever took them was using a major piece of equipment."

"How major? We talking a billion-dollar NASA thing?"

Sikes checked back through his book for the few notes he had taken in his first talk with Stewart. "Here it is. Amy said there was only one other telescope devoted to tracking Earth-crossers . . . a thirty-six-inch Newtonian at Kitt Peak."

"And have you phoned Kitt Peak, wherever and whatever the hell it might be?"

Sikes didn't bother to say no. He went back to his desk, stared at his phone for a moment, then yelled over the din of the other detectives working their own phones, "Bryon! Where's Kitt Peak?"

Grazer's muffled voice came from his office. "The observatory?"

"Yeah!"

"Arizona!"

"What's the area code?"

"Six oh two!"

"Thank you!" Sikes picked up the receiver and called Arizona information. "Who needs a computer?" he muttered.

By the time Sikes had finished his brief conversation with the Kitt Peak National Observatory office, Angie had returned to her desk with her tea.

"So?" she asked.

"The Spacewatch telescope has been shut down for the past ten days. Have to recalibrate it or something. Amy said the photographs were taken six days ago. That was three days ago. So it was shut down when the plates were made."

"Did you ask them if another facility could have taken the photos?"

"They're the only ones doing active asteroid tracking. They're really into it, too. You know you have a six-times-greater chance to be killed by an asteroid than in a plane crash?"

"Then we're all safe," Angie said. "I never fly. Where else could the photos have come from?"

"The guy I talked with said most asteroids are picked up by accident when they cut across exposures being made of other things, so there could be hundreds of telescopes that photographed . . . well, an asteroid. I told them I was trying to track down the source of some photographs I had seen of an asteroid." Sikes drummed his pen against his notebook. "You know, we're going to have to make a decision here."

"What's that?"

"Either we're actually dealing with astronomical photographs or we're not."

"You saw them."

"If it's up to me, then I'd say that's what we're dealing with."

Angie carefully lifted the tea bag from her tea and placed it on a folded-up paper napkin. "You realize that's moving us dangerously back to E.T. and his friends."

"What else could someone photograph with a telescope?" Sikes said.

"Like your old partner said: aircraft."

Sikes closed his eyes with an expression of pain. "Which brings us dangerously back to government involvement."

Angie turned her chair sideways to face Sikes. "Government involvement? That's what Stewart said. So all of a sudden she's gone from suspect to victim again?"

"I don't know." Sikes sighed. He flipped through his notebook. So far he had only used the first ten pages. The rest were blank. He shivered as he realized that there were people alive in the city today whose deaths would take up the rest of those pages. And how many more notebooks to come?

"Earth to Sikes," Angie said.

"All we have is a dead astronomer. No leads on the ballistics. No witnesses from the parking garage. The only person connected to the victim who might know anything about his death has disappeared. Past that, all we have is a mess of possibilities."

"But E.T.'s not one of them, right?"

"Of course not."

"And the government?"

"Theo said it just didn't make sense. And it doesn't."

Angie sipped her tea. "How many more phone calls do you have to make?"

Sikes looked at his list. "I thought I'd try the daughter in Australia." He looked up at the ceiling and yelled. "Bryon! What's the time difference to Australia?"

"Which city?"

Sikes looked at his notes. "Woomera!"

"It's in the middle! Seventeen hours ahead!"

"Thank you!" Sikes looked over at Angie. "You gotta admit he can be pretty impressive at times."

"As long as he's locked up in the next room, sure." She slid her chair back into place. "Tell you what. Talk to the daughter. See if she's come up with anything about anyone her father might have had a problem with, then give me a hand on the restaurant shootings till Stewart's picture goes out on the news. Otherwise, you're pretty well stuck."

Sikes made the call. He got an answering-machine message telling him that Isabel Petty had gone back to the United States for the funeral of her father. Sikes decided they mustn't have a lot of burglaries in Woomera if she could leave that kind of invitation. But just in case someone else was picking up her messages, he left his name and number.

"Okay," Angie began when he had finished. "We got two brothers-in-law. Both fifty-fifty owners in a sit-down catering joint on Robertson. We found 'em in the back room this morning. Both nailed. Both with a gun. Each gun had been fired, but—"

"I got it!"

Sikes and Angie turned to see Grazer come rushing out of his office, photograph in hand. "What did I tell you?" Sikes said to his partner. Grazer laid the photograph on Angie's desk so everyone could see it.

"This guy," Grazer said as he tapped the mystery man. "I

remembered where I saw him." He smiled and nodded in self-contentment and rocked back on his heels as if he had nothing more to say.

Angie smiled and nodded back. "Don't make me hurt you."

"Come on," Grazer said excitedly. "What's throwing us off is the sweater he's wearing. Picture him wearing a black outfit."

"He's a ninja?" Sikes said.

"No, no." Grazer drew three fingers across his forearm. "Three gold stripes on a black jacket. You can do it. It's easy."

"Grazer," Angie said calmly. "I have a gun. Tell me what this guy's name is right *now.*"

"I don't know his *name,*" Grazer said defensively. "I only said I remembered where I saw him. Where we *all* saw him."

"And that is . . ."

"Desert Storm!"

Angie rested her head in her hand. "Grazer, this is not a game. This is a murder investigation. If you waste one more goddamned *second* of my time, I'm going to write you up."

Grazer looked as if Angie had struck him in the face. "I told you. He was in the Desert Storm briefings. You know. Every day from the Pentagon. General Kelly would get up and talk about what had gone on in the past day. Then there'd be all these nameless guys standing around behind him, putting charts up, answering technical questions. Naval Intelligence guys in black uniforms. He was one of them. Three stripes on his jacket. That's a naval commander."

"You're sure about this?" Angie asked.

Sikes took the photograph for a closer look. "You know, I think he's got it." He felt as if someone had fired a gun two inches from his head, but he was convinced that Grazer was right. He really did know everything.

Angie stared at Sikes as if she were reading his thoughts again. "It doesn't have to mean what you think it means."

"A coincidence, right?" Sikes said without conviction. So much for Theo, he thought. So much for Angie. So much for my career.

"Could be," Angie said.

"What's that mean?" Grazer asked.

Sikes and Angie both turned to Grazer and said "Stay out of it" at the same time.

But Grazer slammed his fist on Angie's desk. Then winced as if he had done it too hard. "Now look here," he said with a quaver in his voice. "I helped you two out, and I expect a little cooperation in return."

Angie jumped to her feet the instant Grazer's fist made contact. "You want to help us out, Mr. Detective Three? Go find out what this guy's name is. *Then* you can expect some cooperation."

Grazer snatched the photograph from the desk and bustled out of the ready room. He was back in under two hours.

"His name is Franklin Arthur Stewart," Grazer announced as he reentered the ready room. "Commander, Naval Intelligence. Just as I told you." He tossed the original photograph down on Angie's desk, then dropped another photograph—a black and white 8 × 10—beside it. The new photo showed Desert Storm's General Kelly in front of a podium. Behind him was a large graph on an easel. And beside the easel was the mystery man.

"How?" Angie asked as she looked at the black-and-white print.

"I have a friend in the photo library at the *L.A. Times*," Grazer said smugly. "All their catalogs are on computer. Just punch in Desert Storm briefings, Pentagon, General Kelly. Took less than five minutes to find a shot with Stewart in it." He smiled, giving full vent to his air of superiority. "Such contacts *are* necessary for the efficient investigation of crimes, and I have cultivated them diligently." He folded his arms and waited by the two desks.

"Stewart," Sikes repeated. "You think it's her father or uncle or brother?"

"Looks too young to be her father," Angie decided. "Younger uncle or older brother."

"Now do you let me take part in this case or not?" Grazer asked with a hint of a threat in his tone.

Sikes shook his head. "I don't think you want in on this one, Bryon."

"And why not?"

Sikes was forced to say the very words he dreaded to hear. "We could be looking at some covert, government-sanctioned involvement."

Grazer's smug expression melted instantly. "Government-sanctioned involvement?"

"It really could be a coincidence," Angie said. "Especially if our suspect is related to this guy."

Sikes pushed himself away from his desk and stood up. He'd been sitting too long. "You're always telling me to go with my gut, right?" Angie agreed. "Well, my gut says it isn't a coincidence. My gut says I should go home and put on my blues and get back in a patrol car before Naval Intelligence comes looking for me."

Angie stood, too. She had abandoned any attempt at cajoling Sikes into feeling better. "Look, Sikes. If there is some sort of government connection to this, we'll take it to the captain and leave it in his hands. He deals with the political shit. That's his job."

"Good," Sikes said. "Let's go see him now."

"Uh-uh. First we need to be able to show that it's *not* a coincidence that an astronomy student's got some apparent contact with a government intelligence agency—especially since she was the one who said she was frightened of becoming involved with the government in the first place."

Sikes didn't like the sound of that. It felt like digging his own grave just a bit deeper and a bit faster. "How do we do that?" he asked.

Angie turned to Grazer. "If you can take the pressure, you can come on board."

"But we turn it over to the captain if things get out of hand, right?" Grazer spoke quickly and nervously.

"I'm not interested in getting anywhere near the feds," Angie said.

"What do you need?" Grazer asked with a barely concealed gulp.

Angie handed him the black-and-white photograph. "This was back during Desert Storm. Find out where this Commander Stewart is now, what his duties are. Whatever you can get. Can you do that?"

Grazer's eyes fluttered as he considered his options. "Well . . . I can phone the Pentagon and . . . and ask for him."

"He's in Intelligence, Grazer. Anything they tell you is apt to be a cover story or something."

Grazer chewed on his bottom lip for a few moments. "Well . . . there are a couple of computer data bases I can try. Not exactly kosher, but . . . they might be more accurate."

"Good," Angie said. "You do that." She waved him away, and he walked slowly to his office.

"So what do *we* do?" Sikes asked. He felt as nervous as Grazer sounded.

"You said that Theo Miles's worked on a couple of cases involving . . . the government?"

Sikes was disheartened by how quickly the term "the government" had become a euphemism for "government-directed murder." "Yeah, that's right."

"Then get him in here," Angie said. "If this is going the way you think it's going, we've got to start getting ready to cover our asses."

Sikes sat down heavily at his desk again. This wasn't a homicide investigation. It was a nightmare. "Why would the government want to kill an astronomer?" he asked. But Angie was already on her own phone, and the only one who heard his question was the doll on his desk.

And, for the moment at least, E.T. wasn't talking.

CHAPTER 9

GEORGE CARRIED HIS molecular probe like a weapon, more than sixty standard years of conditioning abandoned. He did not move with the slumped shoulders and aimless shuffle of a slave. He walked with intent and with purpose—exactly as he had been trained not to walk so he would not attract the attention of the Overseers.

But attention was what George wanted.

His footsteps clanked loudly along the open metal grillwork of the hull-access zone. With every fifty paces he passed another transparent portal. And now he knew why they were shaped like teardrops.

The ship wept.

With shame. With embarrassment. For all that had been allowed to happen within its hull.

But no longer, George swore. By victory or oblivion, the reign of the Overseers would end.

Another hull worker with a probe and backpack cowered as George came near, then stared in disbelief that the person who approached with such a forceful stride was not an Overseer. He touched his hearts in a blessing for the mad and the dead as George passed by.

George marched on, ignoring the hot and rapidly uprising wind that circulated the ship's atmosphere within these outermost areas. The pain of his recent wounds had been left far behind him. The mass of his own sealed backpack was no more than starlight on his back. *By victory or oblivion* was his only thought.

He encountered his first Overseer beside the tenth portal he came to. The black-uniformed traitor to his race was about George's age, meaning he was shipborn, and he wore two golden rank badges on his tunic. His spots were dark and formed swirls of interlinked commas. George memorized the pattern.

This line will end, he swore.

The Overseer patted his prod against his open hand and gave George a crooked smile in anticipation of sport. George knew the expression well. He had seen it on the savage youth who had used his prod on Susan.

"Do we have someplace important to go?" the Overseer asked with a hungry grin as George came closer, his stride increasing in length and speed.

But George said nothing. *By victory or oblivion.*

The Overseer braced his feet against the grillwork floor. "That's close enough, cargo!" He gripped his prod in his hand, glaring at George in a manner that would bring any slave of the holy gas to his knees at once.

But George was no slave of the gas. He was a child of the Overseers. Created by their own breeding program. Forged by their own legacy of hate and terror.

He was their match. He charged.

The Overseer saw the madness in George's eye a heartsbeat too late to save himself. He opened his mouth to call the alarm. His hands fumbled on the focus knob of his prod.

And the shaft of George's molecular probe swung through the air with all the force of George's charging mass behind it.

A pink froth from the Overseer's mouth sprayed up in the wind as his body, with a stifled bleat of pain, flew up against the hull and then slid down to the deck beside the portal. His prod clattered on the open deck. George shifted his molecular probe into his backpack and picked up the prod—for the first time in his life touching an Overseer's weapon. More than sixty years of conditioning defeated.

George moved back to the Overseer just as the Overseer staggered to his feet, leaning against the hull, wiping the blood from his chin with the sleeve of his uniform.

Astonishment marked his face. Yet a remnant of his former grin still played across his lips. No individual slave had ever bested an Overseer before.

But the expected expression of fear could not be found on George's face.

"They're going to recycle you bit by bit," the Overseer shouted threateningly over the circulating wind's rush.

"Give me your communications device," George said. His tunic sleeve fluttered in the rising breeze as he held out his hand, the fabric still stiff with the blood that had been spilled by the three-needled testing device.

The Overseer continued as if George had not spoken. "And then they'll feed you to yourself. You'll get smaller and smaller. More and more ravenous. If you have any children, they'll recycle—"

The prod whistled through the air and smashed against the Overseer's face, throwing his skull back against the hull with a hollow thud. The Overseer's eyes went glassy for a moment. He shook his head, then smiled in feral triumph through split lips as he saw George's confusion.

Hearts beating wildly, George stared at the prod. He could tell it was focused to fire, but it had not discharged when it had made contact.

"We're smarter than that, cargo," the Overseer hissed. He spit out a tooth, and it fell through the grillwork, rattling down to unseen depths. "The prods won't work on those who carry the words of power." He held up his wrist, exposing his obscene tattoo. "You're mine. You have no place to go. Nothing to gain."

"And nothing to lose," George said defiantly. "Give me your communications device."

In response the Overseer crouched and raised his hands in a *chekkah*-taught fighting stance. "Come and take it."

George stared at the creature before him as he prepared himself for what he knew he must do. In a faint echo of a childhood ritual he almost began to recite the prayer of guidance to Andarko as he pulled his probe from his backpack. But if there were gods on this ship, then they were locked in other sections of the cargo disk and had never yet walked with George.

He did not finish his prayer. He acted. For the first time in his life George fought back.

He feinted to the right with the tip of the molecular probe. The Overseer lunged. But his reflexes had been dulled by too many years of fighting only those Tenctonese who were influenced by the holy gas.

George changed his attack, withdrawing his probe and ramming the prod against the hull metal beside the Overseer. It fired gloriously, creating a rushing, crackling shower of blue-white sparks that billowed up in the wind, sending streamers of smoke through the open decks twenty feet overhead until the prod's charge was sapped.

George threw the weapon to the deck, and it rolled noisily away, slowly whining as it began to recharge.

The Overseer recovered his footing and stared at the pitted burn mark in the hull, then at George. "Another thousand prods, another thousand years, and you might burn your way through," he said. "It's over, cargo. You're good for nothing, bound for nowhere. Your life is meaningless. Your children and your wife will be *kard-ta* for the—"

The tip of the probe smashed against his throat, and the Overseer fell back, choking. George felt his arm resonate with unsuspected strength, as if he drew power from the thrumming of the power plants themselves. Beyond the portal the stars watched.

"I will watch you die myself," the Overseer gasped.

George swept the probe above his head. He felt the power of the ship move through him. Ten thousand years of rage. Ten eternities, infinities. He felt the ghosts of a thousand nameless races enter into him, fueled by uncountable outrages, measureless despair.

"Cargo!" the Overseer chanted. *"Cargo!"* The ultimate denigration. The person as object. As nameless *thing*.

And the probe swept down as if George were no more than a conduit for the wrath of the stars themselves.

The Overseer groaned and stumbled over exactly where George had intended him to go. His back was directly over the blemish George had burned into the hull metal. The perfection of the hull was now flawed.

George did his work.

He pressed the tip of his probe against the Overseer's chest, then touched the activator switch.

The Overseer tried to push the probe away. George punched him. Flesh to flesh for the first time in his life.

The Overseer's head smashed against the hull again. He took in great gulping breaths. He was stunned and no longer struggled.

George adjusted the position of the probe, pushing it closer and closer to the position of the hull blemish, digging into the Overseer's flesh.

And then the indicator light glowed green.

George waited as the signal went out to the mechanisms that controlled the ship. The Overseer moaned, still not aware of what George was doing. George held the probe steady against the Overseer's black-draped chest as if his arms and hands were made of the same substance as the hull.

The vibration began.

Moving closer.

The Overseer heard it.

The deck rattled. The hull sang, drowning even the rush of the wind. The dark shadow of a hull crawler passed over the portal. The Overseer looked down. Saw the green light. Felt the massive vibration. He pushed frantically at the probe. He squirmed. He squealed. George would not move. He was the ship.

The vibration stopped. The hull crawler was properly positioned. George didn't draw the probe away but kept the Overseer pinned to the section of the hull about to be repaired —about to have its molecules restacked.

There was one brief moment, between the cessation of the vibration and the start of the repair process, in which the Overseer's final terrified keen cut through all the levels of the hull access zone, carried by the air's circulation. And then the hull around his black-clad body glowed orange-white and the crackling and popping of molecular rearrangement began.

When it was clear that the Overseer could no longer pull away, George finally stepped back and removed the probe, no longer needed. The Overseer remained stuck to the hull, legs and arms flailing, mouth gaping, eyes bulging in a dance of terror in which no sound he made could be heard over the hull crawler's work.

At last the orange-white glow faded and the crackling ceased. The Overseer slumped. His head bobbed once, then no more. A thin string of blood and saliva slid slowly to the deck, twirled and whipped by the breeze, then fell through the grilles and down into the bottommost reaches of the ship.

Then George heard a soft metallic snapping sound and stared in wonder as the Overseer peeled slowly forward from the wall and collapsed facedown on the deck.

His back gaped open. As if his spine had been ripped from his flesh, leaving the white fingers of his ribs reaching up from his torn sides, cradling a pool of ruined organs, some still throbbing, not yet aware that the body they served was dead. Then a sudden hot draft howled up through the deck as if the pit of *am dugas* searched to find the *serdos* of the damned.

George looked at the hull where the blemish had been. Where the molecules had been restacked.

A spine of metal grew there, rippling with the bulbous outlines of partial organs and fractured bones that had been transmuted into hull metal by the crawler.

George found it fitting. The Overseer had become one with the lifeless hull of the ship, even as George had been charged with the power of the *lives* that had been lost here.

George smiled. A single sigh escaped his lips. He could smell the heat of the repair, the ozone residue of the prod, the stench of the Overseer's coagulating blood.

And it made him feel cleansed. It made him feel victorious. And it made him feel that he had only begun to fight back.

He turned over what was left of the Overseer's body and searched within the tunic for the communications device. Just as he ripped it from its holder on the Overseer's belt, he heard the sound of running feet.

He clamped the thin metal device and head strap in his hand, then raced off opposite the direction of whoever approached.

And he laughed as he ran, more full of life than he could ever remember.

There was no longer a choice between victory or oblivion. There could only be victory.

CHAPTER 10

WHEN THE PARKING ENFORCEMENT officer tried to get Sikes to move his Mustang from the red curb in front of Hollywood High, Sikes flashed his gold shield and went back to staring at the palm trees overhead. Nobody had ever told him he would have a day like this in the force, and for once he wasn't surprised. He doubted if anyone had gone through a day like this and survived to warn others.

Sikes heard a distant bell ring from inside the school and looked away from the trees to the bottom of the stairs at the school's main entrance. Using all his expertise at covert surveillance, he had carefully parked where Kirby would not be able to see him through the glass doors. If she were able to see him lying in wait, there were five other exits she could use to avoid him. But Sikes had made sure that he would see her at the bottom of the stairs before she would see him.

As it was, they caught each other's eyes at the same time. Kirby actually froze, and at any other time Sikes would have thought the shocked expression on her face was comical. But there wasn't room for humor in his life right now. He pushed against the floor of the car and slid up against his seat back, cupping his hands around his mouth as he shouted her name.

Kirby's shoulders sagged. She was jostled by the other

students streaming past her. But she clearly realized that there was no escape.

Sikes slid back down in his seat as Kirby said something to the two other students at her side—both girls, Sikes was glad to see—then trudged over to her father's car.

"Da-*deee*," Kirby said with a hugely exaggerated sigh, "why don't you just make me wear a T-shirt that says 'geek' on it?"

"They still use the word 'geek'?" Sikes asked. He smiled up at her and was surprised by how easy it was despite the long day. "At least I'm not in uniform like the last time, right?"

"Don't remind me," Kirby said, rolling her eyes again.

Sikes leaned across the passenger seat and opened the car door. "Get in," he said.

Kirby's mouth hung dramatically open. "But I'm going with my friends."

"Not today, kid. Something's come up."

"Really?"

Sikes shook his head. "Remember our deal," he said. "I'll never lie to you."

Kirby dropped her resistance. For all that she complained about Sikes's job, for all that he moaned about her clothing and jewelry, the bottom line was that there was a bond of mutual respect between them. How much longer that could last Sikes didn't know. But it was working today.

"Can I say good-bye to my friends?"

"Just be fast."

Kirby dropped her school bag into the backseat. She paused a moment. "Nothing's happened to Mom, has it?"

"This is nothing to do with Mom."

"Are you okay?" Kirby began to look worried.

"I'm fine," Sikes reassured her. "But I have to get you home." He stopped her from asking any more questions by adding, "I'll tell you all about it when you're in the car."

Kirby didn't lose her worried expression, but she nodded, then hurried back to the steps to speak with the two girls who waited for her, clutching their own schoolbooks to their chests. Kirby was back in under a minute, buckling her seat belt and staring expectantly at Sikes.

Sikes made a U-turn and got into line for the turn onto Highland. "Are you in trouble or something, Dad?" Kirby asked.

"Not really," Sikes said. "But I'm working on this big case

now, and . . . well, I'm going to have to put in some long hours." Go to the mattresses is more like it, Sikes thought.

"How long?" Kirby asked.

"A couple of days, maybe. But they'll be long days."

Kirby thumped back in her seat. "So you're, like, just dumping me at your place until Mom gets back."

Sikes gripped the steering wheel. "I just want to make sure you're inside and out of trouble while I'm at work tonight."

As soon as Kirby realized that her father was telling her that she wasn't going to be able to go out with her friends because he wanted her safely sidelined for the evening, she went over the top. The argument lasted until they reached Ventura. By then Sikes had punched the steering wheel twice, and Kirby, not to be outdone, had punched the glove compartment once, hard.

"You know what really sucks about this?" Kirby said angrily as she came to understand that there was nothing she was going to be able to say to make Sikes change his mind.

Sikes waited for her to tell him.

"You're lying to me." She leaned forward and turned to look at him so he couldn't avoid her. "So much for all this father-daughter honesty crap. You're not telling me the real reason why you're . . . you're locking me up. 'Cause that's what it is, you know. You're locking me up without a trial." She rocked back in her seat and folded her arms. "Locking me up for something *you've* done. Not me. Isn't fair. No way."

Sikes tried to keep his mind on driving. But Kirby had a point. He was locking her up for something he had done. And he *was* lying to her. But he really had no idea how he could tell his thirteen-year-old daughter that her father might be in danger of being tagged by a government-trained assassin. At least that's what Theo Miles had said was the worst-possible-cause scenario they faced. All of them.

Less than two hours ago they had had their council-of-war meeting: Sikes and Angie, Bryon Grazer, and, looking like he had just been fished from a reservoir, Theo Miles. The four detectives had crowded into Grazer's office and in hushed tones had discussed the status of the Petty case. Thanks to Grazer, the status hadn't looked good at all. "First of all," Grazer said as he arranged four neat stacks of file folders by the computer on his otherwise empty desk, "Commander Franklin Arthur Stewart is no longer part of Naval Intelligence. He resigned his commission six months ago."

"For real, or as a cover?" Angie asked. She leaned against a small credenza, jacket off, shoulder holster looking out of place over a pale pink cotton T-shirt.

"For real," Grazer said. He reached into one folder and pulled out a sheet of paper. "Here's a copy of the story that ran in the *Times* when he joined the Fuller Institute." Grazer visibly relished the questioning looks everyone gave him.

"So what the hell is the Fuller Institute?" Theo Miles asked. He was the only one who didn't realize that Grazer was incapable of not telling everything he knew.

"A private research institute for international affairs. Offices in Beverly Hills. It advises businesses and politicians on the current political climate in other countries and makes projections based on likely changes." Grazer pulled what looked to be a press packet from a stack and opened it on his desk. "It's all in this information folder. It's actually quite prestigious. The founder, Amanda Fuller, was a foreign policy advisor to Reagan. People say she was responsible for the hard line Reagan took toward—"

"Do they do any work in astronomy?" Sikes interrupted. He couldn't sit. He paced. Ignoring the looks Theo and Angie gave him.

Grazer ran his finger down a list from the packet. "Closest thing on their list of specialties is technology exchange," he read. "They're associated with research fellows at Brookings, MIT, and a bunch of international institutes."

"So where does that leave us?" Sikes asked.

Theo rolled his head from shoulder to shoulder, and Grazer winced as the clearly audible sound of popping vertebrae echoed in the small room. "You're right where I said you'd probably be," Theo said. "Private research group equals industrial espionage."

"What's the connection to Amy Stewart?" Angie asked. "Other than the possible coincidence that her father or uncle or brother or whatever is employed by the Fuller Institute."

Theo shook his head. Sikes was concerned by his ex-partner's bloodshot eyes and slightly slurred speech. But then, he himself had shown up for his first day as a detective with a hangover the size of the Grand Canyon, so it wasn't really out of place that Theo might be suffering from one now. Especially since his regular shift didn't start till ten and he had come in this afternoon as a favor to Sikes.

"Try this," Theo said, characteristically rubbing his face in thought. "It might even make sense of the coincidence part. The Fuller Institute is working on . . . something to do with technology exchange for one of its clients. Corporate, political, foreign, it don't matter. Part of that technology involves a new aircraft or spacecraft . . . hell, it might even be something to do with optics—you know, what they put on spy satellites and planes." Theo nodded to himself as he saw the others listening carefully. "So the ex–Commander Stewart has some photographs that he wants analyzed. Maybe they're secret. So who can he trust?"

"His family," Angie said. "Amy Stewart."

"You got it," Theo said. "She's an astronomer. She knows about photographs. She can take a look at them, say whether they're real or whatever. But then—"

"Dr. Petty gets hold of them," Sikes said.

Theo shrugged grandly, palms up. His story was done.

"And they have to take the old guy out to get the photographs back," Angie said. "Which means that the killer could have been someone hired either by the institute's client or by the institute itself."

Sikes felt relieved. "And Amy could just have been caught in the middle."

"Remember what I said about your pants, rook," Angie warned.

Sikes felt his cheeks flush as his ex-partner and his new partner exchanged knowing glances. Grazer just looked puzzled.

"So what do we do?" Grazer asked, looking at Angie.

"We sound out the institute," she said. "And thanks to you, we've got a real good reason to. We phone up Commander Stewart and tell him Amy is missing and ask if he can use any of his contacts or resources to help us find her. Yeah, that should get us started. Should be pretty easy to tell if he's up to anything." She left the credenza and went over to Grazer's desk, fanning out all his files, to his immediate displeasure. "How'd you come up with all this stuff so fast?"

Grazer compulsively straightened each folder as Angie finished with it. "Simple, really. I got Stewart's service record through a military personnel data base."

"You've got a friend in the Pentagon, right?" Sikes asked.

Grazer let his face go blank. "I have a friend's password that let me access the system through my own computer," he said stiffly. "But that's all I'm going to say."

"That I doubt," Angie said.

Grazer sniffed loudly and pretended to ignore the insult. "Then, once I had the service record, it was easy to cross-correlate for news clippings and the material we have in the research library."

Sikes was surprised. "We have a library? Where?"

"In the basement," Grazer said.

"So when do we sound them out?" Sikes asked, looking at the other two detectives standing next to Grazer's desk.

"The sooner the better," Angie said. "We should go together."

"Hey! How about me?" Grazer asked indignantly.

"Three of us might be a bit too much police presence," Angie said. "How about if you go back to your computer and your network of friends and see what you can get for us on who the institute's clients are?"

Grazer dug through his files and pulled out a sheet of computer paper. "Here's the list of them. What else?"

Theo Miles took the sheet and began to scan it.

"Well," Angie said, "then I guess you can come with us and, uh, cover the back door or something. Just in case we make any of the people at the institute nervous."

Grazer's eyes brightened. "I can certainly do that."

Then Theo passed the client list over to Angie. "Who's going to be making who nervous?" he asked. "Check this out. Near the middle."

Angie looked at the sheet for a few moments, then passed it over to Sikes.

Sikes groaned. There was no escape from his worst fear. The three middle entries on the Fuller Institute's list of clients were the United States Air Force, the Navy, and the State Department.

"What did I tell you?" Theo said. "What you want to bet it's spy versus spy?"

Angie didn't answer. Her sharp eyes studied Theo, assessing his condition. Sikes didn't want to know what she was thinking. "Sikes tells me you've been on cases where the government might have been involved in a sanctioned homicide," she said.

"That's why I crawled out of my warm bed to be here this afternoon," Theo said.

"What would you recommend we do?"

"I'd recommend you do nothing. You do not want to become involved in any kinda shit like this, no way. You want my opinion, you get yourselves over to the captain's office, and you just sit there like your legs are useless, and you stay there until he's called the FBI."

"Why the FBI?" Angie asked.

"Every time FBI guys get involved in something they shouldn't get involved in, they know it inside of an hour. Washington keeps 'em on a real short leash. All the government-involved cases I stumbled into got transferred over to the FBI and then got conveniently lost. And that's what you want to do right now. Be real sure you haven't got anything at all to do with this one."

"Why not?" Grazer asked. "We are the police, you know."

Theo leaned over Grazer's desk. "Because, junior, if you start messin' around with government hit men, the next thing you know they're going to come sniffin' around for *you*. Even if you are the goddamned police."

Everyone turned to look at Angie. She picked up Grazer's phone. "I'll call the captain," she said as she punched in an extension number. "We'll set up a meeting."

The captain was going to be back at the station house by five. Theo said he was going back home to bed, and he'd appreciate it mightily if no one put his name on any of the reports. Grazer, looking even paler than usual, took his rolled-up shoulder holster and gun from a desk drawer and said he was going down to the target range. Sikes looked at his watch. There was no way of knowing what would happen after they met with the captain. "I'm going to get my daughter at school," he said. "Think I should bring her back here?"

Theo patted Sikes on the back. "Why, that's almost paranoid of you, kid. But Kirby'll be okay." He smiled sardonically. "Tell her the G-men will only be gunnin' for her dad this time."

Theo was laughing as he left Grazer's office.

No one else was.

"I know it's not fair," Sikes told Kirby as he inched along Ventura toward Studio City. "But you've got to cut me some slack on this one." Kirby sat in glacial silence. "I've got to go back to work. If I hadn't picked you up now, then I wouldn't have been there when you got home. Hell, I wouldn't even know *when* you got home."

"Daaad, I can look after myself."

Sikes tried to think of everything his own parents might have said to him in a similar situation so he could be sure not to say the same things to his daughter. But it wasn't working.

"I worry about you, Kirby. I want to make sure you're going to be safe."

He felt Kirby's eyes digging into him. "Dad? Are you sure you're not in some kind of trouble?"

"No, not at all," Sikes said.

"No lying, remember?"

Sikes gritted his teeth. "Okay. A little bit of trouble. I'm in a little bit of trouble." He made the turn off Ventura, heading toward his apartment building.

"*Dangerous* trouble?"

Sikes hated this conversation. Kirby was just a kid. She shouldn't be worried about anything like this. "Aw, look," he said, "I've got my new partner in on this, Theo's helping out, we're all going to meet with the captain—"

"The Captain?" Kirby said, her voice rising. "Did you shoot somebody?"

"No, I didn't shoot somebody," Sikes said as he made the turn into his building's driveway and hit the remote for the garage door. "I just got involved with a complicated case and . . . it looks like we're going to need some help, that's all."

"From who?"

"The FBI," Sikes said. He drove down into the parking garage.

"Cool," Kirby said, impressed.

That's better, Sikes thought. Trust a cop's daughter to trust in authority.

"Dad? Like, no one's trying to kill you or anything, are they?"

So much for no lying. "God, no, honey. Nothing like that." He turned in his seat to back into his parking spot, glad to be able to avoid her eyes. He'd get Kirby settled with some pizza money and her homework and be back on his way in ten minutes max.

"You're sure?"

Sikes pulled on the parking brake and killed the ignition. Then he undid his seat belt and gave Kirby a hug. "At least you know what it's like to worry about someone. But no, no one's out to get your old dad. I just might have to spend a lot of time at the station house tonight, that's all. There's nothing for me to worry about, and there's absolutely nothing for you to worry about either. Okay?"

Sikes sat back. Kirby's expression was wide-eyed shock, as if she hadn't believed a single word he said.

"Come on, Kirby. Don't make this—"

He heard the unmistakable click of a .45 automatic an instant before he felt the cold ring of its muzzle kiss his neck, just under his skull.

"Detective Matthew Sikes?" a muffled voice asked.

"Don't hurt my daughter," Sikes warned.

"Well, that's going to be up to you now, isn't it?"

Sikes started to turn to face his attacker. But a stunning shock of pain burst against his head as a field of stars exploded across his vision. And just before everything went dark, he thought he saw something move against those stars.

Coming closer.

CHAPTER 11

IN THE OPEN CORRIDORS George walked as a slave. His gait was slow. His head hung listlessly. He had abandoned his molecular probe, yet he moved as if its backpack still weighed him down. Thus disguised he made his way to a water hub.

The routine of the ship had not yet returned to normal following the previous *crayg*'s unprecedented torrential release of holy gas. As always, the main corridors were filled with Tenctonese moving from one work station to another or to and from their dormitories according to their shifts. But everyone moved sluggishly, still recovering from the gas overdose. And many were moaning. The sound of their combined voices was like a dirge.

But George knew it would not last long.

Under his tunic he carried the dead Overseer's communication device. It was the same as that which his brother Ruhtra had worn when he had saved Susan and George by leading them into the hidden service tunnels. The Overseers used the small devices to talk to each other from one corridor to another, and to the protected section of the ship where their own quarters were. George had often seen the devices in use as the Overseers gathered data—the location of certain facilities, the actual work schedule for a worker stopped at random in the corridors. It was for exactly that type of information that George had taken the device.

He came to the water hub that linked nine levels near the section of the ship that housed the power plants. The constant background thrumming of the enormous machines was louder here. Vacuum energy extractors, the Elders called them, as if energy could be extracted from nothing. George didn't think it could, but George didn't really care about what the Elders knew. He had come here not to be closer to the power plants but to have many possible avenues of escape open to him in case his plan didn't work.

He trudged down one open metal stairway until he was on the catwalk that ringed the water hub's eighth level. He continued moving along it until he came to a corridor entrance that no one had recently entered. He stepped into it quickly, letting his eyes adjust to the low level of light inside. He peered down into its misty depths. The length of the corridor was deserted.

George walked rapidly down the corridor to a structure support that angled out from the wall and flattened himself against it. If anyone looked down into the corridor from the catwalk, he would be invisible in the gloom. If anyone looked up the tunnel from the end of the corridor, he would be lost in the glare from the brighter light of the hub beyond. He slipped the communications headband over his head and adjusted it so the device covered his right ear valley. His cupped his hand to it as the Overseers did. Then he spoke gruffly: "Location request."

A voice responded so quickly that George almost began to run in fear. It was harsh, almost the type of voice he would expect a machine to have if a machine could talk. "Proceed," it said.

George spoke again, as loudly as he dared. "Cargo designation: Ruhtra, Family: Heroes of Soren'tzahh, Family: Third Star's Ocean."

The harsh voice took longer to reply this time. George wondered if whoever it was had to consult some master list. If the delay was too long, though, George was prepared to throw the device away and flee.

But the voice replied before panic set in. "Dormitory ninety-one, segment four hundred, berth eighty-seven, platform three."

George stifled the automatic impulse to say "Thank you." He had never heard an Overseer acknowledge a communication in that way, and he stopped himself just in time. He leaned forward from the structure support and checked the corridor again. Still clear. For a moment he considered using the device to find the location of his son, Finiksa. But two such requests for members of the same lineage might seem suspicious to whoever had spoken to him. There would be time to find Finiksa after joining the rebellion. And it was fitting that it would be Ruhtra through whom he would join.

George dropped the communications device to the deck and stepped on it, grinding it into rubbish for the scavengers. If he came to a point where he needed another such device, then he would simply kill another Overseer. He found the very fact that he could have a thought like that a sign of his impending freedom. As he ran back to the water hub, he was already planning his route to dormitory ninety-one.

It took George almost an hour of deliberately slow walking to reach Ruhtra's dormitory. He successfully passed three Overseer checkpoints along the way. None of the Overseers was interested in him, and after George had passed through the second pair unchallenged he felt invincible. As he approached the third pair, just outside the main corridor leading to dormitory ninety-one, he even walked up to the Overseers as if he had seen them wave him over. But they simply waved him on, continuing to watch the other gray-clad slaves that moved in an unending chain behind him.

Dormitory ninety-one was almost indistinguishable from George's own dorm, and he easily found corridor segment four hundred. Most of the Tenctonese who lived in this part of the ship were on their rest shift, and the corridor was crowded. Groups of children ran as best as they were able past the tired adults who gathered in small groups. Podlings cried. The air was thick with the smell of old meatgrowth. And for the first time George saw a dormitory as he imagined the Elders must see them, against memories of the open fields of Tencton, a sky of sweet air higher than the ship was thick, a place with room for all the planet's tribes to have vast tracts of land and clear water all for themselves.

For the first time George understood why their religions stressed acceptance. It was either that or madness.

The closer George moved to berth eighty-seven, the more he was stared at by the others who lived in that segment. He did not belong with them, and they knew it.

He came to Ruhtra's berth. The second and third platforms were empty. Gently George shook the shoulder of the frail female who slept on platform one. Her spots were faded by too much sleep.

"Pardon me, I am trying to find the person who sleeps here on platform three. Do you know him?"

The old female didn't respond. George tugged her over. Her face was lined and haggard. "His name is Ruhtra. Can you help me?"

The old female's hand shot out and grabbed George by his neck. Startled, he felt the cold ridges of a crate-moving claw press against his skin. Then two other pairs of hands grabbed his arms and pulled him away from the sleeping platform. George tensed with fear, yet he was ready to fight to the death with the Overseers who had captured him.

But they were not Overseers. They were other Tenctonese, dressed just as he was.

Both of the Tenctonese who had grabbed him were *binnaum-ta,* and they threw George against the corridor wall and kept him there. One leaned against George, pushing his forearm against George's throat. Behind the *binnaum-ta,* the old female rose from her platform. She held her cargo-handler's claw up so George could take a good look at the metal spikes that helped cargo workers keep their grips on heavy crates. He had no idea how she had managed to smuggle the tool from a work station. Perhaps he was not the only one to rob an Overseer.

"Why are you here?" the old female croaked, keeping the claw in view.

George had no quarrel with her or her companions. "I am trying to find Ruhtra," he said, as calmly as he could.

"Why?" she asked. A crowd was gathering in the closed-in corridor.

"Look at my spots," George said. "That's why." His spots and Ruhtra's clearly showed they were related.

The *binnaum* that dug his arm into George reached up with his other hand and picked at George's spots. George tried to twist away.

The old female stepped closer. "Overseers look for Ruhtra. You look for Ruhtra. Maybe you're Overseer." She spat the final frictive click in the word as if it were something to gag on. "Show your wrists."

George held up both his hands and felt his sleeves tugged down. Sharp fingernails scratched roughly at the skin of his wrists in an attempt to peel off any covering he might have there.

The *binnaum-ta* stepped away. George rubbed at his throat.

"Not your dormitory," the old female said.

"It is important I find Ruhtra," George told her.

"If Ruhtra hides from the Overseers, you'll not find him soon."

"I must," George said.

The old female leaned closely against George, making him lower an ear valley to her lips. "Go back to where you belong," she whispered hoarsely. "There is not much time."

George stared at the faint pattern her faded spots made. He looked again at the *binnaum-ta*. *Binnaum* spots were hard to read—they were larger, more melted together in the blending of the other two sexes. But the similarities to the old female's pattern was clear.

George dropped his own voice to a whisper. "Are these your children?" Both *binnuam-ta* were clearly older than George. By rights they should be nowhere near their mother.

A smile flickered on the old female's face. She leaned forward again. "Gather the children," she said softly. "That is what we were told, that is what you should be doing as well. Don't look for your brother. Look for your children."

George felt his spots pucker. Had some order gone out on a network he had no knowledge of? *Gather the children?* Why? Unless . . . of course, he thought, the rebellion is beginning. The rebels have sent out word that we are to gather our children around us. But how will everyone know where their children are?

"How is this possible?" George asked.

But the old female held her fingers to cover her lips. *"Keer'chatlas,"* she whispered. Then she returned to her platform, and her *binnaum-ta* stepped in front of it, thick arms folded over muscular chests, standing guard.

Unsettled by the encounter, George pushed his way through the crowd that had gathered, leaving the dormitory-corridor segments from a direction different from the one by which he had arrived. If the Overseers were searching for Ruhtra, then he wasn't sure why he himself hadn't been stopped at any of the Overseer checkpoints he had passed. Certainly his spots were similar enough that if the Overseers had been shown Ruhtra's spot pattern, then George would have been just as likely to have been recognized. No matter how invincible he felt, George wasn't keen to trust the Overseers to make the same mistake twice.

Five sectors away from Ruhtra's dormitory George fell in with a group of scavengers walking listlessly on patrol. He edged his way into the middle of the group and walked with them for cover, trying to use the time to focus his thoughts. If he felt he had the time, he could go back to the hull access zone, reclaim his molecular probe, and hunt for another Overseer. Enough time might have passed that a request for the location of Finiksa might not appear to be related to the earlier request for Ruhtra's location. But as he recalled the look on the old female's face, George felt sure that there was no time even for that.

Gather the children. Gather the children. The phrase kept running through George's mind. For the rebellion leaders to have put out such a command to be passed on to everyone, they must have been convinced that the origin of the command could not be traced back to them by the Overseers. And since the Overseers had the ability to make any victim reveal his or her or *binn* secrets, the leaders must have determined that the Overseers would no longer have *time* to question enough Tenctons.

It was going to happen soon, George knew. Whatever was to happen, it would happen within a *crayg,* perhaps even a shift. Something was going to happen.

He stayed with the scavenger patrol, his mind churning with indecision. Should he return to Susan? No. She was on a work shift, and he would never be able to gain entrance to her station. Should he return to the hull and retrieve his probe to have as a weapon? No, that seemed wrong as well. If the rebels were going to gain control of the ship, then it would likely have to undergo a translation back into its superluminal mode shortly after so it could begin the long voyage back to Tencton. The hull would not be the place to be during that translation.

There was only one thing that George felt he could do—the

first thing he had set out to do. Find Ruhtra. And, George realized, he knew just where he would find him.

George made his way back to the service tunnels. He returned to the hidden entrance near his own dormitory, then slipped inside when the corridor was clear. If Ruhtra was part of the rebellion and hiding from the Overseers, then he would be hiding in these tunnels. George was certain of it.

He retraced the route he had taken with Susan on the *crayg* they had seen Buck in the water hub. Ruhtra had taken them to an intersection of eight tunnels then, George remembered. Perhaps that was a meeting place. Perhaps that was where Ruhtra hid now. No matter; it would be where George would begin his search.

He moved through the half-height tunnels with confidence. He had killed an Overseer. He had confirmed that the rebellion was nearing its moment of truth. And he was aware of a whole new environment in the ship that not even the Overseers seemed to know about.

He found the intersection where Ruhtra had talked with him. He stopped and looked around carefully. All eight lights glowed by the alien signs beside each tunnel entrance. In the multiple shadows the lights cast, George looked to see if any supplies had been hidden, anything at all that might indicate that someone hid here. But there was nothing.

George noticed a twist of cables in the center of the intersection and sat down upon it. From this vantage point he could look into each tunnel entering the intersection. Ruhtra wasn't here now, but surely someone must come through eventually. And sooner rather than later, given that the rebellion was so close.

George sat very still, breathing deeply, feeling his hearts calm. It felt so good to be doing something at last. So good to be—

"Stangya?"

The word was a hissed whisper. George couldn't be certain he had heard it.

He stood up as best he could in the low-ceilinged space. "I am Stangya," he said in a marginally louder whisper.

A shadow moved between two tunnel entrances, and Ruhtra emerged from between two large vertical pipes. The space between them was deeper than George had realized.

George picked his way across the wires and pipes that snaked across the floor of the intersection and hugged his brother.

But Ruhtra kept his own arms at his side. "You are mad to have come here," he said.

"No," George said. "I have joined the rebellion." His hands gripped Ruhtra's shoulders. "Ruhtra, I have killed an Overseer."

Ruhtra's spots blanched, even in the pale tunnel lights. "Leave here at once. The Overseers will be looking for you."

George grinned, swollen full of new purpose. "No, they won't. The rebellion is almost here, Ruhtra. This is our *crayg* of freedom."

Ruhtra pulled away from his brother and held his hand to his eyes. He seemed to shrink with weariness. "You were never supposed to be part of it," he said.

George didn't understand Ruhtra's reaction. "But I am now," George said. "I *want* to be part of it."

"It's not that simple." Ruhtra collapsed back on a coil of cables. "The rest of us have had years of training. Learning how to keep the Overseers from infiltrating."

George shrugged. "How hard can that be? Their wrists give them away."

Ruhtra shook his head. "They have machines that can remove the tattoos, Stangya. They have devices you're not aware of, devices we've never dreamed of. Not even the Elders understand all of them."

"You don't understand, Ruhtra. I *killed* one. I am part of this, part of you. Part of our people's fight."

But Ruhtra shared no part of George's joy. He only stared at his brother. "I'm so tired, Stangya."

"Then let me fight *with* you."

Ruhtra closed his eyes briefly, then opened them. "You won't be fighting, Stangya. You killed an Overseer. They've probably been tracking you ever since."

George felt a sudden chill trickle through him. "No. You are wrong. How could that be possible?"

Ruhtra looked away from George into the distance. It was like talking to an Elder close to death. "Do you think that in more than a century of this . . . this *lesh* that you are the only one of us to have attacked and killed an Overseer? Do you not remember the stories? The rebellion against the mining controllers on Tromus IV? The battle with the rogue ship?"

George lowered his head in confusion. "I have heard . . . none of those."

Ruhtra looked at his brother in despair. "Because this was not your battle! This was not your war! You were to be free of it to raise your children and honor your wife and carry our line forward!"

George froze as Ruhtra's words echoed through all the tunnels. His voice cracked. "Are you . . . are you not afraid that they will hear you?"

Ruhtra only stared at him. A sudden blue flare erupted against one vertical wall section. Sparks flew. Then another flare, and another. George jerked back and forth, trying to find a place free from the blue fire and sparks that filled the air. But there was no place to go.

The intersection was being sliced open by small mining beams like the one used by the Overseers in the water hub.

"Noooo!" George cried, his voice lost in the howl of the spitting fire.

But Ruhtra did not cry out or move from his position. His face flashed and flickered with blue light, but he showed no fear. He was beyond any reaction. George cried out for the both of them.

The first opening was kicked through in seconds. The edge of the metal hole glowed red. A black shape appeared behind it, then stepped through, one black boot after another.

It was Coolock. A beam weapon in his hand. A communications device around his head.

The Overseer cupped a hand to his ear valley. "Call off the search. We have traced both of them." He grinned in an evil way at George. "Thank you, Stangya. Mighty killer of Overseers." He stepped closer. "Did you really think you could use our own communications to locate your brother?" He swung the beam weapon high and hit George in the ribs, making him drop to one knee, gasping for breath. "Do you think all our checkpoints looked the other way by accident?" He kicked George in the stomach. George fell against the pipes and cables, choking on vomit.

Coolock squatted down by George and lifted his head by the neck of his tunic. "But do not think that you will be executed for your crimes, cargo. That is not going to happen." He slammed George's head against the intersection floor, then lifted it again. "You will wish it to happen, but it won't. Unless you are much luckier than you are now."

George stared at the Overseer through blood-flooded eyes.

"You see," Coolock said with a smile, "I'm not going to punish you. I'm going to *play* with you." He let go of George's tunic, and George's head fell to the deck again. The last thing George saw was Coolock cupping his hand to his ear valley again. And the last words he heard were Coolock saying, "Tell them we have two more players for the Game."

Then oblivion claimed him.

CHAPTER 12

ALL LIVING CREATURES had two hearts, but the ship had dozens. Moodri could recognize the pulse of each.

The power plants sent their subtle vibration through every atom of deck and bulkhead, infiltrating even the dreams of those who slept within their web of infinite energies.

Huge masses of air circulated up against the outer hull to endlessly drift down again from the uppermost levels, through the cleansing 'ponic jungles, and down to the bottom cargo-loading decks, becoming more fetid and stale with each level they descended.

Water thrummed through hidden pipes—hot water, cold water, scalding steam, waste for the treatment plants, salt water for disposal.

Wires crackled with transmitted energy and the exchange of information only machines could read.

Light sped through tubes that could be bent to any shape to flood out through the overhead banks.

The hull crawlers thundered over the outside of the ship like heavy, slow parasites overwhelming a corpse.

And other sounds, perhaps from machines and creatures and cargoes uncounted, resonated dimly from the hidden sectors of the cargo disk and the cut-off bulk of the distant main hull that housed the stardrive and long-forgotten secrets.

Moodri knew them all. And on this *crayg*, as he walked the corridors, head kept low, he heard them all and was heartened because all these sounds, all these pulses were unchanged.

The ship continued, which meant that so close to its destruction, after millennia of plying the dark ranges, it did not sense what fate approached it.

Moodri walked with a strength that belied his years. For more than a century he had fought against the shifting gravity fields of this ship. He had worked at forced labor on more planets than he could easily remember. And he had dreamed of the precise hour when the nightmare would stop. A dream that was close to fulfillment, except for the blindness of those on the council who had once shared his dream with him.

Moodri still could not believe what Vondmac and Melgil had told him. How Buck's task had been handed to a *jabroka*-transformed squad of twenty howling throwbacks to a legacy of Tencton that should never have been revived.

The council's new plan was useless. Moodri did not even have to bother asking the goddess for insight in this matter. Only Buck could bring about the dream of freedom. And Moodri was the only one who could send Buck on his way.

Moodri walked on, his head bent in prayer, concealed by his white robe's hood. He heard a commotion up ahead, near the intersection that led to the infirmary where Buck was being treated. But Moodri did not look up. His own plan was well laid, and he would not deviate from it.

An Overseer slammed him against the corridor wall ten feet further on. It was a female, large of spot and snarling with rage.

"On your way to the recycler, you Tencton *sta?*" she shouted at him.

Moodri did not have to pretend to be startled or frightened. He bowed his head as if unable to speak.

He felt the female's coarse hands search against his robes, looking for contraband. She found nothing. Then she cupped Moodri's chin and made him look up at her.

"What's your pattern, *sta?*"

Moodri made no move to pull back his hood.

The Overseer bared her teeth. "Good," she breathed. "I like cargo with something to hide." She reached out and ripped away the cloth that covered Moodri's scalp, then twisted his head back and forth to examine his pattern. She laughed scornfully at him. "You must be sleepwalking." She pushed his head against the wall in dismissal.

In his mind Moodri sought the peace of the goddess. On his body he arranged an expression of confusion. It went well with the camouflage he had painted on his head.

Spot enhancement was nothing new among the two primary sexes of the Tenctonese. *Binnaum-ta,* always functional, were another matter as always. But when males wished to recapture their appearance of youthful virility, when females wished to disguise how close they might be to the end of their cycles, it was not unknown for members of either sex to darken their spots with dyes and powders. And though the tonal choices were not as extensive on the ship as they had been on Tencton, the powders ground from the dried roots of certain 'ponics plants and fixed in place with subtle creams and lotions were enough to take years off the age of any male or female. Or, in Moodri's case, to add them.

Almost all of Moodri's scalp was pale and spotless pink. Here and there an indistinct mottling of tan showed through, but it was only a faint shadow of what had been—the mark of an Elder who slept most of his days, losing more of his vitality with each unconscious moment until the day his spots would fade completely and his life would end.

Beneath the powders and lotions on Moodri's scalp the proud trident of Family: Heroes of Soren'tzahh and the bold crest stroke of Family: Third Star's Ocean were nowhere to be seen. The female Overseer had no interest in him, and she shoved him out of her way. The recycling squads could deal with him.

Moodri stumbled forward a few steps, replaced his hood, then continued on, head bowed again in seeming prayer. But his eyes searched ahead for the reason for the confusion before him.

Five Overseers stood together. Each held a prod. But where they stood was not an ordinary doorway or corridor intersection. Moodri crossed to the opposite side of the corridor and kept well away from the Overseers. He glanced into the jagged opening and saw with concern that the opening had been cut into the corridor wall by beams of coherent energy. He did not have to see what lay beyond to know that a service tunnel intersection had been exposed. The five Overseers were part of an invasion squad that was going into the tunnels through the new opening one at a time.

Almost imperceptibly Moodri picked up his pace. For years the Overseers had ignored the tunnels except for occasional scheduled sweeps, thinking that they controlled or had sealed all access hatches. But for them to have cut their way into the system here, Moodri knew, meant that they had finally discovered that the tunnels were in use. And depending on whom they had pulled from those tunnels, they might even have learned that the time of the rebellion was near.

Moodri offered up a prayer to the goddess that all had not been lost. If the Overseers had discovered the planned event of rebellion, then they could not help but realize that any such action undertaken *before* the ship was to translate back into superluminal space must have as its goal the landing of the cargo disk on one of this system's planets. If the Overseers managed to send out a fleet warning message to that effect, then other ships would be certain to arrive in this system within two Tencton years, if not sooner.

But Moodri had been cast aside by the council, and there was no one he could seek out to learn why the Overseers had cut into the tunnels here, no way he could learn who had been captured. Only by closely observing what the Overseers did in the next shift would he have a chance to guess what actual harm might have been done.

I pray it was only children playing that attracted the Overseers' attention, Moodri thought. Just as I and the others did when we first came aboard.

He walked on. More than ever the rebellion needed Buck. He was certain of that. He reached the intersection and turned down the corridor that led to the infirmary. He staggered in shock.

The Overseer's prisoners lay on the corridor floor, arms and legs bound in coils of memory wire. Moodri recognized the patterns of their spots at once. They were those of his nephews, Ruhtra and George.

And if George had been caught in the tunnels, if George had learned the secret of the rebellion, then it was only a matter of heartsbeats until the Overseers tortured that secret from him.

Moodri stood before the two bodies on the deck. Both of his nephews were still breathing, obviously only stunned by the prods. He found himself wishing that both had died.

"What are you staring at?"

An Overseer grabbed Moodri from behind, spun him around, and tore the hood from his head again. Moodri blinked vaguely at the Overseer. The Overseer pushed him on. "This one's got one foot in the vats already!" he called to his fellow traitors. They laughed as Moodri stumbled forward. One tried to pull at his robes and trip him, but Moodri pulled away with a move that looked like a simple clumsy misstep rather than the graceful pivot of self-defense that it was.

He continued on his way to the infirmary. His hearts mourned the loss of his nephews, but they were in the hands of the goddess, and there was nothing more he could do for them. Now, more than ever, everything was up to Buck.

The infirmary door opened to reveal chaos. But Moodri could not turn back. He entered and was immediately caught up in the midst of cargo specialists rushing in all directions, and his ear valleys were assaulted by the cries of the wounded.

Along one wall three Overseers lay in treatment harnesses, the bands of soft fabric keeping their bodies suspended above the sleeping platforms beneath them. All three had had some part of their black uniforms ripped away. All three were spattered with pink blood and glittered with heavy sprinklings of antiseptic crystals. They were not attended by the gray-uniformed cargo specialists, though. Instead, two other Overseers worked on them with glowing, sparking medical devices much more compact than any Moodri had seen before.

Other Overseers toiled at the main stations, hastily preparing bandages and medicines. A hand grabbed Moodri's arm and pulled him away from them. Moodri turned to face Cathy.

"They do not need your blessings, Elder. They—" Cathy Frankel stopped talking as she recognized Moodri's features despite the disguise of his false spots. Admirably, she concealed any shock she felt. "The boy is over there," she said curtly, indicating a smaller sleeping platform away from the frantically working Overseers.

Moodri looked over and saw Buck lying on his side, groggily conscious, staring at the Overseers with dazed attention. "What has happened?" the Elder asked before Cathy could rush away.

"*Jabroka*," she said as if pronouncing an obscenity. "Mine workers must have smuggled it on board at the last port world.

The Overseers broke up some sort of suicidal gathering in a 'ponics chamber, and . . . some of the workers took triggering doses."

If not for his camouflage, Moodri's spots would have vanished from his scalp in reality. "How many dead?" he asked. The *jabroka*-enhanced workers were to be the assault force that would take the circuitry key to the bridge.

"Among the Overseers, I think six," Cathy said. She checked nervously to see if any Overseer had yet noticed how much time she was spending with the Elder. "Among the workers, I don't know. They disposed of some of the bodies before I arrived on shift." She looked over at the medical recycling vat. Moodri followed her gaze.

The large transparent tub of bubbling, heated salt water was stained a gruesome rose. Corroding bones danced along its bottom surface, bumped by the circulating liquid that slowly ate away at them. The flesh would have melted in minutes.

Moodri counted eight skulls that he could see. Melgil had said that there were to be twenty workers in the assault force. Now there would only be twelve.

"Go to the boy," Cathy said. "I must help them." She began to move toward the injured Overseers.

"Must you?" Moodri asked.

Cathy looked at him with hatred. "If I do not, then this infirmary will be closed, and I will be able to help *no one*. Including you." She turned to pick up a stack of rolled bandages to carry over to the Overseer medics.

Moodri went to Buck.

The child looked up blearily and tried to smile as he recognized his great-uncle. Moodri could see that whatever drug Melgil had had Cathy give the boy to prevent him from telling the Overseers about the rebellion's plan was still strong in his veins. He took the child's hand. "No need to talk, Finiksa. Melgil told me of your concerns." Buck squeezed Moodri's hand and nodded. "But look closely now. Are these the people you truly wish to help?"

The infirmary door swept open again, and a group of Overseers and workers charged in. Two Overseers carrying a third colleague rushed the limp body of their fallen comrade to an open treatment harness. A single Overseer with an oversized prod pushed a convulsing, shackled worker forward. Following them all two more Overseers dragged a blood-covered body behind them. The body was so large, with such a massively pronounced rib cage, that Moodri knew it was the genetically transfigured body of a worker who had taken a triggering dose of *jabroka*.

The two Overseers dragged the body to an area of the metal floor beside the seething recycling tank. One focused his prod to full strength, then held it to the transformed worker's temple and discharged it. The massive worker cried out as his brain was instantly destroyed, then flopped unmoving against the floor. With that, both Overseers stepped back, and one pressed a control surface near the tank. The section of the floor that held the worker's body rose up on twin hydraulic mounts until it was level with the edge of the tub. Then both Overseers shoved the body into the raging waters.

Instantly the caustic liquid turned deep pink as the worker's skin peeled away in fluttering tatters. Moodri did not look away, and he would not let Buck turn aside either. Those who took *jabroka* lasted longer in the salt, but the end result would be the same.

"He was one of those who were to have taken the key to the bridge in your place," Moodri said quietly. Buck was confused by the Elder's statement, but that was as Moodri wished it to be.

The two Overseers lowered the floor section until it was halfway down, creating a large step up to the tank. Then a third Overseer dragged over the still trembling shackled worker.

"I told you what you wanted," the worker screamed, twisting in vain away from the bubbling tank. "I told you *everything!*"

"Remember, Finiksa. All things come from the Mother," Moodri whispered.

The three Overseers grabbed the worker by his shoulders and his legs.

"They've got more *jabroka!*" the worker shouted. "They're going to take over the bridge!"

The Overseers threw the worker up to the raised deck.

"All things return to the Mother," Moodri said.

"I *helped* you!" the worker shrieked. "You *promised!*"

Moodri touched his hearts. Gently he helped Buck touch his own hearts, too.

The Overseers spun the worker around and flipped him feet first into the tank.

The worker's screech of agonized terror overpowered all the

other sounds in the infirmary. The salt water came up to his waist. For a few moments he stumbled back and forth, trying to keep his footing on the slippery mound of fleshless bones that lay on the tank's bottom as all the while the skin and muscle of his legs were dissolving.

Finally he fell against the edge of the tank and held himself up only by hooking his elbows over the side. Whatever he said was incoherent, lost in great bubbles of blood that flooded out through his mouth and nose as his internal organs were pierced.

The three Overseers laughed, then one used her prod to unhook the worker's elbows and send him sliding down the side of the tank. His face stayed pressed against the transparent surface all the way down, his eyes staring out in eternal horror as what remained of him slowly dissolved into a pink sludge smearing the tank wall.

Only then did Moodri avert his eyes and silently push Buck back onto his platform. It would not do to have the Overseers notice they were being watched by a useless Elder and sick child, not with the scent of blood so fresh in the Overseers' nostrils.

Moodri bowed his head over Buck as if delivering a blessing. "There is much you do not understand yet, Finiksa. Things you have not learned, stories you have not been told. But even in your brief years you must know that what you have just seen is wrong."

Buck stared up at his great-uncle, and Moodri saw in the child's eyes reason to continue.

"Do you remember when you were first taken by the Overseers? Only a child of eight, and they took you to the chamber of your worst fears."

Buck's eyes flickered with the memory.

"It is their way, Finiksa. To find that which is deeply hidden in all of us. Our greatest fear, our greatest love, whatever is most fundamental to our being, and then to use it against us."

Moodri carefully found two spots on Buck's neck and massaged them tenderly.

"Do you remember what your greatest fear was, as a child of eight?"

Buck's voice was restored from the effects of the drug by Moodri's manipulations. "To be alone," he whispered.

"To step into that room was to step into loneliness," Moodri said. "You would have no friends. You would have no family.

No one to care for you. No one to care for." Moodri took Buck's hands in both of his. "It is not just the fear of a child," he said as he continued to bend over Buck, as if ministering to him spiritually. "But do you remember what happened when the door to that chamber opened and the Overseer beckoned you in?"

Buck's eyes stared up at the lights, looking into the past. "You were there," he said with a look of wonder. "I was alone, but you were there for me."

"As I will always be," Moodri said. "You do not need the false family of the Overseers. You do not need the false friendship of those who have yet to meet their fears." He squeezed Buck's hands in a grip of iron. "Believe what I said then. Believe what I say now."

Buck looked deep into his great-uncle's eyes. There was no spinning crystal, no trick of mind control. There was only the purest incarnation of the one power that had enabled a race to survive more than a century of unspeakable slavery and horror.

Buck looked deep into his great-uncle's eyes and saw love.

"Fear no more, Finiksa," Moodri said. "It is your time."

CHAPTER 13

SIKES COULD HEAR his mother yelling at him to get up. He was going to be late for school again. He would have to stand outside Sister Mary Agnes's office door. He would have to reach out to that gleaming brass doorknob. He could feel the slicing sting of her ruler on his wrist. He could hear the righteous anger in her voice. He didn't want to wake up. He didn't—

"Daddy?"

He heard his daughter's voice, and his eyes flew open. The entire right side of his head throbbed as if every one of his teeth had had a root canal. His surroundings were indistinct, hazily lit, and out of focus. But he saw his daughter's face close to his and ignored all other distractions to learn her condition.

"Are you all right?" All the nightmares born in parents on the day their child is born welled up in his heart.

"I'm okay," Kirby said, but he could hear the thickness of old tears in her throat. "You've got blood all over your head, and I thought you weren't going to wake up, and . . ." Fresh tears came.

Sikes moved to take her in his arms and found his hands were tied behind him. He twisted against the wooden chair in which he was trapped. His ankles were tied to the two front legs of the chair. Every movement sent sparks of pain down the right side of his neck. But none of that was important.

"Did they hurt you?" he asked.

He saw Kirby shake her head. She was tied to another chair in front of his, facing him. Her dark hair hung flat and lifeless. Her eyes were shadowed, her skin pale. "They put something over my head," she said weakly. "They told me if I did anything that . . . that they'd kill you." She lost control and began to sob with wrenching gasps.

Sikes pulled on the ropes that bound his wrists, but nothing gave. His only thought was that someone would pay for this. Someone would *die* for daring to harm his child.

But who?

He stopped struggling. He tried to remember. He had been hit from behind in his garage. Someone had held a gun to his head and said his name and—

"Oh, shit," Sikes said. Instinctively he knew that whoever had come for him was connected to Randolph Petty's murder. And if they had already killed once . . . "Everything's going to be okay," he said to his daughter. He doubted if she could hear him over her crying, but he kept speaking, trying to calm her. Through it all he checked out the room they were in. It smelled new. A large window was obscured by a heavy curtain, but light shone in around its edges, giving a soft daylight glow to the air. The soft beige broadloom was thick, the matching walls unmarked. Another band of light entered from beneath the single shut door. Sikes was certain they were in a house, but he could hear no noises that would confirm or deny his guess. There was only the gentle rush of an air-conditioning system. The room was cold.

Eventually Kirby exhausted whatever terrors had gripped her as she had sat watching her unconscious father. Her breathing returned almost to normal.

"Do you know where we are?" Sikes asked her when he felt she was ready to speak.

She shook her head, then tried to wipe her chin on her shoulder. Her face was streaked with tears and mucus.

Sikes tried again. "How long did it take to get here?"

Kirby looked pained. "I don't know," she said pitifully. "I thought they were going to kill you. I thought—"

"Shhh, Kirby, shhh," Sikes said urgently. "We can get out of this, but I'm going to need your help. How did they get us here? What did we go in?"

"A van," Kirby said.

The door clicked open.

"A Chevy Magic Wagon, actually," Amy Stewart said, standing in a halo of bright light from the hallway beyond.

It immediately struck Sikes as odd that he wasn't surprised by Amy's presence, but he wasn't. There was an outside chance that she had been kidnapped, too, he conceded. But somehow he doubted it. "Did you kill Petty?" he asked. It seemed to be the only reasonable thing to say.

"Sorry to disappoint you, but no, Detective Sikes, I didn't. You could say Dr. Petty was responsible for his own death."

Sikes heard the unspoken qualification in her husky voice. "But you pulled the trigger, didn't you?"

"I didn't have time," Amy said calmly. "I was too busy doctoring his computer mail records to give myself an alibi." She almost smiled as she saw Sikes's mystified reaction. "Come on, detective. If a two-bit hacker like Grazer can get into the system, why couldn't I?"

The full implication of what she said didn't hit Sikes for a good five seconds. "How do you know about Grazer?" he asked.

Amy stepped out of the way so another figure could enter the room—a blond man in black pants and a black sweater. The only thing Sikes could see clearly was the .45 automatic he wore in his shoulder holster.

"Why don't we go downstairs?" Amy said pleasantly. "And we can . . . what do you people say? 'Close this case'?"

Sikes stared at her as if ignoring the circumstances. "Does that mean you're ready to give up?" he asked.

"No," Amy said. "It means you are."

As Sikes cautiously walked down the broadloom-covered stairs of what turned out to be a large and mostly empty new house, he saw how Amy Stewart had come to know about Grazer.

Grazer was sitting on a navy-blue couch in the living room at the bottom of the stairs. He was wearing handcuffs and a frown, and his three-piece suit was torn and in disarray. On the other end of the couch Angie Perez's body was slumped sideways, unconscious. A thin trickle of blood had dried near her hairline. She wore handcuffs as well.

Sikes felt his legs threaten to give way. Three cops and a teenage girl taken right off the street—not the sort of crime any rational person expected to get away with. Either he and Angie and Grazer had to fight their way out of here—wherever here was—or they were going to be killed. It was as simple as that.

Sikes's hands were still tied, and the silent blond man with the shoulder holster pushed him onto the couch between Grazer and Angie. Kirby was motioned over to what could only be a La-Z-Boy recliner at the end of the couch. Other than the couch, the recliner, and a few chairs, the only piece of furniture Sikes could see in the room was a tall cabinet of smoked glass and navy lacquer that held a large television and a stereo. He felt he was in a showroom of some kind and not a house after all. The living-room windows were as heavily curtained as the one in the upstairs room.

"They got me in my garage," Sikes told Grazer.

Both men looked around to see if they were going to be told not to speak. But neither Amy nor the blond gunman said anything.

"We got it at the Denny's down from the station house," Grazer said. "Angie got hungry." He sounded as if he were a four-year-old whining.

Sikes turned to his partner. She was out, but she was breathing regularly. "Looks like Angie put up a fight."

"She was warned not to," Amy said.

She stood by the television cabinet. CNN was on, the sound off. There was no sign of the idealistic young student Sikes had interviewed at UCLA. He had a feeling he knew why: It had all been an act. Every word of it.

"Are you going to tell us what all this is about before you kill us?" Sikes asked, then he instantly wished he hadn't because of the look on Kirby's face.

"We're not going to kill anyone," Amy said. She looked at Kirby. "Don't worry. Your father's being an alarmist." She stepped back to shout through an open doorway that Sikes guessed led to a kitchen.

"Uncle Frank, could you bring out some paper towels or something?"

A moment later the mystery man from the photograph in Amy's office walked into the room—ex–Commander Franklin

Arthur Stewart, late of Naval Intelligence. In person he had the same indefinable features and skin color that Amy had, combining the heritage of three or four different racial groups, Sikes guessed. He was dressed in a pair of tan slacks and a light blue sweater, far removed from anything military. He carried a roll of white paper towels.

"The girl could use them," Amy said, pointing to Kirby's sticky face.

"Awfully kind of you, Uncle Frank," Sikes said derisively.

Stewart tore off a handful of towels and gave them to Kirby. Kirby vigorously wiped at her face with them, using both tied hands together.

"So what's next?" Sikes asked. "Some chips and dip and then you send us home?"

"Something like that," Amy said. She looked at the television, then checked her watch. A commercial was playing

Sikes looked at Grazer. "I give up. Do *you* know what this is about?"

Grazer made an elaborate shrug. Then he spoke loudly. "No. But it doesn't matter. As soon as we didn't show up for our five o'clock meeting with the captain, APBs would have been put out on all of us. It's just a matter of time before—"

"Save it, Detective Grazer." It was the first thing Franklin Stewart had said. "There are no APBs going out on you. And your captain knows why you missed your meeting."

Sikes could almost hear Theo Miles explaining how all the pieces were fitting together. If this guy's people had managed to get through to the captain, then their power had to come from a higher source.

"So how are things at the Pentagon these days, Commander?" Sikes asked.

Stewart had the decency to look amused. "I wouldn't know. I work for the Fuller Institute these days. There's no official connection between it and any government agency."

"Except through a bank account in Switzerland?" Sikes challenged. "Or is that passé now? Do you run your money through the Cayman Islands with the drug runners and the other scum?"

Stewart had stopped smiling. "That's quite an attitude you have, detective."

Knowing that he had struck a nerve, Sikes was just about to respond with another attack when Grazer stepped into it.

"What do you expect him to have, talking with the kind of animal that would shoot an old man in cold blood?"

Stewart coolly walked over to Grazer and slapped him so hard the forensic accounting detective fell against Sikes.

"Not bad, Bry," Sikes muttered. "But Uncle Frank didn't kill Petty." Sikes nodded over at the silent blond man with the .45 in his shoulder holster. "Motormouth over there did it."

"Yeah?" Grazer said. The left side of his face was blazing red from the blow.

"Please don't stop, detective," Stewart said conversationally, as if he hadn't just hit Grazer.

Sikes shrugged recklessly. As long as they were talking they'd stay alive, even if they did have to take a few knocks. "It makes perfect sense to me, Uncle Frank. You're the connection to the military. Amy's the brains behind the photographs. And Mr. Happy over there is the government killer. Amy couldn't do it. You were too smart to do it. So you brought in a specialist from Washington. I guess work has been scarce since the good old days in Nicaragua."

Stewart regarded him steadily as if they were predator and prey. "Fascinating. A specialist from Washington to do what?"

"Kill Randolph Petty."

"And why would I want that?"

"Because of the photographs."

Stewart walked back to stand beside Amy. "The photographs. I see. And did I have Petty killed because the photographs were mine and I wanted them back? Or because they were Petty's and he wouldn't give them to me? Or because they were someone else's and he was going to give them to yet another someone?" Stewart took a remote control wand from the top of the television. "You see, I know how your business works, detective. You have a crime, to be sure. But you have no motive. And without a motive you have no suspect. And without a suspect . . . well, you understand."

"I *saw* the photographs," Sikes said. He suddenly wondered if his captors had any intention of killing anyone. Maybe they thought they could stonewall the whole case. Maybe Theo Miles had been right about everything.

Stewart didn't seem to be worried. "But photographs of *what,* detective?" He went over to a small chair and sat down to face the television. "All you saw were a few screens of computer data. Enough to make you *think* you had seen the real thing for . . . for afterwards."

"Afterwards? After what?"

"After the danger has passed," Stewart said. He checked his watch as well. "Ah, here we go." He pointed the remote at the television and the sound came up just as CNN began its science and technology report.

"What danger?" Sikes asked.

But Stewart said nothing. Instead he gestured to the screen as if Sikes would find his answer there.

He did. The lead story concerned a report from astronomers in Russia who had announced the discovery of the fastest-moving object in the solar system—a large asteroid almost five kilometers in length that would intersect Earth's orbit within the next twenty-four hours. The report said that the asteroid would easily miss the Earth at a distance of several million miles, and at the rate it was traveling it would actually leave the solar system. Indeed, there was some speculation that given its speed, the asteroid had originated outside the solar system, and the Russian astronomers were urging that all observatories train their instruments on the asteroid in what might be an unprecedented opportunity to study something from beyond our own sun's influence.

"They don't know what it is, do they?" Sikes said.

"No," Amy answered. "And they won't until it's too late to do anything about it."

"What do you mean, too late?"

Stewart killed the sound as the news went on to another story. He looked at Sikes and scratched at his chin. "Have you ever seen a space probe, detective?"

"Like a satellite or something?" The chattier Franklin Stewart became, the better Sikes liked it. True, the blond with the .45 was still keeping them covered, but Sikes was beginning to hope that they might all survive this encounter yet.

"That's right," Stewart said. "A Voyager, for instance. Or Galileo. Or the Vikings. Most of them could fit into this room. And the better we get at making them, the smaller they're becoming. We keep cramming more intelligence into smaller computer chips. We make instruments more sensitive and crowd more of them together." He stood up and handed the remote to Amy. "The advantage being that the less massive a probe is, the less energy it needs to get where it's going, so the cheaper it is for us to launch it. It's an evolutionary line, so to speak. The smarter we are, the smaller we make them." He stared fixedly at Sikes. "Except for one particular class of spacecraft." He stopped as if he expected Sikes to continue for him.

But Grazer did instead. "The space shuttle."

"Very good, detective."

For a moment Grazer perked up at the praise until he remembered its source. He slumped against the back of the couch.

Stewart continued. "The space shuttle and the space station. Two of the largest, most cumbersome and complex objects ever built by humans. And you know why?"

This time Sikes answered. "Because they have to keep humans alive in space for long periods of time. Jesus Christ. You think there's somebody on that thing, don't you?"

Amy tapped the remote against her open palm. "No, we *know* that there's somebody—or some*thing*—on board that craft."

"It's the only possible explanation for its configuration," Franklin Stewart added. "It's huge. It's hollow. You don't need empty space for scientific instruments. But you do need enormous amounts of space to maintain life."

"You have to grow food," Amy said. "You have to be able to recirculate and replenish your atmosphere. You need room to exercise. Room for privacy—if *they* need such a thing." She shuddered.

"There can be no doubt that that thing is inhabited," Franklin Stewart concluded.

For a moment everyone in the room was silent. Then Kirby said, "You mean an honest-to-God spaceship is coming here?" Sikes couldn't remember when he had heard more excitement in her voice. Not since she was a little girl waiting for Santa Claus, he decided.

"I still don't get it," Sikes said. He had to keep the two talking until he could figure out how to disarm blondie and get Kirby and Angie out of here safely. Thank God Grazer wasn't complicating things and was letting him take the lead. It looked as if Angie had been wrong. Grazer could keep quiet some-times. "So there're a bunch of little green men passing by.

What's wrong with anybody knowing? Why not say hello or something?"

Franklin Stewart gave Sikes a condescending look. "You don't know anything about history, do you, detective?"

Without thinking Sikes nodded at Grazer. "He does." Then held his breath. Once unleashed, Grazer could provoke Stewart into shooting them all just to shut him up.

Stewart addressed Grazer. "Very well, can *you* think of a single instance in human history when one society has made contact with a more technologically advanced second society and *survived?*"

Grazer chewed his lip for a moment. "You know, Sikes, he might have a point."

"Of course he has a point," Amy said. "Look at Native North Americans. They thrived on this continent for centuries. And now, five centuries after Columbus, they're a footnote to history. Decimated by war. By disease. Their land gone. Their culture something to be gaped at in museums and gift shops." She pointed the remote control at Sikes. Her face seemed pinched and tight to him now. He wondered why he had ever found her so attractive. "Do you want that to happen to an entire species, detective? Your *own* species? Do you actually want to attract the attention of beings so advanced they can move nine-times-ten-to-the-sixth tonnes from star to star? Would you care to guess what this planet might look like a single century after any first contact like that? What would happen to our science? Our religions? Our cultural heritage?"

"You can't hide out forever," Sikes said while thinking, We're in the hands of a bunch of racists—planetary racists who've murdered an old man, kidnapped a child, and are holding three members of the LAPD with the blessing of the captain and God knows who else and how high up. Plus, they are completely crazy.

"We won't have to," Amy said. "Someday we'll be out there, too. We'll fly our own craft to other stars. And *that* will be the time to . . . to say hello, as you put it. When we're equals."

"But not *now*," Stewart added. "Not when we're nothing more than trusting indigenous bow-and-arrow users who have never seen cannon before. The risk to the"—he looked up at the ceiling as if searching for the perfect word and found it—"the *purity* of our species' survival is too high."

Sikes was disgusted with them. He didn't want his daughter to listen to any more of this crap. "And you had Randolph Petty killed for *that?*"

Amy nodded. "We traded one man's life for the world's," she said. "I think it has a rather biblical ring to it myself."

"Besides," her uncle added, "Petty was a traitor. He didn't take those photographs himself. They were *leaked* to him. By an astronomical photo analyst at NORAD who thought she knew better than government policy. NORAD enlisted the aid of the Fuller Institute's, um, security division to aid in retrieving the stolen photos."

"NORAD," Sikes said. "So the government *has* known about the whole thing from the beginning."

"We've known about the 'whole thing' since Roswell," Stewart said. "And that was just four clones in a scout ship."

Sikes didn't know what Stewart meant and didn't want to know, but beside him Grazer gasped out loud.

"Why didn't you just kidnap Petty the way you kidnapped us?" Sikes asked.

"Technically," Stewart said, "you're being held in protective custody pursuant to a special White House National Security Directive dating back to nineteen fifty-seven. It's not kidnapping. And the problem with Petty was that alone of all the other astronomers to whom the leaked photographs were given, he was the only one who didn't want to cooperate with us."

"Seventy-two years old, he's got an asteroid named after him, and you shot him for not 'cooperating'?"

"Exactly," Stewart said, glancing over to the silent man with the .45. "Seventy-two years old, an irresponsible and expendable has-been, and he should have known better than to think he could get away with it."

Sikes looked at Amy with contempt. "And everything you told me . . . it was close enough to the truth so that after the fact everyone would think you had been a hero for trying to spread the word. But just distorted enough to make me go running after false leads until the . . . the space thing was headed back to the stars."

"It would have worked," Amy said, "except for Detective Grazer deciding he'd access military personnel files and trigger software alarms. That's when we realized that the cover story would be compromised."

"Tell me, detective, how did you manage to make the

connection to the institute?" Stewart asked, one professional to another.

Sikes nodded at Amy. "Mata Hari left a photograph on her office wall that showed the two of you. And the Desert Storm briefings made your face kind of hard to forget."

"Very clever," Stewart said. "I'll have to remember that for next time."

Sikes narrowed his eyes at the man. "You actually think you're going to get away with this?"

"I already have, detective. Another few hours and that thing will be traveling so fast that it's going to loop around on the other side of the sun and never come back. And tomorrow you will have the choice of signing a standard National Security Oath for law enforcement personnel, swearing never to divulge the classified information you've unwittingly uncovered in the course of your investigation, or spending the rest of your life in a federal prison."

"That will never happen," Sikes said. "And you won't get away with kidnapping and murder either."

Stewart did not acknowledge the threat. "We have before, and we will again."

"It's back on," Amy said before Sikes could reply. She pointed the remote at the television, and the sound returned. An artist's impression of a crater-marked asteroid appeared in a box above the news reader's shoulder as the first story was updated.

British astronomers had just announced that the object—now called the Voronezh Object, after the Russian observatory that had been the first to report its presence—was exhibiting anomalous reflectance characteristics that made it unlike any other asteroid ever discovered. Those characteristics, combined with its speed and trajectory, made the astronomers confident that the Voronezh Object was indeed from outside Earth's solar system.

The newsreader reported that so far there had been little word about the object from American observatories. Unfortunately, several installations that specialized in asteroid tracking had been closed down for repair and maintenance and might, as a result, not be able to participate in the object's study.

Franklin Stewart looked significantly at Sikes. "We were able to shut down twenty-eight observatories around the world just by suggesting that their grants might be up for review. Locking the lot of you up is going to be a piece of cake."

The newsreader went on to say that efforts were underway to attempt to bounce radar and laser signals from the object.

"Hey, that's a good way to say hello," Sikes said.

But Stewart wasn't troubled. "Detective, since the collapse of the Soviet Union, the only country with the capability to mount that kind of effort in only a few hours is this one. And I guarantee you that each radar and laser facility will regretfully report that technical difficulties prevented them from sending out any signals at all. No one's going to talk to that thing."

"Maybe they already know we're here," Kirby said bravely. "Maybe they're just as afraid to talk to us as you are to talk with them."

Stewart nodded. "You've got a smart kid there, detective. It would be a real shame if she had to grow up in a prison."

"Daddy?"

"Don't worry," Sikes told his daughter. "This scumbag isn't going to do anything to us. He's just the kind of creep that's probably keeping space guys away from us in the first place."

Stewart took that as a compliment. "Precisely, detective. That's exactly who I am. The kind of person who is keeping our world free from dangerous contamination. The kind of person who is keeping our world pure."

"Then again," Grazer said slowly, "maybe it's on its way here to land and . . . and take over."

Sikes liked seeing the shadow that passed over Stewart's face at that comment.

"Highly unlikely," Amy said, though she looked almost nauseated at the prospect. "With its present mass and velocity, even if it's using total conversion of matter to energy, it's still not big enough to carry enough reaction mass to have it change its trajectory to rendezvous with Earth."

"Then maybe it's just going to lob a bomb at us," Sikes said, rubbing it in. He looked over at Amy. "Like someone once said, it's a big universe out there."

"Which is why we're staying here, as quietly as possible." Stewart walked out of the room, disappearing into the kitchen. The man with the gun remained unmoving, his gaze never leaving the prisoners on the couch.

Sikes stared at the television screen, at the corny painting of the Voronezh Object. As far as he was concerned, it probably *was* just a big hunk of rock, and Stewart and everyone else were nuts. But with all his might and all his heart, just in case, he sent out his thoughts to wherever they had to go in space and told that baby to *land*.

It would be worth it just to see the look on Stewart's smug face.

Of course, he thought, whatever happens after that is anybody's guess. But it would still be worth it.

CHAPTER 14

THE OVERSEERS, INTENT on their wounded in the infirmary, did not notice when the light panels began flashing to indicate a new shift cycle had begun. But Moodri noticed. This would be the shift cycle in which the ship reached its closest approach to the gravity-well sun. When that moment came, with the ship's trajectory sufficiently altered and its normal-space kinetic energy at its highest level, the ship would translate back into the superluminal realm, hurtling it on onward to Terminus and to oblivion for the Tenctonese.

But it was also the shift in which the ship would make its closest approach to the third planet of that sun—the shift in which the rebellion's plan would at last be enacted.

The light panels flashed, heralding the ship's last hours.

But only if Melgil arrived as planned.

Moodri remained at Buck's side, appearing to pay no attention to the nonstop traffic of Overseers, wounded and otherwise. In the past hour three more *jabroka*-enhanced workers had been thrown into the seething tank of salt water. Two other captured workers had been dissolved alive. From the Overseers' tense exchanges Moodri knew that they suspected that the Tenctonese workers were following some organized plan— only that could account for the breakdown in routine aboard the ship, including the discovery of contraband *jabroka*. But so far the Overseers had not connected the seemingly unrelated acts of rebellion with the ship's close approach to a planet capable of supporting Tenctonese life. To reach that planet would entail the cargo taking over the ship, and that was clearly unthinkable.

As if he were a simple Elder attending to a sick child, Moodri laid out divining crystals around Buck and told him stories of Old Tencton, relating how the Family: Heroes of Soren'tzahh had sailed across the Great Inland Sea to the Central Island, where so many secrets of the Tenctonese race were revealed in the ancient ruins of earlier, yet more advanced civilizations. He told Buck how the hidden strength of each Tenctonese was the body's ability to adjust its genetic structure in response to outside environmental influences over the course of a single generation—perhaps the legacy of genetic engineering performed even before the settlements of the Central Island had been built. He gave Buck the gift of his history so the boy could set forth for the future—the old passing its wisdom to the young, just as Moodri had listened to the stories that his Elders had told on the tribal plains, among the blue fields filled with stars.

An Overseer intruded on them once. His uniform was torn, and his sweat smelled dank with panic as he summoned Cathy imperiously and told her that it was a waste of ship's resources for the infirmary to treat cargo so young and so old as Buck and Moodri. He wanted to throw both of them into the recycler so there would be more room to treat the Overseers who were being injured in the sporadic fighting that was erupting in the service-access tunnels.

From the corner of his eye Moodri saw Buck take hold of a long crystal as if he intended to use it as a weapon. But Cathy told the Overseer that the boy was being treated by the authority of Coolock, and any change in the child's status had to come from him.

The Overseer had retreated at once. Coolock had that much power. They had remained undisturbed since then.

After the shift lights flashed, Buck grew restless. "Isn't it time, Uncle Moodri? Shouldn't I be going to the bridge with my Watcher Group?"

Buck's group would be assembling within the hour. But it would be useless for him to go without the circuitry key that would activate the stardrive.

"We must wait for the key," Moodri said.

"Why can't we go get it?"

"It has been carefully hidden for fifteen years, ever since we tested the design. We cannot go to it. We must wait for it to come to us."

Then Melgil entered the infirmary, his large spots noticeably paler. He hobbled over to Moodri and Buck, cradling his right arm. "There are checkpoints everywhere," he said, gasping for breath as if he had run through the corridors. "The Overseers have closed down the shift except for essential workers. The pressure doors are being closed."

Moodri placed a hand on Melgil to calm him. "The pressure doors must be closed for our plan to work."

But Melgil wasn't calmed. "You don't understand. The Overseers know!"

"The Overseers are confused," Moodri said. "They may suspect many things, but they know nothing. There have been restless times on the ship before, moments of insurrection. Almost all of them following a heavy release of the gas. What they think is occurring now is nothing they have not experienced before."

"But they found the assault squad. They found the cache of *jabroka.*"

"Did you think they would do otherwise?" Moodri drew his friend around so that their conversation would remain hidden from the Overseers still working with the injured on the infirmary's other wall. *"Jabroka* touches something deep within our history. Something uncontrollable. It does not offer us the future, only the past."

Melgil's face was distorted in frustrated rage. "Now it offers us *nothing.* There is no one left who can force his way onto the bridge."

Moodri held out a hand to his great-nephew. "Finiksa has an invitation."

Melgil glared at the boy. "Finiksa would betray us to the Overseers for the sake of a black scarf."

"No longer," Buck said. He looked at Moodri with the peace of the goddess. "I am my father's son, as he is his, back to the crossing of the Inland Sea."

Melgil gazed at the child sharply, and Moodri knew the methods that the *binnaum* used to search within Buck's mind and find the truth. And when Melgil had finished, Buck's shoulders drew up square and proud. "Fear no more," Melgil said, as if in a dream. He put his one good hand on Moodri's arm. "Can it be done with so many of them around?"

"It must be done," Moodri said.

Buck looked confused. "Can what be done?"

"The retrieval of the key," Melgil answered, "from the one place no Overseer could ever search."

The old *binnaum* began to pull back the white sleeve of his robe from his withered right arm. Buck's eyes widened as he saw the network of old scars that ran across its dry and wrinkled flesh. "What the Overseers thought was an accident in the power plants," Melgil explained. "Back before you were born. Fifteen years ago, when the key's design was tested and the ship translated into normal space without warning. Surgery was necessary to reattach bones and muscles."

"And to hide the key," Moodri said. "I shall get Gelana."

Since the shift change, the number of those entering and leaving the infirmary had noticeably lessened. There had been no further corpse disposals or executions, and the injured Overseers, once stable, had been carried out, presumably to better-equipped medical facilities in the Overseers' section of the ship.

Two black-uniformed medics worked on one Overseer in a treatment harness. Another Overseer sprawled, dead, in a second harness. Other than that, Cathy and two other Cargo Specialists were the only people in the infirmary. They were cleaning up the discarded bandage wrappers and spilled blood.

Moodri went to Cathy. "It is time," he said.

Cathy's face was set in anger. "Not while Overseers remain here."

"We have no choice."

"They will close this infirmary."

"The infirmary will no longer be needed." Moodri leaned closer to her ear valley. "When you have completed the extraction, find some excuse to leave here. Gather as many children together as you can and prepare to go to the lower cargo bays when we have landed."

Cathy stared at Moodri in a mixture of alarm and anguish. "Landed?" she said. "But . . . I thought . . ."

"That we would return to Tencton?" Moodri said kindly. He

bowed his head. "Our home is lost to us for now. Perhaps someday we will return, but not until we can face an entire fleet of ships. It is time for us to make a new home."

"But where?"

"Its name I cannot tell you, but it waits for us, Gelana. As it has always waited for us since the day of the coming of the ships. And now, with your aid, this voyage will end and our new home will welcome us." He held out his hand to her. "Come, it is time."

Moodri returned to Buck's sleeping platform. He had no doubt that Cathy would follow. And she did.

She carried a surgical kit in her hands and told Melgil to go over by the work station farthest from the Overseer medics and their patients. Melgil frowned. It was the work station closest to the recycling tank. But he went to it.

Buck tried to get up from his platform, but Moodri told him to stay in place. There could be no break in the routine as long as Overseers were present, and no action could be taken that would attract their attention. "Gelana is skilled. It will not take long. Tell me again what you are to do with the key once you reach the bridge."

In a low voice Buck formally recited his assignment as both he and Moodri watched Cathy at work. "The Overseers in charge of the bridge functions will be working at the green consoles," Buck said. "The stardrive consoles are behind them, painted blood-pink in warning." Cathy prepared a three-needle injector and carefully slipped it into Melgil's shoulder. "The Watcher Brigade will be led across the bridge to an observation area. We will pass between the green consoles and the pink consoles." Cathy peeled the glittering wrap from a scalpel so thin that its blade seemed to disappear when she turned it sideways. "The control surfaces on the pink consoles will be locked to prevent the activation of any controls while we are in normal space." She painted Melgil's right forearm with a sparkling antiseptic liquid. "One control surface will remain accessible and will be marked with a flashing green light. It is the one that must be used to unlock the other controls. That is the port into which I will insert the circuitry key as I pass." She held the scalpel over Melgil's scarred skin.

"Then what will you do?" Moodri asked. It would only be a matter of moments before the key would be removed from its living hiding place. The goddess smiled.

"Alarms will immediately sound, and in the confusion I will run to the bridge-access tunnels and return to the cargo disk."

Cathy made the first cut.

"How long will you have before the tunnels are sealed?"

"No more than fifty double beats."

The infirmary door smashed open. A male Overseer staggered in, carrying the body of a female wearing a black uniform. Her head was almost severed from her body. Her spots were as pale as her skin.

"Help me!" the Overseer shouted.

The Overseer medics turned to him but would not leave their own patients. There was no help that could be given.

"You!" the Overseer yelled at Cathy. "Here! Now!"

Cathy hesitated. Melgil's flesh was exposed beneath her scalpel, his arm cradled in a soft nest of bandages. Blood oozed from the careful incision she had made. And because of that situation she did not instantly respond to the Overseer's order.

The Overseer reacted as if pure *jabroka* pulsed through his hearts. *"Did you hear what I said?"* he shrieked. *"Now!"*

Cathy laid down her scalpel and hurried to him and the body he carried. She looked at the ruin of the female's neck. No blood pulsed from the torn arteries. Moodri could hear the fear in Cathy's voice as she spoke. "I'm . . . I'm sorry, master, but . . . she has died."

Moodri saw the Overseer's arms sag. He felt the loss the Overseer felt as Cathy confirmed the truth the Overseer was afraid to admit to himself. The Overseer stumbled over to an empty treatment harness and laid the body of the female within it. Cathy stood in the middle of the infirmary, unsure of what she should do next. Melgil stared at the ceiling lights, eyes closed, his good hand clutched to the shoulder of his opened arm.

Moodri stood. It was risky, but Cathy needed instruction. She had to be told to return to Melgil and retrieve the key.

The Overseer cried out in anguish. He bowed his head against the female, and when he stood again his face was smeared with her blood. He turned to Cathy. His eyes glowed like mining beams. "Your fault," he spat. "It is *your fault!*"

He lunged at Cathy. She had no place to run. His fist smashed against her face and knocked her to the deck. The other Overseers ignored the assault. It was nothing they hadn't seen before, and they had all seen worse.

"I gave you an order, cargo!" The Overseer punctuated each word with a savage kick to Cathy's ribs. "And you did not respond!"

Cathy's breath exploded from her with each kick. Moodri turned away. There was nothing he could do. Not with so many of them in the infirmary. He saw Melgil pick up Cathy's scalpel with trembling fingers. He knew how important it was to retrieve the key. He cut into his own flesh.

The Overseer turned to Melgil. "What are you doing here?" he screamed. "You filthy *sta!* You have no right to treatment when your betters are dying." He threw himself at Melgil, leaving Cathy doubled over on the floor in a pod position, blood running from her mouth.

Melgil stepped back before the Overseer's rage. His right arm was awash in blood. His left hand held the scalpel. The Overseer reacted as if Melgil intended to attack him with it.

"You dare?" the black-clad monster erupted in fury. "You dare attack me?" With a *chekkah* kick he knocked the scalpel from Melgil's hand, and it clattered against the work station before falling to the deck. "Filth!" the Overseer cried, fueled by grief, by hatred, by the oppressiveness of the ship and the system that had stolen his hearts. "You have no right to be here! You have no right to live!"

He grabbed Melgil before the Elder could move another inch. He butted his head against Melgil's, and the Elder's legs instantly lost their strength.

"You have no right," the Overseer snarled, and he lifted Melgil over his head as if the Elder were no more massive than the robes he wore.

Moodri touched his hearts.

Melgil whispered the name of the goddess.

And then the Overseer threw him into the recycling tank, and Melgil sank beneath the bubbling salt water.

CHAPTER 15

"GROON-CHA! GROON-CHA!" The pulse of the power plants faded beneath the chanting of the crowd—a primal call for blood. Blood that brought back memories for George in the players' cage. Memories of Ruhtra. Of running. Of escape . . .

George remembered running through the corridors, his younger brother, Ruhtra, at his side, small feet striking at the metal deck with the rhythm of the power plants, the pulse of the ship. He didn't know how old he was in this memory, but since he and Ruhtra were together as children he knew it must be before his tenth birthday, before the Overseers came for him. Before he had seen his family for the last time, his mother's hand reaching out to him, his father's eyes so despairing, Ruhtra cradled between his parents, sobbing.

But now, in this memory, Ruhtra was panting, trying to keep up with his older brother's rapid strides, yet never complaining. Their parents had seen to that. How could any child complain about inconsequential matters when so many of their kind lived in such hardship?

"There it is," George rasped. He paused at the corner of the corridor. Ruhtra finally caught up to him. It was mid-shift. The ship was in deep space. The holy gas was at its lowest concentration. Yet the ship had translated. Something was going to happen.

"Did you *look?*" Ruhtra asked, gasping for breath.

"Of course I did," George said with all the arrogance of an older brother to a younger. In fact he hadn't, but he wasn't about to admit it. The ship was more frightening than usual this close to the hull and the locked-off sectors.

"I bet you didn't," Ruhtra said, knowing his brother.

"Did too."

"Prove it."

The argument stopped there. How could George prove he had seen what he hadn't seen? "We'll look together," he said.

Each by himself would have lacked the courage to have come even halfway to the hull when they were supposed to be in the light bay soaking up UV. But together, each afraid of being laughed at by the other, the two brothers encouraged each other in the most foolhardy of pursuits.

Eyes wide, scarcely able to breathe, George and Ruhtra slowly crept forward to the corner's edge and peered around it.

And were transfixed.

Fifty feet directly ahead of them was an enormous viewport —teardrop-shaped like all the others but easily four times the size of any they had seen before and filled with uncountable stars. Without a doubt that proved the bulkhead before them was part of the hull. And most incredible of all, just as the older children had told them, beside that viewport was a *door*.

George and Ruhtra held each other close as they stared at that door and thought about what it meant. A door that opened to the *outside*. An incredible concept.

In the day crèche the Elders had taught them that in space there was no air outside the ship. If the hull was breached, all the air inside would rush out. So why would there be a door in the hull, the children wondered, especially so far away from the cargo holds?

Without explanation the Elders had said that lesson would wait for another day.

And so a trip to the door to the outside had become a secret rite of passage for the children of the ship. Whispered about. Feared. And utterly fascinating. To make the furtive journey to the hull and gaze upon it was almost as important an event in a child's growth to adulthood as the first opening of the *lingpod* flap in boys. But today George and Ruhtra were going to do more than just *look* at the door to the outside—they were going to join that small, select group of children whose spots were dark enough and hearts strong enough to cross the fifty feet of open hull corridor and actually *touch* it.

For George and Ruhtra, separately, such an action would be unthinkable. But together their courage knew no bounds, and no sense.

"You go first," George said. "I'll watch out for Overseers."

"You go first," Ruhtra said. "*I'll* watch for Overseers."

"Are you afraid?"

"No! Are you?"

"No."

"Then you go first."

The exchange might have gone on for hours except for a subtle change in the sound qualities of the corridor. The terrified children, ever alert to the first faint approach of the Overseers' boots, instantly fell silent.

But what they heard made no sense to either of them. It was something they hadn't experienced before.

"Is it a pump?" Ruhtra said nervously.

"Maybe," George said. But the odd pulsing sound wasn't coming from the air vents. It was coming from—

"The door!" Ruhtra whispered in a strangled voice. "Stangya, look!"

George felt his spots twist on his scalp. The door to the outside was *opening.*

He dug the fingers of one hand into the back of Ruhtra's tunic. With the other he clutched at a pipe running up the wall beside him. He waited for the first awful blast of wind that would blow them out of the ship and into space.

But nothing happened.

There was only a gentle puff of white vapor from the bottom of the door seal as the wide metal plate slid upward.

There were no stars beyond the open door. Only darkness.

George still recalled the overwhelming confusion he had felt at that instant—as if everything he had been told about the ship and his place on it had been a lie. *Could* it be possible just to go to the door and *step outside?* Was that all it would take to leave the ship and return to the home his parents told him about? Could it be possible that they had never even left that home? That they had been trapped in the ship all this time for *nothing?*

George felt Ruhtra struggling in his grip. "Let go, Stangya. I want to go outside." The drive to be free was so strong that it overpowered even Ruhtra's fear.

But George could not relinquish his hold on his brother. He couldn't imagine the Elders had lied to him. But then why had they never said anything about—

Something moved in the shadows of the doorway.

Ruhtra shrank back against George. "What is it?" he whispered.

And as the huge white creature stepped out from the doorway George doubted if even the Elders would know.

Years later George would come to understand that the mysterious door to the outside was really an airlock, one of hundreds located along the hull. Sometimes they were used so hull crawlers could move into and out of the ship. Sometimes they connected one ship to another through a long, flexible tunnel. But whatever stepped through the door this time was neither machine nor any living thing George had seen before.

It stood half again as tall as George's father, upright on two widely spaced and massive legs that curved with an extra joint between knee and ankle. The body that was slung between those legs was the same shape as the viewport, sweeping up past narrow shoulders and arms no larger than a child's into a neck that writhed and twisted like a living rope and ended in a stump that held only three horizontal slits, constantly whistling open and closed, fluttering like fabric caught in the breeze from an air vent.

George felt Ruhtra's body shake. He smelled urine.

The creature stopped, then moved swiftly toward the shadows where the two boys hid. Both of its arms worked at the intricate harness it wore. There were implements attached to the harness. Some with blades.

"Nooooo!" Ruhtra cried. "Don't let it! Don't let it!"

George pulled back on his brother as the creature lunged at them. The object it now held in its three-fingered, taloned hand glittered with dozens of metal spikes.

"Stangyaaaa!"

The object swung low, slicing through the air, cutting across George's arm in a spray of pink blood. George gasped but held his position and drew Ruhtra closer to him, placing himself directly between the creature and his brother. And with all the fury his young hearts could give him he screamed: *"Don't you hurt my brother!"*

George still couldn't remember how long he stood like that. The creature kept its distance, slits fluttering as it drew out and manipulated objects from its harness, pointing some at George, whistling into others. But it never moved closer. And eventually it simply left, shuffling with a powerful gait toward a corridor that led only to the locked-off sectors.

It was the first alien life form George had seen. And in all the years and planets since, he had never seen another like it. Sometimes he wondered if it had been one of Those Who Made the Ships, or one of those whom the Overseers served. But the Elders to whom he finally confessed the encounter could not identify the creature from George's description, and in time he began to doubt if the incident had happened at all.

The only other thing he remembered from that day was walking back with Ruhtra, keeping to the smaller corridors so others might not see Ruhtra's soiled tunic. Just before they were to return to their family's dormitory, Ruhtra had suddenly taken George's hand.

"When the Overseers take you," the child had said, "who will protect me then?"

"Mother and Father," George answered.

"But what happens when the Overseers take *me?*"

George was old enough to know there was no answer to that question. But he could not bear to force his brother to face that truth yet.

He held his knuckles gently to his brother's temples. "I will *always* protect you, Ruhtra," he promised. "In Andarko's name."

Ruhtra had held George's knuckles in place. They stood for a long time without talking. And the only sound was the distant pulse of the power plants and the faint splatter of George's blood as it dripped from his arm to the deck. The pulse of the ship. The primal call for blood . . .

"Groon-cha! Groon-cha!"

In the darkness of the holding chamber, George cradled Ruhtra in his arms. At the farthest end of the bench in the players' cage, a third prisoner stared impassively at the thick diagonal bars that imprisoned them. In less than a month he would be named Thomas Edison, but for now he was Zicree, a friend to George and a champion of the Game.

The pneumatic door that led to the Game chamber slid open, bringing dim blue light to the mist that filled the room—the powerless residue of the gas that had filled the ship so recently, now pooling here in the lowest decks. The chanting of the crowd grew louder. Two Overseers passed by, bent over by the weight of the body they dragged. One Overseer followed, grinning maniacally. It was Coolock, and this hellish warren of dark chambers in the ship's bowels was his domain.

"Who's next?" Coolock called out. His deep voice boomed against the hard metal walls of the holding chamber. He stopped by George's cage and clanged his prod deafeningly against the bars. "Ah, you're awake now, Stangya. I've read your records. It's been such a long time since you were here. Feel up to another round?"

George said nothing. He glared at Coolock with rage. It was one thing to execute those who broke the rules of the ship, but to play the Game was barbaric. George knew. He had played it before.

"What about your brother?" Coolock asked with mock solicitude. "Still sleeping, is he? Not fond of the bite of the prod?"

George held Ruhtra close to him, praying he would not wake. They had both been shocked by Coolock's prod in the corridor outside the tunnel intersection where they had been found by the Overseers who had followed George. George had thought the moment that the prod descended upon him would be his last. But somehow he had not been surprised when he had wakened in the darkness of this cage, hearing the high-pitched whine of the *wojchek* in the next chamber. George knew full well that he alone was responsible for Ruhtra's presence here, so he grimly welcomed this brief extension of life if it meant he could pay the price for that mistaken betrayal of his brother. Especially if it gave him a chance to be within arm's reach of Coolock on the way into the Game chamber.

But Coolock had already moved on to other matters. He gazed admiringly at Zicree. "Rest, champion. There will be more important rounds for you to play." Then Coolock turned his back on George and swaggered across the chamber to a second cage filled with other terrified players. "Who shall it be?" he asked them. "Who shall be next to sit at the table?"

George heard a wail of despair as Coolock held out his prod to select the next player. The cage doors rattled as the other Overseers dragged the struggling prisoner to his round with the *wojchek*. Coolock laughed as the crowd cheered. George held Ruhtra. Things had gone wrong too quickly. This was not victory. This was not even the escape of oblivion. The door slid shut, dulling the sounds of the Game chamber and cutting off almost all light.

"Zicree," George whispered. "How many rounds do they play each shift?" He had to know how much longer he might have. If he went first, then perhaps Ruhtra might survive until the rebellion was underway.

Zicree shrugged as if George had asked him about which of two vegrowths tasted better. George didn't understand his friend's passivity. From the chamber came the hydraulic thud of the *wojchek* stopping and locking into position. It was followed by the roar of the crowd as the first high-pressure discharge blasted forth. But the roar did not last long. It had only been vapor and not salt water. The player had survived. The *wojchek* began to whine again. The crowd returned to chanting.

"Are you not frightened?" George asked.

"Of what?" Zicree asked. "To live on the ship. To die on the ship. What difference can there be?"

George wanted to tell his friend that for once there was hope. That a rebellion was underway. But there could be Overseers in the dark, hiding from the prisoners, and George finally understood the importance of revealing nothing. Without *keer'chatlas*, the rebellion would never have advanced beyond a few whispered dreams.

The roar of a second blast of the *wojchek* came from the Game chamber. Again the cries of the crowd died away in disappointment. The *wojchek* whirled again.

"How many rounds will they play?" George asked urgently. He had to know if there was any hope at all for Ruhtra.

Zicree placidly turned to his friend. They had been mine workers together, endless months spent beneath the surfaces of nameless planets—a *jabroka*-induced haze of labor lightened only by the presence of others who could share the burden. But it appeared as if there was nothing that could lift the burden of whatever it was that Zicree now silently endured.

"It doesn't matter what they used to do," Zicree said. "I have heard the Overseers talking. This shift is closed. The corridors are sealed. There is no place for the audience to go. So they will play and play and keep playing."

George dropped his voice to an almost undetectable whisper, afraid that the Overseers might detect his agitation. "Why is the shift closed? Why have they sealed the corridors?"

"Why does it matter?" Zicree said.

The *wojchek* fired. The crowd screamed, almost overcoming the piercing cries of the unlucky player who had just lost his round and his life.

Coolock returned, his boots treading in the smear of blood that streaked the deck of the holding chamber, left by the salt-riddled bodies that were dragged through it to the recyclers. He smiled as he passed George. "Don't worry, Stangya," the Overseer said. "Your time will come soon enough. As will Ruhtra's."

He walked over to another cage. "Who's next?" he asked. "Who's next to sit at the table?"

From the next chamber the captive crowd chanted. The sounds of the *wojchek* being reloaded with its canisters of water and salt clanked from the Game chamber. The Overseers who tended the prisoners stood by the cages and complained that it was going to be a long shift.

And George Francisco knew that one way or another, it would also be the last.

CHAPTER 16

BUCK SCREAMED AS the saltwater took Melgil, but his cry was unheard over the Overseer's shout of rage. The others Buck had seen die in the tank had only been faceless workers. Their fate had been the deserved fate of all who would disobey the Overseers. He had been disturbed by what he had witnessed, even appalled, but he had not been touched by the horror of it until now, when it happened to someone he knew.

Melgil never surfaced. The recycling tank bubbled pink with fresh blood. The Overseer who had killed the Elder turned to face the others in the infirmary, as if daring Moodri or Buck or even Cathy, still on the deck, to protest what he had done.

But Moodri bowed his head and pushed Buck back onto the sleeping platform. Cathy only gasped for breath.

"Should recycle you all," the Overseer muttered. "Useless *sta*. Filthy cargo." Then he grabbed a three-needled injector from the tangle of medical equipment on the work station and lurched for the infirmary door. When it slid aside for him, Buck could see the first purple tinge of holy gas in the corridor. It was not as heavy as it had been in the past *crayg*, but it was apparent that the Overseers were attempting to flood the ship again.

The Overseer medics saw the initial tendrils of gas seeping into the infirmary and immediately began to secure their patients' treatment harnesses to stretcher poles. Within a minute they were carrying their patients from the infirmary, and when the door closed behind them only Moodri, Buck, and Cathy remained.

As soon as he heard the door clank shut, Buck wriggled out of Moodri's grip and jumped to the floor. He felt dizzy for a few moments, but the effects of D'wayn's prod and Cathy's injection had almost worn off. He stared helplessly at the tank of churning salt water. Melgil's pink-stained robes floated on the surface. "What about the key?" he asked suddenly. How could any of this end without the key?

Moodri went to Cathy and helped her to her feet. Her eyes looked into a distance that was beyond the ship. The gas had already begun to affect her. "Do you have any gloves?" Moodri asked. "Any tongs or poles or anything I can use to get the key?"

Cathy blinked at the Elder as if she had never seen him before.

Moodri laid his hands on Cathy's head, his fingers seeking specific points, though Buck did not know why. "Please, Gelana," the Elder said calmly, "the circuitry cannot withstand the corrosion of the salt. Is there any way to drain the tank?"

But Cathy bowed her head. "No equipment," she murmured, her words slurring with the gas. "They give us nothing. The water keeps circulating. No end." She seemed about to faint.

Buck looked from his great-uncle to the tank and back again. Without thinking, he walked over to Moodri and began to speak aloud the words of the prayer for Andarko's guidance. And then, unexpectedly, Moodri put his knuckles to Buck's temple and said, "Of course, Finiksa. You have seen the way."

Buck didn't understand. Moodri left him and walked over to the recycler. He climbed up on the raised section of the deck beside the transparent vat until he was kneeling beside the lip.

"Uncle Moodri?" Buck called out uncertainly.

Moodri smiled back at him. "All that is, is the same, Finiksa. How can there be conflict amongst any of it?" Carefully, deliberately, he began rolling up the sleeve of his robe.

"No," Buck said, running across the room as he finally understood what his great-uncle planned to do.

Moodri plunged his arm into the tank. He bent closer until

his head was only inches from the bubbling surface of the corrosive liquid. His eyes were closed. His face at peace. His arm moved ceaselessly over the bottom of the tank.

Buck pressed his hands to the edge of the raised deck and felt his spots pucker and his eyes expand until he thought they would burst.

Yet Moodri's face remained serene. Salt water dripped from the side of his head, but Buck could see no burn marks. Moodri's arm was submerged to his shoulder, but his uncle did not cry out in pain.

To Buck it was as if a glow of golden light had appeared in the infirmary. He remembered blue fields and drifting currents of stars. He saw Moodri's face in that glow, caught up by the stars, swept into the fields. The constant pulse of the ship's power plants was forgotten. There was a different sound that filled Buck's being. A more elemental rhythm, one that drove the stars.

"Moodri," Buck whispered, scarcely conscious of what he saw or spoke or felt.

Moodri straightened up. His arm glistened with the blood-stained liquid that could dissolve Tenctonese flesh in seconds. And that arm was whole. From the shoulder to the unharmed hand that held a long, slender black slab engraved with an elaborate pattern of golden wires.

Moodri opened his eyes again. Buck wanted to weep. From fear, from joy, from wonder. It didn't matter. What he had seen was something that he thought occurred only in the ancient stories of the days when Andarko and Celine walked among ordinary people.

Moodri smiled at his great-nephew. Buck saw only the light of a thousand suns. His hearts thundered in his ear valleys.

"Careful," Moodri said as he placed the circuitry key on the deck beside him and began to wipe at it with the hem of his robe.

"How?" Buck asked. "I saw . . . in the tank . . . the others *died.*"

Moodri stood up and peeled off his sodden robe, letting it fall into the tank to swirl with Melgil's. Buck stared up into his great-uncle's eyes.

"*Did* they die?" Moodri asked. "Or were they just . . . transformed?"

"I don't know," Buck said.

"In time you will." Moodri held out his dry hand. "Help me down, Finiksa. My knees are not what they used to be."

Buck helped Moodri climb off the raised deck. Moodri took a handful of bandages from the work station and finished drying the circuitry key.

"Encoded in these patterns are all the instructions that are required by the mechanisms that control the ship's stardrive," Moodri said as he held the key out for Buck to examine. It was as long as Buck's longest finger, but as thin as two fingernails pressed together. One side was solid black, the other like the circuitry panels Buck had seen inside the consoles in the power-plant control rooms—fine golden metal patterns against black. "Hide it near the clasp of your scarf and no one will know you carry it." Moodri led Buck to the door. "If you are stopped, tell the Overseers who you are and where you must go. Tell them that Coolock has given you *eemikken* so that you may join your Watcher Brigade. They will know who you are and let you pass."

The door slid open, and a slow wave of purple mist crept in. "What about you?" Buck asked.

"I have my tasks as well." He touched both sets of knuckles against both Buck's temples. "May Andarko and Celine watch over you and guide you in what you must do."

Buck reached up on tiptoes to touch his own knuckles to Moodri's head. "May Ionia watch over you," he said, somehow understanding that to believe in one religion was to believe in them all.

Buck stepped into the corridor, then turned back to Moodri with a sudden panicked thought. "Will I see you again?" the child asked. "I mean, when we have . . . landed."

Moodri touched his hearts. "Of course you will," he said. "Each time you look up at the stars."

Then the door slid shut, and Buck was alone.

But for no reason he could explain, he was not afraid.

CHAPTER 17

BEYOND THE CLOSED DOOR the crowd howled, and Ruhtra clutched George's tunic. Four rounds had been played. The second cage was empty. The next time Coolock entered, his choice would be one of the three—George, Ruhtra, or Zicree.

But George was prepared. He had killed one Overseer this *crayg*. Coolock would be the second. George had already planned his attack. One blow to distract the Overseer. Then grab the prod. Use it as a club. Coolock's skull could be fractured before the other Overseers would know what had happened. It was the only way George could be part of the rebellion.

The door opened with a hiss. The chanting of the crowd was fevered, like howling beasts standing ready to devour the corpses of the losers.

Ruhtra huddled in George's arms, and George made those arms like the iron bars of the cage—solid, unbreakable. What was happening was Ruhtra's worst fear. What was happening was George's fault. He would make it end, just as he had held the creature from the airlock at bay so many years ago.

"Stangya, please!" Ruhtra pleaded. His panic was overwhelming.

George looked into his brother's eyes. "I will protect you," he swore. Repeating the pledge he had made as a child.

Coolock entered the holding chamber, the fall of his boots unmistakable.

Ruhtra shook. "Don't let them take me." His body trembled as if an Overseer's prod had already been discharged against him.

Coolock's voice boomed in the chamber. "It is time."

And Ruhtra collapsed. He was a child again. George's younger brother. Cowering in the corridor as the monster advanced. "I cannot go. Please, Stangya, please."

George brushed his knuckles to his brother's temple. The cage door clanged open. Coolock entered, arrogantly stepping into the cage unafraid.

Zicree waited in the corner, beyond caring.

George and Ruhtra rose together. Coolock moved his prod from one to the other, eyes gleaming with madness and hate. "Now," he said, "who shall it be?" His eyes fell on Ruhtra.

But George pushed forward, looking for his opening. "I will go in Ruhtra's place."

Coolock gazed at George as if carefully considering his offer. He grabbed George's tunic. George made a fist at his side. As soon as they stepped through the cage entrance he would strike.

"You will be a brave player," Coolock said to George, then shoved him sideways, throwing him against Zicree as he grabbed Ruhtra instead. "But *you* will make for better sport!"

Coolock pulled Ruhtra from the cage. George rushed forward, but the cage door slid shut, making all the bars clang as if they, too, shook with fear. Ruhtra screamed and scrabbled in Coolock's unbreakable grip. George plunged his hands through the bars and shouted his brother's name.

But Coolock only laughed, only laughed until the door closed, cutting off Ruhtra's final desperate pleas and the cheering of the crowd.

"Ruhtra," George sobbed against the bars. He had led his own brother to certain death. Was anything worth it? Even a rebellion that had been kept from him?

He felt Zicree's hand rest on his shoulder. "To live on the ship, to die on the ship, what difference does it make?"

George had no answer for him. Only emptiness.

CHAPTER 18

VORNHO STOOD BESIDE BUCK in the corridor lineup and tried to jam a finger under the boy's arm.

Buck twisted, deathly afraid that the circuitry key would fall from his scarf. "Stop it!" he whispered, trying to push his friend away with the most minimal of arm movements.

"Loosen up," Vornho whispered back. "You're a hero, Finiksa, just like me!"

Buck glanced over at his friend and saw that Vornho also wore a second golden clasp of rank on his black scarf. "Heroes of the water hub," Vornho said excitedly. "That's what we are. Wow. Too bad you missed seeing that cargo explode. It was *eech ka*. Real *eech ka.*"

From down the line Watch Leader D'wayn's voice rose in warning. "You two! Keep it down. And keep the line moving."

"Yes, Watch Leader," both boys said at once. Vornho had a hard time trying not to follow it with a giggle.

"Keep quiet," Buck said, "or they won't let us go on the bridge."

Vornho stretched up to see how the line was progressing. About ten pairs of Watcher Youth were in front of them, being guided through a narrow opening into an access tunnel that Buck had never seen before. "Relax," Vornho told his friend, "they have to get us onto the bridge. Haven't you seen how edgy all the Overseers are?"

"So?" Buck asked, afraid to know what that might mean.

"So something's going on," Vornho said conspiratorially.

Buck stared at him questioningly.

"The cargo's up to something. It's obvious, you *vrick*. That's why they sealed most of the corridors and closed the shift. It's like the thing at the water hub."

"Why does that mean they have to get us to the bridge? Why not lock us up in the crèche?"

Vornho rolled his eyes and made the wiped-off-spots gesture across his forehead. "Where have you been, blankhead? There're *jabroka*-fiends all over the ship. Hundreds of them, I heard."

Buck frowned. Vornho was always convinced there were hundreds of some kind of monster roaming the ship. "Then why don't they just flood the corridors with the holy gas of obedience?"

Vornho punched Buck's shoulder. "Don't you get it? They're all out of it."

Buck wiped his own forehead back at Vornho. "Blankhead yourself, I saw the gas in the corridors on my way here."

"Well, yeah, I mean they've got *some,*" Vornho insisted, "but not a whole lot. They used up almost all of the reserves when we were at the water hub. They got the pumps making more of it, but they won't have enough to fill the ship until after we've translated again."

There were only four more pairs of Watchers ahead of them now. D'wayn looked at Buck and Vornho with narrowed eyes, which was enough to make both boys whisper again.

"You're still not making sense," Buck said. "Why does any of that mean we have to go to the bridge and not the crèche?"

"Since there's not enough gas to keep the cargo quiet," Vornho said as if talking to a four-year-old, "the only thing the Overseers can do to disrupt whatever's going on is to put the ship through a *hard* translation. You know how sick you can feel if you're too near the hull for a translation?"

"Yeah," Buck said apprehensively.

"Well, this time it's going to be ten times worse," Vornho said. "They said it'll probably kill all the Elders and a lot of the podlings, but it's only what they deserve, right?"

Buck didn't answer. "What'll it do to us?"

"Nothing," Vornho said. "That's what I've been telling you. The bridge is protected from the translation. That's why all the Overseers not on duty deep in the ship are going to be up there." He grabbed his scarf proudly. "And that includes *us!*"

Then Vornho reached out to shake Buck's scarf as well. Buck couldn't pull back in time and knew in despair that Vornho couldn't help but feel the circuitry key. But D'wayn's hand grabbed Vornho's at the last instant.

"I said keep it down, boys," the Watch Leader said. "Even if you are 'heroes of the water hub,' you still have to set an example for the younger Watchers. Am I understood?"

Both boys bowed their heads. "Yes, Watch Leader."

D'wayn patted their arms. "All right now, into the tunnel, hold onto the rail, and have fun." She guided Vornho and Buck to the small opening. It was barely large enough for D'wayn to fit through, and Buck doubted that any *jabroka*-transformed worker could have made the squeeze. Through the opening Buck could see what seemed to be a wide, moving belt on the floor, as if all they would have to do was stand still and the floor would take them up to the bridge. He found it an exciting concept. Vornho went first and was quickly pulled away with a laugh.

Just as Buck was about to go through, though, D'wayn's hand tightened on his shoulder, only an inch from where the key was hidden.

"Watcher Finiksa," she said formally, "I just wanted you to know that Coolock told me what you told him. I . . . I want to thank you for your support. And I want to tell you that . . . that I will not be so quick to judge members of my own family again."

Buck wasn't quite sure what she meant. "Family?" he asked.

D'wayn touched her knuckles to his temple. "We're all that we have," she said, and for once her voice didn't sound as if it was giving commands. "And if we did not stand together, there would be no order on the ship at all."

Buck had no idea what to say. "Thank you," he mumbled, hoping it was appropriate.

"Thank *you*, spotty head," she whispered. Then she winked at him the way a mother winked at a podling. "You'll be wearing a black tunic before you know it. Now get along with you. Up to the bridge! Up!"

Buck almost fell on his face as he stepped through onto the

moving floor. Vornho was surprisingly close. He had spent the last minute walking against the direction of the floor so he wouldn't pull away from his friend.

"Isn't this *zan?*" Vornho exclaimed.

Buck agreed. The tunnel was tilted and seemed to go on forever, but the floor was dragging them up at an angle without any need for them to walk at all.

Vornho bounced up and down on the springy moving surface, making Buck wave his arms for balance. "So what did D'wayn have to say to you?"

Buck shrugged. "Not much. Just stuff about the water hub."

Vornho looked embarrassed. "Yeah, well, they told me what happened. About you seeing the cargo's clearing charges under his membrane suit and all."

Buck tried not to look at his friend. Moodri had explained about that subterfuge, too: how Buck's memories had been changed to spare him the pressure of trying to lie to the Overseers—something he would never have been able to do on his own.

Vornho gave him a reluctant grin. "Thanks for trying to save me from blowing us all up. But next time . . . *do it faster!*"

Vornho shot both hands out to poke under Buck's arms. Buck lost his footing on the moving floor and tumbled onto his back. He felt the circuitry key fall out from his scarf, but before he could roll over on it Vornho was already kicking it away with his foot.

Buck scrambled to his feet. Vornho held the key close to his eyes, peering at its circuitry patterns intently. "Hey, what the *neck* is this thing supposed to be?" he asked.

Buck looked up the tunnel. They were coming to a large opening where the tunnel ended and two Overseers stood to help the Watchers off the moving floor. Buck grabbed for the key, but Vornho held it out of reach, waving it back and forth.

"Something important, hmm?" Vornho said.

Knowing he had no time left, Buck decided to tell him just how important it was.

CHAPTER 19

GEORGE HEARD THE MUFFLED sound of the *wojchek's* whine. He gripped the bars of the cage as the first discharge blended with the chanting of the crowd.

It spun again. George lost track of how many times. He felt himself spin. He felt himself lost in the darkness. The bars melted from his grip. How could he ever have believed in a rebellion? How could he ever have believed in anything except the ship?

The ship.

He knew what its one name was now.

It was the cry of the crowd in the Game chamber—mindless, bloodthirsty, so blind they did not know that they cheered their own deaths because it was their own kind that fed the Game.

And he knew *what* the ship was now.

It was the Game on a larger scale. Nothing more. Nothing with meaning. Nothing that depended on the direction of Those Who Made the Ships, or thinking machines, or alien beings hidden in inaccessible chambers outside the cargo disk. Those stories were all vain attempts to give meaning to meaninglessness. But George finally understood how unnecessary those stories were.

There was no enemy here. Only mirrors.

Beyond the door the crowd screamed the name of the ship as the final discharge ended another round.

But the Game wasn't over. It would never be over. Not while a single ship plied the dark ranges.

The door opened.

Ruhtra entered.

Dragged by two Overseers. His chest a gaping, glistening hole.

George sobbed his brother's name.

Coolock tapped his prod against the bars. George was consumed by the ship's emptiness. "I'll kill you, you *kakstu!*" he shrieked, arms flailing for the grinning Overseer. "I'll kill you!"

But Coolock bobbed his head just out of George's reach, turning George's rage into nothing more than a children's game. "Who's next to sit at the table?" he taunted. Then his eyes turned to black ice as he answered his own question. "You are, Stangya. You are."

George lowered his arms. Coolock opened the cage. He waited outside as if uncertain what George might do.

But there was no uncertainty in George. Not anymore. He stepped out of the cage, his hands open at his sides. There was no need to attack the Overseer. There was only one need left.

The need to die.

Without even a shove from Coolock, George turned and walked to the Game chamber door.

Willingly he would face the *wojchek*. It was the only victory that was left to him. The only fate he deserved.

George Francisco stepped into the deepest chamber of the ship and prepared to die.

It was the only thing he had left to look forward to.

CHAPTER 20

"D'WAYN GAVE IT TO ME," Buck said.

Vornho stared at him skeptically, the circuitry key still in his hand. They were less than a hundred meters from the tunnel's end and approaching quickly on the moving floor.

"She gave it to you? Just now?"

"Yes," Buck said, stepping up the floor to try and block Vornho and what he was holding from the Overseers at the end of the tunnel.

"So what is it?"

"A circuitry key," Buck blurted, the first thing to come to his mind. "For . . . for some privacy chambers. By the big 'ponics jungle on the top decks."

Buck could see that Vornho wasn't convinced but that he was intrigued.

"They're just for Overseers she said. They can use them whenever they want. No waiting. Lots of *eemikken*. And they keep female cargo up there. Real *poco,* she said. Just for the Overseers."

Now Vornho *wanted* to believe Buck. But he still had one objection. "How come you got one and I didn't?"

Less than fifty yards. "You were supposed to get yours from Coolock, D'wayn said. But he's been too busy with the cargo."

Buck held out his hand. "Give it back to me, Vornho. Not everyone gets them, so she told me not to tell anyone else."

Vornho brought the key teasingly closer to Buck's hand. "Not even me?"

"They were going to take us up there *together,* blankhead. But you're going to ruin everything! The females. The *eemikken* Everything!"

Vornho slammed the key into Buck's hand, then said, "If you're lying to me, Finiksa, I'll peel your spots."

Buck shoved the key under his scarf and wedged it between the clasps. "You'll be too busy having *your* spots licked, mother hummer."

Vornho laughed. He wiggled his fingers beside Buck's ribs. "Eat salt!"

An Overseer grabbed Buck from behind and swung him off the moving floor to a solid deck. "Easy there, young Watcher. Next time ride the belt looking in the right direction."

Vornho stepped off the moving floor between the two Overseers and as he looked up his mouth opened wide. Buck turned to see what his friend had seen. "Andarko," he whispered.

He was on the bridge.

Buck had never seen an open space as large before. The bridge chamber stretched out farther than the food-growth chambers with room for a hundred vats. And the ceiling— Buck gasped—there *was* no ceiling. It was one vast transparent dome of what could only be the same material the hull's portals were made from.

Stars shone all around him. Thousands of them. And forward, in the direction that the ship moved, one star was so large and bright that Buck could see a visible disk almost the size of his thumb tip. It cast long shadows all through the bridge.

"That must be the course-correction star," Vornho said wonderingly. For once there was no hint of challenge in his voice. He sounded just like Buck.

"Can you see any planets?" Buck asked. He wasn't sure what they might look like, but he wanted to know if the world Moodri had told him would be their target was in sight.

"Planets are too small to see," Vornho said. "They're at least a hundred times smaller than a star." He stared all around. "Will you take a look at how big this place is?"

Buck followed along behind a stream of other Watcher Youth between two blue lines painted on the deck of the bridge.

Unlike the decks in the rest of the ship, the floor covering here wasn't made of metal but of something softer, with almost the same consistency as the moving floor in the tunnel that had brought them here.

The scale of the bridge was different, too. Buck could see a dozen Overseers operating equipment consoles similar to those he had seen in the power-plant chambers. But the consoles were at least twice the size they had been in the other parts of the ship. Here the Overseers had to climb up on small metal platforms that had been built before each one in order to reach the control surfaces.

Buck's hearts sank. Would he have to climb up such a platform to use the key?

Near Buck were the sounds of children's excited babble, but from all around came mechanical sounds, odd, almost musical beeps, and strange voices that made Buck think of talking machines. From time to time colored images moved across the transparent dome as if they had been projected there by a hand-held light—lines and circles and sine-script numbers that meant nothing to Buck.

"This is the most *eech ka* thing I've ever seen," Vornho whispered. "Do you think we could ever work up here or anything?"

"Maybe," Buck said. He was distracted by trying to look ahead of the crowd of other children, following the twin blue lines to see where they passed by the pink consoles of the stardrive. He couldn't see them anywhere. "Vornho, do you see any pink consoles?"

Vornho glanced around. "Sure, right behind us."

Buck shivered with fear. He had *already* gone past them. The stardrive consoles had been first on his right when he had entered the bridge, and he had been too caught up in staring through the ceiling dome to notice them.

A loud voice boomed through the enormous volume of the bridge. "All crew prepare for translation."

Buck tried to push past the Watcher Youth gathered behind him.

"Where're you going?" Vornho called.

"We're not close enough to translate," Buck said. Moodri had explained it to him. At translation they would be so close that the course-correction star would fill the portals.

"It's the hard translation," Vornho said as he followed after

Buck, moving through the crowd of excited children. "Not the main one. It's just going to be a bump to knock out the cargo and get things back to normal."

"No," Buck said to himself. Moodri had said others would be waiting to take control of the cargo disk once Buck had inserted the key. But though the bridge was shielded from the effects of translation, if the others waiting elsewhere in the ship were knocked out or killed, then no one would be able to control anything.

Buck stood on the edge of a blue line. The pink stardrive console was ten feet from him. Overseers stood on two platforms that had been built in front of it. They wore dark goggles over their eyes and stared up at the course-correction star as if reading whatever words and symbols were being projected on the dome. Between the two platforms Buck saw the one control surface that was not covered by a clear protective shield. There was a slot in it that his key would fit into. He could reach it without climbing on anything.

"Hey, Finiksa, what's wrong?" Vornho said. There was real worry in his voice.

"Hard translation in thirty seconds," the mechanical voice said.

Buck pulled the circuitry key from his scarf.

"You want to lose that?" Vornho asked in shock. "I thought you were supposed to keep it a secret."

Buck didn't even look at his friend. "Shut up, Vornho. Just shut up!"

Buck sprinted across the deck toward the console.

"Finiksaaaa!"

Buck ignored Vornho's cry. He ignored the sound of Vornho's feet running after him. He reached the console.

"Twenty seconds."

The two Overseers on the platforms to either side looked down at him, ten feet over his head. One of them told him to get away before he hurt himself.

Vornho was at his side. "What are you doing?" He looked at the slot in the control surface, and Buck could see he immediately knew what would fit in it.

"Finiksa, what's wrong with you?" he asked.

Buck began to speak. He had to tell someone. But then another voice called his name. He turned back to the path between the blue lines. D'wayn had just stepped onto the bridge from the moving floor. She waved to the boys, smiling.

"Finiksa, Vornho, come away from there. You'll miss the show."

"Fifteen seconds."

"Finiksa," Vornho said. "What *is* that thing? What will it do?"

D'wayn began to walk toward them. "Come on and join the family," she said invitingly. "We can take better care of you over here." She still smiled.

"Finiksa, don't do anything stupid." Vornho slapped his hand over the key slot. "I won't tell. We're friends. We can stick together, and no one will know."

"Ten seconds."

Buck didn't know what to do. D'wayn was smiling at him. She had called him spotty head. Vornho was his best friend. And Moodri . . . where was Moodri?

Every time you look up at the stars, his great-uncle's voice said.

Buck looked up at the stars.

One was different.

It had a shape—a half circle, blue and white and almost too small to be seen. But it was there, and Buck saw it, almost as if someone had called out to him from it. Almost as if someone wanted him there.

"Five seconds."

Buck turned to face Vornho. He shot his hand out, one finger stiff and ready, and he hit Vornho's sensitive spot on his first try. Vornho doubled over in shock. Buck had never been able to do that before. Vornho's hand came off the key slot. In the distance Buck heard D'wayn gasp aloud.

For an endless moment Buck held the key poised above the control surface, waiting. The fate of two worlds rested in the hand of a ten-year-old child.

But the child was not alone.

Fear no more, Finiksa.

Buck heard the message.

He plunged the key home.

It began.

PART THREE

DESCENT

CHAPTER 1

BEFORE THE SUN SET, CNN had turned over its entire broadcast to live coverage of what it was now dramatically calling "The Voronezh Encounter." Hastily assembled news crews reported live from the Jet Propulsion Laboratory in Pasadena, the Astronomy Department at London University, the Pentagon, the Moscow Academy of Sciences, and an independent television studio in Orange County where two bearded science fiction authors who had written a novel about a giant comet hitting the earth endlessly explained the differences between comets and asteroids. Other than everyone agreeing that the Voronezh Object was damn unusual, no one else around the world had anything else to say because no one knew anything.

Except for those people in a tract house in an exclusive new subdivision in Topanga Canyon, halfway between Santa Monica and Malibu.

Sikes had spent most of the past few hours surreptitiously trying to stretch the ropes around his wrists and asking himself just how badly he wanted to be a cop.

The ropes hadn't seemed to stretch a fraction of an inch, but he knew absolutely that being a cop was not a choice, it was a necessity. There was nothing else he wanted to be or that he *could* be. And that was the root of the dilemma he faced, one that even distracted him from the ongoing CNN reports.

The bottom line was that Sikes had finally realized that Amy Stewart and her uncle and their supporters were going to win this one. The asteroid or the spaceship or whatever it was was beside the point. The reality Sikes faced was that when morning came and that thing was on its way to being another question in a Trivial Pursuit game for the nineties, Sikes would face the choice that Commander Stewart had laid out for him: sign a security oath or go to jail.

And when that moment came, Sikes didn't know what he would do.

The silent man with the .45 was Randolph Petty's killer. Sikes knew that without a doubt. He had seen the smirk on the man's thin lips when he had said as much to Stewart and his niece. He had seen the acceptance of his deduction in their eyes as well. But there was nothing Sikes could do about it.

He had thought about lying. He had thought about signing whatever the hell it was they wanted him to sign, waiting a week, and then going to the media. But he knew that the instant he brought up the threat of the National Security Oath the media would have to check their sources to confirm the story, and he'd be in the slammer. We've done it before, ex–Commander Franklin Stewart had said, and Sikes had no reason to doubt him.

For himself, Sikes was willing to risk a confrontation with whatever shadowy level of the government Stewart took his orders from. But for Kirby's sake, he wanted there to be another way. Even if that way meant signing the oath, saying nothing, and letting Petty's killer go free.

At least I could still be a father to my daughter, Sikes thought. At least I could keep being a cop and lock up other killers.

But what kind of a cop lets a killer go free?

Sikes didn't like the answer to that one. He wanted to talk it over with someone—Angie, who had finally come to and was even more pissed off than Sikes had been, or Theo, probably wearing his chains and hanging out at another strip show. Sikes would even settle for attempting a conversation with Bryon Grazer. But Stewart wasn't allowing anyone to talk anymore, except to request an escorted trip to the bathroom.

Four hours into "The Voronezh Encounter," CNN switched back to a bleary-eyed astronomer at the University of London for the third time in an hour. Amy went into the kitchen. Sikes, Angie, and Grazer sat like the proverbial three monkeys on the navy-blue couch, while Kirby, to Sikes's relief, had curled up in the recliner and fallen asleep from exhaustion.

On television the sleepy Dr. Robin Kingsburgh repeated what she had said twice before about the escape velocity of the sun and the fact that, given the speed at which the Voronezh Object was traveling, it could not be from our solar system. In any event, she added, its speed meant it would not be staying here. Her expression conveyed the impression that she would not be staying either if her interviewer did not come up with a new question to ask.

Sikes sensed the excitement over the object was already dying down. "Hey, Uncle Frank, see if there's a basketball game on," Sikes said, just to bother Stewart. "No one's said anything new for the past hour."

"Good," Stewart said. "That means no observatory has managed any worthwhile observations yet."

Amy came out of the kitchen with a large platter stacked with bread, some kind of sliced meat, and a jar of mustard.

"Gee," Angie muttered, "just like a regular evening at home."

"You don't have to eat anything." Amy put the platter down on the broadloom in front of the sofa. She used a plastic knife to spread mustard onto two pieces of bread and added a stack of mystery-meat slices to make a sandwich. She held it up in offering. "Anyone?" she asked.

"Well, if no one else wants it," Grazer said.

Amy stuck the sandwich in his cuffed hands and ignored his request for a napkin.

"What do you do after this?" Sikes made himself ask her.

"Go back to the university," she said. "Finish my Ph.D."

"Kill a few more astronomers," Angie suggested.

Amy stood up. "I'm not going through all that again. People like you should be thankful there're people like me taking care of the important things in life." She went back to sit in a chair by her uncle. The blond killer with the .45 remained at the back of the room so that Sikes couldn't see him without turning his head.

CNN went back to Orange County and the science fiction writers, who enthusiastically described what an incoming alien spacecraft might look like and how the Voronezh Object did not fit any of the characteristics they would expect.

Stewart laughed scornfully at the screen.

The science fiction writers began talking about the alien spacecraft they had described in another of their books about an invasion of Earth.

"Hey, Uncle Frank, you must've read that one," Sikes said as the cover of the book went up on the screen. "No wonder you're worried. Giant elephants from Mars would scare anyone."

Stewart turned around in his chair. "Detective Sikes, would you prefer to be gagged or simply beaten unconscious?"

"How about letting me use the phone to call CNN so they can get *your* perspective on the object?" Sikes said. "Set those sci-fi guys straight." Stewart got up, just as Sikes had hoped he would, and Sikes glanced at the sandwich platter, fixing the position of the plastic knife in his memory. If he could just provoke Stewart enough to have the man slap him the way he had slapped Grazer, then he could fall off the couch and grab the knife and maybe saw through the ropes before morning.

Stewart stood by Sikes again, almost within arm's reach. "You're all going to be released in the morning," he said coolly. "Whether your captain sends you home or to the hospital is your choice."

Sikes adjusted his position on the couch. He knew just what to say and was glad that Kirby was asleep. "So where are you and your niece going to go after this?" Sikes asked. But before he could finish the insult that would guarantee Stewart's attack, a car drove up outside.

Everyone but Grazer looked to the curtained windows. Grazer was concentrating on his sandwich, being very careful not to drip mustard on his rumpled suit. Headlights sprayed across the living room, then stopped.

Stewart turned quickly to the killer and nodded to the front door. Amy turned off the television with the remote. The killer walked noiselessly across the room, smoothly taking his automatic from his holster. Stewart moved into the kitchen and reappeared a second later, holding another .45. Sikes decided this was not the moment to jump for a plastic knife.

The doorbell rang. It was loud in the half-empty house.

Stewart shook his head at the killer by the door. Then he pointed his gun at Kirby and held his finger to his lips. The message was clear.

Sikes wanted to feel his hands close around Stewart's throat. But he could do nothing.

From outside a muffled voice shouted, "Yo! It's Domino's. The thirty-minute guarantee don't count if you keep me waiting out here!"

Inside no one moved except for Angie and Sikes, who exchanged a look. Sikes saw it in her eyes as well. They were about to find out if there were or were not coincidences in police work.

Someone pounded on the front door. "Yo! Your pizza's getting cold!"

No response. Sikes braced himself. He could feel Angie tense beside him. Grazer's cheeks bulged with sandwich.

"Yo, man! I am telling you I am sick of this shit! You don't pay me for this pizza, I am calling the police! I swear to God I am!"

The killer moved cautiously to the curtained window. He moved the edge of it back with the barrel of his gun and peered outside. He looked across at Stewart and shrugged his shoulders, mouthing something Sikes couldn't make out.

Stewart motioned angrily at the door. The killer went to it, put his hand on the doorknob.

Sikes held his breath. Angie held hers. Grazer pushed the last of the sandwich into his mouth.

The killer opened the door, keeping his gun hidden.

A delivery man in Domino's red, white, and blue stood on the porch, holding three pizza boxes stacked together. "About time, my man. I was just about to eat—"

The killer grunted and fell twitching to the ground, trailing taser wires from his chest.

"Down!" the Domino's man shouted.

Stewart dropped to one knee and swung his .45 up. Sikes leapt from the couch and aimed himself at Kirby. All over the house windows shattered. The concussion grenades went off a heartbeat later.

Sikes hit the floor at Kirby's feet but didn't feel the impact. His ears were ringing so badly that he couldn't tell if a shot had been fired or not. But he could see Kirby's legs trembling. That was a good sign, he told himself. Then he threw up. His body felt like jelly. The house smelled of cordite. He had a black dot at the side of his vision that was worse than anything a flash camera could give him. But he was alive.

He tried to roll away from what he had done to the broadloom. Several pairs of black-trousered legs ran past him, then returned. He felt someone lifting him into the air. Maybe someone was speaking to him, he couldn't be sure.

Strong arms turned him around.

Theo.

Sikes's ex-partner spoke silently, not making sense over the explosions that were still going off in Sikes's eardrums.

"Kirby!" Sikes yelled. "Kirby!" He felt no sound come from his mouth.

Theo helped him turn around. A tall man in black clothes and a heavy flak jacket cradled Kirby in his arms. Kirby looked at Sikes and smiled, tears running from her eyes. Sikes lurched for her, checking her clothes for signs of blood.

He didn't see anything.

He held out his hands to her. Theo grabbed the ropes and sliced into them with a combat knife. The ropes fell to the ground. Sikes took Kirby from the other cop. She pushed her head into his shoulder. He carried her out.

The cold air tasted like freedom.

He looked up to the night sky to give thanks.

The stars were waiting for him.

CHAPTER 2

THE SHIP SCREAMED.

Buck felt the howl of its dying run through his body.

He had no idea what furies he had unleashed. He only knew what Moodri had told him—the stardrive will be activated out of sequence, before the other systems are ready for it. The ship cannot survive the strain. Automatic mechanisms will ensure that the most important part of the ship survives. The cargo disk will be jettisoned.

Buck had less than fifty double beats.

Vornho looked up in shock, his hands under his armpits, sliding across the deck as the bridge spun and the warning sirens screeched. He struggled to his feet as Buck fell back with the first of the shudders traveling through the deck. Vornho threw himself at the stardrive console's control surface. He closed his fist around the key.

"No, Vornho! Don't!" Buck shouted. He didn't know how long the key had to remain in place, how long it would take for the circuitry to work. He pulled at Vornho's scarf to drag him away from the console, but the clasps gave way, no strength to them.

Then D'wayn was behind them both. *"What have you done?"* she cried.

Vornho spun around, his hand still on the key. "Watch Leader . . . this key . . ." He began to yank it from the console.

"Stop him!" Buck pleaded senselessly. But why would she?

D'wayn's spots were dark with rage. She swung her prod up and focused it to full power.

Vornho pulled the key free. "I did it," he said, "Watch Leader, I—"

D'wayn rammed her prod under his jaw, and it discharged with an explosive blue arc. Webs of sparking energy crawled up Vornho's face and scalp. His eyes instantly turned solid white, as if they had been cooked, and blood gushed from his ear valleys and nose and mouth.

The child who had dreamt of *sleema* females crumpled to the deck, and whatever his last sounds might have been, they were lost in the thunder of the sirens and alarms.

D'wayn pulled the circuitry key from Vornho's lifeless hand and crushed it in her own. Only then did Buck realize that she hadn't seen what had happened at the console. She had only seen two boys fighting, and when she had arrived Vornho was the one with his hand on the key, and Buck was the one who was trying to stop him.

"Are you all right?" the Overseer shouted at Buck.

Buck had no words. His best friend was dead, but by dying he had given Buck his life.

"I know, I know," D'wayn said. She swept Buck into her arms and held him close against her substantial bulk. "I should have realized it at the water hub. The way he hesitated before shooting the worker. Even before you tried to warn him." She turned toward the tunnel entrance. "The children!" she yelled. "Get the children to the hatch!"

All was confusion for Buck. The transparent dome swam with projected lines and geometric shapes that seemed to spiral into infinity. The stars beyond moved rapidly, as if the ship spun in space, and the bridge deck began to slant, as if gravity was changing its angle of attraction.

Overseers fell from their platforms by the consoles. Uncounted voices screamed with the sirens. The tunnel entrance was jammed with Overseers and Watcher Youth.

D'wayn barreled into the thickest part of the crowd, screaming for the children to follow her. She wielded her prod before her, shocking every adult she saw trying to put himself or herself or *binn*self before her charges.

The sirens rose to an unbearable frequency. The light panels strobed, sending mad shadows flickering over terror-stricken faces and whitening spots. D'wayn was at the tunnel entrance. She dropped Buck to the moving floor. "Run, child, run!" she begged him. Then she began to pull other children from the crowd and push them onto the moving floor. But the floor was still coming forward, and the frightened, crying children were tumbling together at the end of it, creating even more of a barrier to escape.

The ship trembled. D'wayn swung her prod against a control box on the tunnel wall, and the controls sparked and burst into flame. The floor stopped. She looked behind her. Explosions erupted from the oversize consoles, filling the bridge with fire and smoke. Water began spraying from the walls.

"No!" D'wayn cried, then she picked up a screaming child, grabbed Buck by the arm, and threw herself forward down the sloping tunnel as more and more explosions burst behind her.

The tunnel walls blurred by Buck as his legs thumped in giant, uncontrollable leaps. He cried for Vornho. He cried for the key—how could it have worked in such a short time? And he cried for Moodri and his mother and father and Andarko and Celine and all his people whom he had failed.

And even as she ran, D'wayn heard his tears and lifted him to her again. "Shhh," she said between gasps of breath. "Shhh, little spotty head. We've been expecting this. Everything will be all right."

But Buck did not answer. He knew that nothing would ever be all right again.

It had been his time, and he had failed.

The ship screamed, and Moodri took pleasure in its dying.

The shudders that ran through the decks and walls filled him with satisfaction. The ship would return to the Mother, and Moodri would go with it.

He looked forward to his fate. Of all that his people would need in the years ahead, perhaps nothing was more important than the knowledge that another ship would not come for them. Moodri could give them that at such a small price—his life.

At the instant the first alarms wailed Moodri stepped forth from an alcove in a deserted corridor and walked purposefully for a hidden access hatch. His quick passage disturbed the thin layer of purple gas that lay across the deck. As the council had planned, the Overseers had been compelled to expend the bulk of their gas reserves to quell a rebellion that had not yet begun. Now there was little gas left with which to flood the corridors and chambers, and when the cargo disk landed, most of the captive Tenctonese would be clearheaded enough to run as far away as possible before the inertial stabilizers failed.

Moodri came to the access hatch and easily touched the hidden surfaces in the proper combination. After almost a century of study there were few mechanical secrets that the ship still held. The access hatch puffed open. Moodri peered beyond it. He frowned. The moving beltway in the sloping tunnel beyond was already in operation, as if someone else was already on his way up to the communications substation.

But this was no time to ponder possibilities. The ship was creaking all around him. Fragile pipes burst and sent streams of water and gases into the corridors, swirling into the purple mist. Moodri stepped through the hatch and onto the moving floor. Just like the tunnel he knew Buck had taken to the bridge, this tunnel sloped up through the cargo disk to another part of the ship's main section. The maps upon which Moodri based his passage had been assembled over decades of trial and error at the cost of many lives. But he knew they were accurate, just as he knew that Buck would survive the bridge and set foot on a new world.

Sometimes, when Moodri had visions of his great-nephew's future, he saw himself at Buck's side, though he knew that that would not be possible in the flesh. His own destiny was to ride the stardrive into superluminal space on an uncontrolled translation. He would broadcast the faster-than-light codes that would indicate an unanticipated breakdown had occurred and that the entire ship had been lost on an untraceable, higher-dimensional trajectory. The Elders had penetrated the secrets of the fleet well enough to know that when a ship was lost in such a way, no search or rescue was possible. If a trajectory into the superluminal dimensions was not carefully plotted before it was undertaken, then no return to normal spacetime was ever possible. As far as the fleet would know, this ship would have vanished along with its crew, beyond any hope of recovery, all because of the messages Moodri would send.

He smiled as he stood upon the moving floor, one hand

grasping the railing for safety. Swiftly the floor moved him upward to his final destination. All around him the ship twisted and quaked. Joyfully he sang a peaceful song of Old Tencton, celebrating the dawn that comes on the last day of a voyager's journey. The dawn of home.

He was almost there.

But when the floor took him to the tunnel's end, he was not alone.

A step beyond the deep ridge into which the pressure door would seal itself, Vondmac stood. She wore her robes and leaned on her walking stick, though her spots were so dark and her eyes so bright that Moodri thought she looked younger than she had in decades.

Moodri stepped off the floor and stood on the other side of the door seal. Fine tremors ran through the tunnel walls, and he knew that when they became stronger it would indicate that the stardrive generators had finally reached overload, and the ship would begin to seal each of its sections in preparation for jettisoning the cargo disk. There was not much time.

"It is not right for both of us to go into the superluminal," Moodri said. From behind Vondmac he could see the flash of warning lights and hear distant sirens scream.

"You are correct," Vondmac agreed. "Which is why I shall go *alone* to operate the communications station."

Moodri smiled at her. "How typical that our last conversation in this stage of our existence should be an argument. Please, your knowledge will be needed on the new world. Our biochemistry cannot possibly be compatible with an independently evolved biosphere. Our people will need food."

"Our people will adapt. The engineering of our genes that made us such excellent slaves also makes us excellent survivors."

"This is not the plan that was agreed to."

"The starting conditions have been changed," Vondmac said. "Therefore, we should not be surprised that the results are different from what we anticipated."

"No conditions have changed," Moodri answered patiently. He braced his hand against the tunnel wall as a hard tremor bumped the floor sideways. "Everything is proceeding exactly as we had planned."

But Vondmac bowed her head in disagreement. "One from each family was to have been preserved," she said. "From each family that took part in the rebellion, one was to have remained untainted to continue the line in the new world." She looked up at Moodri. "Stangya was the chosen survivor of the Family: Heroes of Soren'tzahh. But Stangya broke through the walls of *keer'chatlas* and has been lost to the future."

Moodri felt his hearts stir. Vondmac was right. George's actions had not been predicted. His loss was indeed a sorrow. "Finiksa will prevail, though. I have seen him take foot upon the soil of a new world."

"As have I," Vondmac said, "in the hands of those with tattooed wrists." She adjusted her walking stick against the shaking of the floor. "It is not enough that a child survive alone. For how can he progress without knowledge of his past and guidance for his future? The Overseers will give him neither."

The tunnel bucked, and Moodri nearly fell to his knees. "Vondmac, this is not your destiny," Moodri said.

"Melgil was my mate," the Elder said. Moodri was stunned. How long had he known them both and not suspected? "And now I seek no other destiny than to return to the Mother with *binn* at my side." She raised her hand in a gesture of farewell. "See that the seeds of our people grow well in their alien soil." Sudden gouts of pressurized air blew out from the edges of the door seal. Vondmac called out over the terrible rumbling that filled the air. She smiled one last time. "We shall meet again in the fields of stars"—the pressure door began to slide across the tunnel entrance—"and we shall finish our argument then!"

The door closed. The tunnel was sealed. Moodri touched his hearts. He had never won an argument with Vondmac yet, and he supposed he never would.

With a sigh Moodri touched a control on the tunnel wall, and the moving floor began to travel back toward the cargo disk. Moodri stepped onto it, knowing full well that the goddess was teaching him a lesson about being certain of what would happen in his life, even so close to its end. "Just let me know if this will be my final planet," Moodri grumbled in prayer. "My knees are not what they used to be."

He waited for Ionia's answer all the way down the tunnel. When it came it might have been a yes, but Moodri, for once, admitted to himself and to her that he couldn't be certain.

He decided that that was what the goddess wanted him to think, and as he stepped back into the cargo disk he realized that for the first time in almost a century he had no idea what he should expect next.

He rather enjoyed the sensation. It felt like freedom.

The ship screamed, but George did not hear it.

He only heard the thunder of his hearts. The rest of it—the chanting of the crowd, the whine of the *wojchek*—meant nothing to him anymore. All that mattered was his death, and that was only seconds away.

He was dimly aware of a shaking in the deck beneath him. It traveled up the metal frame of the chair in which he was bound by metal cuffs. But he decided it was only the vibration from the rhythmic stomping of the Game's audience. The *wojchek* began to slow. George counted his final seconds of life.

The *wojchek* was a metal cylinder, edged by six evenly spaced nozzles, that spun in the center of the table George faced. When the Game began the *wojchek* stopped, and two of the nozzles aimed out directly for the chests of the two players who sat opposite each other at the table.

The players' chests were bare so that nothing would be hidden from the spectators' avid gaze. Five of the six nozzles would only spray pressurized air from which water vapor would condense, blasting a player with an icy breath, an intimation of eternity. But the sixth nozzle, different each time, would mix and spray forth the contents of two cylinders plugged into place at the table's side. One cylinder held water. The other cylinder held salt.

The horror of the Game was that death was not instantaneous. When the deadly nozzle faced its victim, as it could at any turn, there would be a delay as the cylinders emptied and their contents were mixed beneath the table so that the crowd and the loser both could anticipate the Game's final outcome.

Then a high-pressure blast of salt water would eat its way through the loser's chest, and the crowd would howl in concert with his hideous death scream.

The *wojchek* made its final spin. Only two nozzles remained. One held life, the other death.

George prayed for death.

Alarms rang. He didn't hear them.

The *wojchek* stopped.

The floor shook, and with a sudden lurch the deck of the

Game chamber seemed to change angles. George gripped the arms of his chair for support, though the metal restraints would hold him in regardless.

The chanting of the crowd broke into a dozen whispered conversations. But some among them still shouted, "Push it! Push it!"

The player across from George was the player who had beaten Ruhtra. Coolock stood off to the side, prod in hand and death's-head grin on his face. The grin faded as each shudder shook the chamber, but George didn't care.

The other player looked worried. He faced death as surely as George did, but the shaking of the deck concerned him. He turned to look at Coolock.

"Push it!" George screamed. He pushed his own button beneath his right hand, but it was not his turn, and nothing happened. "Push it!" He called for his own death.

Some of the audience members rose to their feet and began to step down from the bleachers that ringed the chamber. Coolock nodded at the other player. The player turned back to George. More sirens sounded. Growing louder.

"Push it, you *coopr,*" George snarled. It had to end. It all had to end now. Just as it had ended for Ruhtra.

The deck shook. The player pushed the button.

A blast of air sprayed across his chest, and he howled in victory as his restraints popped free.

Some of the audience cheered with him. George slumped in his chair with relief. It was finally over. He could pay the price. He jammed his fingers against his own button, but the machinery beneath the table had not yet reset itself. Nothing happened.

"Come on!" George screamed.

Coolock laughed at him.

A handful of voices weakly chanted. "Push it! Push it!" But most of the audience had left.

George heard a clunk beneath the table.

"Yes," he whispered. "Yes."

He raised his fingers above the button.

The chamber jerked violently, back and forth, up and down. The lights flickered. Coolock plunged to the deck.

The *wojchek* shifted.

The final nozzle no longer pointed at him.

George pressed the button.

The cylinders at the edge of the table chunked into position. Water bubbled out of one. Salt rushed out of the other. He heard them mix together beneath the table.

The nozzle fired.

A stream of salt water arced through the air.

And it missed George.

"Noooo!" George screamed as he rocked against his metal bonds, trying to rip his hands from his wrists so he could throw himself into the jet of liquid death. "I am next! I am next to die! Next to die!"

Warning lights flashed. More alarms. George wept, oblivious to everything except his own failure. And when next he looked up, the Game chamber was deserted. Even Coolock was gone.

"No," George pleaded hoarsely. "No." But there was no one to hear him. He was alone.

George never knew how long he remained in that chair, feeling the ship seem to tear itself apart around him. Eventually he became aware of someone standing beside him. George hoped it was an Overseer come to finish the Game.

But it was only Zicree, placid, serene, beyond caring.

He released the metal bands that held George captive. George didn't move.

Zicree gently tugged on George's arm.

"It's time to go," Zicree said. "We're landing."

And George collapsed in angry tears because, Andarko help him, he did not want to be free. He did not deserve it.

But Zicree helped him from the chamber anyway.

CHAPTER 3

WHEN THE MOMENT of separation came, perhaps only twenty individuals of the three hundred thousand Tenctonese on board the ship truly understood what had brought that moment and what would happen after it had passed.

Moodri was one of them.

He had found a crèche that had been deserted, indicating that the quickly released instructions for the children to be gathered and taken to the lower decks had been successful. Heartened, he had braced himself in a child-sized sleeping platform and prepared for what he knew would follow.

Separation began with a fall.

All power to the cargo disk was shut off for the space of several heartsbeats. The sirens stopped. The lights dimmed. And for a single stomach-wrenching instant there was a moment of free fall as the artificial gravity cut out.

Then the rumble of explosive separation charges roared through the corridors, and by the time it had faded emergency light and gravity had been restored, though neither was as strong as when they had drawn their power from the ship's main section.

In his mind Moodri formed a picture of what the ship would look like seen from afar. The cargo disk was now propelled on a separate course by the force of the separation charges and would appear to spiral slowly away from the enormous bulk of the stardrive section, leaving a crescent-shaped gap in the stardrive's hull and a cloud of hull-crawler machines floating free, caught unawares by the ship's breakup.

The curve of the stardrive hull that had gripped the cargo disk would be veiled in the vapor of lost atmosphere, almost as if it sped through clouds. A similar haze would rapidly dissipate from the edge of the cargo disk.

Then, when the disk had moved about one kilometer distant, the stardrive emergency systems would no longer be able to control the unfathomable generators that gave it the power to slip into other dimensions, and the ship would simply disappear like a dream upon awakening. The stars that had shone behind it might appear to be a degree bluer for an instant, the result of their light being slightly accelerated due to a subtle residual warping of spacetime, but that would be the only trace the monstrous vessel would leave.

Whatever secrets it carried, including Vondmac at the communications controls, were lost forever in realms where nothing could travel *slower* than light.

Moodri smiled in peace as he sensed the ship's final translation. It brought the moment of his reunion with Vondmac an instant closer.

Now there was just the cargo disk spinning through space, drawn by gravity toward the course-correction star. If nothing more was to affect its course, within hours it would be close enough that it would become incandescent gas, and its passengers—no longer cargo or slaves, but *passengers*—would return to the stars from which they were made.

But something *would* happen before then. Moodri knew the plan. And he heard the distant clunkings and rushing of liquids that told him that the plan was underway.

Throughout the cargo disk, automatic emergency systems came to life and prepared to control the flight of an object that had no engines or reaction mass. Moodri was still not certain of the principles involved, though neither had any of the other Elders determined exactly how such a thing as artificial gravity could be possible. But it was artificial gravity that would determine the disk's course now.

Unfortunately, if left to their own internal instructions, the emergency automatic systems in control of the disk would attempt to have the disk follow the ship's original route. The beings within would be long dead by the time it finished its centuries-long voyage through normal space, but the equipment would survive and be reused.

The Elders had taken steps to prevent that.

All through the disk, corridors were sealed off automatically, just as the water hubs had been closed by the Overseers hours earlier. Then the clearing charges that had been planted by members of the rebellion at the time of the water-hub incident fired in precise sequence, blowing apart pumping stations and diverting the disk's water supply according to careful calculations.

Torrents of high-pressure water flooded into the water hubs, which finally functioned as they had been designed to function —becoming holding tanks by which the distribution of mass in the disk could be altered.

As that distribution of mass changed, the artificial gravity generators compensated for the change in stress on the disk's hull. And though it flew in the face of everything the Elders had known about physics, the disk changed course as if the inertia of the water pulsing through it was being doubled as it rushed for the leading section and decreased to zero as it traveled back to the section following.

"Madness," Vondmac had called it when the engineers had first laid out what the alien machines in the disk were capable of doing. But it worked.

Moodri pressed his back and his legs against opposite sides of the sleeping platform as all around him the disk groaned and creaked. The water hubs filled with madly swirling water, the liquid's inertial forces being impossibly focused to provide forward momentum only. In one hub, Moodri sensed, a squad of Overseers had been trapped. And though he touched his hearts as they were swept up by the ferociously circulating flood and spun screaming around the hub's curved and rounded walls until they were broken apart as surely as the ship had been, Moodri found it fitting that they were swallowed by the beast they had served with such equally ferocious hate.

In time the automatic systems would compensate for the damage that the clearing charges had brought and regain control of the disk once again. But by that time, Moodri knew, the disk would have lost so much momentum that it could not possibly escape the gravitational pull of the course-correction star. At that point the automatics would then proceed with their secondary objective of preserving that which the disk carried and would look for an appropriate place to land.

Moodri and the Elders had seen to it that the automatics would not have to look too far to find what their instructions required.

When the creaking and shifting of direction had finally stopped, indicating that the automatic systems had plotted their course and set out on it, Moodri stopped pressing against the sides of the sleeping platform and peacefully settled down to have a nap.

He needed his rest. For though the rebellion had succeeded, in just a few hours the real fight would begin.

CHAPTER 4

SIKES SAT ON THE HOOD of the Domino's delivery car parked in the driveway of the new house. Kirby sat close beside him, and he kept his arm around her shoulder. The night was cold, and they had a blanket wrapped around them. Sikes sipped coffee from a plastic thermos cup. There was still a ringing in his ears, but he could finally hear again. Theo's voice in particular sounded like music.

"You're brilliant, man," Sikes said as Theo came up to him with two large evidence bags. Each held a .45 automatic. "How'd you find us?"

Theo reached out to tousle Kirby's hair. "I didn't *find* you. I just never let you out of my sight. Tailed you to Kirby's school, the whole way home, then tailed the van back here." He looked back at the house. Light poured from its open front door across the small porch and onto the lawn. "And if this isn't a textbook example of a government safe house, then I don't know what is."

Sikes was pleased but puzzled. "Why did you think you had to tail me?"

"Like I said, kid, I've been down this road before. I said if Matt really is up to his"—he smiled at Kirby—"you-know-what in alligators with the feds, there's sure as hell—uh, heck—not going to be any way he's going to get help from the captain. So of course it was up to yours truly—and a couple of friends who had the night off."

"You can say 'ass,' Uncle Theo," Kirby said indignantly. "I'm almost old enough to have—"

Sikes put his hand over Kirby's mouth. There had been eight other cops in on the attack with Theo. "The night off? I thought this was a SWAT operation." Sikes looked down the wide street of the subdivision. There were knots of people in bathrobes and pajamas standing on the front lawns of their dream homes, a few unremarkable cars parked along the curb, but Sikes realized he hadn't seen a SWAT van yet. Kirby gave up struggling and giggled.

"SWAT my a—foot," Theo laughed.

"Ass," Kirby said quickly.

Theo kept going as Sikes covered his daughter's mouth again. "Captain has to authorize all SWAT activities, and I didn't think this was one he was going to sign off on. You and your pals owe your"—he looked at Kirby— "*asses* to Vice tonight."

Sikes was impressed. Theo knew as much about departmental politics as he knew about police work. "So what happens when the captain does find out?"

Theo shrugged. "What can he do? I mean, if I had asked and he had said no, that would be that. But since I acted on my own lawful initiative to rescue a fellow officer, and since we got solid grounds for booking these mother—uh, mothers—on kidnapping, the paper trail is going to be so thick that the captain isn't going to be able to do squat." He pointed a finger at Kirby. "Don't you dare say it, or I'll go in that house and come back out with soap."

"And murder," Sikes added in a flat tone. "Kidnapping *and* murder."

Theo nodded. He held up one of the guns in its bag. "This is from the guy we got with the taser. He didn't have any ID, but we already used a field kit to get his fingerprints. That way we don't have to worry about them going 'missing' at Central."

"He's the guy who killed Petty, all right," Sikes said. "All we have to do is match the bullets from the scene with that gun."

"Well, that's not all, but it'll be a good start," Theo said.

Two cops in heavy body armor came out of the house pushing Amy Stewart and her uncle in front of them with a riot gun. They stopped by Sikes and Theo. Both prisoners wore handcuffs behind their backs.

Sikes held his coffee cup up in a salute. "Hey, Uncle Frank. Now it's your turn to sign something." He grinned unpleasantly. "A confession."

Stewart looked at Sikes with an expression of pity. "You still don't get it, do you? We're all walking, detective. And there's nothing you can do about it."

Sikes slid off the hood of the car and left the blanket behind him. "No!" he said angrily. "You're the one who doesn't get it. This isn't one of your cozy backroom deals anymore. You're not going to be able to have your people call in a favor or two from the captain to sweep this under some stinking little rug. You're in the hands of *cops* now. *Real* cops. Not bureaucratic ass-kissers. You're going down to the station house, and you're all being booked for kidnapping, aggravated assault, and conspiracy to commit murder. And by the time you manage to get through to your paranoid bosses in Washington, it's going to be too late for them to do anything, because none of us will have signed any stinking security oaths, and your photographs are going to be plastered all over the front pages of the newspapers tomorrow, and if anyone—*anyone*—tries to get you off by pulling strings, every reporter in the city is going to want to know why." Sikes trembled with anger, but he felt great. He poured his coffee out on the driveway and watched in satisfaction as it splashed on Stewart's shoes. He looked at Theo. "Right?" he asked forcefully.

"More or less," Theo said, smiling at Stewart and Amy. "Except for that bit about being on the front pages of the newspapers. They'll have bigger fish to fry tomorrow."

Sikes blinked at his ex-partner.

"Hey, some of us have been in the real world tonight," Theo said defensively. He pointed a finger to the sky. "That thing up there? The asteroid whatsit? The radio stations are saying it's changed course like it's some kind of spaceship. It's heading straight for us."

Sikes felt a chill run through his entire body. He had been treating it as a joke, as an impossible possibility. But it was *real*. It *was* actually happening.

Quite clearly he thought, What's the proper reaction to news like this? He had no idea. It was as if the world had turned upside down but kept on going. So many images and emotions flashed through his mind that for a moment he lost track of where he was. Uncle Jack and his telescope. Long summer nights discussing the impossibility of flying saucers and the inevitability of life on other worlds. Dr. Petty with the planets on his wrist. In the desert with Kirby, holding her small and trusting hand in his, watching the dim blur of Comet Halley. It was as if each moment of his life had been meant to bring him to this one night. This last night of the world as it had been.

Without understanding the depth of his reaction, Sikes felt his heart race. He felt the need to look up to the stars and shout out to Victoria, to Uncle Jack, to the world, that whatever was coming for them, Matt Sikes had been among the first to see it. Because he was a cop. Doing his job. Good against evil.

He looked up at the stars, just as millions around the world were doing at that same moment. Good or evil? Which *was* coming for them? What should he do?

But then Sikes saw the grotesquely horrified expressions on Franklin and Amy Stewart's faces and knew exactly what he should do.

Sikes laughed. He laughed uproariously. Gleefully happy that they should be in such distress. They were getting exactly what they deserved.

And now that his first murder case was solved, the only question that remained was, what was the rest of the world getting this night?

CHAPTER 5

IT WAS A SOUND Buck had never heard before. It terrified him. It could be the tortured souls of Tagdot's victims rising up from the dead. "What is it?" he asked D'wayn in fear.

D'wayn looked to the ceiling of the small chamber she and Buck and a handful of other Overseers had crowded into. "Atmosphere," she said grimly. "The cargo disk is moving through air." The floor began to vibrate as it had when the separation had occurred. "We are landing."

"D'wayn! It's your turn!" An Overseer called to her from the far wall of the chamber. D'wayn did not relinquish her grip on Buck's hand. She made him move with her.

There was a machine embedded in the wall. Buck had never seen one like it before. It had an opening at about his eye level, shaped like two circles lying side by side. The rims of the circles glowed with a pale light.

The Overseer who had called to D'wayn nodded at her. D'wayn released Buck's hand, then put both of her own hands into the opening. The glowing opening shrank until it gripped her by her wrists. There was a soft hissing noise. D'wayn closed her eyes, moaning. Then the opening widened again, and D'wayn removed her hands.

Buck stared in fascination. Her tattoos were gone.

D'wayn stepped out of the way as another Overseer came

forth to use the machine. She rubbed the unmarked skin around her wrists, then winked at Buck. "What did I tell you?" she said. "We're prepared for every awful thing the cargo might do. When we're rescued, we will wear the badges of our honor and our courage once again. But until that time, we must be careful."

"Will we be rescued?" Buck asked. Moodri had said no.

"Of course," D'wayn said reassuringly. "As soon as the fleet realizes they have lost contact with us, other ships will come searching."

The rising wail of the atmosphere matched the growing fear in Buck. "But what if . . . what if false signals were sent out? What if the fleet thought there was nothing left to find?"

D'wayn studied him with curiosity. "How could such a thing be possible, child? And even if it were, hidden in the disk are emergency beacons. Once we're safely on the ground, we will simply activate the beacons, and *then* the fleet will come. There's nothing to worry about, spotty head."

Then D'wayn gave Buck a small, sad smile and carefully removed the black scarf he wore. "You will have to leave this behind, too," she said. "Just until the fleet comes, though." She touched her knuckles to his temple. "Wait here while I change."

When it was time to leave the chamber, each of the Overseers was newly outfitted in a filthy gray outfit just like the ones worn by the cargo. Buck was surprised that in such clothes the Overseers looked no different from any other Tenctons. But he had little time to follow through on such thoughts. D'wayn guided him to the chamber door.

"Can you tell the difference in the way the gravity feels now?" she asked him. Buck rose up and down on his toes. He felt lighter, stronger. He nodded. "The disk's gravity fields have been replaced by the natural gravity of the planet we're descending to. That means it won't be long until we've landed."

In his fear Buck squeezed the Overseer's hand.

"You have nothing to worry about, Finiksa. You're a brave Watcher, and we all have faith in you."

Buck tensed. It sounded like a farewell.

"You must leave us now," D'wayn said. "We will all split up for the landing because it will be safer. But we'll be together again soon. I promise."

"How will I find you?" Buck asked. It was important that he

be able to find someone. Who knew if he would ever see his parents again? Vornho was dead. And Moodri might not have survived the violence of the disk's separation. But D'wayn had saved Buck. D'wayn could help Buck survive.

D'wayn lightly touched her head to Buck's, then placed a finger in the center of his spotline and counted over three spots. Quickly she nicked the left edge of the spot with her thumbnail. Buck gasped at the sharp pain. "We will find you," the Overseer said. "Now go! Run as fast as you can down to the cargo bays. And when you get outside, keep running. The disk can't keep fighting the planet's natural gravity for long." She patted his backside. "Scoot, Finiksa! You will be free again! I promise!"

And Buck ran. He didn't know what D'wayn had meant about being free again. He didn't know what it meant to be "outside." At last he realized that he *had* used the circuitry key properly, but what exactly had the act accomplished? Especially if the Overseers could call for other ships to come and get them at any time?

Everything had been a waste, he decided. Vornho's death. Melgil's death. Buck knew if he had just thrown away the key, everyone would still have been safely in space. He and Vornho would have their new scarves, and everything would be fine again.

It was an impossible burden for a ten-year-old of any species, and Buck wept as he ran. He fled down corridors knowing that all the shouting he heard, all the crying, the confusion and the pain, was his fault. He hadn't done what was right. Moodri had confused him with his old crystals and his made-up stories. None of what Buck had done had been right.

In time he forgot how long he had been running, but in that time the howl of the wind had faded and the decks stopped shaking. It was almost as if he were in space again—safe and secure with the Overseers.

Buck stumbled down a long, crowded ramp to the final deck. There was a different smell in the air here, almost as if there weren't as many people around him. The scent of his own kind seemed lighter somehow, the way the gravity felt.

He moved with the screaming, shouting, jostling crowd, pushing his way past Elders and smaller children. Everyone had the same idea. Run. As far and as fast as possible.

There was something wrong with the light now, too, Buck

noticed. It was too harsh, too bright, even stronger than the ceiling banks in the infirmary. He came to the top of another ramp, and since he knew he was on the bottom level, he realized it was the ramp that led down, out of the disk, to the . . . outside.

Buck looked up and saw the source of the light. Straight ahead a large red light bank hung against a distant wall. The light seemed to waver, blindingly bright. Only when the crowd behind him pushed him forward did he realize that the light bank was actually the course-correction star. But why its color was different he didn't know. Maybe because of the transparent wall it shone through in the distance. He wondered if there were other walls on this world.

Buck ran down the ramp. There was dust or grit in the air that made him cough and sneeze. Everyone around him did the same. He felt strong breezes from some enormous air-circulating pump. He heard a high-pitched thrumming of straining machinery but didn't know what kind of machinery it was.

There was a huge dark ceiling above him, and vaguely he realized it was the bottom surface of the disk. He didn't know what was keeping it up.

The ramp ended, but the crowd was moving forward so quickly that Buck had taken twenty steps upon the surface of the new world before he actually knew what he was doing.

Run, said a thousand voices in the crowd. *Run and keep running.*

So Buck ran. The deck beneath his feet was covered in dirt and small broken pieces of rounded metal that pushed painfully through the soles of his thin shoes. But he ran and he kept running.

And he had no idea where it was he was running to.

Moodri had taken up the position he knew had been assigned to Vondmac—standing watch over cargo ramp twenty-seven. He worked with a crew of twenty young workers chosen for their strength and their speed—*binnaum,* female, and male—scanning the departing crowds with him.

Another command had been issued by the rebellion leaders as the Tenctonese had gathered in the lower levels during the descent—no baggage could be taken from the disk.

Whatever waited for them on the surface of this new world, they would face it without the Overseers' prods or cutting beams, without canisters of the holy gas, without *jabroka* or any of the other cruel implements and foul drugs with which the Overseers had ruled.

More than that, the council of Elders had also known that the Overseers had caches of survival equipment stowed away in secret places in the disk. It would have been useful to have shelters and solar stills and blades and ropes and fire igniters, the Elders had known. But each cache might also have a locator beacon, and because of that fear the council would not risk any of those leaving the disk, no matter what other equipment was lost.

So Moodri and the others scanned the departing Tenctonese. Every moment, it seemed, one of the crew would have to run into the crowd to see if the object wrapped in a podling's blanket was really a child and not contraband, but the effort appeared to be working. Since few slaves had any possessions to begin with, the desire to leave with something was minimal, especially considering the urgent orders to run as quickly and as far as possible.

Moodri also looked out over the crowd for spots he might recognize. There were eight times eight exit ramps on the disk, though, so he thought it unlikely he would see anyone he knew. Still he tried. The goddess could be funny that way.

Three hours after the disk had finally settled, it gave a sudden lurch, and the few stragglers that still moved down the ramp shouted in alarm and began running faster. One of the crew who had searched the crowd with Moodri took the Elder's arm and led him to the top of the ramp. "The stabilizers can't last much longer, Moodri. You should leave now."

Moodri knew the young male was right. He and his youthful compatriots could run away from the disk, but Moodri would have to walk—though his knees already felt better in the planet's low gravity.

Moodri clenched the youth's hand in his. "We have done good work this *crayg*," he said.

"We have followed a good plan."

Moodri peered down the ramp at the oddly colored soil that lay beneath them. Obviously the disk's automatics had success-fully chosen a suitable hot desert environment in which to land, far from any of this world's caustic saltwater oceans and where a suitable level of ultraviolet radiation would reach the ground. But he was surprised that no aliens had yet appeared. The disk had been on the planet's surface for considerable time. "Has there been any sign of the indigenous species?" Moodri asked.

"Flying machines fill the sky," the youth said. "We are clearly being observed from a distance."

"Good," Moodri said. "Under such circumstances a long introduction is preferable to a short one. It reduces the chances for hasty mistakes."

The young male gently pushed Moodri along the ramp. "Please, Moodri. It would be such a shame to come so far and miss by only a footstep."

Moodri doubted that even Ionia would be so capricious but dutifully set off down the ramp.

As more of the new world came into view beyond the immense overhanging lip of the disk, he noted with satisfaction that the sky was blue. It was one of his favorite colors, as far as skies went, and he hadn't seen it too often.

There was a pleasant warmth to the atmosphere as well, and little sign of vegetation. More good signs, as they reduced the probability that they had set down on valuable farmland or that they had disturbed local fauna. With an oxygen atmosphere and intelligent tool-users about, Moodri felt quite confident in assuming that the new planet would have plentiful vegetation and fauna. But he was willing to be surprised.

At last he came to the end of the ramp, and because he was more than a century old and had a deep and abiding sense of history, he paused for a moment at its edge, where the metal forged from one world touched the surface of another.

The air smelled dry. It was a good smell. All across the horizon he saw the small dark silhouettes of Tenctonese spreading out from the disk. They would be safe enough when the time came.

Beyond the disk's overhang Moodri saw a vapor trail cut across the blue sky ahead and knew it was made by a flying machine. He waved hello to it, not knowing how advanced this planet's optic systems might be.

He exhaled the last of the disk's air from his lungs, then drew in as deeply as he could the oddly scented air of this new world.

"We thank the goddess for this day."

Moodri set foot on the new world.

"And for each day ever after."

George had wanted to find Ruhtra's body, but the recycling room near the Game chamber was flooded with salt water from the momentary loss of gravity, and Zicree would not let him go in.

Instead they had stayed in the prisoner cage in the holding chamber, where there had been a bench to sit on. Zicree jammed open the cage's sliding door so it would stay open. But he said nothing. George felt each shudder of the disk and prayed it would be the one that would sunder the hull and spew him forth to empty space. But by the time the mad rush of the atmosphere began to howl outside the hull, he knew that option had been forever lost to him.

"How many planets have you been on?" Zicree asked as the gravity lessened, indicating how close they were to the end of the descent.

"I don't know," George said. The thought filled him with sadness. He had set foot on other worlds and did not remember, did not care. "They are all the same."

"This one might be different," Zicree said.

The disk stopped. There was no sound of wind, no sense of motion.

"How?" George asked.

Zicree stood. "This is the first time I have landed on a planet in which it has become my choice whether to leave or stay." He nodded his head as if he had answered a difficult puzzle. "Have you made your choice yet?"

George stared at his friend. He had chosen to die.

"I am going to leave now," Zicree said calmly. He brushed his knuckles against George's temple. "I hope we will meet again."

Zicree stepped through the open door of the cage. Coolock had stepped through that door. Ruhtra had stepped through that door. But only George and Zicree had returned.

Long after Zicree's clanking footsteps had faded away George remained staring at the cage's open door. He knew a little bit about the ship's operation. The cargo disk could not remain near the surface of a planet for long, not without its stabilizers giving out or blowing up or some such thing. But there was nowhere else for the disk to go. Any plan for freedom would *have* to include provisions for destroying the main section of the ship.

George wondered how they did it.

He could find out, he knew, just by stepping through the cage door. He could go to the cargo bay, go down a ramp, and step onto yet another world, and there would be someone else there he could ask.

How *did* they do it?

How did anyone else step through the cage door?

There was no Overseer to lock it. There was no threat of punishment for disobeying. It was up to George and George alone.

He got up and stepped to the edge of the open door. He put his hand through it, part of him free, part of him a slave.

What would it take to step all the way through? George asked.

He didn't know the answer.

He thought of everyone he might ask. He knew they would be outside. He wondered who would be most likely to tell him what he needed to know.

Then it was as if Susan stood before him on the other side of the door, and in her arms was Devoosha.

They were out there, George knew, in a sudden rush. And whether they had the answers he needed to the troubled mysteries of his life or whether they were just as confused as he was, they were waiting for him.

It wasn't an answer, but at least it was a direction. Perhaps, in the end, that was all there could ever be.

No end to a journey. Only the beginning of the next.

George stepped through the door.

He walked slowly toward the cargo bays and the ramps. And he knew he carried the weight of the prisoner cage with him. And he knew that there would be a open door in front of him for a long time to come, with part of him free, part of him a slave, and no one he could ask what he should do until he knew what the question was.

George stood on the bottom of the ramp and stared out at the surface of the new world. He chose to step out onto it. As he did so he swore this would be the one world he would always remember.

He began to walk. And when he was about a mile away, one

of the last to have left the disk, even as the desert floor suddenly lit up all around him, and even as a second later an angry roar cracked the air, and even as five seconds later a giant hand threw him into the soil of this world as the disk exploded at his back, George knew there was no going back.

His new journey had begun.

And there was still another door to step through.

CHAPTER 6

SOMEONE WAS KNOCKING on Sikes's door.

He ignored it. He drained the dregs from the can of Bud on the arm of his easy chair, then dropped it to clatter in the pile of other cans on the floor beside him. He squinted at the vertical blinds that covered the window that gave such a nice view of the apartment building across the road. He guessed it was morning again. But he couldn't be certain.

Whoever it was pounded at the door again. "C'mon, man. I know you're in there." Sikes corrected himself. It wasn't someone. It was Theo Miles.

But Sikes kept staring at the flickering television screen. He had had his set on most of the past week. He supposed most every television set in the world had been on most of the past week. As if something important had happened last week. As if anything could have been as important as what had happened when Sikes had arrived at the station house with Amy and Uncle Frank and Randolph Petty's silent killer. Jesus, Sikes thought. I still don't even know his name.

"Sikes, for Christ's sake, give me a break! I got suspended, too, remember?"

Not that there had been a lot of choice on all those televisions, Sikes knew. Almost all the footage had been the same, no matter what channel he had turned to.

The thing, the flying saucer, the starship—whatever it had been that had crashed in the desert that night—there were only a few different shots of it that anyone had managed to get before it had blown itself to kingdom come the next morning. There were plenty of aerial shots, of course. Every news helicopter in California's Southland and Inland Empire had made it out to the Mojave that day, playing chicken with the military choppers and the jets.

The daytime aerial shots were truly bizarre, showing the things that had been on the . . . the ship, gathered together in tight little clumps across the face of the desert, as if they had to keep as closely packed outside as they must have been packed inside. The lowest count Sikes had heard was that something over two hundred thousand of those things had come out of whatever it was. Some were estimating even higher—as many as four hundred thousand.

"I'll shoot off the lock, Sikes! I really will!"

There was plenty of footage of the military, too. But in the staging areas only, nothing to show what they were doing where it mattered, inside the limits of the quarantine zone that had been set up—huge ditches that had been gouged into the desert floor and pumped full of gasoline, then set on fire to make the Mojave look like Kuwait City all over again.

Sikes swore at the screen each time the cameras showed the aerial night shots—the miles-wide ring of fire cutting a lop-sided circle into the black desert floor. He knew just the kind of people who were responsible for such a senseless, cruel action —he had shared a safe house with them on the night the thing had crashed.

The official explanation for the gasoline was to prevent contamination, as if space germs had to crawl across the desert and couldn't float through the air like every other kind of germ. No, Sikes knew that the gasoline had nothing at all to do with preventing the spread of any space disease. It was an act of intimidation, pure and simple. With emphasis on the *pure*.

Sikes thought if he had just landed on another planet and someone set a moat of gasoline burning around him the first night down, he'd be ready to take the next flight home. He was sure that that was the real reason the fire had been set. But the whole point that the military had seemed to miss was that there wasn't going to be another flight home. That particular airline was deader than Pan Am.

Sikes jumped as a gun went off in his hallway. His front door swung open. "Domino's," Theo said as he burst in, then slammed the door behind him. It wouldn't stay shut, though, and slowly swung open again.

Theo stopped in front of Sikes, slipped his gun back into his shoulder holster, then screwed up his face as if he had stepped into a barnyard. "Christ Almighty, boy, have you taken one step out of here in the past week? It stinks like you're already dead or something."

"Or something," Sikes agreed.

"Oh, I get it," Theo said knowingly, "we're going to be like *that,* are we?"

"Get me a beer," Sikes said.

Theo went over to the blinds and pulled them open, making them rattle obnoxiously and flooding the apartment with harsh light. Sikes kept staring at the screen. Some intrepid soul had gone into the desert with a home video camera that first day and had managed to get back without having her tapes confiscated by the military. In the background of most of the shots she had managed to get, a tall tendril of white smoke hung in the pristine desert air—the aftermath of the early-morning explosion. In the foreground were the first close-ups anyone had managed to get of the things—five of them all huddled together, squatting on the desert floor.

In the footage they looked to be as frightened as the camera operator had said she was. They were dressed in colorless tatters, everyone wearing the same thing, with huge swollen skulls that were covered with what looked to be birthmarks or radiation burns or scabs or something. And they gibbered away in what some experts were already saying was nothing more than animal sounds and not a true language. Every time the camera had pointed directly at them, they had cowered. The most common pronouncement was that the things didn't know what was going on any more than people on Earth did. A lot of the creatures seemed to be dying, too. Always with their hands stretching out, as if asking for something that people couldn't give. Or didn't know how to give.

Theo came out of the kitchen. "Don't you have any real food in this place?"

"Beer or Jack Daniel's," Sikes said. He sort of felt sorry for the poor things. "The number for Pink Dot is on the fridge if you want some Twinkies or something."

"What would you do if Kirby came over?" Theo asked in frustration.

"Kirby's never coming over here again," Sikes said matter of factly. That particular call from Victoria's lawyer—the first of many—had been waiting on his answering machine when he got home, suspended. Perfect end to the perfect day, he had thought at the time. Not only was Victoria planning to lay charges of reckless child endangerment against him, she was sending Kirby to school in Switzerland. Sikes decided that meant their reunion was off. Oddly enough, he hadn't been as upset as he thought he might be.

Theo muttered something Sikes didn't bother to try to interpret, then he went back to the kitchen.

Back on the television, where the really important things in life were taking place these days, as far as Sikes was concerned, other than long, wavering telephoto shots, there wasn't much to see. The military had virtually sealed off a two-hundred-square-mile stretch of the desert before the second night had come. Most of the correspondents on the news shows had concluded that the reason the military had been able to move into action so quickly to secure the area was that they had drawn up contingency plans for just such a scenario. Barracks for the National Guard were already being built on the third day. More damningly, Wolf Blitzer reported from the Pentagon that within fifteen minutes of NORAD determining that the most likely touchdown spot was the Mojave Desert, B-52s carrying nuclear weapons had been scrambled, and they had been continually overflying the quarantine zone ever since. That had been one of the last reports Blitzer had filed from the Pentagon. After the fourth day the news reports had dried up completely. The only substantial break had come on the sixth day, when it was obvious some sort of explosion had occurred inside the quarantine zone, and a Pentagon spokesperson had confirmed that an army Sikorsky transport helicopter had been lost due to mechanical failure. Fourteen people had died in the crash, but their names would not be released. They had not been military personnel.

Sikes could hear Theo doing something in the kitchen but didn't care to know what. He flipped through the channels. One of the locals was showing the demonstrations at the United Nations. They had been going on ever since the world had finally figured out that the United States was not going to let representatives of any other country get within a hundred miles of the Mojave. Some of the protesters carried signs calling for the things in the desert to be nuked. Some carried messages of peace for our space brothers. There were a lot of fistfights.

Sikes changed the channel. Another station was running an interview with two women who claimed that the things in the desert were the result of alien/human breeding experiments, just like the experiments they had been subjected to when they had been abducted by large-headed monsters covered with spots and taken to the very same spaceship that had crashed in the desert. They were quite clear on that. They all recognized the spaceship as the exact one they had been beamed up to. Sikes had seen the interview before. He didn't turn on the sound and kept flipping.

Elsewhere an evangelist held up drawings based on the home video footage showing that what most people thought were spots on the creature's heads were actually the horns of Satan. Across the bottom of the screen ran the chapter and verse citations for Bible passages that described how Satan would send his demons to the Earth in fiery disks. The evangelist said that the Apocalypse was near and that, the creatures should be destroyed at once. Sikes kept flipping.

A retired military officer outlined for an interviewer, with helpful diagrams, how a possible attack on the space encampment might proceed once the army had established that the aliens' intentions were hostile. And their intentions could not be anything but hostile, the retired officer insisted. By destroying their transport vessel, the creatures were clearly announcing that they were on a suicide mission—possibly the precursor to a main invasion fleet that even now could be assembling on the other side of the moon.

Sikes had seen it all. Heard it all. He had watched television for a week and knew all the players. He kept hoping that someone would be able to break through the quarantine zone and manage to snag an interview with one of the things itself. He was tired of hearing *people* speak. It was all useless garbage anyway. Nothing mattered anymore.

He flipped back to the channel that was running the home video footage in slow motion while a zoologist drew Xs on the screen to show how the creatures' joints and musculature might work. Theo came in carrying two plates. Sikes sniffed the air.

"I'm surprised you can smell anything," Theo said. He

dropped the plate on Sikes's lap. Sikes was wearing gray boxers and his favorite, worn-out gray Dallas Cowboys sweatshirt. Now he was also wearing a bit of the peanut butter on stale bagels that Theo had dished up.

Sikes picked up one of the bagel halves. One of the creatures had its face frozen on the screen. "Boy," Sikes said, "don't you think they're wishing they came down someplace else?"

Theo pulled up a hassock and sat on it, facing Sikes and not the television. "I figure they came to the right place, all right. Though I tell you, when they started showing those first shots of all those poor saps swarming out of that thing, I was real pissed off."

Sikes rolled his eyes. "Let me get this straight. We lose a perfect collar, we get suspended, we let a cold-blooded murderer walk free while the captain reams us out *in front* of the killer, and *you* get pissed off because a UFO crashes in the desert?"

Theo patted his chest. "Hey, I spent my entire youth waiting for the saucers to land. I was out there in my backyard just praying for them to come down and get me. Yessir. Let's have a visit by advanced beings. Let's get the cure for cancer, the secret of living in peace, free energy, no more hunger." He shrugged. "I mean, that was the whole spiel back then. If they managed to get here in their saucers, then they had to be advanced, right? So anyway, there I am at home, watching the tube like everyone else, waiting for these super-advanced beings to come forth and plant their flag and take care of all of us—and what the hell do I see when we get our first good look at them?" Theo shook his head. "They were *white,* Sikes. No offense, but goddamn every single one of them was white." He smiled again. "But then another couple of days go by, and it becomes obvious they don't know what the hell they're doing here, and that makes me feel better. I figure the way those guys look, they must be from the bottom rung back where they come from, and they just stole that saucer from somebody else, that's all."

Sikes licked peanut butter off his teeth. He hated peanut butter. But he hadn't realized how hungry he was. "Saucer theft, hmmm? I wonder if we could book 'em for it."

Theo stared at him in silence. After a while Sikes stared back. "What?" he asked.

"Well," Theo said, "could be you and me are going to be able to find out the answer to that question."

Sikes didn't understand.

"We're off suspension," Theo said. "Orders straight from Willie Williams himself. All vacations canceled. All disciplinary suspensions not involving firearms also canceled. For the emergency."

"What emergency?" said Sikes. "Whenever they get around to talking about something other than that thing in the desert, all they say is that the crime rate in Los Angeles is lower than it's been since the night they started bombing Baghdad. *Everyone's* staying home to watch the news."

"Not us," Theo said. He nodded at the screen. "We're going out there."

"The Mojave?" Sikes was more awake than he had felt in days.

"Every police force in the state has been asked to contribute personnel to the AQF. That's the Alien Quarantine Facility. The captain said he sure as hell doesn't want us on the streets, so he 'volunteered' us."

"I'm not going out there," Sikes said.

"We don't have a choice, son. Besides, it'll look good when we come up for our review hearing."

Sikes slammed his fist on the arm of his easy chair and made the beer cans on the floor rattle. "I am *not* going to any review hearing, Theo. The fix is in. I know it."

"So what are you going to do? Quit on me?"

"Damn right."

Theo stood up, cracked his neck with a roll of his shoulders, then walked over to Sikes and picked him out of the chair by a fistful of Dallas Cowboys sweatshirt. "Do I have your attention?" he asked.

"It's all a crock," Sikes said. "Put me down."

"So you can go back to rotting in this pisshole? I don't think so."

Sikes pulled Theo's hands off his shirt and stood looking as if he belonged out in the desert with the other frightened, bedraggled creatures. "Don't you get it, Theo? We *had* them. Amy, Uncle Frank, Petty's killer. You and me and Angie and even Grazer—we worked together. We broke the case. We made our arrests. And we had the evidence."

"So what? Now Angie's in the hospital under observation for her concussion. Grazer's got his chest wrapped because of the three ribs I cracked when I had to give him the Heimlich to keep him from choking on that damn sandwich he was eating when the concussion grenades went off. And Uncle Frank and his crew were better connected than we were. It happens. It's a bitch, I know, but crooks do walk free from time to time. God bless America."

"Well, it stinks!" Sikes said. His voice echoed in the small living room.

"Of course it stinks. No argument from me on that one. But that's not supposed to make you give up like a kid who decides he doesn't like the rules. It's supposed to put you back out on the street to do a better job."

Sikes went to slump back down in his chair, but Theo wouldn't let him. "You can't give up, man. I won't let you."

"I got beaten, Theo."

"You think I've never been beaten, man? You think I've never come home and wanted to put my fist through the wall because some smart-ass gangster hired a better lawyer than the wet-behind-the-ears prosecutor I got stuck with? You think I haven't seen dealers buy a judge or a killer walk because of a procedural error? Face it, Sikes. Every day we're out on the streets we're going to get beaten. That's what it means to be a cop. But what it also means is that we don't accept it. Every time we get beaten we go back out there and we win one. And maybe we win two. And maybe when we get our bloody pension we'll be able to say, Well, I won some and Lord knows I lost some, but by God, I'm leaving this world a better place because I tried my best and I beat them more times than they beat me."

Sikes didn't say anything. He stared at the screen.

"You're going to lose again, son. You're going to lose worse than this one. But you keep at it, you're going to win, too. And that's what counts."

Theo stepped away from Sikes. "You want to sit down and wallow, well, then, you just do that. But if you want to be a cop, you can come with me."

"Out there?" Sikes asked. He looked at the screen.

"Out there," Theo said.

Sikes pointed his remote at the television. It was running the only footage of the saucer that had been cleared by the Pentagon. Before it had exploded. Before they had come out of it. Sikes hit the sound.

There was static. Lots of static. It had been taken by two traffic reporters in a helicopter. The first one on the scene. "I've talked to the military," one of them said, his voice barely audible over the crackling of the garbled transmission. "They've escorted it down. There appears to be a potential—" More static. The picture moved in. This was when it had begun. "It looks like a door is opening—I don't think it is, I don't think it is."

But that *had* been the moment, Sikes thought. The first door had opened then. And everything had changed.

"It's still just hovering," the announcer's voice said. Sikes could hear the excitement building in it. Moment to moment. "It's got—"

More static. More crackling. The helicopter pilot broke in. "This is not a hoax. That thing is *real* out there. Gray in color . . ."

And then the picture had pushed in even further, and the tiny spots of living creatures leaving the saucer were seen for the first time.

In just one moment. Everything had changed.

"Out there," Sikes said again. It seemed to make some kind of sense. He had lost the first round to Franklin Stewart. But that didn't mean he'd have to lose another. And if ex–Commander Stewart didn't want those creatures here, then Sikes made up his mind that *he* did want them. "Okay," Sikes said as he reached out to grab his ex-partner's hand and shake. "I guess that's as good a place to fight for truth, justice, and the American way as anywhere else."

Sikes went into his bedroom to find his uniform.

All it had taken was a moment, but he was a cop again.

It felt damn good.

CHAPTER 7

THE FIRST NIGHT they all thought they were going to die. And many of them did.

Real panic set in earlier in the first day when the disk exploded and the realization spread that there would be no more foodgrowth and no more water. Most of the Tenctonese had grouped together in those initial few hours, recreating the social organization of their dormitories, and had waited for someone to call them to food shift. But the Overseers had vanished, and there was no one left to give orders.

The resistance members were the first to understand what had happened to the Overseers. The hated black uniforms and tattoos had vanished with the disk, and now the Overseers walked among the rest of the Tenctonese, unseen. Here and there, in various huddled masses, individual Overseers were recognized, and as the course-correction star began to move toward the horizon many of the Overseers died—literally torn apart by the savagery they themselves had brutally cultivated in otherwise peaceful beings.

Other Overseers, sensing that the order of the ship was fast breaking down, continued to wield their most powerful weapons—not prods or cutters, but hunger, hate, and fear—as they incited several dormitory groups to self-destruction to reduce their numbers, by claiming that another dormitory group was made up entirely of Overseers.

By nightfall the fighting had begun in earnest, fueled in part by the competition for the first salvaged containers of foodgrowth that had been pulled from the enormous pile of wreckage that was the disk. The children cried. The stars emerged. An unthinkable battle raged—bare hands against scraps of metal and salvaged prods, slave against Overseer, slave against slave. And then, suddenly, all around, the alien horizon walls of flame had roared into life, ignited at a hundred places, forming an outer ring beyond which they could not go.

"We have been welcomed," Moodri said as he stood upon the rock where the Elders gathered, far removed from the rubble of the disk and the greatest concentration of dormitory groups. He pulled his borrowed robe around his shoulders, wondering if the indigenous species of this planet intended the walls of flame to move inward.

"Welcomed to *am dugas,* it appears," another Elder said beside him. She was Nanholt, older than Moodri, one of the three speakers of the council and an architect of the resistance. "Do you think they mean to burn us all?"

"Who can say?" Moodri replied. Thus far all the Tenctonese had seen of the indigenous species had been hundreds of flying machines—some hovering in place, others speeding by a few hundred feet from the ground, still others visible only by the trails they left high against the unnaturally blue sky. Even now, during the night, the flying machines were still at work, visible by the lights that flashed from them.

From time to time Moodri had also seen some of the hoverers descend from the night sky and shine a white beam of energy on groupings of his people. The first time it had happened his hearts had traded beats in horror as he thought an energy weapon was being used, but it turned out to be nothing more than a light, as if whatever flew the hoverer couldn't see by the light of the stars.

Since that kind of limited vision seemed unlikely for an advanced species, Nanholt had suggested that perhaps the light beam *was* a weapon, but one that worked on the indigenous species and not on Tenctonese. A lengthy debate had followed, not helped at all by the rumors that came back to the Elders relating that the indigenous species was, variously, two-

headed, no-headed, twelve feet tall, insectoid, capable of
changing into smoke, and, most disturbingly, possessed black
wrist tattoos in an alien language.

Moodri didn't see much point in taking part in the ill-
informed debate, however, especially without Vondmac's clear
and level-spotted input. They would be meeting the indigenous
species soon enough, and the debate would be moot. In the
meantime there was still the matter of the beacons. Though the
resistance was certain that few, if any, such devices had been
taken from the disk, by morning the disk's wreckage would be
swarming with scavengers. The resistance must be first to find
the beacons and destroy them. Otherwise all that had happened would be for nothing.

The first beacon was brought to the Elders just before dawn.
Moodri had been complaining to Nanholt that the shortness of
the day and night cycle on this world made it impossible to
truly appreciate one or the other in full. Nanholt, who had kept
watching the walls of fire—which, thank the goddess, had not
appeared to advance any closer through the night—had said
that the Tenctonese would adapt quickly, as always. It was then
that a young female was allowed to pass through the protective
ring of resistance members who had positioned themselves
around the Elders' rock. She carried a crumpled gray tunic, and
Moodri could see from the way she held it that there was
something wrapped within.

The female unrolled the tunic for the Elders, and inside was a
black steel cube, small enough to fit in a single hand. Moodri
lifted the hateful thing and examined it. On the side, beneath a
small aperture, a few lines of operating instructions were
printed in sine script. But the aperture was dark, not pulsing
with light. The beacon had not yet been activated.

Moodri passed it to Nanholt. She turned it over once in her
hands, then placed it on the rock beside her. She nodded to the
male and female who had been waiting. One pushed a small
stone into the beacon's aperture, wedging it forcefully into
place. Then the other smashed a larger rock down upon the
beacon, driving the small stone into the device's inner work-
ings.

It took ten blows, but the casing finally split. The rest was
simple. In moments the beacon was nothing more than a
harmless handful of shards and twisted metal. Nanholt

brushed the remains into the sands of the desert. "That's one," she said.

Moodri looked out toward the rubble of the disk, more than a mile away. Already he could see shapes heading toward it in the starlight. And he knew that somewhere in that tangle of destruction three other beacons lay hidden.

"If the goddess is willing, we will have the others soon," he said. "The Overseers appear to be keeping busy with the fomenting of violence, not planning for the future."

Then he narrowed his eyes and squinted at far-off figures that appeared to be moving through the wreckage. He clutched the prayer stones around his neck in worry. The figures there did not appear to be moving like Tenctonese.

And though it was hard to be certain at this distance, some of them did not appear to have heads.

Buck had been found on the fifth day.

A young male with furtive eyes had seen Buck standing in line by a food station. Buck didn't like the food, but it was better than what they tried to feed him on the second day.

On the second day, giant, thunderous, hovering machines had appeared all over the crash site, sending up giant clouds of dust from the planet's deck—clouds that Buck first feared were more explosions. But the clouds were simply the result of the enormous wind the hoverers made, for whatever alien reason, and when they departed Buck saw that cargo pallets had been dropped from them.

Many Tenctonese had gone to the pallets right away, thinking that they would soon be instructed to move them somewhere. But there were still no Overseers. Then some had discovered the cracks in the pallets where crate sides had broken or the contents had spilled. The pallets held supplies.

There were containers of water and packages made from thin reflective metal covered with alien script. The word spread quickly: The hoverers were feeding the Tenctonese without requiring them to do work. It was a miracle, nothing less. Or else, some said bitterly, they had crashed during an alien religious festival when no work *could* be done. But soon enough the Tenctonese would return to being what they were meant to be.

Despite that fatalistic prediction, and others like it, a routine soon developed concerning the mysteriously provided supplies. Each time a pallet fell to the ground from a hoverer, a trio of Tenctons would appear, announcing that they were members of the resistance who had fought the Overseers. Buck suspected they were really Overseers themselves, though, because of the way they organized people into lines and made sure that each person got just the same amount of supplies as all the others.

After his first trip through a supply line, a young female showed Buck how to open his water container by using one of the big pieces of dirt on the ground to poke a hole in its side. The water tasted odd, but Buck saw that everyone else was drinking it with no ill effect, and his lips were cracked. By the time he had finished the entire container, he didn't notice the taste at all.

The thin metal package was another problem, though. Buck used the large piece of dirt to poke a hole in it, then peeled the top part of the package away from the thick brown substance inside. It looked vaguely like meatgrowth, though it was much too dark, as if it had been burned in the crash. And when Buck smelled it, he began choking up the water he had swallowed. Whatever was in the package smelled like excrement. He threw it to the ground in disgust.

However, as he wandered the crash site that day, standing in line after line for more water, he realized that for every torn-open package discarded on the ground he saw other people eating happily from another. He soon figured out that different packages held different substances, and he guessed if he could decipher the alien script, then he would know what was in each.

He got together with a group of other children—none had a telltale scratch on the edge of a spot, though—and began to help them organize a list of what alien foodgrowth was good and what was bad.

The children gathered the empty metal packages from the refuse piles, carefully sniffed each one, then created three categories: Excrement growth, Acceptable growth, and Good growth. Sure enough, the children were quickly able to see a pattern in the odd, angular writing with which the packages were labeled. While most of the markings were the same from package to package, generally the largest symbols at the bottom of each package were different.

Buck's favorites were the packages that carried the symbols: GRILLED CHEESE SANDWICH and SPAGHETTI AND TOMATO SAUCE. In a pinch he could manage to eat the packages marked: HERSHEY CHOCOLATE and HAND SOAP, though he didn't know why they had different symbols, because both had the same texture and taste, as far as he could tell. But the ones to avoid at all costs were any packages marked with STEW, CHICKEN, or LASAGNA. One child who said she was a Watcher Youth and wasn't afraid of anything actually managed to swallow a mouthful of STEW. It was almost as if her stomach had exploded, so quickly had she vomited.

By the morning of the fourth day—though the days and nights were confusing to Buck, neither seemed long enough to make much sense—the children at the crash site had become the key component in a site-wide network of trade in food and water. They could scan the packages that fell from the sky, quickly dividing them into three different groups, then run back and forth between the various dormitory groupings, seeing who had too much water and not enough SPAGHETTI, thus helping the resistance members move supplies around so that everything was equally shared.

The children also realized that there was advantage to be gained in their endeavors. Any liquid container marked with MILK appeared to be the favorite of many adults. The pallets that fell from the sky occasionally included blankets and towels and folded collections of pictures and a strange blood-colored foodgrowth that could be chewed and blown into huge bubbles that made the chewer look as if his or her or *binn* internal organs had erupted from the mouth. The adults hated it, calling it grotesque, but Buck and the other children knew that as long as they had a supply of MILK containers, the adults would gladly trade them packets marked BUBBLE GUM.

While the children ran from grouping to grouping, the adults busied themselves with digging toilet ditches and constructing shelters from the fallen pallets and blankets. Some of the pallets had included rolled-up tubes of some sort of chopped-up vegrowth that didn't have much flavor, but invariably there were ignitor sticks packed with them. With those the adults were also able to construct fires for warmth at night, and funeral pyres for those who had died and whose religion permitted cremation. Many had died, Buck knew, because of the fighting on the first night, or because of hunger or thirst or, among the very old and very young, fear. The smell of decomposition was strong every time the air stopped circulating.

But by the fifth day Buck could sometimes forget that there had ever been a ship or that he had ever done what he had done on the bridge. There was excitement in having so much to do that was new and different without ever being told to do anything.

He decided he liked this world. And he never once wondered what its indigenous species looked like or what it thought about him and his people. He was free, just as D'wayn had promised, and he didn't know how life could get any better.

Then the young male had come up to Buck in a food line by a fallen pallet. He had grabbed Buck's chin and forced the boy to look up at him. Then he had placed a finger on Buck's spotline, counted over three spots, and flicked Buck on the scalp.

"What's your name?" the male asked him, and there was no disguising the tone in his voice.

"Watcher Finiksa," Buck said. He felt the eyes of the other people near him in the line. Everyone spoke of how the Overseers had vanished. Everyone spoke of how happy they were. "Watcher" was not a word that anyone liked to hear these days.

"Come with me, Finiksa," the male said. Then he turned and walked away, and Buck had no choice but to follow. Even five days on a new world was not enough to break the conditioning of the Watcher Youth Brigade.

The male led Buck behind a series of windbreak screens that had been erected around a toilet ditch. He struck the boy.

Buck reeled back. He touched his face where he could still feel the Overseer's slap.

"Never," the Overseer said, *"never* identify yourself as a Watcher! Do you understand me, boy?"

Buck nodded.

"Let the cargo think we all died on the ship. Our time will come soon enough."

Buck nodded again in fear.

Then the Overseer squatted down and smiled warmly at Buck just the way D'wayn did. "So, Finiksa, who was your Watch Leader?"

"Watch Leader D'wayn," Buck said.

The Overseer nodded. "A good officer. One of the best. Did

she tell you what was expected of you now that the cargo are temporarily in control?"

Buck lowered his head.

The Overseer looked around to make certain they were alone. "Do you know about the beacons?"

Buck nodded. "They can call the fleet."

"And the fleet will rescue us. My job is to find one of those beacons. You're going to help me."

"Yes, Watch Leader," Buck said reflexively.

The Overseer held out his finger to Buck. "Don't ever call me that again. My name is T'ksam. You will call me that, understand?"

"Yes, T'ksam."

"Very good." The Overseer stood up. "Follow." He strode out from behind the windbreak screens. Buck stayed with him. But he was confused. T'ksam wasn't heading toward the wreckage of the disk. He was going in the opposite direction.

"Where *are* the beacons, Watch—T'ksam?" Buck asked.

The Overseer glared at Buck, then stepped close. "Don't speak of them where others can hear," he hissed. Then he reached for something under his tunic top—a chain, Buck saw, like a string of prayer stones but with only one item hanging from it.

T'ksam cupped the object on the chain in his hand and let Buck look at it. It was a metal ring, but instead of carrying a decoration it held a tiny, flashing red light. T'ksam moved the ring back and forth. In one direction the red light slowed its rate of flashing. In another it sped up. "This ring will take us to the beacons." He looked out toward the desert, where the wall of fire burned, glowing red by night and staining the sky inky black by day.

"How did they get out there?" Buck asked. He was petrified. That's where the indigenous species was.

T'ksam dropped the ring and chain back under his tunic. "We have plans for every eventuality. Two beacons remained on the disk. Two others were automatically ejected at various altitudes to fall safely away from any risk of explosion." He straightened his tunic. "They're out there, Finiksa. Not far."

"But . . . but aren't the . . . the . . ."

"The *aliens?*" T'ksam said with amusement. "Is that what you're fearful of?"

Buck nodded.

The Overseer smiled broadly. "I've seen them, Finiksa. They are nothing to be afraid of. You know what they call themselves in their language?" He cleared his throat to prepare himself for the alien word. *"Sold'yurz.* And they look even funnier than their name sounds." He patted Buck's shoulder. "But most important, they're easy to kill. In fact, I'll even show you how to do it." He winked at Buck exactly the way D'wayn had. "I think you'd like that, wouldn't you?"

Buck nodded. It was the only way he knew to hide his fear.

On the night of the sixth day George heard alien music. He trudged to its source—a gathering of Tenctonese too small to be a dormitory grouping. There was a large white object beside them, too—a gleaming metallic box with two tiny black wheels. George had seen them being pulled around the crash site by aliens in self-propelled vehicles. He had yet to see an alien himself. Only glimpses of them, covered up in large white overalls that disappeared into a tiny black device that sat between their shoulders where their heads should have been. George felt his spots pucker as he tried to imagine what awful organ must be hidden under the small metal cap and glossy lens of the device. But at least they had two arms and two legs, though he supposed they could also have tendrils hidden under their strange bulky clothes.

George had been told by others that the metal containers were larger versions of the pallets that had been dropped from the hoverers in the first few days when everyone had feared the aliens of this planet were trying to poison them with foodstuffs that would kill them. The metal containers held even more supplies. Equipment as well as food and water. But George had not felt the need to investigate. He had spent his days trudging from dormitory group to dormitory group, trying to find his wife and daughter. He had had no luck. And the piles of bodies were growing daily.

Tired and dejected, he walked through the night toward the music and the large metal container. The music sounded nothing like the group singing that his people had been comforting themselves with as they sat around their makeshift fires, waiting for the impossibly short night to end with rousing songs such as "Ee Take Naz Nahj?". George had the strange thought that perhaps, while he had been searching for his family, the aliens had come into the crash site to entertain their visitors. Wait till they find out we're not just visiting, George thought.

As he got closer to the large metal container, George saw that it was different from the others he had seen. It had two doors on one side, and in the middle was a large, puzzling design— two thick red bars that overlapped each other at right angles. There were tables set up around it, and portable light banks shone from its roof to illuminate the crowd of Tenctonese who stood nearby. The music seemed to be coming from one of the tables. But George only saw a small black object sitting on it, with a series of green warning lights flickering across its face.

As he got closer, he heard people discussing what they listened to. "Can you understand the words?" George asked. He wouldn't even have been able to say that the music had lyrics, alien or otherwise, but he knew from experience that he, along with the rest of his people, would rapidly sort out yet another alien language if necessary, as they had so many times in the past on the different worlds to which they had been sent to labor. The process was already beginning.

"It is a simple language," a young female said.

"The problem is," another added, "there seem to be a great number of them."

George moved on through the crowd. There were windows on the metal object as well, and lights shone out through them. It was like a small miners' barracks, he decided. He wondered if there were any aliens inside.

He stopped beside a *binnaum* and a female arguing over the lyric's meaning.

"*Sanhos'ay* is an actual place on this world, *not* a spiritual absolute. I have asked the interpreters," the *binnaum* said.

"But the interpreters *I* have spoken with have said that the goal of the journey there is to achieve peace in one own's mind. Why would a journey to a physical location be necessary for such a spiritual reason?" the female replied.

The *binnaum* looked impatient. "You're not listening. '*Ellay izza grey'tbig free-ay,*' the creature sings. I happen to know that *Ellay* is the major population center near the crash site, and that a *free-ay* is a major road path for the *carz* we see them operating. Don't you see the resonance? *Ellay? Free-ay?* Their entire culture must be devoted to travel."

The female laughed. "How could any culture get anywhere if its people didn't stay in one place? How could there be any peace?"

"I don't know," the *binnaum* admitted. "But the song clearly says that if you go to *Ellay,* you will become starstuff in just, um, seven—or is it fourteen?—of their *crayg-ta."*

The female's eyes widened in awe. "They can achieve complete spiritual transmogrification in . . . in just a matter of *crayg-ta?"* George saw her spots pale. "What manner of creatures are these?"

The *binnaum* folded *binn* arms knowingly. "When you consider that they're not in service to the ships, even though they're on a common route, we might have to face up to the fact that we've just landed on the world of the galaxy's most spiritually advanced beings."

The female swore softly to herself. The music ended. A chorus of voices asked that it be performed again. George moved deeper into the crowd to see how the music was made, not daring even to consider the possibility that if this *was* a world of spiritually advanced beings, then perhaps the Overseers would be incapable of returning.

The music began again. Oddly harmonic even though it didn't expand through the total range of audible frequencies. George decided it must be a form of artistic discipline, like writing poetry with only specific numbers of words.

He came to the edge of the crowd. He fixed his eyes on the object on the table. The sound *was* coming from it. He decided it must be like the communications devices that the Overseers used and that the performers were on the other end of the connection. They were certainly being patient to play the entire song again.

The female who stood by the music communicator smiled at the crowd that had gathered. She wasn't dressed in a gray tunic from the ship. Instead she wore one of the brightly colored orange jumpsuits that had come from the pallets. She saw George and nodded to him as she had to the others. She glanced away. Then glanced back. She looked at George with curiosity. She gestured to have him come forward.

"Do I know you?" George asked as he approached the female.

"No," the female said. "I am Gelana, a cargo specialist. *We* have never met, but I recognize your pattern." Cathy Frankel traced the backward-pointing trident of the Family: Heroes of

Soren'tzahh on George's head. "I know two of your kin. An Elder named Moodri and a child named Finiksa."

George grabbed Cathy's hand in excitement. "Do you know where they are?"

Cathy bowed her head. "Not now. I saw them in my infirmary just before the crash."

"Together?" George asked.

"Together," Cathy said. "They were both involved in the resistance. I . . . I don't know what happened to them. There was a fight. The gas came. I don't remember much after that."

Somehow that didn't matter to George. Just knowing that he hadn't lost his son to the Overseers was a victory. Ever since he had seen that hateful black scarf around Buck's neck in the water hub he had felt like a failure, as if he hadn't been able to pass on anything worthwhile to the next generation. But this cargo specialist's news proved otherwise.

He clutched her hand to his hearts. "I am forever indebted to you," he said formally.

Cathy gave him an odd smile. "More than you know," she said. She drew her hand away and walked over to one of the doors beside the two crossed red bars. "Come in here." She opened the door.

Not knowing what to expect, George took his first step into an alien artifact.

It was a long white room, blazing with light. It had a harsh smell. He heard the alien music playing outside.

He heard the line they had been discussing.

"Ellay izza grey'tbig free-ay." He could almost feel the immense spirituality that underlay it now.

His senses were overloading in the strange environment. He squinted until his eyes could adjust to the light. He heard podlings squeaking and realized that the room was lined with rows of podling nests. How nice, he thought. The aliens have provided for our children. Someone at the end of the room looked back at him.

"Stangya?"

His spots threatened to lift from his skull as he recognized the sweet voice calling to him.

"Stangya!"

And Susan was running into his arms, and he held her and lifted her against this world's gravity, and the alien music played, and the podlings cried, and little Devoosha squealed in her nest, and for one brief, irrational moment George Francisco felt as if he had come home.

Neither he nor Susan would ever forget Cathy Frankel for the kindness she had done them. And forever after, whenever they heard Dionne Warwick sing their song, they would sigh and remember what it was like to have their dreams come true.

For the very first time in their lives.

CHAPTER 8

SIKES HAD BEEN WORRIED that because he had never gotten around to having all his old uniforms cleaned, he was going to look scraggly on patrol in the AQF. But after three days in the desert even Theo's uniform—a good two sizes too small for the stomach he had grown as a detective—looked as good as anyone else's.

"Come on, admit it," Theo said as they walked from the police barracks to make their six o'clock call for breakfast. "When you were watching all that Desert Storm shit on TV, part of you wanted to be out there, didn't it?"

Sikes fiddled with his hat, trying to make sure that it wasn't making his hair stick out over his ears to make him look like the cops who had arrived from Bakersfield. Mayberry was more like it. "At least in Desert Storm some of the soldiers got to *do* something, Theo. All *we've* been doing is standing around getting tans and searching trucks."

Theo held out his hands and studied the backs of them. "This is about as tanned as you can get, son. Guess that means we've got to be promoted to something new."

"Yeah," Sikes said as they joined the depressingly long line leading into the mess tent. "Like searching trucks *and* cars. Oh, boy, I can hardly wait."

It took them almost half an hour to make their way to the front of the line. When they got there, breakfast looked like it was something that had been brought up from the *Titanic.* Kirby had made better food for him when she'd been five years old.

As quickly as they could, Sikes and Theo left the hot and foul-smelling mess tent and sat outside with their trays on the hood of a Humvee painted basic olive drab. All the desert-camouflaged units were out at the ACP—that was the military's way of saying Alien Containment Perimeter. Also known as a big blazing ditch of gas and oil.

At least the wind wasn't blowing the smoke toward the camp this morning, Sikes thought. So far. He decided he missed his own place, as small and as noisy as the apartment was. Maybe he wouldn't move after all. Who knew?

He gave up on his breakfast. "I thought we came out here so we wouldn't be punished."

Theo mechanically shoveled down what Sikes hadn't eaten. "This is a lot better than any Internal Affairs interview I ever had. Count your blessings, son. With luck we'll be out here long enough that Franklin Stewart's buddies'll forget to send us those Security Oaths. Why don't you just try and let the whole thing blow over?"

"Let a murder case blow over. I'm supposed to feel good about doing that?"

Theo put his now completely empty tray on the hood beside him. "You're just a rook, and you don't need to start out with anything like that mess on your record. Trust me."

Sikes could tell there was more that Theo was thinking that he wasn't saying. He wondered what trouble was listed on his ex-partner's own lengthy record. He wondered how many Internal Affairs interviews Theo had been part of and why. But like seeing him put too much money on the waiter's tray in the strip club, Sikes decided he didn't want or need to know the answer. If it was the wrong one, he didn't know if he could handle it.

"You two Sikes and Miles? LAPD?" That question came from a young sergeant with the letters MP emblazoned on her helmet. She carried a metal clipboard and a pen.

Sikes and Theo hopped off the Humvee. "That's us," Theo said. He adjusted his tie. It helped hide the way the fabric stretched around the buttonholes of his blue shirt. Sikes straightened his gleaming silver badge. He missed his detective's gold shield, too.

The sergeant made two checks on her clipboard. "Okay. Get over to Tent Fifteen by oh seven hundred hours."

"Tent Fifteen?" Sikes repeated. That was in the next layer of the camp that had been constructed. So far he and Theo had been restricted to duty in the outermost layer, searching the vehicles that drove in and out for anything that might have come from the crash site. There were supposed to be five layers to the camp, just like the Pentagon. Everyone was laying bets about what was in the centermost layer, but so far no one had any hard data.

"You got a briefing," the sergeant told them. "Looks like you two boys are moving inside."

Twenty minutes later Sikes and Theo were sitting in uncomfortable folding metal chairs along with fifty other police officers in a large double-walled tent. Sikes recognized two of the others from having worked with them. Everyone was in uniform. The military had insisted on that. The innermost layers of the camp were strictly off-limits to civilians.

A man walked onto a raised platform at the front of the tent at precisely seven o'clock. He had silver hair and wore a black uniform with three gold strips on his sleeve. "Naval Intelligence," Sikes whispered to Theo.

"Thought I recognized the stink," Theo said.

The commander on the stage wasn't Franklin Arthur Stewart, but he might has well have been. Sikes knew without a doubt now that this had been the military's show from the beginning. None of the staggering amounts of equipment that had been assembled in the Mojave in the past ten days had come out of nowhere. Somewhere, somehow, the Pentagon had been ready for something like this. Sikes suddenly remembered he'd forgotten to ask Grazer what Stewart had meant when he said they'd known all about what might happen since "Roswell."

Without preamble the naval commander began to speak. "This is a preliminary briefing to bring you people up to speed about what's been going on inside the ACP. The information you will receive is privileged. Any attempt to disseminate this information before you have been given official authorization will result in your being incarcerated by the military police until such time as this emergency is declared to be over. You will sign letters agreeing to these terms upon your exit from this briefing. Am I understood?"

A sprinkling of gung-ho types chorused back a few "Yes, sirs!" Sikes sank lower in his chair and moaned. They were everywhere.

"Hush up," Theo said. "This should be interesting."

"I guess," Sikes grumbled.

"Ten days ago, as you are aware, what is presumed to have been a spaceship of nonhuman design and manufacture crash-landed in the desert approximately ten miles from this location. Over the course of approximately five hours, between two and three hundred thousand alien beings evacuated that ship, which subsequently exploded. We do not know the cause of the explosion at this time.

"The aliens, despite the reports you might have heard to the contrary, *are* intelligent. They possess a complex spoken *and* written language, and great strides are being made in creating a workable translation dictionary. They also exhibit extremely complex social and familial behaviors, accompanied by clear evidence of religious beliefs, including, we believe, some kind of belief in an afterlife. I say this to remind all of you that what we are dealing with out there are not, repeat *not,* dumb animals or supernatural beings. We have every reason to believe that their culture is at least as complex and meaningful to them as any Earth culture is to us."

The commander walked back and forth as he talked, waving down a few raised hands by saying, "You will have a chance to ask questions at the end of this briefing. Now, on to what we *don't* know about them.

"First of all, there is the matter of the fighting that broke out on the first night after the crash. We still don't know what that was about. We are having limited conversations with a few of the aliens"—more than a few "ahhs" went through the audience at that—"and as our facility with each other's language improves, we hope to learn the details.

"For now, however, we have concluded that there are at least two factions among the aliens, with great animosity between them. Our current theory is that one faction was the prisoner of the second. Whether this means that one faction is made up of criminals or prisoners of war we do not know. For now, however, the aliens have demonstrated a remarkable capacity to organize themselves, to use the supplies that we have provided for them, and to police themselves. Incidents of fighting dropped off dramatically about the fourth day, when we finally determined what their dietary requirements are." He gazed over his audience. "Are there any questions?"

"What *are* their dietary requirements?"

"That is classified information at this time." There was a sound of general puzzlement from the audience. "The aliens have not brought a food supply with them," the commander said. "We have taken it upon ourselves to feed them. Some of what they eat is not found in the normal chain of food supplies, and early disclosure of what those foodstuffs are could lead to hoarding and result in increased cost to the taxpayer." He stared intently at the audience. "You are not military personnel, so I will forgive you your outburst this time. But when we say some information is classified, rest assured that we have a good reason for keeping it that way. Next question."

"What do you call them?" came one.

"As I said, their language is complex. They appear to have many terms by which they refer to themselves. The one that most of them seem to agree upon is, as close as I can say it, *Tencton-ta*. We have begun to call them Tenctonese. The term also works for the name of their language. Anyone else?"

"What are they doing here?"

The commander shrugged. "It appears something went wrong with their vehicle. As you know, the vehicle that crashed here was actually just a small part of what people originally thought was an asteroid traveling toward the sun. That other section of the vehicle appears to have been destroyed in space. The vehicle that landed here could very well be like a lifeboat. As of oh two hundred hours today a secondary containment perimeter was set up around the crash site itself, and a great number of experts are going through the wreckage. We hope to know more about it soon."

"Do you know what planet they're from?"

"No," the commander said. "Its name, we presume, is Tencton, but it's not located in our solar system."

"Are there any more of the vehicles out there?"

"That's classified."

Stunned silence. Then, "How long are they going to stay here?"

"That's classified."

"Can they ever go back to wherever they came from?"

"Classified."

A few of the cops in the audience began to laugh at the repetition.

Someone yelled, "What are *we* doing out here?" There was more laughter. Even the commander broke down and smiled.

"Each one of you has been selected because your service record indicates that you have experience dealing with members of cultures other than your own."

Sikes turned to look at Theo. "What the hell's that supposed to mean?"

Theo chuckled. "It means you're a cop in L.A., son."

"And now," the commander continued, "your government asks you to put that experience to work in a way that very few of you might have imagined."

"We're going to *work* with those things?" someone shouted.

The commander seemed to ignore the question. "Right now this camp supports a classified number of specialists. But that number is in the hundreds, and it's growing every day. Our best people in engineering, physics, computer science, linguistics, mathematics, medicine—you name it—they are all being paired with what we hope are their equal numbers from among the Tenctonese. That demand on our available manpower, combined with support duties for ourselves and especially for those within the ACP, is quite frankly a strain on available specialist personnel. Therefore you officers have been asked to take over all nonspecialist duties requiring contact between humans and Tenctonese."

No one said anything. It was the phrase "humans and Tenctonese" that had done it.

"Are we going to work with them?" a familiar voice called out.

The commander seemed to lose his military bearing for a moment. "Off the record, gentlemen and ladies, it appears we have no choice."

"I know what that's like," Sikes muttered.

There were air-conditioned buses outside the tent to take the police officers to their staging area. But the staging area wasn't where the officers expected it to be.

The buses drove them away from the camp, across the desert, toward the wall of fire and the waiting Tenctonese.

CHAPTER 9

T'KSAM MOTIONED TO BUCK to stay down, and Buck had no difficulty in obeying. He ground his body as tightly as he could into the dirt of the new world, wishing he could pass straight into it.

Both he and T'ksam had heard the approaching *sold'yurz* ground vehicle many minutes earlier, but it had been miles away at the time, giving no indication that it would come anywhere near them.

But the sound of its power plant had slowly come closer, and in the end T'ksam had decided that it would be better to deal with the *sold'yurz* on his own terms. That was why Buck was with him, he had explained, because children could prove to be useful distractions. He told Buck to hide behind a small rise on the desert floor. Then T'ksam had stood up, waved his arms, and called out to the aliens to bring them near.

The sound of the vehicle made Buck's ear valleys hurt. He could smell the stench it put out—as bad as the smoke that blew in from the wall of fire. Then the sound changed, dropping off.

Buck heard an alien voice. But what it said was only meaningless gibberish. They sounded like animals.

T'ksam appeared to be responding to them. *"Help yez. Help help hurt,"* he said. Nonsense sounds.

The aliens replied. Buck heard the sound of metal slamming against metal, then footsteps in the dirt.

"Finiksa!" T'ksam called out. "I've told them you're injured. They're going to come over the rise to look at you. Just lie still and moan. But don't stand up until I tell you."

Buck grabbed handfuls of dirt in his hands as if trying to dig through the desert. He prayed to Andarko that the creatures would not be able to touch him.

The footsteps came closer. More alien words. *Kid* seemed to be the one they used the most.

Buck felt something touch his shoulder. He stiffened in horror. An alien being was trying to turn him over. Buck moaned without even remembering his instructions from T'ksam. He felt himself lifted and turned and—

Buck screamed.

He stared up into two hideously disfigured faces, and he shrieked like the workers who had been recycled alive.

They had no brains.

Their heads were crushed down into nothing more than what lay behind their faces, as if some mad killer had hacked off their skulls with Tagdot's knife.

They had no spots.

It made them both featureless, as if they were engineered food animals with no separate identity.

Buck shook with terror. The aliens were crouching over him as if they planned to eat him. One of them spoke to the other. *Kid* this, *kid* that. Buck covered his eyes with his hands, spilling dirt into them. He drew his arms and legs up to protect himself. One of the creatures grabbed at his shoulders, trying to pull him toward it.

With his eyes still screwed tightly shut, Buck howled, he kicked, he thrashed and punched at the monster. He felt the hands fall away. He looked up.

T'ksam stood behind one of the *sold'yurz*. And in one half of a heartsbeat he braced his hands against the creature's face and chin and spun its head until something crunched, as if there were no muscles in its neck at all.

T'ksam grinned and held out his hands as the creature dropped lifeless to the desert floor. The other monster saw what had happened and jumped to its feet.

"Now, Finiksa!" T'ksam shouted.

His conditioning was stronger than his fear, and Buck leapt to his own feet.

The *sold'yurz* had some sort of prod with a flattened handle, and he swung it at Buck, smashing the boy's upraised arm and face. Buck fell back as quickly as he had risen, not even feeling the impact in the shock of the blow.

The *sold'yurz* spun back to face T'ksam, but the Overseer had already changed position. He rained a flurry of punches across the creature's chest until it fell down on its back. Then T'ksam dropped to his knees on the *sold'yurz*'s chest, making its breath explode from its body. The Overseer leaned forward and wrapped his arms around the alien's neck, and once again there was a crunch.

T'ksam leapt back onto his feet and brushed the dirt from his tunic and trousers. "What did I tell you?" he said to Buck. "It's as if they're made of crystal."

Buck seemed to hear two of every word T'ksam said. He tried to push himself up from the ground, but his left arm had no strength. He looked at it. It was bent as if he had another wrist in his forearm. His face began to throb.

T'ksam was beside him. "You'll be all right," the Overseer said. "A broken arm is a good wound to take from your first battle. Your family will be proud of you." He prodded the sorest parts of Buck's face. "Too bad," he said. "It won't even earn you a scar of valor. Maybe next time."

He stood up and held out his hand to Buck. "If you want, you can examine their vehicle. It's very primitive. I'll hide their bodies."

Buck almost fainted with pain as T'ksam pulled him to his feet. He stared down at the bodies of the dead aliens, fascinated, catching his breath. If he didn't look at the creature's horribly misshapen heads, they weren't all that different from Tenctonese. By their body shapes, one even seemed to be a male and the other a female. He wondered what their *binnaumta* looked like.

T'ksam walked over to their vehicle and came back with what turned out to be a folded shovel. Buck realized that the creatures were dressed in uniforms—oddly patterned in desert colors, but clearly a standard system of dressing. He wondered if these were this world's Overseers. If so, the slaves must be incredibly feeble.

"You go lie in the sun," T'ksam said kindly. "I'll get you back to a medical specialist before you know it." Quickly he began to dig a hole behind the rise. Within minutes there was no trace of the bodies. Buck wondered if he should say a blessing to Andarko and Celine so the *sold'yurz* could find their way past the wall. He didn't know if Andarko and Celine could guide the *serdos* of monsters, but in the end he decided it couldn't hurt to ask. The *sold'yurz* had died doing their work. That had to be good for something, even on an alien world.

Buck looked up at T'ksam. His arm and face throbbed painfully with each double beat. "When they came, were you speaking their language?" he asked.

T'ksam helped Buck walk to the rumbling vehicle. Its power plant was still in operation. "I know a few words. Already we've had representatives speaking with these creatures' leaders, correcting the lies that the cargo is attempting to spread."

Buck sat in one of the vehicle's chairs. It was surprisingly more comfortable than anything on the ship. "Do you know what the name of their world is?" Buck thought that it was important that he know that. He wanted to be able to include the name in his prayers.

"I think it translates as dirt," T'ksam said. "This area we crashed on seems to be part of a tribal tract called *Kwarnn'teen.* At least, they keep telling us that's where we are. Odd-sounding language, isn't it?"

Buck started to nod but stopped. His face felt as if it were catching fire. T'ksam sat in the vehicle's other chair. There was some sort of large valve-release wheel in front of him. He pulled his ring out of his tunic and checked the direction of the beacon they had been tracking. Then the Overseer pushed a lever between the seats, and there was a horrible grinding noise. Buck tensed. His arm blazed with fiery pain. And then the vehicle lurched forward.

T'ksam laughed. "It works just as I was told it works. They have no sense of security." He used the valve-release wheel to alter the direction of the vehicle, then tapped his foot back and forth along the vehicle's floor in front of his chair. He hit a part of the floor that sounded different to Buck, and the vehicle slowed. He hit something else, and the vehicle sped up.

"That's the one," T'ksam said. Then he pushed his foot down, and the power plant roared, and the vehicle moved away from the desert toward a nearby range of small hills. He sang a Watcher's song of victory.

Buck didn't join in. He stared out the vehicle's window without seeing the desert beyond. As the world spun around him in pain, all he could see was the creatures' faces as they had lain dead. In his growing delirium, each one of them looked just like Vornho.

There was something wrong, Buck knew. Something terribly wrong. But he couldn't tell if what was wrong was something in this alien world or something within himself.

Perhaps there is no answer, he heard someone say. Perhaps that is a choice to be made and not a question to be answered.

Buck stared at T'ksam. The Overseer had said nothing.

Buck felt tears fall from his eyes. It took him a long time to realize they were not because of pain.

He thought about choices until he passed out.

CHAPTER 10

SIKES GRIMACED AS the wheels of his Humvee slipped sideways in the desert sand. It was like driving in snow. And he hated driving in snow. That's why he had left Detroit in the first place.

"Easy there, son," Theo said from the back. "We got nowhere to go, and we don't have to get there fast."

Sikes swore as he brought the balky vehicle back on track. There was sweat dripping down his forehead and his nose in the desert heat. Driving in snow and sweating. What could be better? "We're chauffeurs, Theo. We're nothing but goddam chauffeurs for a bunch of men from Mars."

"No, not men from Mars," Miss Laurie said from the passenger seat. Sikes could hear the smile in her voice. She was *always* smiling. "I myself, female from Tencton. Not male. Don't know Mars."

Sikes turned to look at the tall, slim alien at his side, listening to English tapes on a Walkman. Her head was swollen up like a sponge that had been dipped in water. Her scalp was balder than Sinead O'Connor's, and it was covered in hundreds of squiggly-looking freckles. But she had a nice smile, he could give her that. Nice smile and a chipper attitude that made him want to punch the roof and the steering wheel at the same time.

He felt Theo's hand pat his arm. "You let me know when it's my turn to drive."

"Yeah," Sikes said. "Another half hour and you can take us in."

He kept driving across the desert. Looking for stragglers, the official word was. That was the assignment they had been given. Not important enough for the army guys. Just drive through the desert looking for stragglers—Tenctonese who had strayed so far away from the crash site that they were outside the ACP. Sikes had never had a more boring job in his entire life.

So far, in three days of duty, he and Theo—and their ever-smiling Tenctonese observer, Miss Laurie—had rounded up fifteen aliens. Sikes knew that something funny was going on because a few of them sure hadn't been on their own out in the desert since the first night. Most of them looked well fed. A few even wore the orange jumpsuits that had been provided to replace the gray rags they had arrived in. The stragglers' condition told Sikes that the blazing pits of oil and gas hadn't been completely effective in keeping the Tenctonese in the quarantine zone, and the new fencing that was going up to replace the fire pits wasn't doing much better.

"You know," Sikes said for the fifth time that day, *"nothing* out here is what they say it is. The military has gotta be stringing us along again. They got some kind of hidden agenda going on here."

He heard Theo sigh from the backseat. "Kid, the government wants the spaceship. That's all it comes down to, and you can't blame them. They don't want anyone sneaking *out* of the area with any pieces of advanced technology, and they don't want spies sneaking *in.* It's as simple as that."

"Naah," Sikes said. "There's more to it than that. I can smell it, and it *stinks."*

From the corner of his eye he saw Miss Laurie smile at him and then cover her mouth as she laughed.

"Smell it," Sikes said to her again. "You like that, huh? You think that's funny?"

Miss Laurie waved her hand in front of her nose. *"Lee p'sh*—you say: on ship. Everything all time smell *son.* Very very *son.* Like *monk.* You know *monk?"* She looked at the roof of the Humvee and made a grasping motion with her free hand. "Shitty. *Kwen,* that right. *Monk.* Shitty. Bad all time." She gave

Sikes her smile again. "Down here, smell so good. All time good. Breathe deep. No *monk.* You . . . humans complain bad smell. We think good. You think bad. We laugh. Funny."

"Hilarious," Sikes said flatly.

Miss Laurie went back to her Walkman. In the three days Sikes and Theo had been driving her around the Mojave, she had progressed at the rate of a full grade of English each day. At the rate she was going, she'd be speaking better English than Sikes inside of a week. Apparently they were all like that. Their brains were also like sponges. Soaking up everything.

Miss Laurie suddenly pointed over to the left. "There," she said urgently. She took her job seriously, as if work was the most important thing in her life.

Sikes looked in the direction she pointed. Desert. Nothing but desert.

"Two *Tencton-ta. Hend* miles."

Theo held his hand out for Sikes, spreading his fingers. "That's five miles, kid."

"I don't see a thing," Sikes said. He pulled off his sunglasses. Still nothing but superheated glare.

"You know better than that," Theo said. "If Miss Laurie here says she sees two of her people five miles away, then she sees two of her people."

Sikes sighed and changed the heading of the Humvee until Miss Laurie told him they were traveling straight for them. Of course, it had to be over the roughest part of the desert floor, making the vehicle shake like a Piper Cub in a thunderstorm.

How their Tenctonese observer got the name Miss Laurie, Sikes didn't know. All the Tenctonese who were working with humans had been given human names, mainly because humans weren't as fast to learn Tenctonese pronunciation as the Tenctonese were to learn English. It also made it easier to write reports. The human names were given to the Tenctonese by the people they worked with, and it had quickly become clear that the Tenctonese treated their human names as some kind of status symbols. Apparently there was a Tenctonese male working in the engineering section who had been given the name Rover because of his eagerness to please. Even when it had been explained to him what the name actually meant, he hadn't wanted to give it up. In the Tenctonese culture, the briefing officers had told Sikes, names were extremely important and were not given or treated lightly.

But Sikes didn't care. Sikes was getting tired of the whole thing. He knew Kirby would kill him for his lack of imagination and sense of wonder, but when it came right down to it, without ray guns, spaceships, miracle cures for cancer, or an invitation to join a galactic brotherhood, the Tenctonese weren't what a lot of people, including him, had expected space aliens to be. At the end of the day they were just another group of people in trouble who didn't speak the language. And the world was full of those.

According to Theo's soap-opera index, by which he measured the relative importance of news stories by the length of time they managed to preempt afternoon television shows, the Tenctonese crash-landing had scored a record eight out of ten. The air war in Iraq had been a one, and the L.A. riots a two. But now, almost two weeks after the first shock, as everyone realized that any secrets in the spaceship wreckage were going to be hard to come by, "The Young and the Restless" was running again, and the saga of the stranded aliens had been reduced to five-second sound bites on the national newscasts, just like everything else.

It all made Sikes want to go back to where he belonged. He wanted to be a cop again. Even if it meant completely giving in to the captain and signing a Security Oath and living the rest of his days knowing he had let a murderer get away with his crime, Sikes wanted to go back to doing what he knew he had to do. Theo had been right. He was a cop. He'd made his decision, and now there was nothing he could do about it.

He saw a speck on the horizon. "Okay. I see one of them," he told Miss Laurie.

"Adult male carry child. Maybe hurt. Ouch bad."

"Better get the first-aid kit ready," Sikes said over his shoulder. The pressure points for stopping bleeding weren't the same, but the briefing officers had said that bones could be set on a Tenctonese the same as on a human. And if any other treatment was required, that would be the responsibility of the Tenctonese observer that rode with each team.

Two minutes later, Sikes slowed the Humvee by an adult male Tenctonese carrying what seemed to be an unconscious ten-year-old boy, just as Miss Laurie had said. Part of the problem, Sikes could see right away, was that the child's clothes had been taken off. Except for a small gray fabric bundle that was lying on his stomach, the kid was naked. He was going to fry.

Sikes, Theo, and Miss Laurie jumped out of the Humvee at the same time.

"Tell him to cover the kid up," Sikes said. He could see that the boy's face was swollen and that his left forearm had a bad break.

"Sun is good on skin," Miss Laurie said. "Make strong." She walked quickly to the Tenctonese male and began speaking in their own language.

The male cut her off. Sikes didn't understand a single word of what was being said, but he heard the tone in the male's voice. He was telling her to drop dead and mind her own business. Surprisingly, the talkative Miss Laurie shut up. Still carrying the child, the male began to walk toward the back of the Humvee.

"That's it?" Sikes asked Miss Laurie. "You're not going to help the kid out?"

Miss Laurie had lost her smile. "Child okay. Hurt make strong. Go back now."

Sikes looked at Theo. "Hurt make strong?" Theo shrugged. The male roughly put the unconscious child into the backseat, then pushed in front of Miss Laurie and took her place in the passenger seat.

"Hey," Sikes said. "That's where Miss Laurie sits. You get back there."

The male stared at him, and Sikes saw that arrogance appeared to be the same throughout the universe.

"Okay, fine," Miss Laurie said. "I sit back here. He sit there. Okay fine." She said something to the male. He replied. She said to Sikes, "He say you can go now."

Sikes didn't get it. "Well, thank him for his kind permission," he said sarcastically. "What is he, Miss Laurie? Some kind of commanding officer or something?"

Miss Laurie spoke to the male again. He replied again. "His name T'ksam. Ordinary Tenctonese."

Sikes thought his name sounded like someone sneezing. "Tell him he's got a new name. I'm going to call him Sam. You tell him that and it'll make his day."

Miss Laurie explained it to him. T'ksam stared at Sikes with an odd expression. "Sam," he said, as if trying it out. He pointed to his chest. "Sam." Then he pointed to Sikes.

Sikes said his name. The male's eyes widened, and he looked

like he was going to burst into laughter. Then he caught himself. *"See-iiks,"* he repeated. *"See-iiks, See-iiks, See-iiks."* He pointed to his chest and said, "Sam." He pointed at Sikes again, expectantly.

"Sikes," Sikes said, pointing to himself again. "I thought you guys were supposed to be smart."

"Vot keeps urs," T'ksam said, as if trying to keep back a smile.

"What did he say?" Sikes asked.

"You speak the truth," Miss Laurie translated. Even she acted as if some sort of joke was being made.

Sikes didn't get it. It would be five years before anyone explained to him the significance of his own name in Tenctonese.

As they arrived back at one of the main gates leading into the ACP, Sikes noticed that during the whole drive back T'ksam had kept the child's clothes bundled up on his own lap. He hadn't even offered them as a pillow for the kid. Pretty callous, Sikes thought. Maybe they don't care about their kids the way we do.

At the entrance gate, Sikes waited in a line-up of other military vehicles for an MP to wave him into an open vehicle bay for inspection. The gasoline pits had been replaced over the past few days by a pair of fifteen-foot-high chain-link fences that were eventually to form a double boundary around the entire quarantine zone. It was more humane than the ring of fire, Sikes knew, but it made the purpose of the AQF painfully obvious.

Another MP came up to Sikes's side of the Humvee carrying one of the ubiquitous metal clipboards. "What have we got here?" he asked. He wrote down Sikes's badge number as he waited for a reply.

"Five coming in," Sikes said. "Two human." He gave his name and Theo's. "One Tenctonese observer: Miss Laurie. And two stragglers."

"Got names for the stragglers?" the MP asked.

"Yeah," Sikes said, glancing at T'ksam. "This one's Sam."

"Sam what?"

"How the hell should I know?"

The MP frowned. "The computers need at least *two* names to

keep track of them all, detective." He looked across at T'ksam. "Sam, initial I., Am. That should do it." He wrote it down.

"We got a kid in the back, too," Sikes added. "Hurt pretty bad."

"What's his name?"

Before Sikes could ask Miss Laurie to ask T'ksam what the child's name was, the MP looked in at him. "No, don't tell me," the MP said. "I know. He's Buck. Buck Nekkid."

Sikes made a face. He had the feeling that a lot of aliens would be getting their new names this way soon.

The MP walked around the vehicle to finish his inspection, then returned to Sikes. "Unload the child here so we can send him inside in an ambulance." The MP turned away and blew two quick blasts on his whistle.

Sikes got out. Theo, Miss Laurie, and T'ksam followed. Theo went over to talk to the MP as Sikes told Miss Laurie to tell T'ksam that he wasn't going anywhere and to get back into the Humvee. He knew whatever was going on between Miss Laurie and T'ksam was serious because Miss Laurie didn't laugh when he said the word "Humvee." Apparently it had some kind of sexual connotation in their language, but they all seemed too embarrassed to explain exactly what. There were some subjects, it seemed, that none of them would talk about, almost as if they had all been given orders not to talk.

But T'ksam didn't get back into the vehicle. He was still carrying the kid's clothes under his arm. Sikes wished he had his gun, but all the military would let him carry was his cuffs. Not even a nightstick. Nobody wanted to see the Tenctonese with weapons.

"I am not kidding, Miss Laurie," Sikes said, making no attempt to hide the anger in his voice. He could see Theo looking over at him. "Tell Sam to get back in so I can take him to Medical Screening, or I'll have the MPs carry him in." Medical Screening was an absolute necessity for any Tenctonese entering the ACP. Almost all of them had come down with some sort of red rash on the backs of their necks in the first few days after the crash, and though most cases had spontaneously cleared up, there was now a disease resembling pneumonia beginning to spread. Plans were already being made to split up the Tenctonese population into widely separated camps so that any potential alien plague could be more easily prevented from infecting them all.

Miss Laurie stumbled over the words in her own language as if she had to force herself to tell T'ksam to do anything.

T'ksam stared at Sikes and Theo, who now was at Sikes's side. T'ksam grinned. *"See-iiks,"* he said loudly. *"See-iiks, See-iiks, See-iiks."* Then he got back into the Humvee, still clutching the child's clothes.

An ambulance pulled up behind the Humvee, and two attendants got out. One was a human. The other was a Tenctonese in ill-fitting hospital whites. The human let the Tenctonese move the child from the Humvee to a wheeled stretcher. The kid seemed to be coming around. He was mumbling things, and he said one set of words often enough that they almost were clear, though they sounded like another sneeze to Sikes.

"Kleys cawnt zoom," it sounded like, with an odd little click on the end. Whatever *kleys* were, and who knew why they couldn't *zoom?*

But there was something about those words that made the Tenctonese attendant look at the child with worry in her eyes.

Then, before Sikes knew what was happening, T'ksam was out of the Humvee and standing by the stretcher and slapping the child's face.

"Hey! What the hell does he think he's doing?" Sikes said. He felt Theo place a restraining arm against his chest. Their orders said that they were to do nothing to interfere in the aliens' normal interactions amongst themselves. But as far as Sikes was concerned, what T'ksam was doing wasn't normal on any planet.

"It okay, fine," Miss Laurie said nervously. She added her hand to Sikes's shoulder to hold him back. Her grip was surprisingly strong.

The child opened his eyes and looked up at T'ksam, then shouted, *"Kleys cawnt zoom! Kleys cawnt zoom!"*

And T'ksam's hand rammed into the kid's rib cage under his arm, and the kid jerked back as if his neck had been snapped.

T'ksam made a move at the ambulance attendant, and she backed away quickly.

"Who the hell is that guy?" Sikes demanded, struggling to free himself from Theo's and Miss Laurie's firm hold.

"Okay fine," Miss Laurie said, almost desperately. "Sam I. Am. Ordinary Tenctonese."

"The hell he is," Sikes snapped at her. "What aren't you telling us?"

"Tell you everything," the nervous Tenctonese said. "Okay fine. Okay—"

She stopped in midsentence as T'ksam yelled at her. Her hand dropped from Sikes's shoulder. It had been an order in any language. T'ksam walked back to the Humvee and got back inside.

Miss Laurie bowed her head as far as it could go. "He say you can drive Sam now," she said to Sikes. Theo released Sikes.

Sikes turned to Theo. "He was trying to kill that kid, Miles."

"That's what it looked like to me, too. But the kid's still breathing. Remember, we don't know what's normal for them. Maybe it's just a dad beating some sense into a son."

That brought back too many memories for Sikes. "It doesn't work that way, man. It just doesn't work that way."

The MP told Sikes to get his rig out of there. The ambulance had to get past him into the camp.

Angrily Sikes climbed back into the driver's seat. T'ksam didn't look at him. But he did say *"See-iiks"* one more time.

Theo stood with Miss Laurie by Sikes's door. "You not coming?" Sikes asked.

Miss Laurie bowed her large head.

Theo gave Sikes a small wave. "I'm her escort outside the fence, kid. I'll meet up with you back at the mess tent." He walked away with the Tenctonese female. After a few steps he put his arm around her as if comforting her. It seemed like a completely natural thing to do.

Sikes scowled as he started up the Humvee. The MP came over to the side of the vehicle to advise him that the fastest way to Medical was between the fences. The inner fence ran out at the medical compound, and that way Sikes wouldn't have to drive a mile out of his way around the barracks construction sites.

Sikes thanked the MP for the shortcut. The less time spent in the vehicle with T'ksam the better. He slammed the Humvee into gear and kicked up a cloud of desert dust as he drove through the first gate, then hung a hard left. He checked to see what the turn had done to T'ksam, but the male was sitting perfectly upright, still holding onto the ball of gray fabric. He met Sikes's stare, challenge in his eyes.

Sikes turned away. He accelerated. The Humvee roared.

Sand and rocks thundered up against its underside. Sikes hit forty with the chain-link fences rushing by ten feet from either side.

T'ksam had the nerve to chuckle.

Sikes floored it. The Humvee started sliding in the loose soil as he banked to follow the same twists and turns in the terrain that the fence did. He fishtailed on a tight turn and missed an extinguished oil pit by two feet. One of T'ksam's hands shot out to grab the narrow dash.

Sikes gritted his teeth and smiled. There was still a mile to go. He started edging closer to the inner fence, pulling away every few seconds to miss the thick posts. The whole Humvee rocked. The wheels started sliding again. He came closer and closer to the posts.

Then Sikes swore and jammed on the brakes, and the Humvee slid to a stop in a cloud of dust less than a foot away from a pile of fence posts that blocked the whole corridor between the fences. Whoever had dumped the shipment there had left only a few feet of clearance on either side, no room for any vehicle to pass. Sikes kept his hands on the wheel and waited for the dust cloud to blow away. Through the chain-link fence he could see the orderly rows of the white medical trailers that had become the quarantine zone's hospital just beyond the pile of posts. But the end of the inner fence was still a couple hundred feet away.

He opened his door and stepped out into the blazing sun and dry air. The sweat was pouring from his forehead now, and he tossed his hat back onto the driver's seat. His dark uniform was punishment enough in the desert heat. "Come on, Sam. We're going for a walk."

T'ksam got out of the Humvee and stared at Sikes. Sikes pointed past the medical trailers and took a few steps toward the left side of the pile of posts.

T'ksam took his own good time examining the immediate area, then began to walk toward the right side of the pile.

"Hey!" Sikes shouted. His voice was oddly flat in the still desert air. "I'm your escort." He made exaggerated gestures to himself and to T'ksam. *"You* walk with *me.* Get it?"

T'ksam stopped to watch Sikes. He adjusted the rolled-up clothes under his arm.

"What is it with you guys?" Sikes exclaimed. "Half of you learn the language in an afternoon, and the rest of you are dumber than the back end of a truck."

T'ksam waited.

Sikes did his pointing routine again. *"You* walk with *me.* Get it? Sam. Sikes. This way."

As he said both their names T'ksam scowled.

Sikes caught the reaction. "Sam. Sikes," he repeated.

T'ksam's jaw clenched, he turned around, he walked past the posts on the right side. Sikes jogged after him, swearing. T'ksam kept walking.

Sikes fell into step beside him. "I'm getting sick and tired of taking this shit from you guys," he yelled into T'ksam's ear—or at least, what passed for an ear. "Shit. *Monk!* You know, *monk?"* There, he thought with satisfaction, I've learned my first word of Tenctonese.

T'ksam hissed at Sikes as Sikes repeated the alien expletive, as if no one had ever said it to his face before.

"C'mon, asshole," Sikes said with a huge smile on his face, "if I know one word of your language, I bet you know a couple hundred of mine."

T'ksam returned the smile. "Eat *monk,"* he said, then he laughed and picked up his pace, easily distancing himself from Sikes.

Sikes wanted to let him go. He wanted to turn back to the Humvee and just let this alien go. Let them all go. But he had his orders. No unescorted Tenctonese were allowed outside the ACP. He had no choice.

"Wait up, asshole." Sikes broke into a sprint to catch up to T'ksam. As he got within arm's reach, the Tenctonese suddenly spun around and faced Sikes as if he were about to launch some kind of martial arts attack. Sikes made himself laugh. "Am I making you nervous? A dumb little human like me?"

T'ksam snarled something at him.

"Eat *monk* yourself," Sikes said. "Talk English, buddy, or don't bother talking at all."

T'ksam spit onto the dirt at Sikes's feet.

They faced each other.

Then Sikes realized what he was doing.

He shook his head. "Keep walking," he said. He was an officer. He had orders. These people had crashed here and didn't know what was going on any more than Sikes did. It wasn't fair that he take out his bad day—bad week, bad life—on some poor sap a zillion light-years from home.

T'ksam gloated in triumph. He started walking again, his feet crunching against the dry soil. The end of the fence was about three hundred feet away.

"Chee vot!"

Sikes glanced over to the inner fence, fifteen feet away. A Tenctonese female was there. She looked to be about fifty years old, was dressed in the usual tattered gray clothes, had one hand on the chain-link fence, and waved urgently with the other, motioning Sikes over.

Sikes shrugged. He pointed down by the end of the fence. If she wanted to speak with him, she could meet him there.

"Chee vot!" the female shouted again. *"K'ul zoo!"*

Sikes saw T'ksam glance at her. Her mouth widened in shock.

She pointed her finger through the chain-link mesh. *"Na wask vot!"* It was a cry of recognition. *"Na wask vot!"*

Sikes looked at T'ksam. T'ksam didn't look at the female. Instead he started to walk faster.

The female ran ahead along the fence, then grabbed the mesh again and shook it furiously, making an angry metallic rattle. *"Kleezantsun\!"* she wailed. Sikes felt goose bumps rise up on his arms despite the heat. *"Kleezantsun\!"* It sounded like what the kid had been trying to say when T'ksam had punched him out.

Behind the female, other Tenctonese among the medical trailers started paying attention to what she was shouting. More of them began to come up to the fence. T'ksam ignored them all.

The female ran ahead again to keep up with T'ksam's deliberate strides. This time when she stopped it was with a group of others, all ages, speaking quickly amongst themselves and pointing to T'ksam. They all began to shake the fence, sounding like a giant snare drum beating out a march.

And they all screamed out the same word: *"Kleezantsun\! Kleezantsun\!"*

Sikes looked at T'ksam. He could see the Tenctonese was about to break into a run. Sikes didn't know what was going on, but he decided that T'ksam wasn't going anywhere until he could figure this out.

At the same moment T'ksam began to run, Sikes reached out to grab his arm. He missed, but he snagged the bundle of

clothing instead. It fell out from under T'ksam's arm and
bumped to the ground. That was the first time that Sikes
realized that something was hidden in it.

"Hold on here," Sikes said as he stooped over to pick up the
bundle. Even stricter than the orders requiring Tenctonese to
be escorted were the orders forbidding the transport of any
object into or out of the ACP without having it looked at by a
technology inspector. "This isn't going anywhere."

His hand closed on the bundle just as T'ksam's foot connected with his chin.

Sikes went flying back as if he had been slammed by a
linebacker. His fingers clenched tight on the fabric and unrolled it. He looked up from the ground, gasping for breath.
There was a black metal cube lying in the dirt, small enough to
fit in one hand, with one side covered in Tenctonese writing.

A word rushed through the crowd by the fence faster than
"Kleezantsun\" had spread. *"Sobat!"* they cried as if the world
were ending. *"Sobat! Sobat!"*

T'ksam picked up the cube. Sikes got to his feet. "I don't
think so, Sam."

T'ksam snarled at him. Then he said, "You go now."

Sikes rubbed at his jaw and smiled. He knew the guy could
speak English. "I *definitely* don't think so. That thing has to go
through the inspection station."

T'ksam angled his body, putting the cube out of Sikes's
reach.

There were about a hundred Tenctonese pressed against the
fence now. Some were crying. Some were shouting. All were
panicked. The fence shook with an ancient rhythm. Drumbeats
of war in any language.

"I guess this thing's pretty important," Sikes said as he began
to move to the left, making T'ksam shift to follow him.

"Go now," T'ksam said in the same tone he had used to
order Miss Laurie.

"I'm not going anywhere," Sikes said. "And neither are you,
pal."

The fence shook. Back and forth. Sikes made a feint to the
right, expecting to swing in with his left. But T'ksam moved
like something molten. His fingers kited into Sikes's stomach,
slammed against his neck, a foot to his chest, then the cube
came arcing through the air in T'ksam's fist and smashed into
Sikes's nose.

All four blows had landed in less than a second. Sikes felt the desert whirl around him. For a moment he thought he might be in his bed after the party at Casey's, as if everything that had happened in the past three weeks had been nothing more than a dream.

The crowd of aliens roared and screamed, and everything they said was meaningless and yet so clear. They were terrified.

Sikes fell to the ground. Dimly he was aware of T'ksam standing over him, the cube still grasped in his hand. Sikes narrowed his eyes against the sun. He looked over to the fence. They had stopped shaking the chain link. They had stopped shouting and crying. There was silence. He looked at them. They stared at him. And at T'ksam. And at the cube.

And through his blurred vision Sikes saw no aliens. There were only people on the other side of that fence. Frightened people. Lost people. People who had nothing. People who desired only one thing.

Justice.

Sikes stared up at T'ksam. He didn't know what crimes T'ksam might have committed beyond beating a child. He didn't know what the cube meant other than that its presence frightened everyone who saw it. But sometimes details didn't matter. Sometimes there was just right and wrong. It was the same in any language.

Sikes tried to get up, but his muscles cramped and his head fell back against the dirt. A moan escaped the crowd. T'ksam was just a black smear against the blinding sky. But Sikes could hear the sneer in the alien's voice as he said one word perfectly clear, though it made no sense.

"Cargo."

Then T'ksam turned and began to walk away.

Sikes lay flat on his back. The sun burned into him. Dust stuck to his face on each rivulet of sweat. But there was only one thought in his mind, one voice in his heart.

No.

It wasn't over.

It would never be over.

Sikes was tired of being beaten. It was time to win one.

CHAPTER 11

GEORGE CRADLED DEVOOSHA in his arms and sang her a song of Tencton. The little podling cooed sleepily, and his hearts melted.

"I think she needs a nap, Neemu."

George looked over at his mate. She looked so beautiful in her human clothes. He found it to be a good omen that the color used for holy robes on Tencton was the same as that worn by those who cared for children on this new world. Susan held out her arms for their baby. "Here, let me put her in her . . . *bed.*"

They smiled at each other as Susan used the human word. The trailer was filled with tiny *bed-ta* for podlings. In the other trailers nearby were larger *bed-ta* for adults. The humans had asked for all cargo specialists to come to these trailers marked by the *Red Cross* to help the sick and the injured Tenctonese and to teach humans how to do the same. The humans were obsessed with the notion that none should die, no matter how old or how young. These were days of miracles.

That didn't stop the Tenctonese from dying, though. George and Susan had seen the *trucks* arriving by night carrying large metal cans into which the bodies of the dead were sealed. The bodies would be returned, the humans said, when it was certain that they would pose no threat to this world. George wasn't clear on how they would know when the bodies were safe. It had something to do with going to a group of holy elders and asking them to dispense an *Environmental Impact Statement* before a single body could be buried or burned. These aliens were a kind people, George knew, even if they did appear to be hopelessly complicated some of the time.

Little Devoosha squeaked happily in her *bed* and closed her eyes. Susan slipped her arm around George's waist as they stood watching their child. There was a sign on the end of the bed. It read: EMILY DICKINSON. George was very proud that his daughter had been blessed with a human name to bind her to this planet. His mate had one of her own, too: Susan B. Anthony. George looked forward to the day when he would be judged worthy enough to have a job, and the humans would bestow a name upon him so that he, too, could be entered into the records. It would be a thrilling day.

Susan nuzzled George's neck. "I have a *break* in just a few *minutes,*" she whispered into his ear valley. "And I know a trailer where they have lots of *bed-ta* and the doors can be locked."

George's hearts fluttered. But he remembered the Elders' warnings. "Would it be safe?" he asked. So far no one had seen a single human *binnaum,* and the Elders had decreed that all exchange of information about reproduction was forbidden until they had determined if there was any chance that some disaster had befallen human *binnaum-ta* that would make the humans take the Tenctonese's. All mated couples had therefore been emphatically warned not to couple in any location where humans might see them. But George had already noticed that humans respected a locked door. "How long is a few . . . *minutes?*" he purred.

Susan made a humming noise in the back of her throat, and George felt his cheeks flush. "About as long as—"

There was some disturbance outside. They both turned to the window at the same time.

Clearly now they heard the cry again. "Overseer!" someone was shouting. "Overseer!" There was another sound as well, as if the fence by the medical trailers was shaking in a powerful wind.

George glanced down at his sleeping child. "Perhaps I had better go outside—"

"I'm coming with you," Susan said.

They stepped out of the trailer. A crowd was gathering.

"They've found an Overseer," George said as he heard what everyone was saying. "On the other side of the fence."

He held Susan's hand as he pushed into the crowd, feeling the old fear return. Everyone had said that the Overseers were gone. They had died in the crash or remained on the stardrive. The Tenctonese were supposed to be free of them.

George and Susan pushed up against the fence, surrounded now by a hundred of their kind. "No," George said in shock. It *was* an Overseer. T'ksam. The monster who had questioned him in the dormitory and brutalized Susan.

Susan trembled as she recognized T'ksam as well, now dressed in cargo gray and with no trace of a tattoo around either wrist. They could be anywhere, George thought. Everywhere. All around us.

The Overseer walked with a human and that was even more frightening. For the human also wore a dark uniform with a silver badge of rank upon his chest.

George heard the urgent whispers race through the crowd. "Have they come back?" "Is that a human Overseer?" George gripped the fence with a hundred others. "No!" he and a hundred others shouted, and with each cry they shook the fence in the rhythm of a prayer for deliverance.

The Overseer knew he had been recognized. It was obvious from the arrogant way he ignored the crowd that chanted at him. But George could see that his nerve was about to break and—

Sure enough, T'ksam began to run. But at the same exact instant, the uniformed human reached for him and pulled a bundle of old clothes from under the Overseer's arm.

The bundle of clothes unraveled. A dark device fell to the ground.

It was something from the ship.

"What is it?" Susan asked, pressing closer to George.

"I . . . I don't know," George said.

But someone did. The cry went up like a plea to the heavens. "It's a beacon!" "A ship's beacon!" "They can call the fleet with it!"

"A beacon!"

Hundreds of hands shook the fence in terror, trying to tear it down. George looked down the fence to see if it would be possible to get around the unfinished end. But there were armed human guards there, already coming this way to see what the disturbance was.

The uniformed human said something unintelligible and bent to pick up the beacon. T'ksam moved swiftly and kicked him hard. The human fell back.

The crowd moaned. T'ksam scooped the beacon up from the ground.

George held his breath. Amazingly, the human was getting up to face T'ksam again.

"Maybe he *isn't* an Overseer," Susan said hesitantly.

"Then what could he be?" George asked.

"A fool," an old male said, shaking his head. "The Overseer will split what little there is of his skull."

Hundreds of hands still gripped at the fence. But now there was silence instead of chanting.

The human moved against T'ksam, far too slowly. T'ksam exploded in a standard quartet of *chekkah* blows.

The human wobbled back and forth, perhaps already dead, then fell back against the desert floor.

T'ksam stood over the human. He held the beacon aloft in victory.

The silent Tenctonese stood frozen behind the fence, helpless to change their fate.

The human tried to lift his head. He couldn't even do that much.

The Overseer turned and began to walk toward the approaching human guards. George knew that if the humans didn't use their weapons from a distance, they would not survive a hand-to-hand encounter with T'ksam.

It was not fair. To have gone through so much. To have had freedom so close, the bounty of a new world filled with beings who held out their hands to help without asking for anything in return—and now to know that it had all been lost before it had truly been gained.

George felt he was back at the table. He heard the *wojchek* spinning. But this time he wanted to live. He had so much to live for. All his people did.

The human got up.

"George, look," Susan said.

The human began walking unsteadily after T'ksam.

"He is dead already," someone whispered.

The human began to run, his pace gaining in strength with

each stride. The silver badge on his chest blazed with the purity of the planet's sun. George heard the human cry out, and though he knew little English he knew that the cry was inarticulate.

The human was possessed. He cried out with such force that it was almost as if he knew what it was to be a helpless slave himself.

The crowd gasped in awe as the human tackled T'ksam and threw him to the ground.

T'ksam had whirled to see the last moment of the attack but had stared in disbelief at the charging human.

No one attacked an Overseer *twice*. No one.

The human was on top of T'ksam, pounding fist after fist against his face.

The crowd was absolutely still. What they were seeing was unthinkable.

With one blow T'ksam knocked the human from him, then leapt quickly to his feet. The human stood up, too, though more slowly. The Overseer threw the beacon onto the ground and moved toward the human, bent over, spitting hatred in a foul string of words.

In the language of the Tenctonese he called the human "cargo."

"Stangya," Susan asked, "is it possible that he is just an . . . ordinary human?"

George didn't know. He couldn't tear his eyes from the spectacle of courage—or foolishness, he didn't know which— that he and the rest of the crowd were witnessing.

T'ksam lunged. The human dropped to the ground. The Overseer sailed over him, and the human jumped up again, shouldering T'ksam into an uncontrolled fall.

In the low gravity of this world, the arc of T'ksam's trajectory was clearly longer than he had anticipated, and he overcompensated and smashed headfirst into the dirt.

The crowd gasped and then cheered, raggedly at first, and then the cheers increased in strength until it sounded as if there were thousands pressed against the fence.

The human bent over the Overseer. He kicked him in the side. "Yes!" George said. "He knows about the nexus!" Kick after kick rained against the Overseer, and all T'ksam could do was lie there with his arms at his side to protect his sensitive nerve clusters.

The crowd screamed in amazement.

Then the Overseer's arms flopped at his sides. His head rolled into the dirt. It was impossible. But the human had *won*.

The crowd called out its thanks to Andarko and Celine and Ionia and a host of other holy names. What they had witnessed could only be a miracle. There was no other explanation.

The human looked hurt, but he was still standing. Some of the crowd called out to him, pointing frantically to the beacon lying in the desert sand. The human understood. He limped over to the beacon and picked it up. The crowd called out to him to throw it to them. He hefted it in his hand. George couldn't read his alien features to tell what he was thinking.

Human voices shouted. The guards had almost arrived.

The crowd cried out as one in warning.

T'ksam was back on his feet, lurching toward the human.

The human understood the warning and wheeled to face the Overseer.

George couldn't breathe. Surely the human was exhausted. He couldn't withstand another attack.

The human braced himself for T'ksam's charge. But as the human moved to protect himself from a repeat of the *chekkah* quartet of blows, T'ksam changed his attack and grabbed the human's arm, lifted it high, then made a killing fist and howled with the sound of death.

The crowd cried out their horror. They knew what was going to happen. The killing fist. The human was lost.

The Overseer struck. He swung his fist in against the nexus under the human's arm—not powerfully, but perfectly aimed to hit just those nerves that could cause the hearts to falter in their rhythm.

The fist struck.

The crowd groaned. The chain-link fence swayed with their anguish.

The human hung there, supported by the Overseer's powerful grip.

Then the human turned to look at the Overseer's fist in his ribs. Then he turned to look at the Overseer.

The Overseer's spots paled in fear, and George knew why. The human had survived the death blow.

George's spots puckered. He could feel the shudder that moved through the crowd as everyone else's spots did the same thing.

What manner of creature was this being?

Then the human drew back his free arm, and with the beacon firmly in his fist he smashed T'ksam directly in the face.

Pink blood sprayed out from the Overseer's nose, and he collapsed facedown in the dirt of the planet.

It was as if the heavens themselves had burst, so loud were the delirious cries of joy from the crowd.

The human swayed but managed to keep his footing. George was fascinated.

"Look, Appy, he is injured. That means he has *not* been blessed by the gods."

The human looked at the beacon in his hand. He swept his eyes across the crowd calling out for it. The guards were only a few feet away, closing fast.

"Then he *is* just an ordinary human," Susan whispered.

The human's eyes met George's. George felt his spots almost wither. The human's eyes were so alien, so unreadable, and yet . . . there was something in them that George almost understood. As if the creature were about to make a decision.

He wondered if the human could recognize anything in his own Tenctonese eyes. He wondered if two different beings from two different worlds could ever span the gulf between them and their people.

The human glanced away toward the guards. They were almost on him. Then he looked back at George and did something odd. He nodded his head at George, just once. George was certain it was a deliberate gesture, but what its significance was he had no time to consider. Because an instant after, the human pitched the beacon into the air.

The crowd fell silent with a collective gasp. The fate of the Tenctonese and the humans combined spun up against the eerily blue sky. It glittered in the alien sunlight. And it fell perfectly into George's outstretched hands.

Shouting, the guards surged past the human and ran toward the fence. George's hands closed tightly around the beacon. It was too large to pull back through the mesh, but George knew he had only moments to act—the humans were obsessed with anything from the ship. He returned the odd gesture to the human, nodding just once. The human's face broke into a broad smile. Whatever the meaning of the gesture, George felt a sudden connection between them. He found himself hoping it was a good sign for whatever the future held.

Then George slammed the beacon to the ground, close to the fence's edge. At once the force of a dozen hands tore the mesh from the sandy soil, and the beacon vanished into the crowd. George heard the sweet sound of the beacon's destruction as it was smashed into fragments no bigger than the dust of the desert.

"No, Appy," George said in wonder. "He is not ordinary."

The human shouted something at the guards as they gathered around him. He took special care to brush the dust from his uniform. He adjusted the silver badge he wore and gave it a wipe with his sleeve until it appeared as if a second star blazed from his chest.

"Look at the costume he is wearing," George said. "And that badge of honor on his chest. I don't know what he is, Susan, but whatever he is on this planet, that is what I shall become." He felt Susan looking up at him as his people crowded all around in joy, calling out to the human, blessing him to the stars. "Whatever that costume is, I shall wear it. And whatever acts it takes to earn that shield upon his chest, I shall undertake them myself."

"To thank this world for what it has given us?" Susan asked, smiling lovingly at him, understanding as always.

"Yes," George said as the human walked away. "And because it is my choice."

A few moments later, two human guards arrived to clear away the excited, joyful crowd inside the fence and search for whatever might be left of the artifact that had been thrown at the fence.

But there was nothing left to find.

CHAPTER 12

MOODRI GAZED DOWN at his great-nephew and gently touched the focus points on the child's chest and neck that would bring him back from sleep.

Buck woke instantly. Confused but alert. He asked his great-uncle where they were.

"In what the humans call a *hospital*," Moodri said. "Like the ship's infirmary, only larger."

Buck tried to move his arm, and Moodri saw the surprise on Buck's face as he realized his arm had been encased in a chunk of white rock.

"Not to worry, Finiksa. They don't know how to treat broken bones, but they're quick learners. I have great faith in them."

Buck lay back upon his pillow with a sigh, and Moodri could sense the pain and fear the child felt. He had done what was necessary, he had done what his own hearts had said he must, but the burden was too great for a child. He had seen too much death, experienced too much loss. In time, perhaps, he could deal with his actions, but not now.

Moodri touched his knuckles to Buck's temples, preparing to give him a great gift—something no one among his people had had for almost a century: a childhood. The spinning crystal was in his robes, ready to be used again. But there was something else to do first.

"Open your hand, Finiksa. I have something for you."

Buck did as he was told. Moodri dropped a pebble into his hand.

"What is it?" Buck asked.

"The name of this world."

"You know what it is?"

"We all know it. We have known it in our hearts since our journey began."

Buck waited patiently, as if he knew that there was no more need to hurry. That everything would be all right.

"In the language that they speak here, this world is called *Earth.*"

Buck repeated it. It made his tongue tickle to say it.

Moodri smiled. "It has other names as well, in other languages. Older languages. But *Earth* will do for now."

"Earth," Buck said. Moodri could see he was comforted by the sound. But the comfort left him as he remembered. "What about the beacons? What about—"

"Shhh," Moodri said. "The beacons have been destroyed." There was no reason to tell the child about the fourth beacon, still somewhere in the desert where it had been ejected. The humans had cooperated in setting up a strict quarantine zone. In time the final beacon's power would fade. It would not be a threat. In time.

Moodri closed his hand around his great-nephew's fist, making the pebble safe. An entire world in the hand of a child. Right where it belonged.

"Aim see terrata yas rifym vacwa vots tla," Moodri said. May the Earth stay firmly under your feet. It was the first prayer of the new world.

Buck looked up at him searchingly. "Does that mean we're going to stay here?"

"Yes," Moodri said. "We are home."

EPILOGUE

IT WAS LATE. THE HOSPITAL was still. There was only the sound of the nitrogen misters, still humming from the room where Susan and Emily slept.

Vessna gurgled in Buck's arms. George reached out to her and gently traced a finger over her tiny spots.

"How long have you known?" George asked.

Buck shrugged. "The day Moodri took me to the sea. He walked into it, and the salt water . . . it didn't do anything to him. It made me remember him reaching into the recycler and . . ." Buck covered his eyes. "Every day after that he helped me remember more." He looked up at his father. "He still does. Every time . . . every time I look up at the stars."

George took his son into his arms, and for a moment they cradled Vessna between them. "I know," George said softly. "I know." He thought of Ruhtra. There were still some doors to be stepped through.

Buck tried to smile at his father. "Until now I never knew why you wanted to be a policeman."

"I have never forgotten that day," George said. His spots constricted just thinking about it.

"Do you know who it was? The human who threw you the beacon?"

George gave a small laugh. He dropped his voice. "Back then, when everything was so new, they all looked alike to me."

Buck took his father's hand. "I still have the pebble Moodri gave me."

George nodded. "And we still have the dreams, don't we?"

Buck glanced over at the window into the isolation room. "And the nightmares."

Hope as well as despair, George thought. Stars as well as the darkness.

It was simply a question of where one chose to look.

He stood up. "Matthew will be here soon. He will help us. For every Purist scum who tries to do us harm, there is another human who will stand at our side." He went to the window. Buck moved to stand beside him, Vessna secure in his arms.

They stared through the window together, their reflections blending with Susan's and Emily's until they were a single image. George touched the glass with his fingers, but he no longer heard the vibration of the stardrive, he no longer felt the chill of space.

He stared through the window and he no longer thought of staring through the portals of the ship. Not now. It was no longer the time to look into the past. It was time to look into the future.

And there *will* be a future, he thought.

It was the only choice worth making.

And he made it.

INTERLUDE

THE RED CARRALO RUSHED smoothly through the night along the rain-wet streets of the city. There was little traffic now. They were almost at the medical center.

"I never knew you worked at the camp," Cathy said. She had said very little as Sikes had told his story.

"I didn't work there after that," Sikes said. He was surprised by how light he felt, as if he had unburdened himself. He decided he had. He didn't want to have any secrets from Cathy. Not anymore. "The army wanted to court-martial me for throwing that thing into the crowd. There wasn't a whole lot that came off the ship intact. But because I was a cop, they couldn't touch me. So they sent me home. To the hospital, actually. Two months for cracked ribs and . . . all sorts of other junk."

Cathy's voice seemed to fail her. "Did you . . . did you hate us because of what you saw, because of what happened to you?"

"No," Sikes said. "No. I guess I was . . . disappointed more than anything. Here you were, aliens from another world, and when you got right down to it, you were exactly like us."

Sikes saw Cathy force a smile as she spoke. "Well, maybe not *exactly* like you."

Sikes knew what she was trying to say and wouldn't accept it. "No, Cathy. I mean it. More than ever. Exactly like us." He felt his cheeks burn. "In . . . in all that ways that matter, I mean." He locked his eyes on the road. He couldn't believe what he had just said.

From the sound of her, Cathy couldn't either. "Did you really fall in love with . . . with that astronomer so quickly?"

Sikes shook his head. He had figured that one out long ago. "That was my subconscious coming to my rescue. There Victoria was, finally saying that she was willing to try getting back together with me, and whammo, something in the back of my brain said "no way" and opened my eyes to the . . . uh, possibility of other involvements. Happens all the time. Victoria and I weren't meant for each other."

"You feel attracted to females that strongly, that quickly, *all* the time?" Cathy asked with an odd catch in her throat.

Sikes chewed his lip. "Only . . . only when I'm getting into something I . . . I shouldn't be getting into. It hasn't happened for a long time, Cathy." He tensed as he said his next words, like going over that first hill on a roller coaster. "Not since I met you."

The tension was back in the car. Sikes could feel it pressing him into his seat. What more did she want from him? What more could he say?

"Maybe you're right," Cathy said slowly. "Maybe we are the same."

"We just get confused in different ways. That's all," he said. The turn to the medical center was coming up. They were almost there.

Cathy's voice was like a whisper. "We're all lost in different ways, too," she said.

Sikes made the turn. "Just trying to find our way home."

"Do you think we will, Matt?"

Sikes didn't know if she meant humans and Tenctonese or just the two of them. He wasn't brave enough to ask.

"I don't know," he said. "I hope so." On a sudden impulse he reached out his hand and brushed his knuckles lightly against her temple.

At once Cathy's hand came up to touch his. "So do I," she said.

The medical center was before them. And whatever happened next, Sikes knew, their story wasn't over.

It was just getting started.

ABOUT THE AUTHORS

Judith and Garfield Reeves-Stevens are Emmy-nominated scriptwriters, *New York Times* best-selling novelists, science writers, and designers of interactive educational software. In the six years they have been a writing team, they have written six novels, including two "classic" Star Trek novels—*Memory Prime* and *Prime Detective*—and the ongoing fantasy adventure series, *The Chronicles of Galen Sword.* In addition to writing episodes for the animated TV series *Batman* and *The Legend of Prince Valiant,* they have written numerous teleplays, one of which was nominated for a 1991 Daytime Emmy for Outstanding Writing for a Children's Special and was awarded a 1990 Scott Newman Center Drug Abuse Prevention Award. The Reeves-Stevenses live in Los Angeles.